A HIGH MEADOW

A HIGH MEADOW

A Novel

JOHN B. KEANE

MERCIER PRESS

Mercier Press

© John B. Keane 1994

ISBN 1 85635 090 8 *(paperback)*

A CIP record for this book is available from the British Library.

10 9   8   7   6   5   4

TO EDEL
WITH LOVE

A High Meadow is a work of fiction. All the characters and situations in this book are entirely imaginary and bear no relation to any real person or actual happenings.

Printed in Ireland by Colour Books Ltd.

1

THE RAM OF GOD was rudely awakened at five in the morning. Normally he was up and about at six-thirty to drive in the sixty milch cows for the morning milking. This morning, however, the elderly alarm clock which served him so faithfully for years was upstaged by the coarse bawling of his younger brothers, freshly arrived from the nearby village's most notorious hostelry, The Load of S.

The Drannaghy twins, in their thirtieth years, noisily charged into his bedroom without the formality of a knock, announcing at the tops of their drunken voices that the day was well and truly broken.

'Get up you long, lazy hoor,' shouted Murt the taller of the pair whilst his brother Will with a single wild flourish swept aside the bed-clothes, which covered the pyjamaed form of the Ram of God.

'What's the matter?' the Ram called out sleepily.

'Will you listen to the hoor,' Murt addressed his twin uproariously, 'listen to the Ram. I'll tell you what's up Ram. The day is a beauty and there's meadows to be cut. Up now like a good boy and get on the tractor and don't come back from the High Meadow till every blade of grass is cut clean from its bosom.'

'What about the cows?' the Ram asked reasonably.

'We'll look after the cows.' Will gave the assurance from a mouth, stout-stained and spittleful.

Both reeked of stale drink.

'The bull will want watching,' the Ram of God warned. 'Don't turn your backs on him. He's shifty.'

'Not as shifty as a ram though.' Will directed a playful kick in the general direction of his older brother's genitals. Caught unawares as he struggled with his trousers the Ram lost his balance and landed on his buttocks on the bedroom floor. Often enough he had been sorely tempted to take the twins to task if only to knock their heads together but now, as in the past, he decided to indulge their clownish antics.

Drawing himself up to his full height as he buttoned his flies he towered over them although still in his bare feet. At six feet two, lean and paunchless, just gone thirty-five he presented a formidable figure. His hair still curled darkly above a sensitive, thin-nosed face, generous mouth, unintentionally wry. The twins were swarthier, several inches smaller with gnarly features and bushy brows that belied the mischievous humour lurking in their dark-brown eyes. Sober, they could be predictable enough but in drink they tended to exceed themselves especially after an intake of whiskey.

'Mercifully,' the Ram thought to himself, 'they're not whiskey drunk now, merely exhausting the effects of several pints of stout after a night and morning of roistering with the Cronane sisters from Ballybobawn village.'

In the kitchen the table had been laid by Nonie, the girl as she was called although she would be the last to deny that she had been in receipt of the old-age pension for several years. Grey woollen scarf tied round her neck and covering her head she stood crouched over the gas cooker, one of

6

whose jets enflamed the bottom of the frying pan where a pair of rashers and three eggs simmered appetisingly. A cigarette hung from the side of her mouth, its inch-long ash suspended precariously over the pan, its length increasing menacingly as her inhalations contributed to the glow between ash and cigarette.

'Sit there!' Without looking behind her she sensed his presence in the kitchen.

'The tea is drawn. You can pour away!'

Expertly turning the pan's contents she faced him for the first time.

'You'll be starting with the High Meadow then?'

'Might as well while the going is good. You'll call those two for the cows and you'll not forget to warn them about the bull.'

Without answering Nonie expertly transferred eggs and bacon to the waiting plate. The Ram of God made the sign of the cross with customary diligence before slicing an egg in half and impaling his fork in its yolk. Nonie withdrew the cigarette butt from her mouth and blew the ash downwards onto the floor before lighting a second Woodbine from the remains of the first. She sat at the side of the table, one arm draped across the back of her chair, the other resting on the table, her fingers toying with the tassels of the tea-cosy.

'Will I throw a bit of dinner together for you or will you be coming back for it at mid-day?'

'Throw something together if it isn't too much trouble. There's a day's work up there between the three meadows and this kind of weather doesn't last.'

'There's something I've been meaning to say to you.' Nonie took the cigarette from her mouth and laid it on the table as she located cheese and beef

7

in the refrigerator. 'You'd better watch out for yourself my boy! Those two are making plans this long time and I doubt if you're included.'

'Plans!' the Ram echoed the word in mild perplexity as he launched into his second egg.

'You're thirty-five years of age,' Nonie Spillane reminded him, 'and you've a college education. Yet those two boobies would buy and sell you.'

The Ram of God looked at the ageing housekeeper in total perplexity as he buttered a slice of bread.

'And them Cronane bitches, a rough and ready pair, bad as the boys, capable of downing several pints of lager each at a sitting! They don't fool me neither nor their mother. Cute Mollie thinks she knows it all. 'Twould be more in her line to give the right weight in a pound of rashers. Supermarket my arse!'

'What are you talking about?' the Ram asked, not in the least scandalised by her profane mutterings. For the most part when she rambled on thus he took little notice of her.

'I'll tell you what I'm on about,' Nonie exploded as she viciously rended the wrapper from a sliced-pan loaf. 'Those two are set to divide the farm between them. I hear them. They don't hear me but I hear them and that's what they plan if 'tisn't already done. Cute Mollie Cronane is calling the tune and you and me will be for the high road. I have my cottage but what's going to happen to you?'

'Are they getting married then?'

'That's the plan. Sure aren't the four of them day and night below at Cronane's and when they're not there they're in the Load of S.'

Suddenly Nonie raised an admonitory finger

8

and tip-toed to the door of the twins' bedroom. Gently pushing it ajar she peeped inside.

'Like two pigs in a puddle,' she threw the assurance over her shoulder to where the Ram of God was in the process of wiping his plate clean with the remains of a bread slice. Closing the door silently she succeeded in drowning out the noise of the resounding snores. Returning to the table she was silent for a while as she devoted her undivided attention to the making of the sandwiches.

'You know what's going to happen don't you?' She was fuming now.

'I haven't the faintest idea.' The Ram poured himself a second cup of tea.

'Your brother Will and Kate Cronane will move in here when they come back from the honeymoon. Your brother Murt and Noreen Cronane will settle in below at the supermarket until their new house is ready.'

'What new house?' the Ram asked, his interest excited at last.

'The house they're going to build at the western end of the High Meadow. It's all planned by Mollie Cronane. It has to happen soon because the Cronane finances won't stand much more outlay. Those girls are drinking ten to twenty pints of beer between them every night and the twins aren't exactly the last of the big spenders. All you have to do is put two and two together. Mollie is financing everything but she has her bellyful by now. It wouldn't surprise me if there was a double wedding before the fall of the year. You'll be out on your ear this coming winter. Why didn't you get a bloody BA itself? If you'd a degree you could tell the world kiss your arse!'

'Too late for that now.'

The mournful rejoinder stung Nonie to further recrimination. 'Did you think it was going to last forever. I warned you repeatedly that you should pull out. Get a job, look out for your own interests.'

'I'll be all right. God is good.' The Ram spoke resignedly.

'God hasn't been too good to you Eddie boy!' Rarely did anybody call him by his proper name. Few could remember it in the first place.

'If God was good,' Nonie was in full flight again, 'you'd be included in your father's will. He drew up his plan the day you went off to be a priest. You weren't a week in college when the land was theirs. Oh there was a proviso of course. Your education was to be paid for but that was it as far as you were concerned. If your mother had been alive itself!'

THE NOONDAY ANGELUS sounded from the village church two miles distant, the rich tones languorously imposing themselves on hill and valley and lingering faintly long after the final chimes had tolled. As soon as the first note assailed the hair-bedecked ears of the Ram of God he alighted from the tractor, formally crossed himself and sonorously recited the prayers of the holy Angelus.

Crossing himself secondly at the close of the recital he strode purposefully to a corner of the meadow where he had at daybreak deposited the satchel which contained his lunch. First, however, he would treat himself to a sojourn in his pale, unwrinkled pelt beneath the ascending June sun. He thought about a brief immersion in a pool fed by cold spring waters in the next field but, he told himself: 'Better be sun-kissed than bathed. I can bathe any time but the sun may not be shining tomorrow.'

The Ram of God lay on his back in the southern corner of the High Meadow. Overhead a lark sang exultantly, straining its tiny voice-box until the sky seemed to overflow with the trilling mixture of joyous exclamations. As if by heavenly command the other sounds of the meadow were hushed into barely-discernible background subservience. 'You would swear,' the Ram of God spoke to himself, 'that proprietorship of the meadow was his by divine right and yet there is no impertinence, no intrusion. His timing is perfect. This is the best part of the day, the part that most deserves acclamation.'

No sooner had the outline of the carolling lark vanished into the bluebell sky than the Ram of God drifted into a pleasing slumber. He lay with his rolled-up shirt and trousers under his head, his large, gnarly hands folded over the ghastly white of his stomach.

Near to where the Ram lay, a bobbing finch chirped happily past, glad to be in the shade of the dense whitethorn which formed a dividing hedge with the neighbouring meadow. Gradually an all-enveloping hush descended. As if by common consent the birds of the air and the denizens of the undergrowth succumbed to the mid-day lull. Activated by the unfamiliar heat the meadow was transformed into an incubator of growth and development. Instinctively the Ram stirred in his sleep and turned over on his stomach to escape the inevitable burning brought about by over-long exposure to the scorching sun. He grunted contentedly

11

savouring the natural glow which pricked and coloured his back and buttocks. He lay thus for a half-hour and would have slumbered longer had not the distant sound of a female voice alerted him to his nude condition. Not daring to raise his head he listened, his eyes fully opened as he endeavoured to determine from where the voice was calling. It was certainly a girl's voice and it was his name that was in question.

'Ram! Ram! Where are you?' It seemed to be coming from the direction of the gate which offered the only access to the High Meadow.

'Ram! Ram! Where are you?' the distant queries persisted. Lying flat on his back he first drew on his trousers and then his shirt. Shielded by the tall grasses all around he retied his flies, located his socks and wellingtons before raising his head to ascertain the identity of his unexpected visitor.

She sat astride the six-bar gate, her long legs tucked behind the third bar for balance, her palms resting on the uppermost, a pair of folded exam papers held firmly in her mouth as her eager eyes searched the meadow.

'Over here Mary!' The Ram of God waved both arms as he called out to the sixteen year old. Lithely she leaped from the gate and ran towards him, the papers now clutched in her right hand, her long legs tripping over the shorn sward, leaping the uniform rows of tufted swathes, sometimes pirouetting, other times tumbling but all the time reducing the distance between herself and the Ram of God who stood now with hands on hips, a broad smile etched on his unshaven face, his eyes twinkling in appreciation at the unrestrained limberings of the flowering adolescent whose presence illuminated even more the bright enclosure of the High

Meadow.

'Mary Creel,' the Ram of God thought, "tis a wonder she can laugh and sing at all with the father she has and the mother little better than a mute drudge. The eldest of six in a home where poverty is rife and love is at a premium and yet she skips and dances as though she were the light of her father's eye, her mother's pride and joy, an heiress to vast estates and title most high.'

'How did you get on?' the Ram asked as she handed over the pink examination papers, the colour to indicate the higher grade English classification.

'I think I did well,' Mary responded breathlessly.

'Let's see how well you really did my girl!' the Ram spoke with mock severity as they both sat on the rapidly drying meadow-grass. He asked several questions and seemed pleased with the answers. He fingered the stubble at the forefront of his chin and asked several more. He expressed satisfaction.

'I also think you did well!' He returned the papers which she folded neatly and thrust into her frock pocket. The Ram was certain he had seen the frock before. It could be that it was a cast-off of one of the better-off girls in the village of Ballybobawn where Mary resided in one of the council houses at the eastern side of the village although it was more likely an examination gift from the Presentation nuns in the convent which Mary attended in the town of Trallock some seven miles to the west of Ballybobawn.

'I don't know if I got this right or not.' She knelt by his side and placing one hand on his shoulder pointed at the final question in the second part of the paper.

13

The Ram of God was deeply touched. Here was this beautiful, burgeoning girl placing infinite trust in a man whose reputation as a one-time philanderer, rightly or wrongly, exceeded that of any other within a radius of twenty miles. Silently he thanked God for endowing him with the grace to be able to respect and revere a creature of such naïveté and innocence. He followed her finger carefully, intoning the question and providing the answer all in one breath.

'I got it right.' Mary joined her hands in delight and rose to her feet.

'Have you had anything to eat?' the Ram asked.

'Well no,' Mary answered with some hesitancy. 'I came here straight from the school bus. Nonie told me you were in the High Meadow.'

'Sit down. Sit down,' the Ram commanded expansively. 'There's surely enough here for two.'

In the satchel was a pint-sized flask of tea, an enamel mug, chipped but clean, an apple and three stout, well-stocked sandwiches.

'You take this,' the Ram said tendering the apple. 'I can't imagine how it got in there. I never eat apples.'

He poured half the contents of the flask into the mug and added some sugar and milk which Nonie had thoughtfully provided. They ate silently, relishing each mouthful.

'I didn't realise I was so hungry,' Mary admitted after she accepted half of the third sandwich.

'The meadow is a great place for the appetite,' the Ram explained.

THEY HAD KNOWN EACH OTHER for two years, ever since Mary came to assist Nonie Spillane on a part-

14

time basis across the summer. Her first day had very nearly been her last. Will, the smaller of the twins, had lured her into one of the bedrooms on some pretext or other while Nonie was cycling towards the village. Fortunately the Ram of God happened to be in the vicinity. He would have passed through the farmyard as was his wont on his way to one of the outhouses but some undefinable force arrested him. He stopped in his tracks suddenly aware of a deadly silence. He sensed that something untoward was happening but where? He listened, holding his breath lest he miss out on a tell-tale indication of the foul presence which he now knew to be at work somewhere.

The scream which suddenly shattered the quiet was unequivocal in its urgency. It was a despairing, panic-filled plea. The Ram charged into the farmhouse praying fervently that he might arrive in time. In the bedroom Will Drannaghy, a crazed look on his face, savoured every movement of the struggling girl held firmly around her slender waist, her back pressed against his unyielding stomach.

Seizing him by the scruff of the neck the Ram had cuffed him smartly across the face, knocking him to the ground.

'Are you all right?' He put the question gently to the terrified girl. She nodded, the shock still evident on her face.

'You sure?' Again she nodded.

'Up you!' the Ram shouted to the cowering twin. He helped him to his feet.

'You go to the kitchen and wait for me.' He spoke in tender tones to Mary who seemed now to be none the worse for her ordeal.

'Try that again,' the Ram said to his badly shaken brother, 'and I'll kill you.'

A brief look of protestation died on the twin's face as he caught the Ram of God's cold eyes. He suddenly felt it to be in his best interests that he remain silent.

'If the girl reports you,' the Ram spoke matter of factly, 'you'll get at least twelve months but that's nothing to what I'll do to you if you ever interfere with her again. Now we'll go down to the kitchen where you'll apologise and assure her that you'll never even look her way again.'

Later the Ram explained to Mary that she could, if she wished, complain to her parents or go to the local guards' barracks.

'I don't believe he'd have done you any serious harm,' the Ram assured her, 'although what he did was bad enough for anything. The trouble is that if you complain him to the barracks you might come worse out of it than he. However, in the final reckoning, it's you who must decide.'

'He's apologised and I think he means it,' Mary had said, 'so it might be best to forget it.'

'I think that's wise,' the Ram had agreed, 'and you have my assurance that nothing like it will ever happen again.'

Mary settled in happily after that. Each evening he walked her to the outskirts of Ballybobawn village and watched after her as she took the left hand turn along the road which led to the nearby council houses.

Midway through the summer of the second year he was relieved of his responsibilities when she had told him there was no longer any need for his guardianship. It happened one evening as they neared the cross. A teenage boy appeared in the distance as if from nowhere and was about to vanish into that place from whence he first took

16

shape when Mary waved urgently before making her excuses to the Ram of God.

Feeling pleased with himself the Ram turned for home, glad that she had altogether forgotten the episode involving his brother Will nor had Will breathed a word, not even to his twin.

THE LUNCH OVER THEY walked to the highest point of the meadow, their gazes sweeping the sun-drenched valley where lay the drowsy village of Ballybobawn. Far away to the west the shimmer of the distant sea dazzled the eye and in between a warm haze hung between land and sky. Everything was now subject to the early afternoon lassitude. Soon it would lift and the cattle in the fields around bestir themselves before resuming the grazing of the fragrant pastures. The ripe meadows too would be subjected to fresh onslaughts. The bustle of the forenoon would slowly return as the afternoon traffic resumed its bustle, to and from Trallock on the right, to and from Cork on the left. The Ram of God examined his watch.

'Glory be to God!' he shouted in mock alarm, 'it's half-past one in the day and there's a whole third of the High Meadow remaining to be cut. Haven't you got anything to do my pretty miss?'

'I have. I have,' Mary called back as she ran towards the gate. 'I have to go to Ballybobawn for the groceries. Nonie Spillane will kill me.'

The Ram folded his arms and surveyed his progress. There was a time before the advent of the rotary mower when it might have taken as many as three full days to dock the High Meadow. Now with the ancient but still perfectly functioning Ferguson 135 he could easily cut as much as two and a half acres in the hour. Two and a half more hours and he would be through. Then he would move on to the three other meadows, each approximately thirteen acres.

Of the one hundred and twenty acres which made up the farm almost fifty-nine acres were devoted to meadowing. Drannaghys' was the last remaining substantial farm in the district which had not, as yet, changed over to silage. By the Ram of God's reckoning the three lesser meadows lower down ought to be sufficient to carry an extra twenty milch cows with a change-over. The Drannaghys ought also, by all the known norms, to be the laughing stocks of the countryside when it was so patently obvious that they were losing profits hand over fist because of their dependence on a hay crop. As it was, however, nobody was laughing because of the circumstances which obtained at the farm. The Ram, as everybody well knew, was no more than a glorified servant boy, dependent on his brothers for the bite and sup and a weekly wage which was modest enough by local standards. The Ram, as anybody in Ballybobawn would tell you, had no claim at all to the Drannaghy place. It was the exclusive property, dwelling house, outhouses, barns and machinery of the twins Murt and Will and here lay the crux of the matter.

All three brothers were only too well aware that a change-over to silage would increase the milk yield which was below their allotted quota. It would also make more land available for fat stock or grain or even beet. It would reduce the amount of work involved in the day-to-day running of the farm. Unfortunately for the twins they could not agree on a precise method of change. Since the beginning of their relationship with the Cronane sisters the plans, which had been professionally drawn up for the transition to silage, were stored with the deeds of the farm and other moulding documents in the family safe, a hiding place, without lock or key. The twins, influenced by Mollie Cronane, the belligerent matriarch who ran the family supermarket unopposed and was making fair bids to dominate the entire village together with a large part of the contiguous countryside, decided to postpone the implementation of the silage plans until the farm was legally divided and each twin was free to put his own plans into operation.

'That way,' Mollie Cronane shrewdly pointed out, 'you'll be able to back each other up instead of crossing one another the length and breadth of the day.'

Mollie privately complained to her silent husband Tom that the joint courtship was now proceeding for a full five years.

'It's time,' said she one sleepless night, 'to put the boot in!'

As a consequence of this decision she called the daughters together early the following morning and directed them to the musty sitting-room which was used only for the entertainment of important visitors such as nuns or priests or relatives who might be holidaying from the distant USA.

Mollie first drummed one finger on the breastbone directly above her daughter Kate's ample cleavage and simply said, 'Sit down there Madam!' She executed an identical manoeuvre with Noreen. When both girls were comfortably if inextricably seated in the rather inadequate and venerable armchairs she produced a ten pack of tipped cigarettes from her own cleavage, lit one, inhaled deeply and returned box together with matches to that well-protected spot where they had earlier rested.

Mollie addressed herself first to the older daughter. The information which she wished to solicit was simply whether or not they were still determined to marry the Drannaghy twins. On being assured that they were she tendered what she believed to be sage advice.

'Then marry the hoors,' she said, 'or ye could be beaten to the draw. I don't care what means ye use but I want positive results before the summer is in its bloom.'

This ultimatum was issued the morning after Easter Monday. Less than three months elapsed before they triumphantly announced to their delighted mother that the marital altar was well and truly in sight.

'Did they propose?' Mollie asked.

'Yes,' the girls had answered in unison.

'And was there rings?'

'Not yet,' Kate answered, 'but we'll have them the weekend. As it is we have better than rings.'

'And pray,' Mollie demanded, 'what could be better than rings?'

Kate came forward a step answering brazenly, 'I'm two months gone and this one here is three.'

That night Mollie slept soundly for the first time in months, her early fitful snoring abating quickly and giving way to a richly satisfying repose which lasted for several uninterrupted hours. In the morning she twined her beads around her podgy fingers and whispered the Rosary.

'I could not,' she told herself between decades, 'have carried those two another week. I must have invested in a hundred and fifty casks of lager these past five years. Now they'll be nicely settled, thanks be to God and His holy Mother, within a stone's

20

throw you might say and two better customers for a supermarket you wouldn't find if you were to scour the countryside. It will have to be a double wedding but, far more important, it will have to be quick.'

Tom Cronane, her husband and nominal head of the Cronane household, feigned sleep when his daughters made their dramatic announcements. He had become embittered over the years by his wife's parsimony towards him. How often had he watched as she plied Murt and Will Drannaghy with red and white wines from the beleaguered supermarket whilst he sat parched, a mute witness to their boisterous celebrations. 'Dang the lot of 'em,' he said to himself as for the thousandth time he surrendered himself to the tender embraces of his night-time partner Madeleine Monterros, the heroine of his adolescence, from the time he first saw her in *Mexican Paramour* at a Sunday matinee in the town of Trallock. Sometimes he had little difficulty in conjuring up her heavenly face but other times despite his most committed concentration the lovely features which enraptured him failed to materialise.

THE RAM OF GOD alighted from his faithful Ferguson at half-past three in the afternoon. The last of the meadow grass lay at his feet. It had taken him eight hours, not counting the lunch break, to get the better of the twenty acres. The crop was heavier than usual and would have a likely yield of two and a half tons to the acre. He stood for a moment admiring the long parallel swathes, the earlier mowing wilting as it dried, the more recently cut reflecting the brilliance of the afternoon sun, generating more heat now than at any other time of the day. If the fine weather continued the crop would be ripe for the first turning any time after mid-day the following day. If it held fine there would be a second and third turning before the introduction of the baler on the third day, but first things first, the Ram of God reminded himself as he mounted his iron steed and made tracks for the adjoining meadow.

The thousands of bales scattered over the High Meadow were testimony to the industry of the Ram of God. By the fourth day he had broken the back of the baling. The new grant-aided baler was the envy of the countryside and already he had accepted several commissions from local small farmers. He should be able to make inroads into the outside work as soon as the home meadows were baled.

2

MOLLIE CRONANE WAS OUT of bed with the first
light on the last day of June. The fine weather
which arrived three days earlier, contrary to all
forecasts, still prevailed. The night before, at the
end of its final news bulletin, Radio Éireann confi-
dently predicted that the trough of high pressure
directly overhead was unlikely to be deposed for
several days. Mollie was no lover of fine weather.
People seemed to eat less. She knew from experience that the heat produced an indifferent attitude
to food. Almost every household in Ballybobawn
produced its own lettuces and onions and there
was an abundant supply of freshly-run sea trout.

The nearby river Ogle, largely unsupervised by
water-keepers, played host to thousands of these
most palatable of seasonal visitors chiefly during
the closing days of June. For the vast majority
there was no return journey. They ended up on the
tables of rich and poor alike, particularly the latter
who were the poachers-in-chief of the locality and
who did not tire so easily of the fishy fare, day in,
day out.

Mollie sighed deeply and arched her plump
arms over her dark head at the same time
stretching her short, bare feet under the mahogany
desk. Her brain had grown weary from the changing compilations of the various expenses which the
forthcoming weddings would involve. She poured
herself a cup of tea and lit her first cigarette of the
day. As she relaxed before drawing up a final as-
sessment of the financial demands which would be

made upon the family resources she heard the barely discernible sounds of the gently plopping hooves on the roadway outside the window of the tiny office which was attached to the supermarket proper. She rose instantly and went to the main shop window which afforded an unrestricted view of what was happening outside at any hour of the day or night. Upon beholding the horses she frowned.

'Tinkers' nags!' she spat the words out viciously. Tinkers, in strict terms, they were not. The antecedents of some may certainly have been itinerant tinsmiths with limited skills but the owners of the off-white and skewbald horses congregated uncertainly at the cross of Ballybobawn were now possessed of no apparent skills save the driving of Hiace vans which had replaced the traditional horse-drawn caravans so common to previous generations.

The tinkers involved here, as Mollie knew well, were of the settled variety possessed of council houses in nearby Trallock or one of the many other towns and villages as far north as the city of Galway. Gradually they would converge from all over the south and west of Ireland on the town of Killorglin where every year was held the great fair of Puck. The itineraries of those farthest away began several weeks before. Others departed at later dates right up to the very eve of the festival depending upon their proximity to the colourful mid-Kerry town.

Mollie noted the trio of fettered mares which brought up the rear. If the fettered animals were so near the main herd it meant that they had dined across the star-filled night in a field not all that far from where they were now gathered. Mollie was always angered by this annual incursion into her bailiwick.

'They're no bloody asset!' she repeatedly told her family as she cautioned about the dangers of relaxing their vigilance for even a single moment while these unwelcome visitors remained in the supermarket.

Mollie was correct in her suspicion that the horses had grazed locally. A short while before, just as the first cocks had begun to crow, they were driven from a poorly-fenced field on the outskirts of the village by a flaxen-haired garsún and a red-haired girl, both barely out of their teens. There was no noise, no giddy-ups nor rump-smacking. The horses sensed the urgency of the unspoken commands and responded by heading unswervingly, without whinny or bustle, for the gap through which they had entered. Only their affrighted eyes registered their alarm. Their instant co-operation suggested an awareness as sensitive as their masters that the powerful, clover-filled mouthfuls, ravenously filched whilst the native herbivores slept or rested, were not theirs by right. Only now at this late stage of their leisurely pilgrimage were they beginning to add flesh to the once well-defined ribs and slack rumps of a harsh winter and late spring. Eyes still filled with uncertainty they lifted their delicate nostrils into the morning air. Suddenly the boy and girl reappeared as though from the ground and silently ushered their noble charges towards the council houses at the end of the village.

'You'll have the Hiaces along any time now,' Mollie spoke wearily to herself, 'and after the Hiaces you'll have the women with babes in arms and they pretending they never heard of dole or childrens' allowances and what harm but many of them are helping themselves to double doses or even more.'

Tom Cronane sat erect in his bed. Although still half-asleep he smelled the equine contingent the moment they halted at the cross. His eyes still remained closed. There was a bemused look on his wrinkled face. The voices of the young itinerants came to him from far away as he nodded his drowsy head confirming to himself that what he smelled and heard was part of the annual migration to Puck Fair.

They would spend a week, maybe ten days, in the boglands to the west of the council houses. From now until October there would be rich pickings for the horses in the myriad passages which criss-crossed the boglands. Odd, Tom often thought, how they never dallied on the return journey; probably had too many other festivals to visit before the frost of late autumn nights put paid to their wanderings. He lay back on the bed and scratched his lower abdomen. His thoughts drifted to the dark-skinned Madeleine Monterros.

Downstairs his wife of the puckered face glared at the final reckoning, then pursed her rich lips into a soundless whistle. Gradually her features relaxed into a becalmed state of resignation. This, in turn, was replaced by a triumphant smirk. She would at least be relieved of the responsibility of providing for two unmanageable daughters and there was the added compensation of procuring two weddings for the price of one.

One hundred and eighty guests at ten pounds apiece came to eighteen hundred pounds. Flowers would account for an extra hundred. Then there was the question of a wedding cake; at least two hundred Mollie reckoned. Clothes, to include dresses for brides and bridesmaids as well as the immediate family, had come to a thousand and to arrive at this figure she had been obliged to cut her cloth without room for flounces or frills. Fortunately, the four boys already possessed presentable suits.

Finally, there was the matter of settling with the clergy. There were some in the parish who might give more but the vast majority would give far less. After the most careful consideration she had arrived at a figure of two hundred pounds. To be fair to the parish priest, Father O'Connor, he was neither a grasping nor a demanding man and would cheerfully or so it seemed have accepted any amount she might choose to give him. Mollie told herself righteously that the presbytery account for groceries would have to reflect her investment. Father O'Connor's reply when questioned regarding matrimonial fees was to suggest whatever a family could afford. Everybody in the parish said he was easily accommodated. His curate, Father Hehir, according to himself, had the life of Reilly and spent most of his time perfecting his swing on Trallock's recently-developed golf course.

Mollie lit the third cigarette and looked at her watch. The time was eight-fifteen. She located a referee's whistle in the pocket of her apron and went to the foot of the stairs which led to the bedrooms. First came a well-sustained blast which lasted for several seconds. This was followed by several shorter blasts ending with a second sustained summons before she paused to regain her breath and inhale deeply from the cigarette.

She idled at the foot of the stairs for half a minute or so before repeating the calls. All the blasts, long and short, had one thing in common. They were all shrill and all calculated to penetrate the deepest sleep. The four Cronane sons made their appearances on the landing simultaneously. They knew better than to dawdle when their mother took to the whistle. Upon beholding her matriarchal form at the foot of the stairs they descended silently and solemnly. In order of age downwards they were Cha, Sammie, Donie and Tomboy. Normally the daughters, Kate and Noreen, would arrive downstairs before the boys but of late they were afforded preferential treatment because of their special conditions known only to themselves, their parents and, of course, their husbands-to-be. Today she would allow them to sleep until noon. All that was now required to send her carefully-wrought plans awry was a miscarriage. She would take every possible precaution to ensure that this did not occur.

After lunch they would drive to Trallock where she would see to it that they were publicly displayed before the curious eyes of town and countryside, eyes that were capable of vetting her charges comprehensively with seemingly cursory glances. Now was the best time for the physical exposition Mollie had in mind. In a few short weeks the girls would be showing. In stature they were small like herself. She recalled that she had looked as if she had been carrying for six months after only three months of pregnancy. The girls would be out like barrels in no time at all. First they would visit the leading draperies and shoe shops, not that she had the slightest intention of purchasing anything but the girls would be seen to be possessed of their natural shapes and that was all that Mollie wanted.

As her sons prepared their breakfasts Mollie advanced several steps up the stairs and blew her whistle once more. This time she indulged in just two sustained blasts but each was of such duration that even the boys were obliged to stuff their ears with their fingers. At length Tom Cronane appeared on the landing. He wore a white silk dressing gown over his pyjamas.

'I'm not deaf,' he called down with undisguised annoyance.

'I know you're not deaf,' Mollie threw back, 'but we have a priest to see this morning and I have to go to town after lunch to finalise the arrangements for the reception.'

'You can put away the whistle,' her husband spoke peevishly. 'I'll be down as soon as I shave and dress.'

Tom was more bitter than usual on the occasion. The sound of the whistle had caused Madeleine Monterros to vanish from his dreams.

Tom was almost twenty years his wife's senior and now at sixty-five he looked more like a man in his eighties. Over the past year he had grown prematurely senile. Nobody was more aware of his decline than Mollie. He himself refused to acknowledge that any change had or was taking place. Mollie, for her part, was more annoyed with him than sorry for him. He had grown extremely cantankerous of late but mercifully he hadn't touched a drink for almost three months.

When Tom drank he persevered until he had utterly exhausted himself. Sometimes his alcoholic escapades would last for several days at the end of which he would take to his bed and remain there for the best part of a week until his health partially returned. His most recent outbreak had very nearly

29

been the death of him. He was just not physically capable any more of containing a sustained intake of intoxicating liquor. Most of the population of Ballybobawn awaited his next alcoholic foray with mounting interest. He had never let them down in the past; it wasn't likely that he would in the future.

MOLLIE CRONANE, NEE PURLEY, originally came to work in Cronane's as a domestic at the age of twenty.

'The only reason,' she confided to a friend at the time, 'why I am demeaning myself is to make enough so that I can go to England and from there to Australia. There's no future for girls like me in this part of the world. There's nothing thought of us. I have no fortune and although I'm not bad-looking I'm no raving beauty either. The best I can hope for is a small farmer or a labouring man, maybe a tradesman if I'm very lucky. I've seen enough poverty and I don't want to see any more.'

Mollie Purley was unfair to herself when she suggested that she was not bad-looking. She was, in fact, an attractive young woman with a curling dark mass of hair and darker, sparkling eyes as well as a lively disposition and a buxom figure which rarely went unnoticed by members of the opposite sex. Before descending from her humble home in the nearby mountains to the Cronane General Store, as it was then, she had already turned down several offers of marriage. She had only taken one seriously. He was a small farmer in his late twenties but the land was encumbered by substantial debts and she had shied away from the prospect of a continuation of the lifestyle which she had been used to all her life.

Mollie's other suitors were either middle-aged or elderly and while at least two were comfortably off she could not see herself, by any stretch of the imagination, wasting her young life on either. She had seen the debilitating changes wrought on other girls who succumbed to the prospect of security. After ten or twelve years and several children they grew old before their time. Holiday-making exiles home from England and America were often hard put to recognise the friends and companions of their youth. Husband and children took precedence over all else as a matter of course. It was fashionable under the circumstances for over-worked mothers to neglect themselves. To be seen to be indulging themselves would have been con-trary to tradition, a sort of betrayal of the accepted martyrdom which went with all too many poverty-stricken marriages. The girls who carved out infin-itely better lifestyles in exile privately thanked their lucky stars while at home on holiday.

Mollie was aware from the beginning of Tom Cronane's drooling shenanigans and while she did nothing to encourage him she made no attempt to assume a mantle of false modesty while he was in the vicinity. Tom's mother Madge took a more jaundiced view of the likely effect this sonsy addi-tion to her staff might have on her bachelor son, now in his fortieth year. She resolved to get rid of her at the earliest opportunity. After three months in service Mollie accumulated enough money to cover the fare to England and to allow her a few days' relaxation before taking up employment in pursuance of her declared intention to settle in Australia.

One day in the course of her upstairs duties

31

she found herself making up the bed of her mistress Madge Cronane. To her surprise the door of the small safe which she always found closed was wide open. At first she suspected it might be a trap but from the bedroom window she could clearly see Madge standing, hands folded, at the other side of the street engaged in deep conversation with Tom Dudley the proprietor of Tom's Tavern.

The first interesting item to catch Mollie's eye was a post office savings certificate held jointly by Madge and her husband Charlie. The investment involved amounted to twenty thousand pounds. She rose quickly and went to the window in order to ensure that Madge was still engaged in conversation. Assuring herself that the exchanges would last for some time she instituted a more leisurely search of the safe. There were two insurances jointly held and both due to mature in less than four years. Mollie Purley was pleased to note that one would benefit the holders by twenty thousand pounds and the other by twenty-five thousand pounds. There were numerous bank statements but even to Mollie's untrained eye it was evident that the current account overdraft was minimal.

Finally there was a sizeable jewel box which when opened showed itself to be filled with Victorian sovereigns. By Mollie's reckoning there must surely be two hundred. The fact that the jewel box which was possessed of a lock was left open convinced her that a trap had been set. There was also a cigar box filled with bank notes of varying denominations. Madge Cronane was still holding forth to Tom Dudley whose interest seemed to be waning for now he was beginning to hail passers-by in the hope that a rescue would be forthcoming.

When Madge returned to the shop she went

straight to her bedroom. From an adjoining room, where she was in the process of tidying up, Mollie listened attentively to the muted jingling of the sovereigns. At that moment a strange voice came from the foot of the stairs.

'Are you there Mrs Cronane?' came the unfamiliar, stentorian call.

Madge did not answer immediately. She was checking the bank notes against the figures in a passbook which rested on top of the safe. After a while she came to the landing. Unaware of Mollie's presence in the nearby room she went part of the way down the stairs.

'Thank you for coming sergeant,' she addressed the serious-faced custodian of the peace in low tones. 'I suppose you could call it a false alarm,' she said taking him by the arm and walking him as far as the front door of the store.

Mollie came in her bare feet to the landing where she had no difficulty in picking up every word. She knew Sergeant Holly by sight. Like all of her kinfolk in the mountains she lived in fear of uniforms. Collecting her shoes she climbed to the attic which was her bedroom.

As she sat on the hard bed she was overcome by a cold fury which, when it subsided, was followed by a resolve which revealed a dimension in her that she had not been aware of previously. Mollie made up her mind there and then that she would never go to Australia nor indeed for the moment would she cross the Irish Sea as had so many of her ilk unless it was for a holiday in the distant future. She would fix Madge and some day too she would have her own back on Sergeant Holly.

From that moment forth she set her cap for

Tom. She did it subtly and guilefully so that Tom believed he was the assertive party but time was of the essence if Madge was to be outsmarted. From the limited outlook of her background and upbringing the stakes seemed unbelievably high to Mollie but she was possessed of all the trumps. All she had to do was play them with care.

The inevitable happened of a sultry evening in late July. Madge went with a party of friends to Trallock in order to attend a funeral. To assuage any suspicions which the older woman might entertain Mollie asked for permission to spend the night at her home in the mountains. Madge readily acquiesced. The removal of the remains would take place at eight-thirty. Even if Madge were to return from Trallock directly after paying her respects Mollie would have plenty of time to complete the planned operation.

For the occasion she chose a black threadbare frock which she had recently outgrown. The tight-fitting cotton accentuated her breasts and buttocks so that she would present a voluptuous rather than a plump figure when she would enter the sitting-room. She combed her hair in the privacy of the tiny bedroom for the umpteenth time. She decided to forego stockings. The black patent, high-heeled shoes contrasted favourably with the creamy silk of her calves. She loosened a second button on her front. She needed to be striking and provocative as well as sensual on that vital first entrance. He needed to be smitten with such force that he would follow blindly to his mother's bedroom which was the unlikely location chosen by Mollie for the gamble of her life. The satisfaction which she would derive from being conscious of the place of surrender would far exceed any joy which she might derive from the act itself.

Tom sat reading a trade journal when Mollie Purley entered to ask if he might have the correct time.

'Time!' he murmured without looking up to see who had asked. 'The time is twenty minutes to eight.'

'Will I draw the curtains?' Mollie asked.

Tom looked up for the first time.

'Curtains!' he returned, his mouth open, his interest instantly primed.

She did not await his reply but slowly crossed the room before utilising every contour of her barely concealed figure to draw the curtains together.

'Sit down! Sit down a minute for God's sake!' he called out desperately as she was about to leave the room.

'I'd love to,' said Mollie as she stood framed invitingly in the doorway, on her face the most apologetic and disarming of smiles, 'but I have so many things to do upstairs.'

'Upstairs!' He whispered the word to himself brokenly. He found himself unable to swallow. His mouth suddenly turned dry.

'Upstairs!' He repeated the word as he rose unsteadily to his feet.

She did not close the door behind her. Her perfume beckoned like an invisible finger in her wake. He found his teeth chattering as he climbed the stairs. He had never felt so light-headed.

In the bedroom her back was turned to him as she smoothed the pillows on his mother's bed. When he seized her urgently from the rear she exclaimed in tones which were far from aggrieved that he was exceeding himself. When he ripped away the flimsy front of the cotton frock all she said by way of protest was 'No, no Tom! You mustn't!'

Tom acted as though he hadn't heard and truth to tell it was quite possible that he truly hadn't, so faint had been her vocal objections. Not in the least deterred either way Tom laid her out lovingly on his mother's bed. She indulged his every whim, was at once limp and gymnastic, girlish and womanly, tantalising and fulfilling. She overwhelmed him as she herself seemed likewise to be overwhelmed. Sometimes she mewed like a kitten. Other times she clawed like a cat. She grunted, groaned and snorted as well as producing a whole range of sounds, exciting and original, which made the ears of her conquerer tingle and his pulse quicken as it had never quickened before. Finally she swooned when the limp figure which had been so assiduously astride her dissolved panting by her side, the ravages of the demanding rampage showing on his pinched but grinning face.

When Madge Cronane arrived home from the Trallock funeral she found the lights on and the curtains drawn in the sitting-room. When her son failed to answer her calls she quite rightly presumed that he had gone to bed early. Before bolting the doors for the night she paid a hasty visit to Tom's bedroom. She was about to knock gently on the door but refrained when the reassuring sounds of his profound snoring assailed her ears. He rarely snored and never like this. He must have put in a harder day than usual.

The wench Mollie Purley had gone to her home for the night and good riddance thought Madge. In fairness, however, she was obliged to concede that the creature was an outstanding worker, possibly the best domestic she had ever employed but there

36

was something there that made her wary something sinister that she could not quite define. She
had thought of giving her notice at the end of the
three months which had just expired but could find
no adequate grounds. Her latest efforts to ensnare
her had not succeeded either. There was nothing
tangible which she could hold against her and yet
Madge was certain that the mountainy girl boded
no good for the Cronane household. Her every
instinct warned her that prompt action was an
absolute necessity. Within the next few days she
decided she would make her move. The girl would
have to go.

Mollie and Tom involved themselves in three
further sessions of unchaste dalliance and although in Tom's eyes none was as lustfully fulfilling as the first he was, nevertheless, enthralled
with this captivating and sultry cailin from the
mountains. Tom was certain that the rapturous
heights to which they had initially ascended might
again be scaled if sufficient time was put at their
disposal. As it was the meetings were hurried and
furtive and took place in such diverse places as the
turf shed, the back seat of Tom's Morris Oxford
and finally in the little attic bedroom one morning
while Madge Cronane was attending early mass at
Ballybobawn parish church.

This was to be their last clandestine encounter.
Shortly afterwards Mollie informed Tom that she
was expecting a baby and that he was the father.
Tom could not quite make up his mind whether he
should laugh or cry. He had been in many an entanglement but he had never succeeded in making
a girl pregnant before. This made him want to
laugh, to exult in his prospective fatherhood. However, the thought of his mother's reaction was so

chastening that he wished the ground would open and swallow him up. He decided that marriage was the only honourable course open to him. His decision was reinforced by the thought that he would have undisputed legal access to the transcendent favours of Mollie Purley for the remainder of his natural life.

The marriage was celebrated in the parish church and the reception was held at the Arms Hotel in Trallock. Instead of squandering every penny of the Cronane fortunes, as everybody said she would, Mollie extended the empire further and eventually transformed the ramshackle premises into one of the most modern supermarkets in the county. Her mother-in-law failed to show up at the wedding but her absence in no way detracted from the celebrations. She purchased a small house on the outskirts of Ballybobawn and spoke neither to her son nor her daughter-in-law for several years. In the end she relented when the children began to visit her, prompted by Mollie, now generally accepted as the overlord of the village and its surrounds. The children benefited from their grandmother's will but not a penny did she leave to either her son or daughter-in-law.

TOM CRONANE DID NOT come downstairs until ten o'clock. He headed straight for the sitting-room where he found the *Irish Independent,* as usual, awaiting him unopened on his favourite armchair. Despite his premature senility he could still read without spectacles.

'My mother says do you want breakfast Da?' The question was posed by his oldest son Cha, a

38

powerfully-built, squat young man of twenty with the dark eyes and round countenance of his grandfather. He was a dour-looking fellow, the only male member of the family retained by his mother to work permanently in the supermarket. The girls, Kate and Noreen, were usually on call whenever they were required. The three other sons, Sammie, Donie and Tomboy the youngest, were still schoolgoing. Sammie and Donie were in their pre-Leaving Certificate or intervention years. Tomboy had just completed his Intermediate Examination. All three were celebrating the start of the summer holidays which would last until early September when the new comprehensive school in Trallock would reopen.

'My mother says if you're not having breakfast Da to know would you go with her to the presbytery to see Father O'Connor?'

Tom answered his oldest son with a voice full of irritation. 'Will you tell your mother that I will not be available until I have the paper read!'

'And how long will that be Da?' Cha's question was respectfully intoned.

'How in Christ do I know?' his father replied sharply.

'Say half an hour Da?'

'All right Cha. All right boy. Half an hour then.'

Tom rarely worked in the supermarket. The encroaching senility restricted both his movements and timing. His second visitation of the morning was from his three other sons.

'What is it now?' he asked.

'Da,' Tomboy the youngest and most articulate acted as spokesman, 'we're going to Trallock to get our hair cut for the weddings.'

Tom Cronane puckered up his already wizened

face. 'But the weddings are three weeks away,' he argued.

'Yes Da,' Tomboy went on patiently, 'but our mother don't want us looking too freshly barbered.

'You see Da,' Tomboy explained, 'our mother has given us the money for the haircuts all right but she's refusing to give us any pocket money until the weekend.'

'All right. How much?' Tom injected as much resignation as he could muster into his voice.

'We were thinking of twenty pounds between us seeing as it's the start of the holidays.'

'How much?' Tom exploded.

'A tenner between us would do grand Da.'

Tom thrust his hand into his fob pocket and withdrew a roll of notes. He peeled off a ten-pound bill. He held it between his fingers a while before parting with it.

'By the way,' he asked innocently, 'how much is a pint of cider now?'

'Ninety pence,' Tomboy blurted out the price without thinking. Sammie and Donie held their breaths.

Tom extended the hand which held the tenner.

Tomboy came forward to accept it.

'Did I see you with a woman lately Tomboy?'

The blood drained from Tomboy's face.

'Drink and women,' his father shook his head solemnly.

Tomboy pocketed the bank note and nodded in agreement. His father must have seen him walking with Mary Creel. He waited for the old man to say more but he became immersed in his paper.

Later, after he read the paper, he was joined by Mollie at the front entrance to the supermarket.

'Are you ready?' he asked.

40

'Just hold your horses a minute!' She lifted a restraining hand.

'What's up now?'

'That's what's up,' Mollie returned, pointing to a travelling woman who had come into view further down. 'I'm not leaving till she passes by.'

Mollie recognised her from previous expeditions to Puck Fair. She had been a constant visitor to the shop until Mollie had identified a frock worn by one of her clan as being the property of Cronane's supermarket. If she had stolen one article from the well-stocked shelves then by the Lord she had stolen more! Mollie Cronane was without mercy for those who plundered her hard-earned possessions.

The travelling woman entered the village with a heavy step and a sad face. Her swollen belly, loosely covered by a smock in dire need of washing, attested to her advanced pregnancy. She paused, sighed audibly and placed the palm of her right hand between her ample breasts and uprising midriff. After a few deep breaths she proceeded at a leisurely pace towards Ballybobawn cross. The drama of her contrived movements was lost on the all but empty street. Only a member of her own semi-settled community would know that all her manifestations of despondency were part of an established ritual beloved of her kind and that they carefully concealed her real feelings.

Bob's Katie as she was called, for no other reason than that she was married to Bob, was as happy as she could possibly be. Was she not on her way to the great fair of Puck in a daffodil-coated, span-new Hiace van. Would she not be meeting there with all the members of her own clan and would not the drink flow free for the greater part of a week. Bob's Katie had seen hard times, harder than most of her equals and she surely wasn't going to let the good times go by without acknowledging her good fortune and how better could she do that than by playing the role of a martyred tinker woman on the point of having another babby! If she was only gone the five months itself what the devil harm was it to make the most of her situation. There would be no danger of a beating in Puck no matter how drunk her man might get. Her brothers would be there, not that they would be likely to take her part but Bob Latty wouldn't want her going around with a mark on her face. In her condition he couldn't very well strike her elsewhere. Anyway her husband would spend far more time in the town than he would at the encampment and when he came home she didn't have to be there. The children would look after each other. Bob's Katie would be free for the first time in a year. She looked forward to the drinking sessions and the music and the ballad groups, the bags of French fries, the hamburgers and the hot dogs. Puck Fair was fairyland and if she and her kind were barred in most of the pubs they could always have a drink bought for them by one of the settled community and claim right of tenure until it was drank. It wasn't that the publicans looked down on the fraternity of travellers but it was a fact that many of the visitors invariably ended up fighting.

Bob's Katie knew Ballybobawn well, not much good in it but pickins' all the same. It had been better in her mother's time. God be good to her, the old woman used to say, 'Collected proper 'tis worth more nor a hundred saucers of flour!'

'There's no flour now,' Bob's Katie spoke to herself, 'nothing but the shop bread and amen says me to that for you'd want a good fire to bake and good fires were scarce in them winters. No flour but if a wan's face is like the mother o'sorrows and wan's mouth is poor enough there's always a few to be gathered.'

'She's better off than most behind the doors she's knocking at,' Mollie made the observation out of the side of her mouth as they watched Bob's Katie approach.

'God spare you the health missus would you have e'er a copper?' Bob's Katie didn't look directly at Mollie. She looked instead at her feet. When no reply was forthcoming she raised her head and looked Mollie straight in the eye.

'E'er an oul' copper missus and I'll pray for you.'

By way of reply Mollie drew the air in forcefully through her nose, upsucking rheum, snot and saliva from her nasal recesses, mustering all three in the mouth. Then from pouted lips she squirted the malicious spittle in the direction of Bob's Katie's feet. The tinker woman moved sharply backwards, very nearly losing her balance in the process.

The spit was Mollie's reaction to the thievery the pregnant woman had perpetrated upon her over the years.

'Now, now,' Tom turned on his wife, 'there's no call for that.'

Bob's Katie passed on slowly.

'Be wary missus,' she counselled in a whisper, 'or your spit will be blown back into your gob.'

3

IN THE VILLAGE NOTHING stirred. The long street which comprised most of the built-up area was deserted save for occasional dogs stirring themselves only to scratch.

From the fields all around there came the drowsy sounds of numerous mowing machines but if one was curious and approached the entrance to the Load of S one would hear the clicking of pool balls as the exponents of this new indoor diversion squared off, cues in hand, in solemn confrontation. At the bar counter on a high stool sat Mickey Creel, father of Mary, balefully surveying the meagre remains of the proud pint which had earlier filled his glass. He looked around at the pool players and their absorbed audience in the forlorn hope that some generous and understanding soul would issue the order for replenishment. Fat chance! All the other inmates of the bar, and there were many, were recipients of social welfare like himself and would argue that they had no more than enough to satisfy their own needs. Through multi-coloured drapes of strip plastic an inner sanctum was barely visible to the casual observer but if he was a perceptive person he would observe several fascinated viewers, drinks in hand, watching a television film in which three nude and youthful contortionists were engaged in the more bizarre forms of sexual activity.

Mickey Creel's more recent preference was for the Load of S rather than Tom's Tavern where he had spent most of his adult life. In the Load of S there was always a passing trade. It had become a landmark during its short lifetime and a mecca for the type of braggart visitors who felt it was necessary to buy rounds of drinks for hangers-on in order to establish themselves as men of consequence. Mickey Creel knew to the dram when the buying-power of such interlopers was exhausted. Silently he would sidle from his stool, and before anybody was aware of the fact, he was seated hopefully at either the Widow Cahalane's or Tom's Tavern where, alas, the likelihood of free drink was more remote. After a sojourn in the wilderness he would return to the more fruitful Load of S in the hope of finding his former benefactors gone and a new crop of blusterers waiting to be ratified by a carefully-compiled mixture of blandishments and flattery.

It was an occupation at which Mickey Creel had become expert. He learned over the years that even the most unlikely sources could sometimes show a profitable return with circumspect investment. There were bleak occasions too when he was obliged to muster every last nuance of cajolery in order to obtain a lowly half-pint of stout which was the cheapest measure of alcoholic drink available. Passing strangers whose business took them through Ballybobawn at night often wondered at his uncanny ability to remain upright while he staggered homewards at the conclusion of his day-long imbibitions. He was never known to fall. Despite hairbreadth escapes from night-time traffic and unexpected obstacles such as rubbish bins and other dangerous obstructions he had yet to be brought to his knees on his return journey.

MARY DEPARTED AS usual for her home in the village. She took her leave earlier than was her wont in order to catch one of the specially-hired buses which would take her and scores of other young boys and girls to the annual end-of-school dance which was being held in the recreation hall of the new community school in Trallock. It was Mary's first such outing. Tomboy Cronane would be there or at least he had promised he would.

Mary did not bother to ask her father's permission. Instead she asked the Ram of God if it would be all right. Her mother had already approved and so had Nonie. The Ram was dubious at first as he felt he did not have the authority to give her permission but in the end he gave her his blessing. In normal circumstances it would have been sufficient to seek her father's permission. Circumstances, alas, were never normal in the Creel household when Mickey was drinking heavily and drinking heavily he was at this particular time for on that very morning he had commandeered the family allowance money and despite his wife's protestations did not return a single penny. He spent the entire day drinking in the Load of S.

The Load of S closed its doors after a long and profitable innings due to the fact that the dole and family allowances fell on the same day. Alas, when Mary returned from Trallock after the dance, she found the entire family huddled together at the rear of the house to which familiar spot Mickey Creel had expelled them with kicks and blows for no apparent reason shortly after midnight. Silently, after she confirmed that her father was fast asleep, the family had returned to the house.

AS THE LOAD OF S disgorged its patrons on the stroke of midnight Sergeant Holly made the observation, to himself, that not one of the public house's numerous patrons was employed. Not one in fact had been employed for a period of over six months and there were some who had never engaged in a full day's work in their lives. Most complained that there was no work available but it was Sergeant Holly's guess that work was the last thing many of the patrons wanted. Some, on their own behalf, worked in the bogs but only to an extent which would provide them with winter firing. Others, a goodly number of handymen and labourers, indulged in a few days' work now and then on a cash-on-the-line principle. This way the parttimers were not accountable to the tax system nor were they obliged to make the normal social-welfare contributions.

'This is an extraordinary country,' Sergeant Holly commented whilst he and his only aide, Garda Thomas Connelly were engaged in a routine patrol of the village. 'Here we have a situation where only the unemployed can afford to drink on a regular basis and to any great degree of drunkenness. On Thursday, which is dole day, the Load of S is never empty. Tom's Tavern also draws its share and while the Widow Cahalane's mightn't be exactly chock-a-block she's not deserted either. If those pubs were depending on the employed sector they'd have to close down. If the Load of S was put up for sale in the morning it would make the most of a quarter of a million pounds; a quarter of a million in a village where there isn't a single factory!'

Garda Connelly shook his head in disbelief.

'The farmers do all the work,' the sergeant continued, 'and the unemployed do all the drinking.

Something's got to give sometime. The money's going to run out.'

'Do you think the last of 'em are gone home?' the garda asked.

'No way,' the sergeant scoffed. 'There are four or five farmer's still left in the Widow's but we won't bother them; they couldn't come any earlier. It's silage time. They'll be up with the crack of dawn, drink or no drink.'

'Tell me about the Ram of God,' Garda Connelly put in the request as they moved down the street.

'Let's take a look at the itinerants first before they move on to Puck. What do you want to know about the Ram?'

'His name for one thing.'

'Well his real name is Edward Drannaghy. Nobody seems to remember who tagged him with the name Ram of God but it stuck and it's going to stay stuck.'

'Was he a ladies' man then?'

'Not particularly,' Sergeant Holly returned. 'To put it in a nutshell Thomas, rumour has it that the Ram is the father of a child, that he was seduced by his first cousin's wife who came expressly to Ireland from New York so that she could conceive within the circle of the family. The scheme had her husband's blessing. The couple were childless and desperate for a family of their own. It wasn't a commonplace occurrence but it has been known to happen. In fact there was an instance of it in my own countryside in Galway. Anyway the lady in question came to Ireland for the sole purpose of making herself pregnant by one of her husband's relations. There was a Drannaghy family in Cork city but apparently no member of that branch measured up to the lady's requirements. She vis-

48

ited another branch in the county of Waterford and wasn't all that elated with what she saw there. Then she came to Ballybobawn. The Ram's father was alive at the time and he received his nephew's wife with open arms. In fact everybody liked her. She wasn't fast or game or anything like that. She was a fine-looking woman. The minute she clapped her eyes upon Eddie Drannaghy she knew that her search had come to an end. It didn't matter to her that he was a clerical student in one of the country's leading seminaries.'

'You said she was a fine-looking woman,' Garda Connelly cut in. 'Could you elaborate?'

'Well,' Sergeant Holly searched for words which might provide a more accurate description, 'I'll tell you just one thing about her and I'll tell you no more. If I had been her cousin I would have accommodated her anywhere, any time. Does that answer your question?'

'Yes it does,' Garda Connelly replied.

'This whole business took place fifteen years ago and but for a piece of bad luck the Ram might have gotten away with it.' The sergeant stopped in his tracks and removed his cap in order to scratch his head.

'If the Ram had any experience in such matters he would have suggested a safer location as soon as she had declared her hand. Trouble was he was what we call a cock virgin and didn't want hand, act or part in her scheme. There are few of us, my dear Thomas, proof against the wiles of a woman if that woman happens to be beautiful as well as being artfully designed. Resistance melts like butter on a hot griddle. Remember I knew the woman. I spoke to her on several occasions. I would never have believed then that she was hatching such a plot. The whole village loved her. The twins, they were just kids then, followed her everywhere. The old man doted on her but the Ram of God kept his distance. They say she first stole to his bed in the morning light and that he was powerless to resist her. One thing is true and that is that she was seen in his arms in what we will call compromising circumstances one summer's evening in the field next to the one they call the High Meadow. There's a lovely hazel glade there and there's a stream. Add to that the fact that the weather was fine and that the seductress from the Land of the Mighty Dollar decided she was going to bathe in a pool which was the most attractive feature of the stream. It would be my guess that this was the first time it happened. She selected her locale with great care. She selected her apparel with even greater care, that's if you could call it apparel for all she had on was a bikini.'

'But how was he found out?' Garda Connelly asked.

'I'm coming to that. If you'll be patient and bear with me I'll tell you the full story. What the American lady didn't know at the time was that she was followed from the farmhouse by the twins. They were right little bastards then and they're no better now. The Ram was in the High Meadow turning hay when he heard her call. Naturally he went to see what she was up to. When she emerged from the pool he was carried away. I know I would be. Can you imagine it Thomas, this fine, full-bodied woman, with nothing but a few wisps of cloth covering her! Can you imagine the water droplets sparkling like diamonds on her skin and can you picture the laughing smile on her face?'

'I sure can,' Thomas Connelly sighed. 'How well

I couldn't have a cousin like that.'

'Well,' the excitement disappeared from the sergeant's voice. 'One thing borrowed another. The poor fellow was like putty in her arms. He had no chance at all Thomas.'

'What happened then?' Thomas asked eagerly.

'What happened then was that the twins appeared from nowhere. They saw all that took place and they broadcast it to anyone who would listen all the way down to the cross of Ballybobawn. By nightfall the story had travelled far and wide. Maybe it was the twins, who christened him the Ram. Later he was to be labelled the Ram of God although I honestly cannot say who was responsible. It was a first-class monicker under the circumstances. Thankfully the only person who didn't hear about the lovemaking session was the old man, the Ram of God's father. He never quite grew accustomed to the sobriquet which he dismissed as an out-of-taste prank by the twins. The American woman wasn't in the least bit mortified or so everybody said at the time. The Ram went with her to Shannon in order to see her off and did not come back for two whole days. There is no direct evidence to suggest that they continued with their illicit relationship before she departed but I'll lay you a pound to a penny Thomas that she was well and truly sired before boarding the plane that was to take her back to New York. It's a matter of record that a daughter was eventually born to her, her birth coinciding with the prescribed period of nine calendar months after her visit. I'm sorry for the Ram. He was the only loser in the whole bloody business.'

'In what way?' Thomas asked.

'Well he was wrongly branded for one thing. He

had never been involved with a woman before that. In fact he was an exemplary young man. He lost his place in the seminary to boot. I know the Ram and this must surely have broken his heart. Dammit man you're up there one day on a pedestal and the next down in the muck. Another man would have cracked up when the full story got out or at the very least he would have left the country or even the place where he was born. Not the Ram of God. He kept his head down and his mouth shut and he forgave the twins. When his father died he hung in there and carried them on his back until now. They're sitting pretty and again the Ram is the loser for he's out on his ear the minute the Cronane gang move in. Some men are born to suffer Thomas. I hope you won't take it unkindly if I tell you to watch your footwork when you're dealing with the damsels in this neck of the woods.'

'I won't mind sergeant,' Thomas replied with a smile.

Both men paused at the junction which led to the council houses. The lights were still on in many of the front windows and upstairs rooms.

'They'll sit up awhile now,' the sergeant explained, 'after the beer, maybe eat a bite, relieve the bladders a few more times before hitting the sack. It's a good life provided you don't worry about not working and most of them have stopped worrying about that long ago. Their fathers worried and their mothers slaved and all for nothing. These people know they won't starve. They might hunger occasionally but they'll never be short of the price of a drink. They're telling us something Thomas and we're not listening. They're saying that they don't give a damn any more. They're free and their freedom is being subsidised by a state that is totally lacking in imagination. These people are not prisoners like the workers in Trallock. They're not tied to machines or assembly lines. Instead of being dehumanised they're liberated. There's no revolution in the offing here. They have colour television, hot and cold water, enough to eat, the prospect of a good booze-up at least twice a week and they have their pornographic movies. They haven't been sacrificed to progress like their working brothers. In fact they have no intention of being sacrificed to anything. The national conscience doesn't exist around here any more.'

'The itinerants have a good life,' Thomas fuelled the fire of his sergeant's disquisition.

'A better life than you and I Thomas. They don't have to get up in the morning. One of the children will see that the horses are secure. You won't catch them eating like us just because it's dinner-time or supper-time or breakfast-time. They'll eat when they're hungry. It's true that they neglect themselves but it's their choice. Bad weather doesn't suit their lifestyles but they're truly free and again they're subsidised man, woman and child for the fifty-two weeks of the year.'

There were three Hiace vans parked at the encampment. All were relatively new, one daffodil, one Caribbean blue and the third vermilion. There were also three makeshift tents. The ashes from three fires still smouldered on the camp's outskirts. From the tents came satisfied snoring of a kind never before heard by Thomas Connelly. It was gentle, it was even and it was musical.

'You're listening to the sleep of the just Thomas,' his sergeant informed him. 'It's a sound rarely heard by the settled community.'

As they moved on the sounds of slumber were

interspersed by a series of long, drawn-out expulsions of intestinal wind.

'Hear that!' Sergeant Holly raised a finger, "tis as though they were telling us how little they care. Oh they're free Thomas. Their only problem is thinking up new places to go before returning to their council houses for the winter.'

After they had passed by a dog barked half-heartedly, a child cried out briefly and silence, save for the gentle snoring, descended once again on the sleeping encampment.

On their return journey through the village both policemen stood for a while at the cross.

'What time are you Thomas?' Sergeant Holly asked.

'I'm quarter to one sergeant.'

'All this talking has made me dry Thomas. What would you say if I suggested that we repair for a spell to the Widow Cahalane's and partook of a pint or two?'

'I'd say it was a very sound suggestion sergeant but will they let us in?'

'Oh they'll let us in all right Thomas,' the sergeant assured him, 'but will they let us out?'

IF THE RAM OF God had been eavesdropping while Sergeant Holly recalled his version of events for Thomas Connelly he would have been forced to concede that the sergeant had given a reasonably accurate account of the folly which had bedevilled him during the height of that summer fifteen years before. He might add or subtract a little from what the sergeant said but he would have made no major correction. Undoubtedly, the sergeant's version about what might or might not have occurred

54

during the two-day interlude before Lorraine left for the United States was only conjecture but again the Ram would probably verify that it was near enough to the mark.

Lorraine Drannaghy nee Dupree was all the things the sergeant said she was. She was also ruthless and yet passionate. The pair broke their journey to Shannon and spent a night in Limerick. This was followed by a night in Galway. The Ram could never bring himself to recall the details of their love-making. As he drove home from Shannon in the family Ford which his father had placed at Lorraine's disposal for the length of her stay he stopped at a scenic viewpoint on the banks of the Shannon River which skirted the roadway. He stood, without moving, for a full hour, his gaze fixed, unseeing, between the clear sky and the unfractured expanse of river water. They kissed before she boarded the plane but it lacked the rapture of those earlier kisses which eventually led to the fullest possible relationship. He sensed that she could not wait to be aboard the plane. He knew from that kiss that it was all over, that he would never see her again. In a way he was relieved. She had been too much of a burden for him. At the time she had been thirty-five and he twenty.

As he looked out over the placid stretch of water between the counties of Clare and Kerry the turmoil in his mind refused to abate. A pair of cormorants, one flying barely above the other and both perilously close to the surface, flew up-river, the faint whirring of their wings reminding him of the almost soundless disrobing of his freshly departed love.

There was nobody to whom he could turn after Lorraine left. He prayed incessantly, chiefly to his late mother, for counsel and forgiveness and to the Virgin Mary that the sickening sense of guilt which weighed upon him might in some way be absorbed into the abundant heavens where its malign influence would expire in their immensity.

'I had no chance. No chance at all.' He whispered the words to himself as he sat against the harvester and allowed his eyes to take in the loveliness of the tiny hazel grove which flanked the pool on all sides but one. Here were willows of a fading green, some browning ever so slightly after the long drought. The setting had not changed all that much in fifteen years.

He had seemed like a vegetable to his family and neighbours. He was lucky to have the farm work. Working in isolation suited him. He could not endure human company in a work-place. He kept his mind to himself and this was a mistake. He should have turned to somebody.

Fortunately, there had been the sage advice of Nonie Spillane. Nonie's heart went out to him as she watched him come and go silently. He rarely spoke. One night they were sitting alone in the kitchen. The summer had passed and there were late August rains pattering against the windows.

'You'd want to gather yourself,' Nonie said.

'How's that?' he answered absently.

'How long since you were at confession?'

He declined to answer. He sat looking at the floor.

'Go down this minute to Father O'Connor. He'll be still hearing.'

'I can't,' was all the answer he gave her.

'Go down now,' she had persisted, 'that poor man will forgive you anything. You need have no fear on that score and take this.' She thrust a five pound note into his hand. 'Go into the Widow's and throw back two balls o' malt for courage.'

Nonie was right as always. Father O'Connor could not have been more helpful. The Ram received absolute forgiveness and left the confessional with a powerful determination to pursue his vocation. He took no drink on his way to the confessional but afterwards he spent Nonie's fiver in the Widow Cahalane's. The Widow was taken somewhat by surprise when he entered. She was uncertain whether or not she should dispense the glass of stout which he ordered. While she was making up her mind her twelve-year-old-daughter filled the pint for the handsome, thoughtful twenty-year-old. They could say what they liked about him. In young Patricia Cahalane's eyes the Ram of God was an innocent and forlorn young man who had been through enough without incurring the displeasure of her self-righteous mother.

Much to his surprise before the winter snows had whitened the High Meadow he found it difficult to conjure up the least impression of the feelings which haunted him across the summer and autumn. In the spring of the following year he had all but forgotten her. Then, alas, it was too late. Disaster struck through the medium of an anonymous letter. News of its arrival came as a total shock to him.

Returning to college in early October the Ram applied himself with renewed zeal to his studies. The daily time-table began at six o'clock in the morning beginning with the Rising Bell which was the signal for vacating one's bed, winter and summer. This was followed by meditation and prayer. At seven o'clock mass was celebrated. Breakfast was served at eight followed by study and lectures until twelve-thirty when a light lunch was available. Dinner was served at the unlikely hour of three-thirty in the afternoon followed by further study until five-thirty. At seven o'clock there was spiritual reading followed by tea, bread and jam at seven-thirty. At nine o'clock evening prayers were said. Then came ten o'clock and Lights Out.

Most young men with such torrid experiences of the recent summer so fresh in the mind might rebel at the dreary routine; not so Eddie Drannaghy. He revelled in the demanding discipline. There were some breaks in the rigourous routine. There were exercises and games on Sundays after dinner. There was the occasional play and concert enacted by the students themselves.

Eddie Drannaghy was a model seminarian. He was his old self about the house and farm during the Christmas holidays. He devoted his spare time to study, never once lingering in Ballybobawn or Trallock after the seasonal and Sunday masses. Already in his second year he had taken honours in Latin and Greek, Logic, English and History. In the October of the following year he would be sitting for an honours BA.

Then one day after a long and cheerless homily from a visiting spiritual director he was surprised when he was called aside by the dean of studies as he left the chapel where the talk had been delivered.

'Edward,' the dean began with what in Eddie Drannaghy's eyes was spine-chilling solemnity.

'Yes Father?' he had answered meekly. The dean clasped his hands close to his chest and swallowed soundlessly before sucking in his breath. This tactic was one which he never failed to employ prior to uttering some dictum of unusual importance.

'The president has instructed me to inform you,' the dean rose to his full height of five feet two inches as he continued, 'that you are to report to his office at precisely seven o'clock this evening.'

'But,' Eddie had protested fearing the worst, 'I have a spiritual reading at seven o'clock.'

'The president is well aware of the college time-table. You will present yourself at seven and not a moment later.'

'Yes Father.'

The dean stood for several moments as though to ensure that his words were taken properly to heart and that there could be no possibility of a misunderstanding. Seminarians, in their junior years, as he was all too well aware, were great warrants for misinterpreting the most simple of instructions when these might conflict with their own interests.

'Could you by any chance tell me Father,' Eddie ventured, 'what I might be wanted for?'

'I daresay I could,' the dean returned at once, 'if I were so disposed. However, in the light of what has been revealed to me I think it is far too serious a matter for further discussion in public. See that you present yourself at seven.'

'Yes Father.'

Short as their exchange was Eddie feared the worst. For a moment he considered leaving without a word to anybody. He could take a boat to England. However, to leave the grounds without special permission meant to incur automatic expulsion and since he had not yet been condemned he decided to brazen it out. He tried to recall some other misdemeanour which might merit a special interview with the president but nothing came to mind. It had to be something external. His conduct within the walls was always impeccable. He had, in fact, been commended on more than one occasion by the dean of studies although there had been the distinct impression in his delivery of the president's summons that his attitude was no longer friendly.

During the five-thirty to seven study period Eddie found it impossible to concentrate. He had never before been summoned before the president. Some of his friends had, usually for some breach of college rules, such as persistent late rising or horseplay within the confines of the college. He fervently wished that he would be charged with some such triviality. He closed the text book which lay open in front of him and resorted finally to prayer until the time came for his visit to the presidential office where already were seated the president Monsignor Gresham, the vice-president Father Claffy and the dean of studies Father Morrikan. They began their deliberations at six-thirty and had not arrived at any conclusion.

Father Morrikan was speaking. 'If what the letter says is true monsignor we seem to be faced with a situation which has no precedent.'

'No precedent to our knowledge Father.'

'Of course monsignor,' Father Morrikan voiced immediate agreement.

'If it is true how do you propose to deal with it?' the vice-president, Father Claffy asked.

'It's not what I propose to do Father,' the monsignor responded gravely, 'it is what the law says in relation to the matter that will take precedence over what any of us might think and the law requires in this instance that if Edward Drannaghy is guilty he expels himself.'

'On the word of an anonymous letter-writer!'

Father Claffy shook his grey head with an even greater gravity than that shown by his president.

'Since my ordination to the priesthood,' the vice-president continued 'I have received a grand total of seven anonymous letters which is considerably less than the average priest receives. I have consigned each and every one of those letters to flames. I will confess that because of initial ignorance and curiosity I read the first two but after that, upon satisfying myself that there was no name at the end, I folded them in my fist and cast them into the fire.'

'And most commendable too I'm sure,' the president amended drily, 'but I am in the unfortunate position Father where I am obliged to read all mail affecting the seminarians. I do not approve of anonymous letters but I must confess that this particular one is not in the least mischievous nor is it offensive. The author's only concern would seem to be the welfare of the seminarians and the good name of the college.'

'I can't go along with that,' the vice-president sounded distinctly unhappy. 'There is nothing as odious or as mischievous as an anonymous letter. I have seen the harm they have done. If we accept Edward's guilt on the basis of this prurient discharge from a sick mind we are letting down the good name of the college.'

'Let me assure you Father,' the president raised his hands as though he were imposing a blessing upon a congregation, 'that we will definitely not be assessing guilt or innocence on the basis of this letter. What I propose to do is put the contents of the letter before him and simply ask him whether they are true or false.'

'You must do what you must do,' the vice-

61

president spoke as though he intended washing his hands of the matter.

'May I say something monsignor,' the dean of studies cleared his throat and sucked in his breath.

'By all means Father. That is why you have been invited here, to say your piece.'

Father Morrikan cleared his throat secondly. 'I'm not sure that what I have to say has any relevance but I feel duty bound to say it. It is true that there would be many an unsolved murder but for the reliance of the police on anonymous information. I too would be wary of anonymous letters but if an anonymous letter does more good than harm then there is something to be said in its favour. I read somewhere recently that the police, in fact, rely on anonymous tips more so than routine detective work for the solving of all kinds of crime.'

'We are not talking about crime here Father,' the vice-president cut across him.

'And neither is Father Morrikan,' the president came to the dean's aid. 'What he is trying to do is show us that anonymous material can help in all forms of investigation and what I am doing here is conducting an investigation and, therefore, I propose to present Edward Drannaghy with the accusation made in this letter. I cannot ignore the letter. That is why you are both here. We have been seminarians ourselves. We are not likely to do the young man an injustice. I thank you for your analogy Father Morrikan.'

The ecclesiastical triumvirate fell silent and exchanged anxious looks as the mantelpiece clock spelled out the hour. Before the chimes expired there was a tentative knocking on the office door.

'Come in,' the president called at which the door opened slowly, revealing the tall, pale-faced student whose future lay in the hands of the three men who confronted him.

'Sit down Edward,' the president's jovial command was designed to put the young man at his ease. The gesture failed lamentably for the chair upon which Edward Drannaghy sat betrayed his true feelings. It seemed as though it would disintegrate at any moment.

'I'll come to the point Edward,' the president spoke in reassuring tones. 'It is with some reluctance that we have summoned you here and please do not think any the less of us for hauling you before us as it were. I have here before me a letter purported to have been written by a devout woman who happens to hail from the parish of Ballybobawn or so she maintains. It is an anonymous letter and it is a disturbing letter and it has to do with you Edward and let me say here and now that I am convinced that you will immediately set all our minds at rest by declaring unequivocally that the contents of the letter are false. I will not read the letter as it contains some material which is not relevant to the business in hand. I will simply say to you that this woman accuses you of being the father of a child which was recently born in the city of New York and that you further were involved in a disgraceful affair with a married woman who happens to be the mother of this child. All you have to say to us Edward is that you are not the father of a child and that you were not involved with this American woman. Say that and you will walk from this room with our sincerest and most heartfelt apologies.'

Edward hung his head, his eyes closed, his

whole frame shaking.

'I propose we end this inquisition forthwith,' the vice-president rose and rested a hand on the seminarian's shoulder. 'The boy is obviously distressed beyond words.'

'Be good enough to sit down Father. We have a duty to perform.' The president's tone made his displeasure clear.

The vice-president withdrew his hand but did not sit down immediately. To do so, in his opinion, would be to renege on the seminarian altogether. Of the three clerics present he was the only one who had been at the receiving end of such a tribunal. In his case there had been acquittal after a lengthy and unfair examination, most of which had little to do with his alleged misdemeanour which had to do with nothing more serious than breaking a window. When he sat down there was an uncomfortable silence. He was the first to speak.

'Proving paternity has always been one of the more bewildering and inconclusive aspects of litigation and to suggest that the contents of an anonymous letter should be taken seriously in this regard smacks of lunacy.'

'We are not in a courtroom Father.' The rebuke came from Father Morrikan.

'I am well aware of where we are,' came back the sharp retort.

'That is not the impression one gets,' Father Morrikan, assured of the president's tacit approval, knew that he might be exceeding himself but felt constrained nevertheless to make the next proposal.

'I think we should proceed with the questions which the president first posed which were, as I recall, was Edward involved or was he not with the

American woman? I propose the boy should be asked if he is in a state of grace and if his vocation feels threatened. Are you in a state of grace to the best of your knowledge Edward?'

'Yes Father.'

'And does your vocation feel in any way threatened?'

'No Father.'

'On your word as a seminarian,' the next question came from the president, 'will you deny that you had an intimate relationship with this woman?'

Edward Drannaghy hung his head.

'Will you deny that you are the father of her child?'

'I cannot answer that,' the seminarian replied.

For the first time a puzzled look appeared on Father Morrikan's face. There was anger in his voice as he put the next question.

'Did you have an intimate relationship with this woman Edward?'

'Yes Father but I could not help myself Father.'

'Then it is possible that you are the father of a child?'

'Yes Father.'

'And the woman in question was a married woman?'

'Yes Father. She used me. I know that now. I had never before been involved in any way with a woman nor have I since that time. I have confessed and been forgiven by my parish priest Father O'Connor. I want to be a priest more than anything in the world. This most regrettable incident has fired my resolve to devote myself to my studies and to the service of God and my fellow human beings. I made a terrible mistake, a mistake that I will never, never make again. I wasn't prepared for what happened. I'm truly contrite and I will ask each of you to forgive me as Father O'Connor has forgiven me.'

The saddened trio nodded and murmured assent.

'Of course we forgive you my boy,' a note of kindness entered the president's voice, 'but it will not be possible for you to stay on here.'

Edward had burst into tears upon hearing the decision. He spoke brokenly to himself, 'My father ... the village, the neighbours. What will I do?'

The answer was voiced by Father Morrikan. 'You'll find your father will be forgiving just as Father O'Connor was.'

'But what will I tell him?'

To this there was no reply. To suggest a fabrication would be a negation of all the principles on which their faith was founded.

'Could you give me a second chance?' he blurted out the plea as he lunged forward on to his knees, his fingers entwined in pitiful supplication.

After a decent interval Father Claffy helped him to his feet and returned him to his chair. 'It isn't your fall from grace alone Edward. There is the unfortunate business of the nickname which, according to the letter, has replaced your Christian name in your homeland. We have to think of the other seminarians and, of course, the college itself. Far be it from me to condemn you my son. Alas, it is an exceptional deviation and our duty is clear, unpleasant and all as it is. Let us not speak of words like expulsion. This is not a drumming out. Look at it as the beginning of something new. There is nothing to stop you from taking your degree at the National University.'

The president went on but his words were lost

on the dejected figure sitting before him.

Now fifteen years later most people had lost interest in the Ram of God's far-off trespass. The rising generation, some of whom had been sketchily filled in by their elders on the Ram's one-time waywardness, either forgot it instantly or dismissed the whole business as a triviality. There was a new liberality abroad in the land, a liberality of which the Ram might not altogether approve but it had given him back the prospect of a normal life. He knew now that he would always be walking on a moral slack wire and this was more than most men knew. He also knew that he was the equivalent of a hare whose hindquarters are but a shade ahead of the hound's tooth. All men, he knew, were continually treading the slack wire of circumstance.

'The balance is the thing,' he said, 'preserving my balance so that I won't let myself down again.'

4

THE RAM OF GOD, now in his thirty-fifth year, sat silently on one of the high wooden stools in the licensed premises of the Widow Cahalane. Occasionally his fingers beat a slow, rhythmic tattoo on the polished counter. He had been sitting thus for over an hour.

The partially-consumed pint of stout which confronted him was the third of its kind which the widow had dispensed on his behalf. Occasionally she looked up anxiously, wondering at the sensitive face, now taut, the pursed lips cogitating on God-alone-knew-what and the silence into which she dared not intrude, not that he was likely to rebuff her if she spoke but she felt that to trespass would be to violate some unutterable profundity which he might be endeavouring to resolve.

She knew all about him. When it first came to her attention all those years ago that he was the father of a baby girl somewhere in the United States she was scandalised but now it didn't seem to matter at all. So much was happening everywhere. So much was changing. Many of the mortal sins of yesterday were the venial sins of today. She found the whole pattern of deterioration incomprehensible and disturbing. She might seem, because of a surface meekness, to have submitted to change but in her heart she would never condone anything that might conflict with the deeply-held religious tenets which dominated her upbringing. She kept her own counsel and she would hold fast to the end no matter what. She fervently wished the door would open and present her with a customer with whom she might pass the time of day, anything to dispel the intense silence which the Ram's presence imposed. Absently he lifted his glass and slowly drained its contents.

'The same again missus.' He spoke the words without looking directly at her. Before rising to fill the order she brushed some invisible motes from her skirt and selected some equally imperceptible specks from her woollen cardigan. She used the diversions to convey the impression that she was not in the least perturbed by the unnerving reticence of her solitary customer. She need not have been so concerned. The Ram of God was hardly aware of her existence. After supper there had been a violent confrontation between himself and his twin brothers. The three were seated at the kitchen table with Mary Creel. Nonie sat by the open door, an empty tea cup in one hand, a cigarette in the other.

Murt, the taller of the twins stretched his legs under the table, making contact as he did with Will's indrawn feet. The smaller twin reacted by stacking the plates within reach on the supper table, a chore usually left to Mary Creel or Nonie. Neither action escaped the notice of Mary or the Ram. The latter tensed visibly knowing that a showdown was at hand. Mary excused herself and gathered the plates which Will Drannaghy had stacked. Nonie Spillane, cigarette in mouth, unaware of the covert exchange between the twins, took up her position by the sink, relieving Mary of the ware and cutlery which left the table bare for whatever pronouncement either of the twins might make.

Every man, woman and child in Ballybobawn

knew of the forthcoming weddings but the prospective grooms had yet to declare their intent officially to their brother. The Ram was not in the dark, however, having been briefed on numerous occasions by Nonie whose sources were legion. Mary knew what every girl of her age in Ballybobawn knew, that the twins would be marrying in a hurry, Will to Kate Cronane and Murt to Noreen.

Will Drannaghy opened the proceedings as he revealed the tidings in his usual circuitous manner.

'You'll be able to manage on your own for a fortnight or so?'

The Ram nodded agreement.

'You can hire a man if needs be.'

The Ram shook his head.

'No need for that. The hay's done and the corn is a long way off. No need for a man.'

'Good,' Murt spoke next. 'We'll be back after two weeks. He'll be going one way,' here he indicated his twin, 'and I'll be going another but we'll be both going the same way if you follow my meaning.'

The pair burst into peals of laughter which suddenly stopped with the realisation that a more important pronouncement had yet to be made. During the exchanges there had been no subduement of the ware-washing which was being conducted at the kitchen sink although the ears of both females were strained to the utmost.

'When we come back we'll be taking over.' Murt looked to Will to come to his aid.

'When we come back we'll be taking over,' he said, echoing Murt's pronouncement and then he added with a carelessness which did not quite come off, 'that's to say we'll be taking over altogether.'

Both anxiously watched the Ram's face. The message did not seem to have sunk in. All that the face registered was genuine perplexity.

'What in the name of Christ is that supposed to mean?' The question was put by Nonie Spillane.

'This is a family matter,' Murt threw back curtly.

'Well Goddamn you for an impertinent whelp,' Nonie screeched the words at him. 'I was a member of this family before you were born. I was a member of this family when your two arses needed wiping and I was a member of this family through every up and down we ever had. Now explain yourself or I'll give you this dishcloth across the mouth.'

Will turned suddenly on the ancient housekeeper and launched into a counter-attack.

'When we come back from our honeymoons there will be a new woman taking over here and since there's no need here for two women full-time that means that someone will have to go. Now you'd hardly expect me to throw my own wife out on the road so you know what it means don't you?'

'Oh I'd be going anyway,' Nonie retorted proudly. 'I wouldn't demean myself by doffing my cap to them two lardy lumps of Mollie Cronane's. I'll serve my betters and I'll serve my equals but I won't be a housemaid to trash!'

'Should she be listening to all this?' Murt pointed a finger in Mary Creel's direction.

The Ram made no answer. The heat of the exchanges had taken him by surprise.

'It's time I was going anyway,' Mary solved the problem of her presence by reaching for her coat which hung from a rickety wooden rack to the left of the fireplace. She would have much preferred if she had been allowed to stay but she consoled herself with the thought that Nonie would reveal all in the morning. Casting an anxious and what she hoped was a reassuring smile in the Ram's direction she hurried out of doors into the balmy evening.

As she dawdled along the roadway which would take her to the cross of Ballybobawn she could not help but dwell on the contrast between the older and the younger brothers. It was hard to credit that they were members of the same family. The twins were crude, arrogant and blustering, the Ram gentle, considerate and, most of all, superior; there was no other word that fitted him so well. She suspected that his services would no longer be required around the farm as soon as the twins returned from their honeymoons.

Behind her Mary left an uneasy silence, broken only by the scratch of a match on the side of its box as Nonie Spillane lit another cigarette. Nonie had a long-standing habit of never inhaling the first draw from any cigarette. As soon as she had blown the smoke aloft she turned on the twins.

'Seeing as you'll have a new woman here you might as well have my notice here and now. The minute you come back I'll be gone and if it's any news to you I'd have taken off years ago but for him.'

She pouted the second exhalation towards the Ram.

'Where would the pair of you be but for him? You wouldn't have a shilling in your pockets or a shirt on your backs. I declare to God but I can't recall a single day in the past ten years when I didn't find the stink of liquor from you. 'Tis hard to conceive that the two of you came from the same womb as your brother. Two more foul-mouthed or two more dirty-mannered wretches a body would be hard put to find if they were to search the entire land from top to bottom.'

Nonie paused breathlessly but she had not finished.

'I have my pension and my cottage and that leaves me beholden to none. But what of this man that worked here like a slave for the past fifteen years? I want to know.' Her voice was at its shrillest since her onslaught began, 'and I want to know now what sort of settlement he can expect before he's thrown out on the road.'

'Settlement!' the twins echoed the word as though they had never come across the likes of it before.

'Settlement!' Nonie hammered home her demand.

'He's not a cripple,' Murt shot back. 'He'll have no bother getting a good job managing a farm somewhere. According to you he has no equal in that regard.'

'That's not what I'm talking about,' Nonie persisted. 'I want to know how much cash is to be settled on him before he leaves this house for good.'

'That's none of your business,' Will Drannaghy came to his brother's assistance, 'and I'll thank you to keep your mouth shut or you can get the hell out now.'

'That's no way to talk to the woman that reared the two of you.' There was stern reprimand in the Ram's tone.

'We'll talk whatever way we like and you'd better listen. We are not obliged to offer you a single penny and we have the advice of a senior counsel on that. But here's what we'll do. You can have the car, we'll be getting new ones anyway and on top of that there's a thousand pounds to keep you going 'till you get a job. I'm not finished yet,' Will Drannaghy raised his voice as Nonie attempted to interrupt, 'but there will be sweet damn all if everything isn't to our liking when we get back. We don't want to part enemies. You're our brother and a fair enough brother as brothers go although in your eyes we were never anything but upstarts. There's no better man to work a farm. We'll grant you that. We believe we're doing the right thing by you. There's others wouldn't give you a button.'

'Well sweet Christ if that isn't the greatest load of bullshit I ever heard! That car is a wreck and a thousand pounds wouldn't buy a good ass and cart.'

The twins chose to ignore Nonie's latest outburst.

'Well?' they asked in turn.

The Ram sat silently as though he was not the subject of the dispute which had taken place. By way of reply he arose and went as far as the kitchen door. Behind him the twins sat waiting. From the doorway he could hear the faint pipings of a distant lark as well as the mixed notes of thrush, blackbird and robin as they trilled and throbbed with song in appreciation of the balmy serenity which the evening had induced.

'There's always solace out of doors,' the Ram whispered the thought to himself. Far down the narrow roadway he could discern the distant figure of Mary Creel. She raised a tentative arm and waved in his direction. He waved back before returning to the tension-filled kitchen.

'I find the terms acceptable and you needn't worry about the place while you're away but I feel that Nonie is entitled to something. After all she's given her life here.'

'She's always been paid,' Will returned at once.

'And she's always had her holiday pay which no one pays around here,' Murt added.

'I have plenty, thanks be to God,' Nonie said without bitterness, 'but ten thousand pounds would be a fairer figure than the one they've offered you.'

'Like yourself Nonie I'm well pleased. I have plans. I won't need much where I hope to go.'

'You're a cruel pair of bastards,' Nonie stood with hands on hips the contempt showing clearly on her face as she addressed the twins. 'You're getting away with murder but by God the good times are over and you'll remember me when them two Cronane viragoes have you spancelled.'

Murt jumped suddenly to his feet.

'You have a neck talking about our wives-to-be like that. You better pack your traps now before I kick you out through that door. Come on. Out with you. We don't have to take that from anyone.' He fairly danced with rage on the tiled floor, his clenched fists pressing against his thighs.

'Do you hear me talking to you?' Murt was shouting now.

Even Will, who was generally the more aggressive of the pair, was taken aback. Then it began to dawn on him, as Nonie crumpled on to a chair, ashen-faced and shocked, that Murt was playing a game, a game fraught with danger but a game nevertheless. Normally neither he nor his twin took the slightest notice of Nonie's diatribes having become accustomed to her colourful censures from childhood. If they had been asked they would have cheerfully admitted that they regarded her offensives as more in the nature of badinage rather than actual abuse. Before the Cronane sisters there had been other girlfriends. Invariably Nonie showered abuse on their heads too even though she might never have laid eyes on the objects of her wrath.

Will became fully alerted to Murt's stratagem when the taller twin suddenly turned and dashed the cigarette from between Nonie's fingers. He wasn't surprised for he knew well the depths of cunning to which Murt could sink. Slowly he rose from the table behind the figure of the Ram who instantly erupted from his seat the moment Murt dispossessed Nonie of her cigarette. Will greatly admired Murt's manoeuvre of keeping his back to the Ram while he faced Nonie.

'No more smoking while you're in service here!' Murt issued the command as he trod upon the cigarette.

'That will do!' The stern command came from the Ram of God who could hardly believe his ears.

For years Will had envisaged a situation similar to the one which now obtained in the kitchen. Often in their cups the twins had considered ways and means of deposing the Ram from his unassailable position of pre-eminence in the Drannaghy household. They came to the inevitable conclusion that there would have to be total surprise if he was to be physically overcome.

'Leave over Murt!' The Ram spoke with quiet authority but to no avail.

Silently Will spread his feet well apart and flexed his muscles in his eagerness to join with Murt in the assault. He would move the moment his twin moved, not a second before. The cuffing which the Ram administered after the incident involving Mary Creel still rankled. He had been in the wrong. He would not deny that but the severity of the backhand loosened a tooth and left him with a headache for days. He felt that a verbal caution would have been sufficient.

Murt was speaking again. 'Hand over the cigarettes and matches. Quick now. I haven't all day.'

'You go kiss my arse!' Nonie recovered sufficient of her composure to make the rejoinder.

Murt bent and seized her by the shoulders before lifting her to her feet where it seemed his intent was to shake the cigarettes and matches from their hiding place. Gently but firmly the Ram laid a restraining hand on his shoulder. It did not dawn on him that his younger brother was being deliberately provocative. The moment his hand rested on the shoulder Murt turned and smashed a tightly-clenched fist on to the Ram's jaw. As the Ram staggered backwards Will swung wildly and made contact with a glancing blow on the forehead. He had no sooner committed himself to the swing than he knew that his anxiety had grievously affected his timing. Had he made proper contact the Ram would not now be reeling backwards, out through the kitchen door. Rather would he be lying on the flat of his back or at the very least sitting on his posterior in such a confused state that the remainder of the demolition would have been less than a formality.

Terrified that he might regain his balance the twins followed quickly almost impeding each other in their desire to hold on to the initiative. Still staggering backwards, clear of the kitchen, the Ram of God fell on his back, on to one of a line of rhododendrons which fronted the house. It helped to break his fall. If the twins had been less eager and more cautious they could not have failed to notice

77

the beginnings of a grim smile which barely manifested itself at either side of his mouth.

In some ways it's just like old times, the Ram thought, except that the playfulness of their youth is sadly absent!

As he extricated himself from the rhododendrons he feigned confusion lest the twins be alerted to the fact that he was in full possession of his senses. Holding his head between both hands he reeled about the tiny front garden pretending to be incapable of defending himself. Scenting victory the twins rushed at him from either side, each with the right hand swung fully back and the fists clenched to the utmost. The Ram of God seized each hand, at the same time, and with a skill born of ancient habit, banged the skulls of his would-be conquerors together with sufficient force to acquaint their proprietors with numerous stars and other heavenly bodies already well-known to them. Satisfying himself that they were incapable of a second assault he released them. They quickly withdrew to a safe distance lest he repeat the punishment.

'We were only clowning!' The excuse was proffered by Will who sat now on an adjacent window sill, his head covered by his hands. Murt, for his part, seemed incapable of any speech, other than a deep moaning sound to indicate the agony which he was undergoing.

'You'll think twice,' the Ram of God spoke without malice, 'before you attempt a caper like that again. In spite of what you tried to do I'll still undertake to run the farm until you come back but you have to admit that you're treating Nonie shabbily!'

Shamefacedly the twins exchanged glances, each silently urging the other to make some sort of concession.

'Would five hundred be all right? After you're paid and the cars and honeymoons paid for there won't be an awful lot left.'

'Five hundred is better than nothing.' The Ram assented. 'Go in now and apologise to her. That's the least she deserves.'

Still ministering to their aching heads the twins went indoors.

'YOUR PINT MISTER DRANNAGHY.' The Widow Cahalane clung to her life-long practice of waiting at the counter until each order was paid for. She might have returned to her seat at the counter until such time as the Ram emerged from his reverie and then reminded him that payment was due but she clung instead to her motto of payment upon delivery.

Often there might be several customers awaiting her attention while a client fumbled through several pockets in search of money to discharge his debt. She never exhibited the least signs of impatience no matter how long the wait. She would stand calmly, a palm extended over the counter, her eyes looking everywhere but at the customer who was holding up the proceedings. Sometimes a stranger would grow tired of waiting and walk out in a huff but the regular customers realised that it was her policy to always seek payment on the spot. Customers, regular and otherwise, were not above indulging in bouts of forgetfulness if the Widow was unavoidably distracted while awaiting payment. Eventually she allowed the wait for payment to supersede all other matters, no matter how pressing.

The Ram of God handed over his money. As she placed his change on the counter she noticed the fresh weal on his forehead.

'A fall surely,' she told herself, 'for he's not the type of man to get himself into a brawl. None of my business.' She returned to her seat, folded her arms and awaited the arrival of the next customer.

For the first time the Ram of God peered into the mirror which was fastened to the wall behind the rows of bottles. The mark on his forehead had become more pronounced but he was thankful that his jaw had not swollen. He forgave the twins although he was perturbed by the cowardly nature of the attack. Their aim had been to bring him down a peg. Seeing him on the flat of his back would have sufficed. If they meant him real harm there was nothing to stop them from taking advantage of him during his sleeping hours. If his mother hadn't died so young things might be different for the twins, different for him too. Then he had been away at college for those two vital years. He saw the change every time he came home, gradually evolving from being simply wild to becoming almost ungovernable. If he had been at home he might have directed them, set them the example which his declining father could not. They would make poor farmers. They had been late risers all their lives and late risers they would remain and there was nothing the incoming Cronane women would be able to do about it. Still he wasn't without hope for them, not if Mollie Cronane became involved. Mollie was tough and tight-fisted. If Mollie had her way little of the farm income would end up in the Load of S.

The Ram of God did not hear the door open or see Patricia Cahalane as she entered. After some

80

time when he looked in the Widow's direction to see if she was still there he noticed the smartly-costumed girl who had somehow mysteriously taken her place. God knows he knew the girl well enough; Patricia Cahalane but it had been a long time since he had seen her at such close range. She had grown even more beautiful in the intervening years. She had taken her BA with second-class honours, her higher diploma a year later at twenty-one after which she had been immediately appointed to the Secondary School of Trallock Presentation Convent where she taught English and Mathematics, was beloved of his friend Mary Creel and of the nuns themselves who cherished her as a student and even more as a teacher. He silently trotted out the statistics to himself, all acquired over a period from Mary Creel whose firm belief it was that the sun, moon and stars shone out of her English teacher.

'We have a mutual friend,' Patricia broke the silence in the certain knowledge that it would never be broken unless she made the first move.

'You wouldn't be referring to Miss Mary Creel by any chance would you?' the Ram asked with a smile.

'None other,' came the quick response followed by one of the most wonderful smiles the Ram of God had ever seen. Not just did her lips quiver but her large hazel eyes shone with a radiance that seemed to illuminate the entire premises. She used the smile to take better stock of the tall man with the sensitive face. So this was he who was playing father to Mary Creel. Strange that in such a tightly-knit community they never actually found themselves alone together but then, of course, he wasn't the gregarious type and there was that rather sad business so many years ago. It still affected him or so Patricia surmised but he would return to the Church; of that Patricia was absolutely certain. In fact Mary suspected that developments were already taking place in that respect. There had been a letter from a religious order in Southern California. It was the only letter in the morning post and he had been at pains to keep its contents to himself. After he finished the milking he washed his hands in the kitchen sink, never taking his eyes from the letter which Mary placed on his side plate. The twins who entered the kitchen almost immediately in his wake favoured the epistle with curious glances. If they made a closer inspection they would have noted the name and address of the religious house from which it had been dispatched.

With a hand scarcely dry the Ram of God took possession of the letter and departed to the privacy of his room.

'I'd say he'll be for the road soon,' Nonie confided to Mary as they made up his bed later that day. There was no sign of the envelope or its contents. He had never been so secretive about a letter before. All other correspondence received over the years had been unwittingly exhibited on top of the pile of books which dominated the table by his bed.

'He won't go out of the blue,' Nonie said sadly, 'but go he will and that's as sure as the swallows will go. He'll tell us any day now. It had to come. The announcement of the marriages was the spur he needed. He'll tell us when everything is settled. You and me will be the first to know.'

'But California!' Mary used the word as though it belonged to another planet.

'Where else girleen?' Nonie saw the logic of the situation at once. 'Nobody will know him out there.

He'll be just another priest, not the Ram of God.'

In the Widow Cahalane's Patricia suggested that it might not be inappropriate if the Ram were to cover the angry weal on his forehead with a piece of sticking plaster. The Ram of God conceded that it might be the proper procedure under the circumstances whereat Patricia, without another word, entered the rear of the premises and returned straightaway with a tin box which contained medicaments of various kinds. First she located a bottle of twenty volume peroxide, a cleansing agent for cuts and scrapes which her mother swore was without peer. Removing the cork she poured a small quantity on to a fragment of cotton wool. She came outside the counter and as though it were the most natural thing in the world applied the wet wool to the afflicted area. Leaning across the counter for the sticking plaster her thigh accidentally brushed against his knee.

'Sorry,' she made the apology in the most casual of tones. Another man might have foolishly misinterpreted her action as an invitation to something of a more familiar nature. The Ram of God, although physically aware of her presence, sat doggedly on his stool, his hands behind his back, a full suffusion colouring his face. As she applied the plaster he could not help but notice the calm-inducing loveliness of her hazel eyes. He looked into those same eyes for several seconds until her face assumed a faintly quizzical, faintly amused look.

'Is there something odd?' she asked when she knew full well that instead of asking questions at such close range she should be moving away, her nursing completed.

He reacted as if he had not heard.

'Why am I standing here?' Patricia asked herself. 'After all,' she thought, 'this innocent man is the property of God and I am trespassing on sacred ground.'

Brusquely, rather too brusquely she felt afterwards, she informed him that there were chores awaiting her attention in another part of the premises. After she left, the brightness which enlivened the bar seemed to vanish.

'If,' the Ram told himself, 'she stayed where she was for another few seconds I would most certainly have attempted to take her hand in mine and thank her most sincerely for dressing my wound. On the other hand,' he thought, 'that might have been the wrong thing to do.'

All in all he felt he acquitted himself well and was in no way likely to be in the least enamoured of her in the future. Her presence made him realise that his vocation was still intact. He felt, however, that he would always regard her as a powerful obstacle on the long and hazardous road towards priesthood.

She stayed in his thoughts for days but there was no diminishment in his freshly-found resolve to resume where he left off on the road to holy orders. Anyway, he long believed that a vocation which did not encounter obstacles was not a genuine vocation. There had to be real trials and tribulations. He fell once and had paid the high price of spending fifteen years in the wilderness. He would not fall secondly.

5

IN THE CRONANE SUPERMARKET Mollie Cronane stood with folded hands surveying the empty street. It was still early in the day. At the farthest corner of the shop her oldest son Cha was engrossed with the weighing of potatoes which he transferred in quantities of stones and half-stones to plastic bags, carefully marking the price on each finished package.

Mollie decided against another cigarette. She felt that she was already smoking far too many. The tensions and pressures brought on by the forthcoming weddings were responsible for a hundred-per-cent increase in her daily intake. Each and every one of the invited guests had signalled acceptance and the presents were coming in with invigorating consistency over the past week, and yet, Mollie could not shake off a harrowing premonition of impending disaster. Everything was moving too smoothly. Too many things were falling into place too easily. She found herself lighting another cigarette.

She decided against calling her husband although he rarely slept until this late in the morning. The time was but a few minutes short of the noonday. She climbed to the landing and blew the whistle on three separate occasions. Not even a mumble of protestation reached her ears save a deep and even snoring which carried quite clearly to where she was standing. He might grumble later that he had left instructions to be called at ten o'clock, that she should have persevered when he failed to respond. Mollie decided she would cross that bridge when she came to it.

There was a restlessness about him lately which made her apprehensive. She was well aware too of the furtive looks which he cast in her direction from time to time. There was a stealthiness and a guilt about him which, however hard he might try, he could not quite manage to conceal. She could only conclude that he was girding himself for a monumental booze-up. If this was true there was nothing in the world she could do to prevent him, apart from locking him in his room and he would never stand for that despite his senility. He had his own money. She could never be quite sure how much nor did she know where he kept his bank book or post office book. The rest of the savings were in joint accounts with herself but she was well aware that there were substantial reserves, not that she worried over-much about the amount of money he might spend. He wasn't what you would call a mean man but he didn't exactly suffer from squandermania either.

All the portents for a sustained shaughrawn were becoming more evident as the days went by. He was hard to spot. From imperceptible beginnings such as a tiny sip from a noggin bottle of whiskey, hidden in the most unlikely place, he would graduate, day by day, until at the climax of the skite he would be drinking in excess of a full bottle of whiskey in the round of a day, not to mention several glasses of beer.

There had been a time, not all that far away, when he might consume double this amount on a daily basis over a period of a fortnight. Then suddenly it would end and after three or four days in bed, on a diet of chicken broth, mashed potatoes and soft-boiled eggs, he would present himself to the public as upright and as sober as a lifelong member of the Ballybobawn Total Abstinence Association.

Even Tom himself knew that three or four days steady drinking would be sufficient to stupefy him but he had a rare cunning when it came to husbanding his health and strength as his drinking progressed to its finale.

Only his son Cha knew that Tom Cronane had taken the first step on the perilous road to alcoholic satiety the evening before. Cha saw him enter the store at the rear of the supermarket. There was a furtiveness about him which alerted the oldest son. He watched unseen from another entrance as the old man sat on an ancient fowl crate. From the recesses of the crate he withdrew a tiny bottle of vodka. Cha guessed it contained a glass of the transparent liquid.

Tom flexed his shoulders several times as he held the bottle firmly in his right hand. He then shook his head vigorously and moistened his lips. His next act was to blow his nose after which he cleared his throat.

Cha thought for a moment that his father was about to embark on a stave of a song but all his parent did was to raise his noble head and fasten his eyes on some remote clime which existed in the vast world beyond the doorway.

For a long while he sat contentedly looking into space. Then with painful protraction he unscrewed the tin cap and flung it recklessly over his shoulder. It was a movement possessed of the most profound symbolism. Cha fully understood although he would be hard put to explain if asked. Tom did not drink immediately. He felt the slender jowl with

the tip of his tongue and was overcome by a powerful shudder at his first taste of alcohol in four and
a half months. He had, so far, not even swallowed a
solitary drop and yet the taste quickened his pulse
and set his body trembling, dismissed all other
forms of thought, bending his mind to nothing but
the prospect of the gulp that would douse his arid
brain and send the familiar spirit coursing through
his bloodstream, inflaming his thoughts, disturbing and distorting until nothing mattered,
nothing in the whole wide world, except the next
swallow.

With an animal grunt which frightened Cha he
raised the bottle clumsily to his lips and swallowed
half its contents. Nothing happened for several
seconds. Then Cha was astounded to hear a cackle
which reminded him of a frightened hen. It was
made more hideous by the fact that it was uttered
by a human. It was followed by a long session of
heavy breathing during which Tom slumped forward on three separate occasions as though in re-
pentance for what he had done. Leisurely he raised
the bottle to his lips for the final time and drank
slowly, holding the liquor in abeyance in the jowl of
the bottle as he allowed a slow trickle to enter his
mouth. He left the building and flung the bottle into a briar patch close by the outhouse. As Cha
watched him enter the dwelling house he surmised
quite correctly that his father would go straightaway to his bed.

'TOM! TOM!' IN THE name of Christ will you get out
of it.'

'Are you aware that it is one o'clock in the afternoon?'

Tom Cronane turned over and lay on his other side, hoping the abrasive voice would go away. Could it be, he felt, as a hand shook his exposed shoulder that he had been dreaming? But it had been so real – the warmth and tenderness of Madeleine's body, under the buffalo robe by the glowing camp fire.

Irritably he opened his eyes to behold the angry face of his spouse, the redoubtable Mollie Purley. Bemused, his gaze wandered from her puckered features and took in the familiar surroundings.

Tom's palm felt the sheets beside him but there was nothing, not even a trace of warmth where her body should have lain.

'What's all the rush?' he asked petulantly as soon as he realised that the tender episode with Madeleine Monterros was no more than a dream.

'Remember yesterday?' Mollie reminded him, 'you warned me to call you early. You said you wanted to go to Trallock to buy a suit for the wedding.'

'So I did. So I did,' he conceded reluctantly.

'Get something dark this time,' Mollie counselled, 'bright colours don't suit you any more. Navy now would be more in your line.'

'We'll see! We'll see!' He was still irritable as he sat on the side of the bed.

'Do you want something to eat?' Mollie asked from the doorway. Tom considered the question for a moment.

'I think I'd like a fillet steak,' and then after a pause, 'a good fillet with plenty onions and mushrooms but no potatoes. I'll settle for bread instead.'

'Very well your lordship!' Mollie curtsied in mock respect before exiting.

In the wardrobe Tom located a heavy black

overcoat. Thrusting his hand inside the lining near the rear slit he smiled triumphantly as his fingers came in contact with his personal post office and bank books. He opted for the bank book. The maximum amount available at any one drawing in the post office was fifty pounds which would be ideal if his only project was the advancement of the drunken spree initiated so tentatively the evening before. There was the question of the new suit, however, and for this he would need considerably more than the fifty available from the post office. The suit would cost a hundred at least. Drawing on his trousers he placed the bank book in the hip pocket. He looked at his watch. Five minutes after one, plenty of time before the Bank of Ireland in Trallock closed its doors for the day.

He would take the car, of course, this to divert suspicion. He had never been known to drive under the influence. He would have a few in Trallock, three slowly sipped whiskies undiluted and just one glass of beer, a tiny swallow at the time after each sip of whiskey. His mouth watered at the prospect. His hands trembled in heady anticipation. A trickle of spittle ran down his jaw. This was the most exhilarating part of the entire proceedings.

In the bathroom the tantalising odour of frying onions wafted upwards for his further titillation. He shaved with a will, anxious now to implement his plans without further delay. In the bedroom he chose a white shirt and vermilion tie. Discarding his trousers he transferred the bank book to the breast pocket of his best suit, a light grey tweed which he had not worn for some time. He brushed his rapidly thinning hair with the utmost care. Too many precious ribs would be squandered if the treatment was rough and ready.

He surveyed himself in the full length mirror on the inner side of the wardrobe door. Not bad, not bad at all for a chap in the autumn of his days. If only she were here, his dream girl, his constant night-time companion, his sultry partner of a thousand rapturous escapades.

'Madeleine!' he whispered the name softly over and over.

From the foot of the stairs came the sound of Mollie's whistle. His steak was ready and his onions and his mushrooms, a fitting base for the liquid diet which was to follow.

That night he left the Widow Cahalane's at a respectable hour. There was no need to remind himself that he had enough taken. By then the whole of Ballybobawn was aware that Tom had embarked on another booze up. Mollie displayed neither annoyance nor concern when the news was brought to her by young Tomboy that his father was on his way home from the Widow's.

'He can't be too bad,' she told her youngest, 'and at least he'll have it put behind him for the wedding.'

'He's taking the two sides of the street,' Tomboy informed her.

'He has the same right to the street as them nosy bitches that will be charting his progress,' Mollie reminded her son.

They sat silently in the sitting-room, heard the door open, listened apprehensively as he negotiated the stairs and breathed sighs of relief when they heard the bedroom door close behind him. He threw himself on the bed and was asleep in an instant. Later Tomboy and another of the brothers undressed him and turned him on his side in the bed. Mollie herself made regular inspections to make cetain that he was all right.

'One down and two to go!' she had announced resignedly.

'One down and three to go!' her son corrected.

'Not this time,' Mollie spoke with authority, 'two more days is all that's in it if there's that much at all. Let us forget about your beloved father for the moment Tomboy and let us turn to yourself. I've been meaning to have a few private words with you for a while. You're blushing already I see.'

'No I'm not,' Tomboy shot back.

'Maybe not,' his mother agreed, 'but you may before our conversation is finished. I know all about the cider Tomboy but it's not that I'm worried about. Youth is entitled to its fling and I don't begrudge you and your brothers a few bottles of cider so long as you don't overdo it. You've been seeing a girl lately Tomboy.'

Mollie produced a cigarette, not to cover her son's undoubted embarrassment but to provide herself with the time to frame her next question. After what she adjudged to be a suitable period she spoke again.

'Do I know her Tomboy?' Tomboy hung his head.

'Mary Creel isn't it Tomboy, the drunkard's daughter?'

Tomboy was about to protest but thought better of it.

'You've seen her mother Tomboy haven't you? Of course you have. Well that's exactly how Mary Creel is going to look in ten years time. Remember that when you get the urge to see her again. You have arranged to see her again haven't you?'

When Tomboy made no answer his mother rose

and struck him a stinging blow on the side of the face with the palm of her right hand.

'Answer me.' She shrieked the command.

'Yes,' Tomboy answered. 'I'm supposed to be seeing her again.'

'You are not to look at her, speak to her or tarry with her ever again. You hear?'

Tomboy nodded eagerly.

'Give me your solemn word on that?' Mollie awaited his reply, legs apart, hands on hips, willing and able to strike again.

'You have my word,' Tomboy was pale-faced now.

'I had a good gander at Mary Creel yesterday,' Mollie Cronane spoke half to herself, half to her son, 'and I didn't like what I saw. With a pedigree like hers anything is possible. Wouldn't you agree?'

'Yes mother. I would.'

'And then we have her out at Drannaghy's with the Ram of God. That's a nice combination that is. Wouldn't you say so Tomboy?'

'Yes mother,' came the meek response from her youngest offspring.

'If by any chance you go back on your word you'll walk out of here for good with nothing more than the clothes on your back and you'll never darken this door again and that's as true Tomboy as my mother is in her grave this night.'

FOR THE SECOND EVENING in a row Mary was surprised by the absence of Tomboy Cronane. There was no sign of him at the usual place. It eventually dawned on her that he did not want to see her any more.

Shortly before her father arrived home from the

Load of S Mary confronted her mother in the kitchen of their home. The younger children were all in bed.

'Mother I have to talk to you'.

Maggie Creel looked long at her daughter's pinched face before denying her request.

'I don't want to talk to you Mary. I don't want to hear anything from you. I don't want to hear anything that will make the cross I'm carrying any heavier. I don't want your father laying the pair of us out cold on the floor of this kitchen. I'll talk to you some other time Mary but not now girl.'

'But mother!' Mary protested.

'But nothing!' her mother screamed back, a look of terror on her face as she listened to the approaching footsteps of her lord and master.

6

THE ANTI-CYCLONE WHICH DOMINATED the skies over Ballybobawn throughout late June and early July gave way to cloud and to light, variable winds. There were occasional rainfalls but these were light and of short duration. It was generally believed that the fine weather would return. In the freshly cut meadows the aftergrass began to shoot and already the familiar green was beginning to usurp the light brown of the hay stubble.

In the High Meadow the Ram of God surveyed the greening acres with growing satisfaction. All that remained of the bales was a score or so in one of the upper corners. Soon the meadow would be empty.

As he loaded the fragrant cargo on to the wooden trailer he paused for a moment to acknowledge the presence of an ascending lark over his head. Only a churl, he told himself, would ignore such a heavenly rendition. He wondered if it was the same lark who had so sweetly serenaded him on the high noon of the first day's cutting.

'He blessed my endeavours at the beginning,' the Ram looked upwards into the empty sky, 'and now he blesses them again at the close. Surely I should be on my knees in thanksgiving for all the good fortune which has attended me lately. How easy it is to become remiss in these matters. How simple to forget the source of all good things!'

So saying he threw himself on his knees, unmindful of the prickly aftercut. Meticulously he made the sign of the cross and closed his eyes as he intoned the five decades of the Rosary. Afterwards, hands clasped behind back, he made a slow circuit of the meadow, reciting the sacred Litany of the Saints, his face happily upturned, his fingers now entwined, his palms brought forward and pressed against his abdomen as he worshipfully reeled off the names of the heavenly host in thanksgiving for all the good that had befallen him; for the survival of his vocation and for his acceptance as a third year seminarian in Saint Rowland's College in Southern California, although he would willingly agree that the good offices of Father Mortimer O'Connor, parish priest of Ballybobawn, played a large part in his acceptance. He had accompanied him when he went to see the bishop of their own diocese.

'If there's ever anything you want Edward,' the bishop promised as he was leaving, 'you are to get in touch with me at once. I will always be available no matter what. It's not an easy time for seminarians or for any of us so you will remember where I am if you need me.'

'He's not a bad oul' skin when you get used to him,' Father O'Connor declared as they sat down to a meal and a bottle of wine in the Ross Hotel. 'Like most bishops the poor fellow has to watch himself all the time. We can all make false moves Eddie my boy, all of us except bishops. I wouldn't be a bishop if you gave me the sun, moon and stars. I like to work discreetly, unobserved, if you get my drift and you can't do that if you're a bishop.'

Sometime in the immediate future he would inform Nonie Spillane and Mary Creel of his decision. He would inform his brothers as soon as they returned from their respective honeymoons. He already notified a delighted Father O'Connor who embraced him upon hearing the wonderful tidings. They decided that it was news best kept under wraps for awhile but now, he felt that he owed it to Nonie to let her into the secret and, of course, Mary Creel.

Never before in his life had the Ram of God felt so elated. A feverish excitement bubbled upwards from within his being and brightened his features. It was, he felt, as if a heavenly spotlight had been turned on him which would direct his feet henceforth through all manner of trials and tribulations. It was a feeling which transcended all that was earthly and commonplace. He felt like extending his arms towards the heavens and exclaiming to all the world that he had been exalted and purified by the grace of God. Instead he submitted himself to the restraint by which he believed he would be bound forevermore and meekly continued with his recital of the Sacred Litany:

All ye holy Apostles and Evangelists,
All ye holy disciples of our Lord,
All ye holy Innocents,
Saint Stephen, Saint Lawrence and Saint Vincent,
Saints Fabian and Sebastian,
Saints John and Paul,
Saints Cosmas and Damian,
Saints Gervase and Protase and all ye holy Martyrs,
Saint Gregory, Saint Ambrose and Saint Augustine,
Saint Jerome, Saint Martin and Saint Nicholas,
All ye holy Bishops and Confessors, pray for us,
All ye holy Doctors, pray for us.

Quite soon the Ram of God found himself back where he started at that spot where he had parted from the tractor and trailer with most of the Litany remaining to be said. He paused for awhile with bent head as he recalled his past sins and begged God's forgiveness before resuming where he left off:

Oh Lord deliver us from sudden and unlooked for
death,
From the snares of the devil,
From anger and hatred and every ill-will,
From the spirit of fornication,
From lightning and tempest,
From the scourge of earthquake,
From pestilence, famine and war.

As he completed the second circuit of the High Meadow he continued with the recital pausing every so often to beat his breast and beg forgiveness for the sins of the past. As he finished, the tones of the evening Angelus floated serenely upwards from the parish church in Ballybobawn.

'Good god!' he said aloud, 'the day is gone.'

He applied himself without another word to the work in hand, mounting his tractor and speeding to where the last of the bales stood in isolation.

Luckily he was exempted from the evening milking because it was felt that priority should be given to the drawing-in of the last of the hay. On each of the other trips he was accompanied by Murt whose job it was to remain aboard the trailer and stack the bales uniformly in preparation for the downhill journey to the farmyard where the hayshed was already partly filled.

Murt remained behind on this occasion to assist Will with the milking while the Ram gathered the last of the bales for the final journey to the farmyard. 'Let it rain now if it will,' he declared triumphantly, 'or let it pour because he's a poor farmer who hasn't his meadows emptied.'

After the bales were safely aboard the Ram of God took a final turn around the High Meadow. As he mounted the tractor for the downward journey he thought briefly of Patricia Cahalane. He found it difficult to conjure up her features although he had no problem recalling the large hazel eyes, their infinite calm and the amusement lurking deep when something puzzled her. Odd that he should think of her after his uplifting and prayerful circuit of the meadow.

She was taller too than he had imagined. From a distance she seemed to be of medium height. It was only when she drew near that the extra inches revealed themselves in her willowy length. There was a gracefulness about her movements which suggested an undeveloped capacity for some form of athletic conversion but she didn't seem to him to be the type who would seriously involve herself in conventional sports such as running or jumping. He imagined she would be more inclined towards lawn tennis perhaps or basketball. In opting for the latter he had surmised correctly. She was coach to the school's basketball team, an indifferent outfit, good one day and bad the next but always deriving maximum enjoyment from their activities.

Her mother, the Widow, was still an attractive woman. Although in her early fifties she had managed to preserve her figure and sometimes looked like a slightly plumper version of her daughter. The Ram of God suddenly recalled that Patricia's name had once been linked with Willie Halvey, proprietor of the Load of S, although he rarely appeared there, entrusting its operation to a manager and staff of two girls. Willie had numerous business interests including a block-making unit on the outskirts of

Trallock where several workers were regularly employed. As well as that he owned a half share in the profitable Trallock Arms and was linked with other highly successful enterprises all over the county.

He had originally purchased the Load of S in a ramshackle condition from its elderly owners and changed its name from the somewhat misleading Fisherman's Retreat to the more up-to-date Load of S which he felt would better reflect the new clientele who were in the main, according to Willie, as scruffy a lot as you'd find anywhere. Willie's age was estimated by those who claimed to know about such matters to be somewhere slightly in excess of two score. He was a glum sort of individual rarely given to diffuseness and fond of keeping his own counsel. Rumour had it that, on the basis of no more than casual acquaintance, Willie had faced into the Widow Cahalane's one evening and asked the proprietress if he might speak to her daughter. According to some eavesdroppers who were present in the public house at the time Willie was ushered into the Widow's kitchen where Patricia was immersed in the correction of some English essays.

'Yes?' Patricia asked politely as Willie whipped off his hat and drew up a chair without being invited. He sat silently for awhile as though he didn't know quite where to begin.

'It's nice and mild outside,' Patricia opened, feeling that he needed some form of priming before he could be induced to disclose his business.

'I won't put a tooth in it now Patricia if you don't mind,' he began.

'I don't mind Willie,' Patricia answered, the amusement beginning to flicker in her hazel eyes as Willie cleared his throat.

'My accountants inform me,' Willie went on, 'I

100

am worth something in the region of one and a quarter million pounds,' He paused in order to allow this hitherto undisclosed piece of information to register. Satisfying himself that Patricia was suitably impressed he proceeded with his inventory.

'They also assure me that each of my business interests is viable and likely to be more viable in the future. I am, I may say, no cock virgin if you will forgive the use of the term but I feel that all my cards should be on the table, face upwards, if we are to do business together. What do you think?'

'What do I think of what?' Patricia returned innocently as she endeavoured to formulate some sort of response for the inevitable proposal.

'Of my situation,' Willie Halvey replied.

'You're a wealthy man,' Patricia answered, 'no one would deny that.'

'So what do you say?' Willie sat back in his chair, spread his short legs and waited for an answer.

'What do I say to what for God's sake?' Patricia pretended to be flustered.

'Are you going to marry me or aren't you?' He blurted out the words as he rammed his hat firmly back on his head. Patricia realised that there was now no scope for indecision.

'No!' she replied firmly. 'I will not marry you. I'm grateful and flattered but I have no notion of marrying now or at any time.'

'Would that be your final answer?' he asked without emotion.

'Absolutely,' Patricia answered.

Rising from the chair he tipped his hat and made his way into the bar where Sadie Cahalane sat in her accustomed position behind the counter.

'Stand over here till I talk to you.' Willie Halvey removed his hat for the second time that night. Now convinced that his primary goal was no longer realisable he outlined his wealth to the widow before laying his proposal before her.

'I could never marry again,' she answered his request simply and he knew from the sincerity of her tone that the same answer was likely to be tendered to whomsoever might make such an offer. He returned his hat to his head and shrugged his shoulders before faring forth into the rain storm which was brewing outside.

On his way to his car he consoled himself with the thought that he had proposed to the two handsomest women in his native village. That they happened to be mother and daughter was purely coincidental. What mattered, in his estimation, was that they were the best available. He would dispense with the idea of marriage for the moment but he wouldn't let up on it. Time had a way of changing things, even in Ballybobawn.

AS THE RAM OF GOD drove slowly downhill, his mind preoccupied with the hazel eyes of the Widow's daughter, he scarcely noticed the figure of Mary Creel sitting astride the gate. When he did he raised a hand in recognition expecting her to return his salute. Nothing happened. She sat trance-like, her young form hunched forward, her knees tightly drawn together. He waved a second time expecting her to vacate her perch and open the gate but there was no reaction of any kind.

'Come on Mary,' he called, 'stop the day-dreaming and open the gate.'

When she failed to move he drew to a halt no

more than a few yards from where she sat.

'What's the matter?' he asked more perplexed than annoyed as he noted her unsmiling features. It seemed to the Ram of God that for some reason known only to herself she was determined to remain where she was. The impression he got was that there was some sinister presence outside the meadow from which she was trying to shield him. Her normally parted lips were tightly sealed. There was no trace of the ever-engaging smile. Her body was taut, the white of her knuckles showing clearly as she grasped the uppermost bar of the iron gate. The Ram of God dismounted uneasily, reluctant now to demand an explanation for her abnormal behaviour. All his instincts forewarned him of an imminent and calamitous disclosure. What else would transform such a bright and playful teenager? Gently he took both her hands in his and forced a reassuring smile.

'It's all right Mary,' the Ram of God whispered, 'you can tell me. Whatever it is I'll understand.'

She suddenly burst into tears and threw her arms around his neck.

'It's Will,' she blurted out.

'Will?' Angrily the Ram held her at arm's length. 'What's he done to you Mary?'

Mary bent her head.

'There's been an accident,' she whispered. 'Will is dead!'

'How can he be dead?' the Ram asked in disbelief. 'I was speaking to him only a few hours ago. He was as alive as you or me. What are you talking about?'

'He's dead Ram,' Mary burst into tears a second time. 'I saw him. It was the bull.'

'The bull!'

'He came up behind him and knocked him. I didn't see it. All I heard was a shout and then a terrible scream. Nonie saw him attack. She ran to the milking parlour for Murt but he was dead when Murt got there.'

'You're sure he's dead?'

Mary nodded.

The Ram buried his head in his hands.

'Where's the bull now?'

'Murt turned him into the field next to the house.'

'Is Will badly maimed?'

'No,' Mary spoke earnestly, 'you'd notice nothing. Nonie rang for the doctor and the priest. Murt sent me here.'

'How's Murt?' the Ram asked brokenly.

'He seems badly shocked.'

'He would be. There were none as close as those two.'

'We had better go down,' Mary took him by the hand and led him to the tractor.

'You'll be able to drive?' It hadn't escaped her that he had been severely shattered by the terrible news.

'I'll be all right.' His face was bloodless as he lifted her on to the tractor and placed her on one of the bales. He stood for a moment, a hand resting on the side of the gate.

'You're absolutely certain he's dead?'

'He's dead beyond doubt,' Mary answered tearfully.

The Ram shook his head as he mounted the tractor. 'I've lost count of the number of times I told them to get rid of that bull. Only the other day I warned Murt that he wasn't to be trusted.'

The bull, Friesan by strain, shifty by nature

had for some time sought diversions other than the mounting of the hederacious heifers and cows he so faithfully serviced since they had been granted the freedom of the pastures earlier in the year. He regularly took stock of each of the three brothers in turn, rarely looking directly at them, averting his bloodshot eyes when one drew near but upturning showers of dust and clods over his powerful shoulders as he pawed the ground beneath, always making clear his hostility whenever he was taken by one of his uglier moods.

Other times when he would return from the pastures with the herd he could be as docile as a lamb, content to dawdle aimlessly in the vicinity of the milking parlour until such time as his charges were released. Happily in their midst he would proceed with bent head back to the grazing which had been so unreasonably interrupted by a visitation from one of the trio who had been in his sights for so long.

'When a bull looks at you,' the Ram once heard an old farmer talking to his late father, 'it's not out of curiosity the way a cow might look at you or a bullock. No sir, when a bull looks at you he's wondering what kind of a kill you'd be. Ninety-nine percent of the time you're safe but the only reason you're safe is because it doesn't suit the bull. He doesn't have the advantage. When he has the advantage he'll let you know.'

'Never, never, never trust a bull!' It was a caution uttered by every farmer to every farmer's son since time immemorial and yet even those who so sagely tendered the advice in the first place were often the victims themselves.

WILL DRANNAGHY LAY STRETCHED on his back,

his hands turned downwards and inwards over his abdomen, his powerful chest crushed as though it was no more than pasteboard. Murt stood akimbo over the body of his dead brother, his head bent, mouth open, a semi-erect parody of the still figure at his feet.

He had not hesitated to confront the bull after Nonie called him. Pike in hand he forced the enraged creature to retreat from the sprawled body of his twin. Nonie and Mary contributed in their own ways and it may well have been the joint distractions – Mary with a chair, Nonie with a bucket – which finally left the bull undecided before he eventually retreated through the open gate which Murt closed quickly behind him.

Murt held the lifeless body in his arms, repeatedly calling Will's name to no avail. Then suddenly he whispered an act of contrition into the unreceiving ear of the dead man before laying him lovingly on the ground and adopting the watchful pose in which the Ram and Mary found him.

The Ram of God knelt by Will's side and bending down looked for signs of life. Finding none he repeated the act of contrition and rising, placed his hands about the inert Murt, kissing him on the forehead. All the while Mary stood silently watching her heart went out to the grieving brothers. Nonie emerged from the rear of the farmhouse with the news that Father Hehir, the curate, was on his way. A doctor from Trallock had already left the town and Father O'Connor had taken it upon himself to convey the grim tidings to the Cronanes.

'Should we say the Rosary or something while we're waiting for the priest?' Nonie asked the Ram.

'Tell me first how it happened,' he directed the question towards Murt but it was clear that the

106

surviving twin was so deeply shocked that he was unable to reply. Drawing near the Ram, Nonie spoke in a whisper.

'The bull was standing against the gable there looking at the ground when Will passed on his way to the parlour. Like a flash he butted him in the back and knocked him. The next thing he was on top of him with a foreleg at either side of his chest. There was no escape. I called Murt but when Will screamed I knew 'twas all over.'

'Had he drink taken?'

Nonie nodded.

'He had the sign of the village on him all right,' she said sadly.

Mary Creel moved close to Murt Drannaghy and took one of his gnarled hands in hers. Murt stared at her uncomprehendingly, looking away absently before fixing his benighted gaze on her once more. Gently she raised her other hand and touched his brow with her fingers, finally resting her palm gently against his cheek. Slowly the trance-like look gave way to one of sorrow. He pressed the sympathetic hand to his face, his powerful chest heaving uncontrollably until the pitiful tear-releasing cries of despair vented his agony. The Ram went immediately to his other side, his arm firmly around the quaking shoulders.

When Father Hehir arrived a few moments later he stood respectfully until Murt recovered sufficiently to properly observe the proceedings. Kneeling by the dead man he turned to the onlookers and explained that the simple ceremony would consist merely of the rite known as the Short Anointing, 'which means,' Father Hehir was at pains to point out, 'that I shall anoint him on the forehead alone.'

107

So saying he placed his stole round his neck and knelt by Will's side. With the thumb of his right hand he applied the holy chrism with the accompanying words of heavenly pardon: 'I absolve you of your sins.'

There followed a few moments of silence before Father Hehir completed the rite with the words: 'Through this holy anointing may the Lord forgive you what ever sins you have committed.'

Father Hehir rose slowly to his feet and solemnly addressed the tiny gathering.

'As we stand,' he spoke in low key, 'we shall recite a decade of the Rosary and pray that the good God will have mercy on his immortal soul.'

Father Hehir had almost reached the end of the decade when young Doctor O'Dell from Trallock arrived on the scene. Satisfying himself that Will was indeed dead he set about establishing the cause of death. Hot on his heels came Sergeant Luke Holly who tendered his sympathy to the brothers and Nonie Spillane.

'The last thing I want to do at this time Eddie,' Luke took the Ram of God aside and spoke in confidential tones, 'is to intrude upon your grief but there is the question of the animal. Would that be him beside the gate?' The sergeant pointed to where the Friesian stood pawing the green sod, his earlier fury somewhat abated but still intimating that visitors would be unwelcome.

'He's the boy.' The Ram of God answered with a futile shaking of the head.

'Have you made up your mind what you'll do with him?' Luke asked. When no answer was forthcoming the sergeant stroked his chin.

'The usual thing with a dangerous bull,' he explained, 'is to have a lorry come from the factory.

We could put a few cows aboard with him to keep him quiet. From the looks of him the best place for him is inside in a tin. We'll take Will's body into the house now and I'll round up a few of the neighbours. We'll get that black and white devil into an outhouse and wait for the lorry.'

The sergeant paused and with a quizzical look surveyed the taller man for a moment 'or I could shoot him here and now and we could have the carcass removed tomorrow?'

'No!' The Ram of God was adamant. 'I'd appreciate if you rounded up a few of the neighbours. We'll house him and put a few cows in with him to keep him quiet.'

'Then that's the way it will be my friend.' The sergeant laid a hand on his arm. 'I can't tell you how sorry I am Eddie.'

'I know that Luke,' Eddie replied. 'You're a great help to us.'

The arrival of the Cronanes into the kitchen of the Drannaghy farmhouse was heralded by the piteous wailing of Kate, Will's intended. Supported by her mother and her distraught sister Noreen, her grief-stricken face was tear-stained and blotched. She threw herself across Will's body, laid out on the kitchen table until such time as it could be claimed by the undertaker and readied for laying out in Ballybobawn's solitary funeral parlour which had been built only the previous year by Willie Halvey.

The heart-rending cries of Kate Cronane filled the kitchen and brought home the full extent of the tragedy for the first time. Even Nonie Spillane was moved. The tears coursed down the young face of Mary Creel. The only dubious aspects of the tragedy were the occasional piercing ululations of

Mollie Cronane. Between Mollie's forced outbursts she took time off to look around the kitchen. Ancient but spacious she thought.

Noreen prevailed upon her sister Kate to take a seat. Neighbours were beginning to arrive, women, their heads covered, men with caps in hand

'Good Christ on his cross,' Nonie Spillane whispered furiously to the Ram, 'there isn't a drop of drink in the house. Make out a list and I'll send Mary down to the Widow's. Patricia will deliver.'

Looking around Nonie could see no trace of Mary in the kitchen. Muttering incoherently to herself she went in search of the schoolgirl but she was nowhere to be found. Nonie was mystified. She had no way of knowing that the answer to the riddle lay with Mollie Cronane. No sooner had the visiting mourners spread themselves around the kitchen than she had casually approached Mary. She stood next to the grieving girl for a moment making sure before she spoke that nobody was within earshot.

'Get yourself home out of here,' she hissed. Mary looked at the older woman in astonishment unable to believe her ears.

'Go on now or I'll give you the back of my hand. Go on!' She raised the hand as though she would strike.

Mary Creel stood undecided. She looked in Nonie's direction but the housekeeper was engaged in earnest conversation with the Ram. Mary looked directly into Mollie Cronane's eyes. They were narrowed to slits, hate-filled and bloodshot. Mary found herself trembling all over. For a moment she was reminded of the bull.

Mollie was voicing a final threat. 'If you're not gone from here this instant I'll drag you by the ears to the door.'

Dejectedly, without looking behind, Mary made her way to the door and beyond. She might have turned and sought the protection of Nonie or the Ram. She was certain that help from either would be assured. She felt, however, that it was hardly the time for parading her own troubles.

Her father Mickey made his way to the Drannaghy farmhouse shortly before the pubs closed. Rumour had it that the whiskey and beer would flow there during the wake. The body had been removed to the funeral parlour but the mourners were expected to make the journey to the farmhouse to offer their condolences.

The bull was successfully dispatched to the factory. A neighbouring farmer took charge of the transferral from cowhouse to lorry. He was assisted by Sergeant Luke Holly and several neighbours. Afterwards he called to the house to pay his respects. He found the Ram in a thoughtful mood by the front door.

'Did he finish his job itself?' Joe McCallum asked. He was a spare man, tall and serious with little time for frivolity or indeed any pursuit other than farming.

'Did who finish his job?' the Ram asked.

'The bull of course,' Joe answered.

The Ram found himself smiling in spite of himself. It was just the sort of thought that would occur to his neighbour. The Ram knew that the question was not posed out of idle curiosity.

'There are three or four heifers still to be covered,' he told Joe.

'All mine have took,' Joe spoke without pride, 'so there's no work now for my Aberdeen Angus. He's only the two years but he's as fervent a polly as ever went astride a cow. Besides he's a quiet chap. I'll drive him up tomorrow on the sly. You won't need getting a new bull or the artificial insemination. This chap will finish the job for you.'

'I'm mighty grateful Joe.'

'Not at all man for God's sake!' Joe threw back expansively. 'What else is neighbours for and won't it be a worry off your mind. Anyway he fancies 'em. Don't he see 'em often enough through the hedge.'

BOB'S KATIE TRUDGED THROUGH Ballybobawn like a woman in labour. She walked with bent head, not out of the mock servility she so often utilised for soliciting but rather availing of the immunity always afforded to women in her condition. She did not have to look where she was going although, without once seeming to look up, her footsteps inevitably directed her to the Cronane supermarket at the very heart of Ballybobawn. She had heard about the killing; it was the talk of the village.

Behind Bob's Katie was a second travelling woman who walked hand in hand with a red-haired girl of no more than ten. Bob's Katie turned into the Load of S where her promises of prayers and novenas fell on deaf ears. Further in she could see a group of younger men, their interest completely absorbed by a television set, the screen of which explicitly showed a young lady disporting herself without the aid of clothes or headgear. From where Bob's Katie stood she seemed to be posing for a pair of equally naked young men who eagerly awaited her favours.

'What's the world comin' to at all sir?' She addressed the question to a middle-aged man who sat drinking a pint of stout near a mirror where the

112

happenings on the television screen were fully reflected.

'Would you have e'er a few shillings sir to know would I feed my childer?' she asked as she peered through the front window at the supermarket across the street. No one there save a young man!

'Why don't you go in to the back room there and show that fine figure of yours to them young lads. You've a bigger belly than any of them young doxies on the screen.'

Bob's Katie threw him a withering look as his jibe drew guffaws from those within earshot.

She hurried into the street where she paused to convey the most imperceptible of signals to the second woman who happened to be her daughter, a sixteen-year-old with body and looks mature enough to help her pass as a woman ten years her senior.

The daughter, Bob's Biddy, crossed the empty street and entered the supermarket through the side door, all the time holding her younger sister by the hand. From the moment she entered she found herself subject to the most obdurate scrutiny by Cha Cronane. At the time there were two other women in the shop. Both were in the process of filling trolley cars with their requirements

'How much a pound is the sausages sir?' Bob's Biddy asked.

'Eighty-five pence a pound,' Cha informed her, never taking his eyes off her hands.

Bob's Biddy handed the pound of sausages to her sister and produced a purse from her coat pocket. She counted out the exact amount. Cha accepted the money and waited.

'Have you spuds sir?' Bob's Biddy asked.

'Over there,' Cha pointed towards the front entrance, 'just to the right.' Vigilantly he followed her movements as he stood with folded arms. It was just possible, Cha told himself, that the poor woman was decent enough. Just because one or two were branded as thieves was no reason why they should all be branded. Try telling that to his mother!

Before she went upstairs Bob's Katie took off her shoes and transferred them to a canvas bag attached to the dress under her shawl. She had entered through the front door, ignored by the shop's two customers and unseen by Cha whose sole preoccupation was the scrupulous surveillance of the only visible travelling folk in the supermarket at the time. Rightly or wrongly he followed the guidelines laid down by his mother.

'When a tinker woman comes in you must drop everything until she goes out!'

On the first landing Bob's Katie paused for breath. Standing on one bare leg she listened intently. From the room on her right came the sound of snoring. No call for alarm there! That would be the oul' fella, spun out for sure from his three days on the rantan! Noiselessly she opened the bedroom door. He lay sprawled on his back. As she drew near she wasn't in the least revolted by the smell of excrement and vomit. Expert fingers ran through the pockets of the coat and trousers which were thrown on the floor at the foot of the bed. Concluding her search Bob's Katie drew back disappointed. Twenty-seven pounds! She'd expected more. Her eyes took in the contents of the room; time to move on.

In the next room were two beds. She guessed it was the girls' room. She was sorry to be sure for the wan that lost her man but wasn't that the way

114

o' the world! None of us can expect to go free from sorra!

The next room was Mollie Cronane's. Bob's Katie knew the minute she opened the door. By the bedside was a safe and miracles of miracles – the door was open with the ring of keys nearby on the floor. She fell on her knees, her belly plopping in front of her like something apart. She first opened the cash-box.

'My heart will surely be heard downstairs,' she told herself as she beheld the heap of notes resting inside. There were several cheques and a few postal orders. The cash would do nicely thank you! She left everything else. Anything other than cash always spelt trouble especially with a man as careless and greedy as Bob Latty.

'There's two thousand pounds if there's a penny,' she placed a hand under a fold of the shawl and placed the empty box thereon. With another fold she wiped the box carefully before returning it to where it had reposed before she moved it.

'Never in a month of Sundays,' Bob's Katie congratulated herself, 'would Mollie Cronane leave that safe open. She had something else on her mind poor woman.' Before rising she dealt with the safe handle, meticulously wiping it clean of all prints. She administered the same treatment to the door-knobs of each of the three rooms not forgetting to blow a kiss towards the recumbent form of Tom.

On the landing she paused and listened long and well. It would never do to slip up now at this the ultimate stage of her foraging. She bided her time on the landing before descending two steps at a time as soon as she heard her daughter's voice at the side door. Cha stood with his back turned to the descending Bob's Katie. Hands folded, his eyes remained glued to the departing figure of Bob's Biddy. Satisfied that she had put sufficient distance between herself and the supermarket for a return to normal trading he turned around. All was as it should be, the two female customers still absorbed by their own wants and the street outside empty of humanity.

Cha's thought returned to the awful fate of the twin Drannaghy. Often in nightmares he had fled similar bulls escaping death only by the skin of his teeth. He wished he could have accompanied his mother and sisters. Mollie had been adamant when he suggested they close the shop.

'Time enough for that the day of the funeral,' she had replied coldly. 'You make sure you stay open until eight o'clock. Then go up and change your father. I'll be back as soon as I can.'

'Will I tell my father?'

'Waste of time,' Mollie spoke from long experience. 'I'll tell him in the morning when he's some way sober.'

The other members of the Cronane household Sammie, Donie and Tomboy had hitched lifts to Trallock immediately after their suppers, less than a half-hour before news of Will's death reached the supermarket. Primed by Tomboy and Donie Sammie had lifted a ten-pound note and a five-pound note from his father's trousers pocket. It had been the simplest of thefts. For a moment he was tempted to take a second tenner but his conscience got the better of him and he settled for the sum earlier agreed upon by himself and his brothers. They also decided to hitch back from Trallock the moment the football game ended and to spend their ill-gotten gains in the back room of the Load of S. After they arrived in Ballybobawn Cha broke the

116

terrible news.

Later they stood at the cross waiting for darkness to descend. Three times during the half-hour they spent there Mary Creel passed by. On one occasion she was accompanied by a sister, on another by a brother and finally on her own. Each time she saluted the trio but only two acknowledged her. Tomboy had kept his eyes firmly fixed on the ground.

Sammie and Donie, aware of their mother's injunction, made no attempt to rib Tomboy as they might normally have done. There were questions both would have loved to ask such as the extent of the intimacy in the now defunct relationship. Neither felt any great sense of pity for Mary Creel.

Cha Cronane, concealed from view of the street by a large cardboard advertisement, saw Mary pass to and fro. Cha was also aware of his mother's mandate. He was angry with Tomboy.

'If she were my girl,' he whispered the words wistfully to himself, 'I wouldn't let her pass by.'

7

IT WAS AFTER ELEVEN o'clock when Mollie Cronane returned to the supermarket. It never occurred to her until she collected the evening's takings from the cash register that she might have forgotten the keys of the safe. After a search of her handbag she tried her coat pockets but found nothing. As she hurried upstairs to her bedroom she had already begun to fear the worst.

Later as she sat upstairs with Sergeant Holly she explained that she had never before, since first becoming mistress of the house, forgotten to close the safe and return the keys to her handbag or pockets.

'We both know who did it,' she said as the sergeant and Garda Connelly searched for clues.

'I have no idea yet who might be responsible,' the sergeant made the admission to Mollie's obvious annoyance.

'What kind of a shagging mope are you?' she demanded. 'It was Bob's Katie, that thieving wretch from the encampment. Wasn't her daughter downstairs while she was above!'

'We'll need proof,' Sergeant Holly reminded her.

'And if you move fast and stop shag-acting around here you might find that proof!'

'All right Mrs Cronane you've had your say. Now I'll have mine. I'll get on to Trallock straightaway and have them send out the two squad cars fully manned. Meanwhile Garda Connelly and myself will wait near the encampment until they arrive.'

118

'And I can tell you, you size fourteen fool that you'll find no trace of my money!'

ON A HIGH, GRASSY bank overlooking the Ogle river, the clan of Bob Latty sat in deep contentment, some surveying the full moon, others the shining river, the younger members stretched out in the dreamless sleep of abandon.

'That's a great moon,' Bob Latty addressed himself to the upper regions from where the orb of night shed its bountiful rays on settled folk and traveller alike. The nearby encampment had swollen to four Hiace vans, three caravans and several rude shelters. The last would be hurriedly abandoned should there be persistent rain.

All the adult members of the settlement occupied the river bank in whose drought-lowered waters the trout and salmon were returning to their normal habitats after a sustained barrage of gravel and stones from the itinerant children.

Puck Fair was no more than a week away. The Lattys, Bob, his wife Katie, their daughter Biddy and the several younger children had dined well. Fragments of cooked ham, cow's tongue, assorted sausage meats, biscuits, buns and cakes were scattered everywhere. There was no adult in the gathering who was not possessed of at least a six pack of beer whilst some produced partly filled bottles of whiskey, from which they swallowed carefully, providing added bite to the beery intake.

'Nobody loves a full moon more than a tinker!' Sergeant Luke Holly made the observation to Garda Thomas Connelly in whispered tones from behind the willow clump where they concealed themselves fifty yards upriver from the peaceful gathering.

'How do you make that out?' Thomas asked in equally subdued tones.

'I don't know for sure,' the sergeant whispered back. 'Maybe it's due to the nomadic existence they favour from time to time. It brings out the poetry and the nostalgia. See there's one of the women singing.'

Bob's Biddy, unaware of the law's presence, had risen to her feet and was shrilly singing:

> *Sure I won't be a nun*
> *And I can't be a nun*
> *All the priests in the parish*
> *Wouldn't make me a nun.*
> *But I'll go to the fair*
> *And a young man find me there*
> *Sure he'll put me such a way*
> *As I can't be a nun.*

On went the irreverent ballad, the full company joining in the chorus every so often, Bob's Biddy dancing now in her bare feet, not to any prearranged measure but in tune with the quickly accelerating handclap of her fraternity until she decided to collapse on her behind in the centre of the ring. Her shape, features and face were carefully noted by more than one young man in the gathering.

Earlier one of the suitors in question made the journey to Trallock for the drink and provisions so evident along the river bank. The money was supplied by Bob Latty out of the fifteen hundred which his wife had handed over to him. She offered five hundred to her daughter Biddy but the girl declined on the grounds that there was little luck accruing to money acquired in such a manner.

'I'll store it for you then.'

120

'Don't indeed!' Bob's Biddy shot back, 'for the lad I have my eye on won't see me short.'

Bob's Katie was on the point of chiding her for her want of foresight but she said nothing. 'Young girls is entitled to their dreams,' she reminded herself. 'A young wan should make the most of her dreams before her belly rises.'

She hid eight hundred pounds where nobody would find it. She'd want it soon enough. Wasn't she married herself before she was fifteen and wasn't Biddy only a year older nor that and wouldn't she want what she could lay her hands on before the fall of the year maybe. 'I'm what the world made me. I wouldn't be what I am only for them that's in the middle of plenty. I was supple as Biddy once God bless me and then the little beads of morning dew slipped inside me and I was spancelled for evermore. 'Tis such a small thing puts a hobble on a woman. Still I have a few hundred pounds to the good at last.'

Behind the willows Luke Holly looked at his watch for the umpteenth time that night.

'I make it two minutes to twelve. What about you?'

'The same,' Thomas Connelly verified.

'Let's move. The two squad cars will arrive in the camp in two minutes time.' Sergeant Holly moved silently in the shadows of the ancient alders which darkened the river pathway save for where the tinkers sat in the moonlit clearing. Emerging suddenly from their cover the scattering which they expected their arrival to precipitate never materialised. It was at this precise moment that the squad cars from Trallock entered the encampment. Luke Holly quickly deduced, from the absence of panic, that visitors were expected.

'Have a drink sergeant?' the invitation came from Bob Latty.

Thomas Connolly was surprised when his superior accepted the outstretched bottle of whiskey. Wiping the jowl as he made sure that none of the lawmen from Trallock were watching he indulged in a liberal swallow and after a pause another of shorter duration.

Despite the most intensive search of the encampment and its surrounds nothing incriminating was found. The female garda who had accompanied the raiding party had searched each of the itinerant women from head to toe and found nothing. When one of the younger policemen revealed, unwittingly, that a sum of twenty-three hundred pounds had been stolen, he little realised that he had convicted Bob's Katie of a heinous crime, that of withholding eight hundred pounds from her man.

'You can hand it over now,' he told her after the guards left, 'or I'll bate it out of you at my aise!'

'You may wonder,' Sergeant Holly explained later to Thomas Connolly, 'why I accepted the drink and why I drank so deeply. I don't have to tell you why but here goes anyway! Firstly, it would have been bad manners to decline the offer. The onus was on me to prove that it had been purchased by ill-gotten cash and I had no proof of that. Secondly, when in the name of Jasus am I ever again likely to drink two glasses of good whiskey at Mollie Cronane's expense? Finally, and most importantly, when I need information about crimes like rape or murder, the men with whom I shared Mollie Cronane's whiskey won't forget their partner in crime when it comes to putting the finger on the right man.'

After a somewhat heated conference with the

superintendent of Trallock garda division and the
drivers of the two squad cars the senior officer de-
creed that the local pair should stalk out the encampment after dark.

'The money is hidden somewhere along the
banks of the Ogle River, not far from the encampment and sooner or later somebody's going to come
and reclaim it.'

The superintendent was adamant despite Luke
Holly's protestations that the money was nowhere
near Ballybobawn.

'They have a system of laundering and distri-
bution second to none,' he explained, 'and sending
us to the river at night is just a waste of time.'

'Well indulge me then like a good man,' the
superintendent returned sarcastically, 'and don't
make my job any harder.'

Luke guessed that he was under pressure from
the chief superintendent who, no doubt, was under
pressure from Mollie Cronane. At the conclusion of
the briefing the superintendent took Luke to one
side.

'I hate to have to say this Luke,' Joe Chaney
opened, 'and I might as well tell you there's no man
I respect more but there are ugly rumours and
there have been anonymous letters regarding yourself and the Widow.'

'What the hell are you talking about?' Luke
asked angrily.

'I don't believe any of it so I won't say any more
on the matter except to be careful.'

'Careful of what man?'

'Now, now!' the superintendent chided although
there was a hint of mollification in his tone.
'There's none of us hasn't had an anonymous letter
written about him at one time or another so let's

forget it.'

'Sure,' Luke commented drily, 'but a letter from Mollie Cronane would be something you couldn't forget.'

The letter contained no more than what Mollie hinted privately to Ballybobawn's more malicious gossips, that the sergeant's sense of detection was rendered absolutely ineffective by his after-hours devotion to the Widow Cahalane.

'He's knocking her off every night when the bar is closed,' she insisted when even the most receptive scandalmongers expressed total disbelief. Mollie persisted with the outrageous fabrication in the hope that repetition would beget suspicion.

DURING THE NIGHTS FOLLOWING the robbery both civic guards spent hours on end concealed by the dense cover which the river banks afforded. They arrived after dark and took up their positions as near to the encampment as they dared. On the third night of their vigil the lawmen were assailed by a steady downpour. They came unprepared but managed to remain partly dry for a while by availing of the shade provided by the leafy branches overhead. Towards morning a fresh wind sent the drops raining down upon their heads and shoulders, drenching both to the skins. In the barracks they slept until noon of the following day, attending to routine duties during the afternoon and evening and returning to the river bank after the sergeant conveyed a verbal report to Superintendent Chaney in Trallock.

'Do you really think you should jack it up?' the super asked.

'We'll give it one more night,' Luke suggested.

'They should be pulling out for Puck tomorrow and if the money is hidden in the vicinity of the camp tonight's the night they'll go for it.'

'All right Luke I'll leave it in your hands.'

'That's something you should have done in the first place,' Luke said as soon as he put down the phone.

As dark was falling they arrived at the chosen spot making sure, as usual, that their approach went unnoticed by the residents of the encampment.

'What's this?' Thomas asked as he noticed a neatly wrapped package at his feet.

'Looks like a bottle,' he said as he lifted the object nearer his eyes.

'Powers Gold Label!' he exclaimed in disbelief, 'and it sealed to boot. Whatever possessed them to go in for Powers Gold Label?'

There was no answer forthcoming from Luke who never indulged in any other brand of whiskey. It was the encampment's way of informing them that their presence had been accepted from the beginning, that the inhabitants were sorry for the inclemency of the previous night's weather and that they would be departing for Puck Fair the following morning.

'What do you think we should do with it?' Thomas asked.

'I think we might take pattern from the old Irish proverb Thomas.'

'And what proverb would that be sergeant?'

'In rough translation Thomas – let us drink for those who cannot drink.'

'There was a lot of commonsense in those old Irish sayings sergeant.'

'There's one for every occasion Thomas.'

'And if there wasn't sergeant it would be no bother to you to compose one.'

Later, after half the bottle had been consumed Luke recalled how he had known Bob's Katie's mother.

'She was one of the Cafferkey's of Clare, a fine brave woman with the hair swept back on her head and coiled behind into a bun. We used to admire their caravans when they passed on the road below us. We had a farm. The brother is still there and still single like myself. God what a sight they were and they trekking to Galway for the races, the caravans painted down to the spokes of the wheels with all the colours of the rainbow and more besides, with squares and diamonds and circles and semi-circles and designs so psychedelic I can't bring them to mind. There would be the goats and the dogs and the ponies following behind and when the cobs drawing the caravans grew tired, man, woman and child would walk the road without a bother, ten, twelve and often fifteen miles in the day and all they ever stole was a few sods from a reek of turf or the fallen branches from a tree. Old Meg Cafferky, Bob's Katie's mother, was a brave woman surely. I saw her in Kilrush one day and she opened a blackguard's head with an iron kettle. Her man was outnumbered and she stepped in. What a warrant she was to make paper flowers! and her husband knew how to make a tin panny or a milk gallon or whatever. They were real tinkers, industrious too not like a lot of these shifty bastards going today. There was a lot thought of those folk and they were welcome in the countryside whatever about the towns. Listen Thomas my boy! What would you say if we were to return to the day-room and finish off what's left in this bottle. It would make a few nice mugs of punch before we took to our beds. It's a bit late for the Widow's and the chill of last night's wetting is still in my bones.'

'I wouldn't say no sergeant,' Thomas replied.

As they walked through the main street of Ballybobawn their progress did not go unnoticed. It rarely did but on this occasion there was more than one sleepless female gazing idly and otherwise on the street below.

From her second storey front room Patricia Cahalane was surprised to see the custodians of the peace abroad at such an hour. She examined her watch. Twenty minutes past two. Time, she felt, to return to the bed she had vacated half an hour before when sleep had failed to come.

'Why the hell should I worry about him,' she thought, 'when it's certain and sure he doesn't worry about me? How dare I read anything into those few moments we spent alone in the bar.' Nothing happened, a smile perhaps, a careless brushing of bodies and yet as far as she was concerned everything had happened. 'Just as well he's off to California and that's probably the last Ballybobawn will ever see of him. Just as well I'm a reserved virgin and a preserved virgin who was never in the slightest danger of losing that which my mother believes should be cherished more than any other commodity in the world, should be safeguarded with a zeal and commitment until the day I face the altar rails of Ballybobawn parish church with the man of my choice by my side.

'Just as well he doesn't call to the pub on a regular basis because as sure as hell I'd be out there chatting him up for better or for worse and just as well I'm not the romantic type for nothing is surer than that I'd be strolling up in the general

127

direction of the High Meadow in the long summer evenings and maybe dropping in to see Nonie and Mary for a chat and a cup of tea. That's as sure as blazes what I should be doing if I had an ounce of gumption but no! Let him lose his vocation through some other means. I would never have it on my conscience that I came between him and his God.'

Mollie Cronane had been chain smoking for over an hour. Unable to sleep she sat in her dressing gown by the window. Earlier that evening there had been a council of war in the downstairs parlour. The upshot of the stormy proceedings was that a man would have to be procured and procured fairly quickly to take the place of Will and he would have to be a man who would move into the Drannaghy farm come hell or high water in the course of time but meanwhile the wedding would take place as planned.

Inside the central window of the storey beneath sat the sisters Kate and Noreen.

'Is the Stringer McCallum still interested?' Noreen took her time before posing the question. She might well be rushing her fences.

'I would imagine he is,' came back the morose response.

'And the McCallum farm bounds the Drannaghy's and the Ram would surely have no objection and he such friends with the Stringer's brother Joe and it would surely suit Joe for he'd be free to bring in a woman.'

'Easily said but how would I go about it?'

'You wear the black a while yet and let things to me. Hold the bone as my mother might say and let the dog follow!'

'I have nothing better to do,' Kate agreed resignedly.

'Do you miss him bad?' Noreen, again ventured the question, hoping that it wasn't posed before its time.

'I miss him but I never loved him. He was as much my mother's choice as mine. Hop a ball to the Stringer in God's name and don't I be left rearing a bastard!'

THE RAM OF GOD TOOK careful stock of the Cronane sisters as the grave-diggers lowered the coffin into the seeping trench which they had excavated the evening before. There was no thump of clods on the timber coffin. Instead a coarse green mat was drawn across the gaping wound which would be filled in at leisure as soon as the last of the mourners had departed.

Kate Cronane was supported on the one side by her sister Noreen and on the other by her brother Cha. Mollie Cronane stood close by, her arm linked to that of her husband Tom whose trembling hands were partially steadied by her proximity. The Ram of God's were not the only pair of eyes to be absorbed by the stance of the sisters. They stood pale-faced and unmoving. Neither made the slightest attempt to answer the funeral prayers which had preceded the laying on of the mat. Father O'Connor and Father Hehir departed immediately after the obsequies. Traditionally, after the departure of the clergy there was a time for lamentation and for other manifestations of heartfelt grief. The rustic audience felt cheated when no sound escaped the tightly pursed lips of Kate. When she was led away meekly by her brother and sister many of the onlookers exchanged looks of puzzlement. Some verbally denounced this unprecedented

129

flouting of custom the moment they found themselves free of the sacred confines of the graveyard. Older mourners shook their heads regretfully reminding each other that it was all due to the changing of the times.

The more knowledgeable onlookers said that Kate wouldn't be Mollie Cronane's daughter if she didn't turn her face from what was over and look to what lay ahead. This was, in fact, precisely how Kate was beginning to adapt herself to the tragic circumstances in which she found herself. If the graveyard congregation felt cheated she felt that she was the victim of downright robbery. Now that the initial grief had passed and Will would never enter her life again it was time for alternative arrangements.

The Ram of God was puzzled by the absence of any display of emotion especially since she had wept so copiously upon first beholding the lifeless body on the kitchen table of the farmhouse. He felt disappointed rather than cheated or was it possible that, like himself, she was unable to give proper expression to her grief. The Ram was aware that she was carrying Will's child. Concern about her future must surely outweigh most other feelings at this time. How would she cope with the future? What were her expectations? What would people say when the whole truth came out? It was the Ram's considered opinion that these questions were sufficient in themselves to fully occupy anybody's mind. As he saw it a situation had arisen which was so fraught with problems that it did not bear thinking about.

Meanwhile he concerned himself with the present. There were the Drannaghy relations from Waterford and Tipperary and there were cousins on his mother's side. There was still plenty of drink remaining from the night before. On the Ram's instructions Nonie had purchased sufficient edibles at Cronane's to cope with whatever relatives and neighbours might look in after the burial. Both the Ram and Nonie were baffled by the continuing absence of Mary Creel. It was, they agreed, a most unusual departure for her. Neither could recall a solitary day's absence since she first came to work at the farmhouse. Both tried to remember if they had been guilty of some unintended slight but then they reassured themselves that she would be the last person to take umbrage at anything, always directing the limelight away from herself and never complaining.

'I'll give a call to the house,' Nonie promised. 'Life isn't easy for that family.'

Mickey Creel arrived late to the farmhouse to offer his condolences and accept the glass of whiskey which Murt thrust into his hand. He drank several glasses and numerous bottles of beer before returning to his home and routing his entire family from their beds, berating and scolding them at the top of his voice and striking out at those who didn't vacate the kitchen quickly enough. Fortunately he fell asleep quickly. After a while the drunken snores, rippling and crackling, assured them of a few hours respite. Silently they stole back into the house grateful to be serenaded by the now even tenor of the contented snoozing which carried to several houses at either side of the Creel home. Until he awakened temporarily, some hours later, to relieve his bladder for the first of many times, there were frequent alarms in the shape of rasping snorts and booming breakings of wind. The Creels, mother and children, took little notice. They slept, fitfully, until morning.

Nonie called, as promised, to the Creel household. Immediately afterwards she informed her master, 'It was exactly eleven o'clock and all I could hear was snoring. I knocked and I waited and when I got no answer I knocked again. I saw the curtains move in the kitchen window and threadbare curtains they were to be sure. I waited a while and the curtains moved once more. It was then I got the bright idea to knock at the window. After a few minutes the curtain was drawn and I saw the worn face of poor Maggie Creel and she looking at me as if I was a process server.

'Where's Mary?' I called in through the window.

'The poor cratur started to make signs that Mary was sick.

'"Let me see her," I called but all Maggie did was to shake the head and motion me to be on my way. I suppose she was afraid I might wake Mickey out of his beauty sleep.

'"Christ almighty woman," I screeched at her, "let me talk to the girl. I won't keep her a minute."

'The curtain was drawn and that was the end of that. 'Tis not the end of me though because I'll call back and I'll make it my business to see Mary some way.'

'It's very sinister,' the Ram of God said.

'I don't know what that's supposed to mean,' Nonie went on, 'but as sure as hell there's something cockeyed going on somewhere and I don't like one bit of it.'

'Maybe if I called,' the Ram suggested.

'No! No! No!' Nonie responded, 'you keep away from there. I'll try it again tomorrow and the day after if that don't do the trick.'

8

'MURT HASN'T DRAWN A sober breath since Will's burial,' Nonie complained, 'and what way is that for a man to behave and he getting married in a week's time. It's my guess that with Will gone he hasn't the taspy for taking on them Cronane's on his own. He'll be up against all of 'em you know, Mollie and the two daughters and the rest. In the name of God man a regiment of soldiers wouldn't handle that gang!'

'Do you reckon that's why he's drunk all the time?'

'That and the fact that he can't accept Will's death. Neither one of them was ever able to cope on his own. One always depended on the other. Murt reminds me of nothing but a bird with one wing. He'll never be the same.'

'When I'm gone,' the Ram of God tried to sound reassuring, 'he'll pull himself together. You'll see. He's making the most of his free time because he knows that when I'm in California he'll have to shoulder all the work.'

'And I tell you,' Nonie was adamant, 'that he's lost without Will just as Will would be without him. He's going to drink himself into an early grave,' she warned, 'and if you ask me maybe that's the way he wants it.'

'And I tell you he'll be fine when the honeymoon's over,' the Ram had countered.

'He won't be fine,' Nonie had persisted, 'he's only half a man since Will died. He has no interest in anything, least of all in getting married.'

'You're an alarmist Nonie,' the Ram placed a hand around her shoulder, 'believe me he'll be all right.'

'You don't hear him talking to himself at night the way I do and you don't hear him pacing the room calling Will's name. It goes deeper than you imagine. It's like half of him was cut off.'

'You'll see,' the Ram spoke with conviction, 'the responsibility will bring him to his senses. Remember he'll be married with a child on the way.'

'Well on the way,' Nonie added. 'When you're gone this place will fall apart. Mark my words!'

'Let him drink. Let him mourn. He knows what he's doing. He's making the most of my presence here. He'll pull himself together when he has to.'

'You might convince yourself,' Nonie blew on the top of her cigarette butt and used it to light the fresh cigarette which replaced it, 'but you'll never convince me. This place will be sold and you'll see strangers ruling the roost here. What do you think is going to happen now that poor Will is under the clay? Noreen Cronane wouldn't know a milk bucket from a piss-pot but they'll get a man for the sister, more like as not a man hungry for land, the likes of the Stringer McCallum or some other hero from around the place that would marry a hag as long as there was land going with her. The Stringer or whoever 'tis going to be will fall in for Will's half of the farm and you'll be where you always were, on the outside looking in. It's no use shaking your head. You'll be studying for your white collar but there's no changing what's going to happen here unless you exercise your legal claim.'

'That's all guesswork. I know full well I have no legal claim. Will's share reverts to Murt.'

'No it doesn't,' Nonie cut across him vehemently. 'It reverts to the next of kin and the next of kin are his two brothers. The position at the moment is that Murt owns three-quarters of the farm and you own a quarter.'

'Since when did you start studying law?' the Ram asked astonished that she should know so much.

'Luke Holly,' Nonie spoke matter of factly as if she were in the habit of consulting the sergeant over legal matters every day of the week.

'And where did Luke hear all this?'

'In a pub,' Nonie responded drily. 'He was drinking with a solicitor after the court in Trallock the day before yesterday and he put the facts before him, mentioning no names of course.'

'Well it makes no difference to me one way or the other. I'm on my way to California,' the Ram reminded her. 'Murt is welcome to the farm and anyway I have no notion of taking my brother to court.'

'I don't know what kind of a fool you are! You'd want your head examined surely. Suppose you tire of the seminary? You're not a boy any more you know. You mightn't take so quickly to the studies and you might not take at all. Suppose they throw you out, that you're not suitable? Anything can happen and you'll be a long way from home.'

'When I come back from California Nonie in three years time you'll be calling me Father and you'll be kneeling down to receive my blessing. Let's have no more now about the farm. I'm leaving all that behind me forevermore.'

'Yes,' Nonie reflected as she drew deeply upon her cigarette, 'but will it leave you behind?'

In spite of his apparent disinterest in pursuing the matter further he was still curious. 'Have you something on your mind?' he asked.

'Nothing,' Nonie told him, 'except that God makes his own plans for all of us.'

FATHER MORTIMER O'CONNOR PAUSED for breath as soon as they reached the summit of the hillock which marked the western boundaries of the High Meadow. At the older man's insistence they had walked from the farmhouse. He explained to the Ram of God that he had long entertained a wish to do so, having last undertaken the scenic ascent when the Ram's mother was alive.

'A shame she died so young,' the old priest shook his head sorrowfully, 'we were very good friends. She was a woman of great piety and charity. It must have been a great blow to you.'

The Ram nodded his head. It was a subject on which he was reluctant to dwell. Even in his private thoughts he tried not to recall the happy memories. His mother had been his whole world. He could not recall shade or shadow, sorrow or anger in her presence. The women of Ballybobawn and the countryside around said that she had been badly lost, that she had been taken for granted by a doctor who should have known better.

'She died in childbirth wasn't it,' Father O'Connor recalled not realising how painful were such recollections for his protégé.

'Yes,' the Ram replied, 'childbirth. The twins were the death of her.' He had overheard Nonie convey her simplistic conclusion to a number of other females who attended the wake. He had been filled with hatred of his infant brothers for months afterwards but when he began to realise how helpless they really were he had assisted in their rearing with the now deceased Nanny who spent several years in the farmhouse before retiring. She had, however, first assured herself that Nonie and young Eddie were capable of carrying on.

'We once walked up this way you know,' Father O'Connor stood looking down at the distant village as he reminisced. 'It was shortly after she got married. I was new here the same as herself. I decided a courtesy call was in order. Your father was at the cows and she invited me to accompany her on a stroll. We became friends.'

'I remember you used to call to the house a lot when I was a youngster.'

'I remember you as a boy Eddie. You were a particularly quiet lad. I recall you were nearly always by your mother's side.'

'I'll be in Southern California in three weeks Father.'

'So you will, so you will.' Father O'Connor clapped his hands with delight. 'You'll write?'

'I'll write regularly Father.'

'I have the utmost faith in you Eddie.'

'You don't know me that well I'm afraid.'

'Is there something I should know Eddie?'

'I don't know if it even warrants your attention Father.'

'Then it's better out than in Eddie. I'll be the judge of its importance.'

'There's a girl in my thoughts Father.'

'There was many a girl in my own thoughts Eddie. I wouldn't be much of a man if I didn't admit that. Is she a local girl?'

'Yes.'

'Then my boy you'll be shut of her as soon as you board that plane for by all accounts the women of Southern California would take a man's breath away.' They both laughed.

'You'll always be troubled by something Eddie. I often think that temptation was especially invented for priests but I know now that it isn't so. Your problems are universal problems. They are the very essence of commonality. Try to remember that always. It's the great truth but alas it's not profound enough for some of our more intellectual theologians. I'm often forced to smile when I hear Churchmen speak of profundities. The more profound they become the more obscure they become and nearly always they do more harm than good.'

'Is it all that simple Father?'

'Of course it is my son. There's nothing profound about life Eddie. In fact there's nothing profound about anything.'

'You should be in Maynooth Father.'

'I am where I belong Eddie and a priest who knows that, knows all he needs to know. Whenever I hear somebody say that he has heard or read something which is profound what he really means is that he is more mystified after this so-called profundity than he was before.'

'I know exactly what you mean Father. It's reassuring to hear a man of your experience speak like this.'

The Ram of God was delighted that the subject of his mother had been replaced by Father O'Connor's endearing brand of logic. Not everybody would agree with him but, in Eddie's considered opinion, he always made sense.

'The trouble with the world Eddie is that the pseudo-intellectual and the thwarted academic are finished without regular doses of undiluted obscurity. They will persist in denying that complication and obscurity are the chief ingredients of profundity. Life is not profound Eddie. Life is simple, a time of worrying, hoping, playing, piddling and puking and loving of course, if one is that way inclined. The conclusion alas is always the same. These are the simple facts of the case my boy and all the profundities in the world won't change them.'

They stood silently for a while as the setting sun lingered over the distant sea, its crimson surrounds of sky and ocean paling by the minute, the stars gaining brightness as the first of the night sounds, the sharp yelping of a vixen, intruded on the silence. From a distant covert came an answering bark, high-pitched and ritualistic. The countless other sounds hushed and stealthy, furtive and deadly, established the reign of night. Still the two men, priest and acolyte, both subservient to the great transformation, stood without moving, their respectful silence a fitting prayer of acknowledgement to the new order of night.

As they turned to resume their downhill journey from the High Meadow Father O'Connor lay a hand on the Ram's arm.

'You'll be all right Eddie. Remember that the stronger the vocation the more visitations you will receive from the devil. His agents are numerous and innocent. They know not that they are being used. Do you understand?'

'Yes Father. I understand.'

'We are only men Eddie but we may turn to God and his blessed mother when temptation stalks all around us. I have no fear of you. You will make a good priest but it won't be easy. It wasn't easy for me and I happen to know that it wasn't easy for our good friend the bishop. Nothing worthwhile comes easy Eddie. You will remember that won't you during those moments of weakness and

139

doubt?'

'I'll remember Father.'

'There used to be a brook up here somewhere and a pool,' Father O'Connor, realising that one could go on and on and defeat one's purpose, deliberately changed the subject.

'Yes,' the Ram of God replied. 'It's in the next field. If we go over to the opposite hedge you'll hear it clearly although the water is low enough due to the fine weather.'

As they crossed the meadow the wind stirred the lengthening aftergrasses to life. The rich lispings came and went like human whisperings.

'Yes, yes!' Father O'Connor called out excitedly. 'I can hear it. It's faint but I can hear it.'

'You should hear it in high water,' the Ram spoke proudly and proprietorially, anxious to render a true account of the stream's past performances. 'A right torrent it is after a heavy fall of rain Father.'

'I can well imagine. Is there anything to beat a stream in spate, the songs, the surges, the cascading white of the broken water. Seems as if these gentle waters are merely tuning up in readiness for the floodwaters. Then we'll have the full orchestra, eh, Eddie?'

'The full orchestra indeed, Father.'

Father O'Connor had climbed the hedge which divided the High Meadow and the Pool Field as it was called locally.

'All the fields have names don't they?' he called down to Eddie.

'Every one,' the Ram of God called back.

'It was the same on my father's farm. We had the Sheep Field and the Linen Field and the Bittern's Meadow and the Cuckoo Glade. What a tragedy it is when they're all drained and the hedges flattened and there's one big field where you had four or five or even more. History is wiped out Eddie. The names are gone forever. It's agricultural cannibalism. I often ask myself if it's right or proper.'

'It can't be right Father.'

'Maybe not Eddie but it's legal. I can see the pool.'

'Yes,' came the reply from the Ram of God who had joined him on the hedge.

'See how it glimmers in the moonlight!' Father O'Connor seemed quite carried away. 'What a romantic spot Eddie. Almost makes one wish for youth again and for the lost dreams of long ago.'

For an awful moment the Ram feared that maybe the old priest was referring to Lorraine Dupree and to the incident which put paid to his primary aspirations towards the priesthood but no; that wouldn't be the old man's style. He would never stoop to such common innuendo. He wasn't a man of the world or so his friends said but he was an honourable man in all respects.

IT WAS TWENTY-FIVE MINUTES to twelve when Luke Holly and Thomas Connelly knocked at the rear door of the Widow Cahalane's. They were admitted by Patricia who recognised the prescribed code of four knocks, one following immediately upon the other and the second pairing with a much longer space between.

'Who's out?' she asked observing the caution upon which Luke had insisted.

'Knowing the knock,' he had told her firmly, 'is no guarantee that there are friends outside.

141

Acknowledge the knock by all means but make sure you ask who's there.'

They proceeded through the kitchen towards the bar. Thomas, shy and quite overcome by the looks of the widow's daughter, led the way.

'I'll have a pint of stout Thomas,' Luke indicated his choice but remained behind to converse a while with Patricia Cahalane.

'How's things?' he asked in his fatherly way.

'All right thank you.'

'Is there something wrong?' he asked detecting what he guessed to be a certain restraint.

'Not with me,' she said turning her head away.

'Am I in the doghouse then?' he asked when no elaboration was forthcoming.

She turned quickly.

'You know you'll never be in the doghouse with me,' Patricia relieved him of his cap and placed it on her head.

'Suits you better than me,' Luke told her. 'Come on now. Tell me what's the matter.'

'There's nothing the matter,' Patricia assured him. 'Have you noticed my mother a trifle down in herself lately?'

'Your mother?'

'Well not exactly down, more I would say in the want of cheering up. I mean there she sits behind the bar all day when she isn't scrubbing and scraping in here and never a compliment, never a word of praise.'

'Are you serious?' There was a look of concern on Luke's face.

'That's the way it seems to me,' Patricia told him with all the innocence her face would register. She returned the cap to his head.

'You'd better go into the bar and whatever you

142

do you must promise me you'll forget our little conversation.'

'I promise.'

In the bar there were three farmers drinking peacefully in a corner reserved for their equals. All farmers great and small who frequented the Widow Cahalane's by day or by night made straight for the same corner as soon as their orders were dispensed and paid for. There was an ancient fireplace at one side and it was this hallowed spot, or so Luke maintained, which was the attraction. Being countrymen it reminded them of the hearths of their childhood now almost universally replaced by Stanleys and Hamcos and other established names. Luke and Thomas sat side by side on two wooden stools fronting the counter. Luke's eyes rested on the aristocratic nose of the Widow as she knitted a winter cardigan for her only child. If she had but once lifted her head he would have looked into the hazel eyes, so like those of Patricia, as he had so often looked in the past. So deep were the eyes in question that he had never found what he was looking for or so he felt. And what was he looking for? Easily answered. He was looking for anything, a sign of some kind, the least evidence of response, of awareness, of reaction to the way he felt about her.

'I am fifty-four years of age,' he reminded himself. 'I have been sergeant in Ballybobawn for twenty-five of those. I have never drank in any other pub but I could not pay this particular woman a compliment if it were to save my life and thereafter my immortal soul. She has no idea how I feel about her and how the hell could she when I have never given the slightest indication of my true feelings for her. I'm sure she'd collapse if I were to utter the least thought of my heart.'

'You're here a long time sergeant.' Thomas broke in upon his thoughts, 'and maybe you could tell me something.'

'What something is that Thomas?'

'What's Ballybobawn really like sergeant?'

Without taking his eyes from the Widow, so intent upon her knitting that no word came her way, Luke lifted his pint and went a full halfway down before taking it from his lips.

'There are undercurrents here Thomas more powerful than the backwash of a harvest tide. There are men here Thomas whose feelings are so deep that they dare not commit themselves to declaration. In backwaters like Ballybobawn, Thomas my boy, true love lurks sweet and hopeless. It is there in an everlasting state of ripeness underneath the surface, terrified by the ignominy of rejection should it allow itself to bloom. There are strong, silent men in this very neck of the woods Thomas bound to silence, harbouring love illicit and true for the most unlikely females. You'll never know what's in a man's mind Thomas and you'll never know what's in a woman's either for she don't know herself. Drink up like a good man and we'll have two more.'

As the Widow Cahalane filled the empty glasses Luke noticed the same things he always noticed, the frail shoulders, the figure which defied the years and the hair impeccably groomed with never a rib out of place.

'I swear to you Thomas,' the sergeant spoke in a whisper, 'that I have heard what few men hear.'

'And what would that be sergeant?' Thomas asked, a serious note entering his voice.

'The purr of unrequited love Thomas is what I

have heard. The night winds strum the chords of its passion my boy but the melody's not for the common mob.'

The sergeant paused to shake his head in appreciation of his disclosure.

'A lot goes on then?' Thomas also shook his head more in bewilderment than curiosity.

'A lot goes on Thomas but not all of it is hidden. There are in the parish of Ballybobawn five thriving cases of illicit entanglement so discreetly indulged that only myself knows about them. There are three damsels in this very village Thomas whose wares are available to all and sundry, free gratis and for nothing. We may boast only one penis exposer but in the matter of animal buggery we can hold our heads high. I am aware of one depraved agricultural labourer who is in love with his donkey, another from whom no enclosed heifer or cow is safe and yet another whose taste runs to fowl. It's a sorry world Thomas but it takes all kinds. Nobody knows better than a village sergeant.'

'What fairy tales is he telling you now?' The Widow Cahalane smiled benignly as she placed the pints of stout on the counter.

'Not fairy tales,' the sergeant returned. Then with a courage which surprised him: 'I was just telling him what a beautiful looking woman you are, what a refined woman and what an enchanting woman. All in all I managed to convey to him that you are a gorgeous creature entirely and that's more than I said about any woman in my entire life.'

There followed a silence during which the Widow Cahalane was unable to close her mouth. It hung open with no sound issuing forth. She did the only thing she could do under the circumstances.

She removed her spectacles, blew gently upon the lenses and with a spotless white handkerchief which she produced from the inside of her sleeve, polished the lenses and returned the spectacles to her patrician nose.

'Tis a fair description of her all right,' Thomas concurred, entering into the spirit of what he believed to be no more than light-hearted raillery.

'Ah sure if the truth was told,' the sergeant went on, 'you'd be hard put to find the right words to do her justice.'

'You didn't make a bad fist of it at all now,' Thomas conceded.

WHEN THE PUB WAS empty Sadie Cahalane sat pensively over a cup of tea in the kitchen.

'You're in a thoughtful mood,' her daughter laid the work which she had just completed to one side.

'I don't know whether to laugh or cry,' came the wistful response.

'Is it something you want to talk about?'

'Oh dear no! It's the very last thing I want to talk about.' Sadie was emphatic.

Patricia poured herself a cup of tea. Her mother sighed gently and removed her spectacles for the second time that night. Using the same handkerchief which she had used earlier to clean the lenses she now vainly tried to absorb the moisture which had appeared in her eyes.

'You're crying mother!' Patricia rose and sat by her mother's side.

'I was thinking about your father. He'll be dead twenty years this Christmas. You still can't remember him?'

'Not really, just a vague recollection. But what

made you think of him tonight?' Patricia asked innocently.

'I think about him every night,' Sadie chided gently.

'Yes but you don't cry after him every night. In fact I haven't seen you cry after him since I was conferred.'

'Maybe I should be crying after him every night,' Sadie spoke the words sorrowfully.

'I often wonder why you never married again?' Patricia knew she was on tricky ground. It was a subject which was never aired. Her mother had always frowned on conversations which tended to take such a direction.

'I never married because I was never interested.' She blew her nose loudly before replacing the spectacles.

'And are you interested now?' Patricia asked tongue in cheek.

'I don't know what you're talking about,' Sadie replied but Patricia noticed that there was a flush to her face as she rose to go upstairs to bed.

LATER AS THEY STOOD at the cross of Ballybobawn both Luke and Thomas remarked in turn on the tranquillity of the night time scene.

'There can't be many quieter places in the world just now,' Thomas observed as he absently took note of several white moths which winged their ways in and out of the arc of brightness thrown outward by the light of the street lamp over their heads.

'Quiet is hardly the word Thomas. Sultry nights like these are never quiet. They only seem quiet. However, I see no likelihood of rape, murder or arson so I think we may feel free to return to our barracks but wait! What's this?'

'It looks like Murt Drannaghy sergeant.'

Thomas had no difficulty in identifying the drunken figure who staggered from the rear of the Load of S.

'He's pretty bad.' Luke watched as the surviving twin endeavoured to open the door of his car.

'He's been like that every night since Will died.' Thomas' disclosure was common knowledge in the village. Murt never rose before midday. After a meal he repaired to the Load of S where late in the afternoon he was joined by Noreen Cronane who remained with him until nightfall when he would turn a deaf ear to her entreaties to go home.

'Let him drink the bloody death out of his system,' Mollie Cronane advised. 'Just as long as he shows up sober for the wedding. We'll straighten him out in jig time when the honeymoon is over. There'll be no Ram then to mollycoddle him and we'll have the house to ourselves.'

'He's acting strangely mother,' Noreen insisted when her mother argued that all that mattered was getting Murt to the altar. 'He was always headstrong and wild but he was never like this. He doesn't laugh any more either.'

'It's all right Murt,' Sergeant Holly assured Murt Drannaghy when he reeled back against the car upon beholding the two men in uniform. 'Just sit in here to the back with me and Thomas will drive you home. You can collect the car tomorrow. In you go now.'

Silently Murt allowed himself to be driven home.

'You must understand Murt,' Luke advised him, 'if you go near a car again in this condition you'll

148

be put off the road. We're making an allowance this time in view of your brother's death but don't let it happen again.'

Murt, however, seemed to be shut away in a world of his own. The truth was that he could no longer see a role for himself in any sort of activity. Neither he nor Will had ever joined anything as individuals or participated subsequently as individuals. Murt's mental balance had become lopsided without his twin's presence. The frustration drove him to the Load of S where he drank himself into a semi-stupor.

He found himself incapable of confronting the new and inadequate person that he had become. It was like looking in a mirror and seeing nobody there. Suddenly there was no echo where there had always been an echo. There was nothing but desolation in every room, in every landscape, in every situation. Murt knew for sure that he was mortally wounded, that there could be no recovery, that his only hope of redemption lay dead and buried.

9

MADELEINE MONTERROS LAY IN Tom Cronane's arms, her body melting against his. He held her gently, his heart throbbing, her heart matching. He raised her aloft, surveying her supple form as he tenderly spun her with powerful hands. Then her eyes found his and compelled him to lower the body that longed for his.

A voice seemed to penetrate to the very centre of his love-crazed brain. It so irritated him that he unconsciously bruised the tender buttocks of his beloved with his crude fingers. The calls persisted, however, and came in quick succession now with a maddening and unrelenting intensity. Deafened beyond endurance he released his hold on the lovely Madeleine and sought refuge from the clamour by covering his ears with hands reluctantly torn from the willing flesh he would ravage.

Reality struck him most forcibly when he found himself unable to shut out the ear-splitting commands which now seemed to be coming from directly over his head. He averted his gaze from the open mouth which called out to him and sought the countenance of his beloved Madeleine. By all the powers she should have been beside him in the bed but she was not. She was nowhere to be seen.

'Where is Madeleine?' he asked forthrightly of Mollie, as though she were to blame for the disappearance of his companion.

No answer was forthcoming. A blank look replaced the one of exasperation on his wife's face. It did not occur to her to ask who Madeleine might

be. Of late he had been in the habit of asking foolish questions

'Madeleine!' Tom asked angrily. 'What have you
done to her?'

'Stop the fooling like a good boy and get out of
that bed this minute. You're wanted downstairs.'
Mollie would brook no further nonsense.

Grimly Tom realised that he was where he had
always been, in his bed above the supermarket in
Ballybobawn. Of late he found it more difficult to
return from the heady presence of his beloved.

'Come on!' Mollie called out uncompromisingly,
'your gallivanting is over for another while my boy.'

As she spoke she whipped off the bedclothes
and opened the two windows which looked down
on the main street of Ballybobawn. Silently her
sharp eyes took in the thoroughfare from end to
end. Nothing stirred. Little ever did at that particular time of day. There was always a lull common to
all villages between the hours of two and four.
Occasionally a straggler from the council houses or
the outlying cottages would appear briefly on the
deserted roadway before sidling into Tom's Tavern
or the Load of S. Sometimes the silence was broken
by the noisy passing of a tractor drawing a trailer
filled with freshly-cut silage but there were hour-
long interludes when not even a car would pass by,
nor animal, nor human – not even a bird of the air
would alight between the houses. This was particularly true of summertime.

Even the God-forsaken countryside of Mollie's
childhood was more endearing. There, at least, one
could see the shapes of men working in the bogs
and meadows, the women hanging out the washing
on hedgerows, the cattle grazing in the low-lying
fields, ass and horse-drawn carts setting out for

town or returning from whatever mysterious business it was that took people away from their lawful labours on a summer's day when hay or turf might be saved. Then there were the ass, pony and horse-rails of turf on their way to Trallock, to house-holders too lazy or too grand or too busy to harvest their own.

There was always something in the countryside but never anything in a village street. Occasionally an unseen hand would rearrange the curtains on a window after hidden eyes had searched, fruitlessly, for the slightest diversion. In the countryside there were sounds all around; the murmuring of insects; the calls of wildfowl; the singing of the smaller birds and there were butterflies; butterflies of every hue brightening the long afternoons. No butterfly paraded itself in Ballybobawn's main street! There were few sounds, if any, not even those of the children who had enough sense to remove themselves to the river-banks. One could easily stifle here like most of the miserable wretches who peered out from the cover of their blinds and curtains, or the idle men who sought refuge from reality in the Load of S with its pool tables and poker machines and pornographic videos, not to mention the fruit machines and the card games! Otherwise the village was tolerable. The supermaket did a thriving business, the afternoon apart, and even if it did not Mollie had enough to carry her over nicely thank you!

'What time is it?' Tom asked with customary petulance.

'Time to get up,' Mollie replied without taking her eyes from the street or fully breaking off from her reverie. After a while she said, 'it's after half-past two. The day is all but gone!'

'What's up anyway?'

Mollie took her time before answering.

'All will be revealed as the man said when you come downstairs. There's some people below so you'd better not delay.'

Without another word she crossed the room and silently closed the door behind her, leaving him to make the most of her limited disclosures. Silently he cursed her as he fumbled at the foot of the bed for his trousers. He had made a surprisingly fast recovery from his last binge but he was far from contemplating another. His time had not come. When he was good and ready he would break out again. Mollie had not informed him of the theft until the investigation was in progress. If ever a man needed justification for a full-blooded binge that was surely it. The thought of the good-for-nothing, so-called tinkers squandering the hard-earned supermarket takings enraged him. He knew the gardaí would be powerless. There was only one cure for the thieving itinerants and that was the double-barrel, barrel after barrel into their stinking encampments and then the petrol bomb to the vans. That would teach them to interfere with God-fearing, industrious people.

So great was his fury he was unable to draw his trousers above his knees. He found it necessary to sit on the bed. What was all the bloody mystery about now? Why couldn't she tell him out straight what was wrong? That was no way to leave a man, mystified and full of anxiety not knowing what misfortune had befallen his household. He dressed hurriedly lest the foreboding fermented by his spouse drive him towards a drinking bout for which he was ill-prepared.

When he came downstairs and entered the

153

kitchen he was surprised to see Joe McCallum and his brother the Stringer seated at the table with Mollie and his two daughters. His sons, Sammie, Donie and Tomboy stood in the background. The Stringer vacated his chair immediately and despite Tom's protestations he was made to accept the offer of a seat. Mollie produced a packet of cigarettes from the recesses of her cleavage, extracted one and lit it. The Stringer stood behind Kate, his hands resting proprietorially on the sides of her chair. A long silence ensued as if by tacit agreement while Tom settled into his seat and entwined his fingers on the table in front of him as he awaited an announcement. He looked from one face to another but his expectant glances elicited no response.

'So what's it all about?' he asked.

It was Joe who answered.

'There don't seem to be no sign of Murt Drannaghy,' he explained.

Tom said nothing. He knew Joe well enough. In his own roundabout fashion he would come to the point.

'We've tried high and low,' Joe went on after a while, 'but he don't seem to be nowhere, that is nowhere he can be seen.'

'You mean he's missing?' Tom suggested.

'Yes,' Joe agreed, 'you could say he was missing if you like but he could be thrown down drunk somewhere or he could be gone off on a skite. He's been drinking drop-down these past weeks. He don't know whether he's coming or going poor fellow since Will was killed.'

The Stringer's bony right hand found its way to rest on Kate's right shoulder. She responded by dabbing both her eyes with the handkerchief which he tendered with his free hand. Mollie's face registered approval. The Stringer had first called the previous Sunday night at the invitation of Noreen. He had been present at the funeral but he felt that because of his past friendship with Kate something in the nature of more personal condolences might be required. He was made welcome by the entire household, Noreen saw to that. Now he stood close by, willing and eager to make any sacrifice his rediscovered relationship might demand.

'He could be anywhere,' Tom sounded hopeful, 'asleep in a ditch somewhere or in some shady corner of a field on the farm. What of his car? Has anybody seen his car?'

'There's no sign of the car.' The Stringer spoke for the first time.

Tom Cronane took careful stock of him, marvelling at his leanness. He was flesh and bone to be sure like any other human but the flesh was scarce and the bone only too apparent. Tom recalled what people were fond of saying about him: 'The Stringer will never fatten until he has a farm of his own.'

'Has he ever gone missing before?' Tom asked.

There were negative murmurs all around.

'When was he last seen?'

'At the Load of S last night around half-past twelve.' The answer was provided by Tomboy Cronane. Normally he might have expected rebuke for being so familiar with the comings and goings at the countryside's most notorious public house.

'Which way did he go when he sat into his car?' Tom senior asked choosing to ignore the fact that his son might have been patronising the Load of S which indeed he had been and in the company of his brothers Sammie and Donie. It was their inaugural visit. They were at first appalled and then excited by the obscene scope and revealing nature of the pornographic film on view behind the flimsy screen but its very repetitiveness palled towards the end.

'Which way did he go?' Tom repeated the question.

'I don't know,' Tomboy replied.

'Find out. You two go with him. Ask around.' He addressed himself to all three of his sons. The trio hurried for the door, glad to be contributing. Mollie preened herself. She had been right to awaken him from his foolish dreams. He had a head on his shoulders. When it came to organising things, whatever else his faults, he was without peer. Of course, he had the brains and the education. There was nobody would deny that.

'Have the gardaí been notified?'

'They have to be sure,' Mollie responded.

'And who pray was responsible for that?' Tom asked angrily.

'It was nobody here I assure you,' Mollie shot back. 'The Ram was the informant. When he discovered that Murt hadn't slept in his bed he searched the outhouses and the farm. When there was no trace of the car he went to the barracks.'

'We'll be the talk of the bloody country and nothing at all wrong maybe except a drunken man asleep in his car. What do you think Joe?'

Joe McCallum was a man never given to hasty responses. He fingered the bristle on the point of his jaw and bared his uneven teeth as he pondered the question. There were many answers he might make but he always felt his credulity was at stake whenever an answer was expected of him. Even if the question had been an insignificant one where the answer would make no great difference to anybody Joe would have spent the same amount of time preparing his answer.

'I don't know Tom,' he ventured after a lengthy period of intense jaw scratching. 'It's hard to know what might have happened. All I'll say is that I don't like it. I don't like it at all. If things were right the car should be somewhere between the Load of S and the farm.'

All present exchanged anxious glances. Joe never spoke lightly whether the subject was calves or bullocks or a missing man as was the case now. Tom addressed himself to his daughter Noreen.

'When did you see him last?' he asked not unkindly.

'Last night,' Noreen answered.

'How did he behave?'

'When I left him at half-past ten he was drunk the same as he's been since Will was killed.'

'And did you promise to meet again tonight.'

'Well that would go without saying,' Noreen answered.

'I wonder if the Ram knows anything?' the Stringer spoke for the second time.

'If the Ram knew anything he'd let this house know at once,' his brother Joe answered. Later word would come that a female patron and a friend from the council houses had left the Load of S at the same time as Murt. He had been unsteady on his feet but had located his car without difficulty and driven off but not in the direction of the Drannaghy farmhouse. He had driven towards Trallock town but had turned to the left at the end of the village on to the narrow road which ran all the way to the coast and to the strand from which the farmers of Ballybobawn and district had drawn sand and sea-wrack for generations as fertilisers for their pastures.

Tomboy's announcement was greeted with dismay. Noreen beat the table with her clenched fists before rising to rush screaming to her room.

'Now, now, now!' her father called after her, 'there's no need for that.' His tone lacked conviction however. He turned for comfort to the McCallums.

'We might as well notify the Ram. He's entitled to know.' Joe obviously feared the worst.

'You boys come with me.' Tom gave the order to his sons, 'and fetch Cha from the shop. We'll want every man we can get. We'll find Murt for sure and he'll be safe and sound.'

'Four days to his wedding and to go off like that!' Mollie shook her head in bewilderment.

'He'll turn up,' Tom spoke with authority, relegating Murt's shaughraun to no worse a misadventure than any of his own. He too had been missing in his earlier years for as long as three days at a time and no one had worried. Murt would show up and Tom would not allow a solitary drop of intoxicating liquor inside his lips during the wedding or during the run-up to the wedding but when the celebrations were well and truly over he would treat himself to a well-earned skite.

THE RAM OF GOD sat at the head of the large table in the kitchen of the Drannaghy farmhouse. Opposite him at the other end sat Sergeant Luke Holly, his cap on the table before him. To his left sat Tom Pearson the veterinary and to his left Garda Thomas Connelly. That morning both policemen had scoured the countryside within a radius of five miles but no sign did they find of the mis-

sing man or his car. Tom Pearson who had a reputation as a diviner deduced that the Drannaghy
twin was somewhere near the shoreline ten miles
to the west of where the party sat. A silence settled
on the foursome after a lengthy exchange concerning the likely location of the absent Murt.

'Prepare yourselves for the worst!' Nonie cautioned as she poured tea all round. 'Remember he
hasn't drawn a sober breath since we put poor Will
under. On top of that the sleep is gone astray on
him and then there's the prospect of being latched
for the remainder of his natural life to the Cronanes. Wouldn't that drive any man out of his mind!
Tom Pearson is right. The shore has him claimed.'

'I've been wrong before Luke as you know well,'
Tom conceded after a sceptical response by the
sergeant.

'I know,' Luke agreed. And then grudgingly, 'but
you've also been right and that's what worries me.'

'It can't do any harm to take a drive to the spot
you pinpointed,' Thomas Connelly advised.

The Ram of God rose from his seat and stood
framed in the doorway.

'He's drunk somewhere, in a pub in some distant village, in a ditch or a dyke or maybe even in a
hotel or guest house. He was always careful about
his night's sleep.'

'And I tell you,' Nonie Spillane countered instantly, 'that his sleep is gone. Don't I hear him
nights and he walking the floor talking to himself.
How many times have I told you!'

The sergeant rose and stood in the centre of the
kitchen.

'I've already notified Trallock and Superintendent Chaney has suggested that if he doesn't show
up for the evening milking a full scale search

should be mounted. Meanwhile Thomas and I will make the journey to the shore.'

'How can I help?' the Ram of God asked.

'You might spread word among the neighbouring farmers to keep an eye out for the car. If he shows up for the milking let us know at once.'

The sergeant donned his cap and motioned to his acolyte.

As soon as word spread that the gardaí had been seen heading for the shore a large number of villagers and those outside the village who found themselves with nothing to do turned left on the Trallock road in search of whatever diversion the search might offer. The farming community, of necessity, stayed put until evening when the cows would be milked and the everyday chores completed. Then they conscientiously participated in the search. Murt was, after all, of farming stock and, therefore, one of their own. As the Ram of God drove towards the sea he wondered at the awful turn of events which saw him lose one brother and place another in jeopardy. Deep down he feared for Murt who had never been so set in his ways since Will's death. He was a model of consistency, never varying the routine which took him from farm to pub and pub to farm.

The Load of S experienced one of the quietest days in its short but colourful history. One way or another the vast majority of its patrons made their way to the sea where it was rumoured that Murt Drannaghy might well be drowned. Not even the promise of a new release of pornographic films halted the flow. The television was, after all, only make-believe and could in no way be compared with the real-life drama which might be in the offing.

Nonie knew for a certainty that Murt would never again cross the threshold. She had seen the despair in his eyes during his rare moments of sobriety. She knew enough to understand that he would be totally incapable of facing life and particularly marriage to Noreen Cronane without Will by his side. With Will alive it had been a game, a challenge, heightened with fun, something they would take on together and in their stride as they did everything else.

Knowing Murt and his attachment to Will, Nonie was forced to conclude that there had been no other option open to the surviving twin.

10

TRABAWN STRAND RAN ALONG the coast for three miles. At high tide no more than thirty yards separated it from the water, at low tide two hundred.

The sand deposits were still deep despite the depredations of local farming interests. There were as yet no rocky outcrops protruding from where the ongoing excavations had reduced the level of the lime-rich deposits but here and there recently formed clusters of speckled pebbles and darker encroachments of shingle began to surface with increasing frequency.

Trabawn was rarely used by holiday-makers, day-trippers preferring the allure of more established resorts to the south and the still more spacious sand expanses to the north which extended for several miles. Trabawn was greatly favoured by elderly people and others who sought seclusion and long, uninterrupted constitutionals where only the sea birds intruded. There was neither hotel nor guest house, nothing save the undulating dunes which formed the gloomy backdrop to the sea's immensity. Occasionally there were ships to be seen, slow-moving tankers for the most part, heading for the ports of Foynes and Limerick further up the wide estuary of the Shannon.

Trabawn was a regular habitat of countless sea birds, and in season when the pale salmon made their perilous up-river journey to the spawning beds there were sizeable but ever-declining catches by net fishermen drawn from the locality. In winter the long strand was deserted save for the bird population swollen by the arrival of starving migrants from the freezing wastes of Scandinavia. There was no caravan-park, no lifeguard, none of the joyful sounds of summer. Its lack of appeal might be attributed to a certain, almost undefinable suggestion of repellence which manifested itself most during windy weather.

At the northern end of the strand there stood the remains of a derelict pier much in use when the herring shoals fed off the banks which once formed part of the coastline. Time and tide had wrought the changes which reformed the contours of that part of the estuary and now the banks were no more although locals cherished the belief that the shoals would return inevitably as part of the great universal plan which took no account of man's involvement. Several generations had passed but the great shoals and their offshoots regularly by-passed Trabawn.

The pier, which extended into the sea for over a hundred feet, was still traversible from its base founded on the bedrock beneath the sand to the nose which was almost covered at full tide. Here, at noon, thirty-six hours after the disappearance of Murt Drannaghy, a large crowd had assembled. Some were regular strollers but most had little if any recourse to the sandy expanse up until that time. The crowd had been gathering since morning, many from nearby Ballybunion chock-a-block with visitors at the time, others from Ballybobawn and Trallock and the farmlands for miles around.

For as far as the eye could see groups of people walked along the shore casting their eyes eagerly about them for surfacing bodies or whatever the sea might choose to retch out of its mysterious depths. A small number had climbed the sand dunes which overlooked the strand, the better to scan the sea with binoculars and with the naked eye but if the sea had hold of Murt's mortal remains it was not yet prepared to yield them up. The sea, in this respect, was beyond caring. A drowned body might surface and it might never again be seen. It was the way of the sea. Natives of the place confirmed this with solemn and ponderous shaking of their heads when questioned about the likely whereabouts of the body.

In a patrol car which was parked out of the way of the curious and the ghoulish the Ram of God sat with Sergeant Luke Holly and Garda Thomas Connelly. Close by was another patrol car where Superintendent Chaney of Trallock and three young policemen sat. Thermos flasks were handed around amongst the occupants of both cars and sandwiches were eagerly devoured. Most had been present on the beach since shortly after dawn.

When the Ram arrived at the beach at six-thirty the patrol cars were already in evidence, their occupants, aided by binoculars and a powerful telescope, evenly disposed over the shore and dunes, constantly studying the face of the unrelenting sea for non-integral features. Neighbouring strands and beaches would be searched later, if necessary, with equal vigilance.

When the first of the crowds began to make their way towards the pier Superintendent Chaney took it upon himself to marshal the more exuberant into search parties allotting each prescribed areas so that overlapping might be eliminated. The superintendent, a veteran of thirty years' experience, was a man who kept his mind to himself. He believed in the maxim that there was more to be gained by listening than by holding forth. He did not expect the body of Murt Drannaghy to surface on that day or any other day. He was convinced that Murt was sitting in his car somewhere but he would not be prepared to say whether he was dead or alive. Luke Holly suggested to his superintendent that it might be best to call in the sub-aqua squad which was based at the Garda Training Depot in Dublin. He reluctantly agreed and already the squad was on its way and expected at one o'clock.

'Nonie makes a bloody great sandwich,' Luke gratefully accepted a second offering from the Ram of God. The trio had covered ten miles of coastline since their arrival at Trabawn.

'Eat something,' Thomas handed one of Nonie's sandwiches to the Ram.

'I'm not hungry.' The response sounded dejected in the extreme.

'What a turn up!' The Ram spoke to nobody in particular. 'A few short weeks ago I had two brothers and now it seems that I have none.'

'I wouldn't say that,' Luke cut across him, 'Murt could show up for this evening's milking. Who's to say?' Luke went on to mention instances of men from the Ballybobawn area who had gone missing in the past. Thomas who sat in the rear leaned forward and laid a comforting hand on the Ram's shoulder. Thomas, a man of few words, his thinking governed by his mentor Luke, expressed his sympathy the only way he knew how.

'What next?' the Ram thought as he looked out over the shimmering expanse of the estuary.

On the dunes Patricia Cahalane with a party of nuns from the convent in Trallock looked towards the patrol car in which the Ram of God sat. She turned her gaze in that direction for the umpteenth time. She saw him several times throughout the morning. On one occasion they were within hailing distance of each other. She was tempted to approach him, to sympathise or offer some words of support. He was alone at the time, looking out to sea as he walked some ways behind Luke and Thomas. She would have liked to accompany him, to walk silently by his side after he acknowledged her presence. She allowed the opportunity to pass. Her caution won out as usual and she succeeded in convincing herself that there would be talk, that it would have been unmannerly to abandon the nuns however temporarily, especially since they had politely commandeered her that morning for the express purpose of participating in the search.

It would be lunchtime shortly and she would be expected to drive south along the coast to Ballybunion, there to provide a repast for her precious charges in one of the resort's better eating places, maybe even a round of sherries beforehand. They would, of course, make all manner of protestations but the gesture, nevertheless, would be expected. She would prefer to remain where she was in order to be abreast of the activities but she promised herself that the lunch would be a hasty one and that they would return immediately to Trabawn since word had spread that divers were already on their way from the city of Limerick.

The Cronanes, Tom and his four sons, Cha, Sammie, Donie and Tomboy walked in single file close by the sea. They walked barefoot. All made fruitless excursions from time to time into the water. Mostly their attention was attracted by drifting seaweed and once by a curious seal which surfaced far out after a fishing currach had passed with its nets dropped in the hope of recovering a body. Shortly after noon Tom issued instructions to his second son Sammie to take the car and return to Ballybobawn where he would be provided with a sufficiency of sandwiches and flasks of tea to sustain them for the remainder of the day.

Tom could have sent Cha but there was the danger that his mother might hold on to him and send one of the girls back instead. Cha was a dependable sort, a good man in an emergency, Tom told himself, and although his youngest son might lay claim to the title of favourite Tom knew that he would find himself turning to Cha in a crisis. Although never expressed in words both knew that a bond existed between them. Odd, Tom thought, that it took an occasion of tragedy such as Will's death and the likelihood of Murt's to bring them closer. Both would have felt uncomfortable if any feeling manifested itself. It was sufficient that the awareness of mutual reliance and other deeper bonds were known to both.

Mary Creel and her thirteen-year-old brother Jonathan sat near the highest point of the dunes. They had arrived at Trabawn at ten that morning. They were both hungry and tired. They had gladly accepted a lift on the outskirts of the village from the genial Tom Dudley, proprietor of Tom's Tavern. Mary was informed of Murt's disappearance by her mother who overheard it through the open window of the kitchen. Hastily she breakfasted on bread and tea. There was neither jam nor butter since she had relinquished her position at the Drannaghy farmhouse. Arriving at the strand, on Mary's injunction, they kept to themselves although their eyes swept the sea as meticulously as any. Like Patricia Cahalane Mary would have liked to offer words of sympathy to the Ram but she could not bring herself to face him.

Two of her menstrual cycles had come and gone without relief. The subject was absolutely taboo between herself and her mother, the latter informing her that she would put an end to her own life if Mary was to reveal anything of a shameful nature. She lived in abject terror of her lord and master. Mary knew that her own situation had reached the point of no return. She would have to do something drastic and she would have to do it soon or else brazen it out for as long as she dared and eventually present herself, repentant and sorrowful, before the reverend mother of the Presentation Convent. It happened to other convent girls, not many, only a distinguished few Mary reminded herself scornfully. She longed most of all to tell the Ram and Nonie but her overpowering sense of shame prevented her. She could go to her teacher Patricia Cahalane but again the oppressive shame held her back. She sighed as she drew her slender legs upwards behind her thighs. Involuntarily a hand shot downwards to her midriff. She withdrew it hastily wondering if her brother had noticed the move. She need not have worried. His eyes were glued to the sea.

Mary tried to reassure herself with the thought that there was no need for immediate alarm although something would have to be done. She would do anything to rid herself of the unwanted burden which had formed unbeknownst after that night when she had foolishly drank the cider at Tomboy's insistence. She wanted to believe him when he told her it was harmless.

'It's not as if it were vodka or gin,' he had assured her, 'it's only cider. Even children drink it.

What can happen?'

Vaguely she remembered the interlude in a field at the roadside. It was almost as if nothing had happened but to allow herself to be hoodwinked again was unforgivable and stupid. Served her right although it was cruel ill-luck. Other girls who played around with every Tom, Dick and Harry had escaped scot-free. She would never have consented had not Tomboy threatened he would abandon her unless she agreed. At least nothing was showing yet as far as she could ascertain and that was something. Soon, all too soon, she would begin to show in deadly earnest and that would call for deception and camouflage until the inevitable must happen. It was a prospect which would be shelved until the final reality. It simply did not bear contemplation.

'Can I go down?' The request came from young Jonathan. All the search parties were now converging on the pier where a blue van with a canoe attached to its roof had just drawn to a halt. From its interior a group of young men spilled out into the sunlight which temporarily replaced the drab shadows caused by a morning of drifting grey clouds.

'You may go but don't go on the pier itself and come back here in half an hour.'

Jonathan took his leave without a word, rolling down the side of the steep dune, his slender body gathering momentum as it turned over and over before coming to rest at the base. For a moment he feigned loss of consciousness, opening his mouth and allowing his tongue to protrude before suddenly rising with a joyous whoop as he darted across the strand to where the young divers were now donning their suits and preparing their equipment.

Mary had not seen Cha Cronane as he strode across the dunes to where she sat, head now resting on knees, as she balefully eyed the shimmering sea. She looked up startled when he spoke.

'I thought you might care for one of these,' he said handing her a sandwich wrapped in transparent tissue. Mary accepted gratefully. Without being invited to do so Cha sat by her side. Neither spoke while Mary bit deep into the sandwich. She relished every mouthful, careful not to appear too ravenous whenever she found her benefactor casting a shy glance in her direction. When Mary finished eating Cha proffered a second sandwich.

'Your brother might care for that,' he said, 'when he comes back.' Cha did not look directly at her when he spoke. He looked instead at the incoming sea. The flowing tide had completed half of its inward journey. In a few hours most of the strand would be covered. Two of the police team replete with diving apparel and oxygen tanks stood ready to enter the water at the nose of the pier.

'Are you all right?' Cha found the utmost difficulty in mouthing the question, hardly knowing what his query might imply and more importantly, how it might be received.

'Yes. I'm all right,' Mary returned but Cha realised as he looked directly into her eyes for the first time that everything was not as it should be. The cause of her trouble was unknown to him but he rightly guessed that it was no frivolous matter. Here was a lovely young girl with a problem which was weighing her down, which was taking its toll on her looks and on her disposition. Cha without realising what he was doing gently took hold of Mary's hand. It was an impulsive act, carried out instinctively. Surprised although not alarmed she drew her hand away but regretted it immediately when she saw the hurt on his face. She made amends by momentarily resting a hand on top of his, exerting enough pressure to assure him that she appreciated his concern and had not taken offence.

Cha longed to say more, anything whatsoever to protract their togetherness. He wanted to ask her if she had lost interest in Tomboy and if so to tell her that he cared for her more than he had ever cared for anybody but he could not bring himself to utter a word on this subject. Instead he told her that he would have to rejoin his father and brothers.

The Cronanes hurried together to the pier which had now been cleared of onlookers to facilitate the activities of the divers who were set to enter the water. The level had now reached the half-way stage which meant that there was no current of consequence to be reckoned with. At high and low tides there was a powerful flow with an extremely dangerous undertow but between tides there was no movement of water in the pier's vicinity. Sergeant Hickson, in command of the six-man diving squad, was already well aware of the dangerous conditions which existed at high and low tides. He knew that the local name for the current was the Trabawn Race and that it was one of the most treacherous of its kind along the entire coast.

The Ram of God and Luke Holly remained on the pier as the six-man team of divers entered the sea. By their reckoning if there was a car in the water it would be roughly fifty yards from the nose of the pier. Their judgement was based on the likely time the car entered the water and the state of the tide at the time. The last sighting of the car had occurred at one o'clock in the morning of the previous day. A pair of cyclists, one male and one female, had been obliged to dismount and seek the cover of a nearby hedge or be struck down. At the time there had been a full tide so that if the driver had driven straight to the pier and thence to a watery grave the current might be expected to carry the vehicle a considerable distance before it filled with water and sank.

Following the plan devised by their sergeant the divers swam outwards from the pier to a distance of one hundred yards. Because of the clear conditions prevailing in the water the sweep was a comprehensive one since it enabled the divers to swim further apart than they might otherwise do. After several minutes in the sea the divers returned and climbed on to the pier where they indicated to the sergeant that they wished to speak privately with him. There were some exchanges out of earshot of the onlookers but it was impossible to deduce from the guarded expressions on the faces of the search party whether or not they had met with any success.

There were excited whispers among the large crowd when Sergeant Hickson's face assumed a look of the utmost gravity. He listened intently while the leader of the group conveyed the findings of the team. The sergeant nodded grimly at the conclusion and cast an anxious look in the direction of the Ram of God. Slowly he approached the tall figure who stood with his hands hanging limply as if he already sensed that the news would be tragic. The Ram of God looked downward awkwardly at his feet as the sergeant drew near. Thomas Connelly placed a hand upon the Ram's shoulder when the sergeant shook his head to indicate that the worst had happened.

'I'm sorry.'

'You're sure?' Luke asked.

'Well,' Sergeant Hickson gestured helplessly with his hands, 'we can only say that the car is the car in question and that the man inside answers the description of the missing man. There will be formal identification as soon as we bring the body ashore and, of course, there will have to be a coroner's inquest but that's another day's work.'

Luke and the Ram accompanied Sergeant Hickson to the end of the pier where the divers extended their sympathy and awaited their sergeant's order for the recovery of the body. At a nod from their superior they silently slipped into the still sea and disappeared underwater.

'Did he make any effort to get out?' The Ram of God forced the question to his chattering lips.

'Apparently not,' the sergeant answered. 'He's still strapped in the driver's seat with his hands clutching the wheel. Even if he had managed to get out there is no way he would have made the shore, not with the Race flowing so quickly. At least we have the body. If the Race had got hold of it there's no telling where it might show up, that's if it ever did show up.'

Sergeant Hickson shut himself off suddenly, realising that he might be over-indulging himself in technical aspects which the next of kin might not altogether appreciate at this particular time. He would never get used to the role which he was obliged to play all too often across the months of summer. Although hardened by experience he, nevertheless, always found it to be a disheartening business. Saddest of all was when he found himself with the awful task of announcing a young person's drowning. He could never bring himself to look at the inconsolable faces of the shocked parents. He had children himself.

Luke came quickly to his assistance.

'Having the body,' Luke explained to the Ram, 'means that his remains will not be lost forever, that he will be buried with his own and that, at least, is something.'

The Ram of God nodded his understanding.

'It has been suggested,' Sergeant Hickson spoke in a low key in what he hoped was a tactful manner, 'that we bring the body ashore now without further delay before the tide comes in and the Race starts to run.'

Again the Ram of God nodded agreement.

'The car can be recovered at any time so there's no problem there,' Sergeant Hickson concluded.

Later as the body lay on the pier, awaiting the arrival of an ambulance which would convey it to Trallock General Hospital, the Ram was relieved to discern an almost joyful look on the twin's face. There seemed also to be an emanation of gentleness that he had not noticed since Murt was a boy. Death, it seemed, had removed all traces of the coarseness and ugliness which had been regular features of the now composed face for all of its adult life. If Murt had entertained misgivings when confronted on the sea bed by the awesome prospect of death they had not conveyed themselves to his face. Certainly there was no trace whatsoever of the terror which might be expected to transmit itself to his blackened features. There was instead an aloof dignity. Death failed to mask the feelings which had transformed Murt's commonality to its present serenity. There were also, the Ram noted as he turned the head slightly on his lap, certain almost

174

imperceptible similarities to his late mother. There was chiefly about the mouth, a veiled suggestion of achievement which he recalled only too well from the distant days when he and his mother would resolve a problem together. It was as though Murt conveyed to those who might think otherwise that he finally slipped the traces of confusion and turmoil which bound him and once again became inseparable from the scallywag brother whose departure left him unbalanced and defective. Now at last all of that had been put to rights and the face which should have borne at least some aspects of the hideousness of death was unaffected.

'Poor fellow solved his problem the best way he knew how,' Luke explained to Thomas as they stood at a respectful distance from the brothers.

'And I'll tell you another thing Thomas,' Luke spoke in a whisper, 'this leaves Ballybobawn with the biggest balls-up since the civil war. I can't figure it out. There's only one person with the capacity to resolve a problem of this size and that's the lady mayoress of the village, Mollie Cronane herself and even Mollie will be hard put to sort out this one.'

The same thoughts occupied Tom Cronane's mind as he stood with his sons among the large crowd of onlookers around the pier. He saw further than Luke, however. He realised that the solution lay with one man and no other and that man was the Ram of God. The Ram could simplify or the Ram could complicate and all anybody could really do at this point in time was wait and see.

There were other eyes focused on the Ram. Looking up briefly he noticed the concerned features of Mary Creel. He smiled instinctively and raised a hand. For a moment he forgot the situation in which he found himself and would have risen so that he might have words with his young friend. He wished to reassure her about the welcome which always awaited her at the farmhouse, to tell her of his and of Nonie's concern and to assure her that there was no need for awkward explanations but she vanished suddenly into the crowd and was nowhere to be seen.

Patricia Cahalane was another who was moved to tears by the pathetic scene on the pier. She would have dearly loved to approach him but to do so would be the equivalent of going on the stage before an audience. When the nuns in her company moved forward on to the pier she decided to accompany them, believing that it was their intention to sympathise with Edward. Her mortification brought a blush to her face when the members of the Presentation order knelt together, the senior of the party opening with the first decade of the Rosary. Patricia had no option but to kneel as well and to recite a decade when her turn came.

The Ram sat where he was, Murt's head still resting on his lap, murmuring the responses in unison with the sympathisers from Ballybobawn and surrounds, the curiosity-seekers and the elderly folk who would have been drawn to the strand anyway as a matter of course. Then his eyes caught Patricia Cahalane's and for the briefest of moments she allowed the hazel eyes to linger before transferring them to the beads held loosely between her fingers.

Oblivious to the ascending prayers the gulls overhead cried raucously as one of the flock attacked another and the entire colony went screaming down the sky. The Ram of God looked upwards, the prayer stilled on his lips, a faint smile appearing on his face. The twins would have enjoyed such a disruption.

11

FATHER MORTIMER O'CONNOR, PARISH priest of
Ballybobawn, sat smoking his pipe on the ornate
garden seat which had been a gift from the parishioners of nearby Trallock town where he had served
as senior curate for fifteen years. Around him in
the presbytery garden a cloying stillness prevailed.
Not even the accustomed murmuring of the bee
population intruded upon his thoughts. The smoke
from his streamlined, apple-bowled, brierwood,
another gift, this time from his housekeeper,
ascended the still air without resorting to twist or
twirl, the long plume dissolving only after it had
fallen foul of the mild air current above the garden
wall. There were conditions attached to his indul-
gence. His housekeeper had stipulated, after pre-
senting him with the gift, that it should only be
used out of doors, not that she minded a man
smoking indoors; she would insist that she enjoyed
the aroma of perfumed tobacco but she had read in
a magazine that fresh air diluted the damaging
pungency of pipe smoke, rendering it less harmful
to throat and lungs. Rather than argue the point
the mild-mannered cleric opted for the garden
whenever he felt in need of a drag. As his eyes followed the trail of ascending smoke he recalled the
events of the week which had just ended.

There had been many visitors to the presbytery
since the burial of Murt Drannaghy which had gotten the week off to the most dismal of beginnings.
Father O'Connor's first call was from his bishop. It
was, unfortunately, not as amiable as might be

expected. The bishop rang earlier that morning explaining to the parish priest that he would like to visit on his way back from Limerick later that evening. His Lordship arrived earlier than expected and surprised the pipe-smoking parish priest in the garden. Dismissing the older man's apologies for not having been at the front door of the presbytery to meet him the bishop went purposefully to the point of his visit. Refusing the offer of refreshments he withdrew a letter from his pocket and handed it over to the priest.

'See what you make of that Father like a good man and take your time. I'll have a dander around the grounds while you're perusing it. I may look into the church. I'll slip in by the sacristy. No need to alert anybody. I need the privacy to sort out a few matters which are causing me some concern.'

The pipe fell from Father O'Connor's mouth as he read the well-worded epistle. Was the bishop aware that pornographic films were being shown at the premises known as the Load of S and if so what did he propose to do about it? Father O'Connor read the letter a second time after recovering his pipe. Was the bishop aware of the fact that teenagers male and female had access to these disgusting side shows and would he not agree that Ballybobawn made Sodom and Gomorrah look like tidy towns winners.

The ageing parish priest was still in a state of shock when his superior returned to the garden.

'I had no idea,' Father O'Connor blurted out the words abjectly.

'Of course you hadn't,' the bishop, taking account of his obvious chagrin, agreed.

'If I had known I would have visited the place. I would have denounced it from the pulpit.'

'And given them free advertising!' The bishop made no attempt to conceal his scorn.

'You must know Father that the country is undergoing a period of moral decline right now. It may get worse and certainly we do not want to fuel the fires. Ballybobawn is not the only village where pornographic films are on show. Indeed they are also to be seen in so-called respectable homes. The Church has never experienced a more serious threat to its authority. The family which is the very backbone of the Church is imperilled as it has never been. The most disturbing tales of debauchery reach my ears daily. The youth of the country is the target for the vendors of these shameless exhibitions. Unless something drastic is done quickly the average family may not be proof against this onslaught of immorality and it's not just immorality. Honesty and decency are going by the board all over. A stand must be taken. Unfortunately, the pulpit no longer possesses the power to effectively chastise those who would destroy what we hold sacred. People are just not taking our castigations as seriously as they used to. The tragedy is that it must get worse before it gets better. The people, unfortunately, must experience the evil effects before they realise what has happened to all they once held dear. You have a sergeant here?

'Yes of course.'

'And is he aware of what's happened at this Load of ...' The bishop searched unavailingly for an appropriate word.

I'm sure if he knew he'd put a stop to it right away.'

'We shall give him that opportunity Father. Is he a discreet fellow?'

'Oh yes my Lord, the very soul of discretion.'

'You will summon him here before the weekend and you will relay to him my concern and you will stress that if I hear as much as a whisper from this day forth about pornography in public houses in this village I will report the matter to his superintendent and if that doesn't bring results I will present myself before the minister for justice.'

'But, but, but my Lord!' Father O'Connor was spluttering now, 'it's only an anonymous letter and it has been my experience that anonymous letters are often malicious rather than well-intentioned.'

The bishop, who was pacing around, stopped dead in his tracks.

'I did not come here this evening to be lectured about anonymous letters,' he thundered. 'Do you think that this letter is my only source of information?'

'I'm sorry my Lord. I spoke out of turn.'

Mollified the bishop resumed.

'I'll leave the matter in your hands Father and I must warn you that I will accept nothing less than positive results. How's Hehir by the way?'

The question caught Father O'Connor by surprise.

'He's out right now but I'm sure he has no complaints.'

'I'd be surprised if he had. How's his handicap?'

Presuming that the prelate was interested in the curate's golfing progress Father O'Connor responded proudly that it had never been lower.

'Like the morals of the parish which he so conscientiously serves! Forget I said that Father. It was uncalled for.'

'Of course my Lord.'

Father Harry Hehir was a type of priest once unknown in the countryside. In the bishop's eyes the curate tended to run with the hare and hunt with the hounds. He was also a great fellow for consoling widows and divorcees and was known to hold the most liberal views on marriage and sexual attitudes. He was also a dab hand at figuring centrally in social occasions and for having his photograph in local papers. The bishop felt he was over-quoted and felt that too many regarded him quite wrongly as a spokesman for the diocese. Harry the Hare, journalists called him privately but it was out of a sense of astonishment at his ubiquity rather than disrespect. Father Harry was always available and prepared to comment off the top of his head on topics ranging from the non-availability of contraceptives to the desirability of abortion clinics. Trouble was, the bishop was obliged to concede on reflection, more and more people tended to take him seriously.

THE SECOND VISITOR WAS Edward Drannaghy. The Ram of God had come, in the first place, to discharge his financial obligations in respect of his brother's obsequies, the chief of which was the High Mass which Father O'Connor, Father Hehir and a curate from the parish of Trallock had celebrated for the repose of the soul of Murt. It was the second such transaction between the parish priest and the same bereft party in all too short a time. As soon as the money changed hands both men sat in silence, knowing that a serious debate about the younger man's future was in the offing. The older man spoke first.

'You'll be wanting a postponement in your departure for Saint Rowland's I take it.'

'Yes Father.'

'Not for too long I hope. As you know the opening term is a brief one but it is also the most important one.'

'Not for too long Father I assure you but my affairs at the moment are in the most complicated state imaginable. I hardly know where to begin to sort them out. My whole world has changed completely in the last few weeks.'

'But your vocation is still intact and that's what is most important.'

Father O'Connor was at his most reassuring. 'Time my dear Edward will lessen your grief and the trauma you are experiencing now will be but a memory. Meanwhile we must make contact with the president of Saint Rowland's and acquaint him with all that has happened. You may let that in my hands. I'll find out how much time you may safely forfeit before setting out for California. I'll phone at the appropriate time.'

At this point in the conversation the Ram of God thrust his hand into his trouser pocket and withdrew a wad of notes.

'There's a hundred here Father,' he informed the parish priest. 'Phone calls to California are expensive and if this isn't enough I'll reimburse you fully as soon as we find out the cost.'

Father O'Connor nodded gratefully as he pocketed the money.

'We could reverse the charges,' he suggested suddenly.

'No, no!' The Ram of God declined the suggestion.

'Tell me Edward if there is any way in which I can be of help?'

'Maybe later Father. First I have to find out the precise legal position with regard to the farm. I propose to do that right away. In fact the family solicitor has sent word that he would like to see me. When he clarifies matters I'll come directly here and we'll talk again.'

FATHER O'CONNOR'S THIRD IMPORTANT visitor of the week, outside of the normal trickle of parishioners across the midsummer season, was Mollie Cronane. She came late and under cover of darkness. She came after careful consideration and she came with a disposition so generous that Father O'Connor was more than agreeably surprised. He was on the point of retiring for the night when the doorbell summoned him. He was alone in the presbytery at the time. The housekeeper, a widowed woman from the locality, slept in her own home although she spent most of her waking hours in her place of employment. Father O'Connor ushered Mollie into the sitting-room.

The first proposition put by Mollie to the parish priest was one he had not expected.

'If you wish to smoke your pipe Father I might have a cigarette to keep you company.'

In the absence of his housekeeper and in view of the fact that his caller might need the cigarette to break the ice Father O'Connor felt that the indoor smoking injunction might be temporarily lifted.

'I suppose you know what brought me Father,' Mollie shook a mournful head, wiped a tear from her eye and filled her lungs with cigarette smoke.

'Naturally,' Father O'Connor spoke with a voice full of understanding, 'you'll be wanting your money back.'

'What money would that be Father?' Mollie asked innocently.

'The money you paid me for the weddings.'

'Oh that money!' Mollie feigned surprise. 'Ah sure there's no need at all for that Father. You hold on to that. Won't there be other weddings Father with God's holy help.'

'With God's holy help,' Father O'Connor echoed dutifully.

'And if there isn't itself Father can't you say a mass or two for the repose of the souls of the poor boys that left us the way we are, God pity us!'

Father O'Connor was relieved. A post-dated cheque was the best he could have offered if Mollie had demanded her money. Ballybobawn was a poor parish, not quite the poorest in the diocese but very close to that most dubious of distinctions. Making ends meet was the chief task to be faced every day. He knew that his curate, a decent sort in Father O'Connor's books, had no financial worries, having a modest income at his disposal from parental investments apart altogether from the pittance which the parish was obliged to pay him.

'I was talking to Tom only this morning Father. Discussing our plight we were and wondering where in God's name would we turn.'

What Mollie said was true. Tom woke earlier than usual, not having ventured during the night to meet Madeleine Monterros for the first time in weeks. 'Why don't you have a talk with Father O'Connor,' Tom suggested. 'Put your cards on the table and see what he makes out of the mess.'

'Tell me now what brought you?' A greatly relieved Father O'Connor leaned forward encouragingly.

'To begin with Father,' Mollie opened, 'I can't begin to tell you about the shame and the humiliation I feel over having to tell you my sad story.'

'Now, now, now my dear Mollie you're in the presence of a friend. Anything that's in my power to do I'll do with a heart and a half to bring you from your troubles.'

'Oh 'tis a shameful tale I have to tell you this night Father O'Connor, a shameful tale indeed.' Mollie cast a glance at his face out of the corner of her eye and saw that he was suitably concerned.

'You might not know our story Father,' she continued, 'for you are a saint to be sure but there's others that has us blackened throughout the parish and beyond. My daughters as you know Father were to be married to the Drannaghy twins and now they're worse than widows without pensions or without the belongings and property of the men they were to marry. What are they going to do at all Father, two innocent girls that put their trust in their husbands-to-be and now to be thrown aside without as much as a copper to support them.'

Father O'Connor's confusion showed in his face. The girls had been stricken with tragedy sure enough but it wasn't the end of the world. They were young and the Cronanes were well off, millionaires by parochial standards, so what was all this about their not having a copper? More mystifying still to the parish priest was the reference to the belongings and property of the men they were to marry.

'I'm not sure I fully understand you?' He took the pipe from his mouth and looked into the bowl, its contents no longer ruddy.

'God help us in our plight Father,' Mollie rushed to enlighten him, 'my two little girls are with child. I can't believe it for it was only this very day it came to my notice. It's the time that's in it Father. God knows they were brought up decent and they got the finest of example if ever any pair got it. There isn't a holier or a more Catholic home in the parish of Ballybobawn. Since the day I was born, that I may be struck dead, I was devoted to the Sacred Heart of Jesus and poor Tom, my own Tom, who doesn't know what's after happening to him, and who never had a sinful thought in his head. Oh mother of the divine God what are we going to do at all Father? We'll be the talk of the parish and the parishes beyond and those innocent babes will be brought into this cruel world without fathers or without homes and the only title they'll ever have is the title of bastards.'

With exquisite timing Mollie burst into tears, covering her face with her hands. Then came the sighing and the sobbing, sufficient to move the most hard-hearted man in the world to pity and a caring cleric like Father Mortimer O'Connor to tears.

'My dear Mollie,' he rose and placed his priestly hands on her bent head as the platitudes began to flow. 'God never closed one gap without opening another.'

Having spoken, the deeply-disturbed priest removed his hands and joined them together as he moved around the room.

'God's help is nearer than the door,' he spoke in Irish before resorting once more to the speech of the foreigner as he sometimes referred to the English language.

'The darkest hour is before the dawn.' He repeated the age old cliche as he continued with his circuit of the outsize room. Mollie, between sobs, managed to produce another cigarette from her handbag. Father O'Connor addressed her from the farthest corner of the room. First he lifted the smokeless pipe aloft as though to command her undivided attention. Then as his wrinkled visage assumed a gravity relative to the message he was about to impart he slowly pointed the pipe in the direction of his visitor.

'Trust Tom,' Mollie spoke to herself as she watched the inspiration illuminate the old priest's face. 'Tom knew what he was doing when he sent me here.'

'There may not be,' Father O'Connor spoke aloud as though he were addressing his flock of a Sunday morning. 'There may not be,' he repeated his opening line, 'a crisis here at all. We are all instruments of the Lord but few are given the opportunity of fulfilling ourselves. We have, however, in our midst a man who may resolve our problems and who not only has just now become an instrument of the Lord but has been already chosen by the Lord.'

Father O'Connor came forward and re-occupied the seat he had vacated.

'I don't understand you Father,' Mollie managed to successfully conceal the smile which threatened to surface.

'I am referring to Edward Drannaghy, the brother of the deceased twins and the natural uncle to the babes your daughters will bear one day. Edward Drannaghy is a God-fearing and pious young man who hopes to serve the Lord as I endeavour to serve Him and I am sure that when I speak to him he will not turn a deaf ear to your plight. What sort of settlement have you in mind?'

Mollie drew on the cigarette before answering.

'The farm Father!'

188

The simplicity and forthrightness of her answer took Father O'Connor by surprise. If he had not been already seated there is no doubt but he would have been compelled to avail of a chair. He placed his pipe in his mouth and realising that there was no succour to be drawn from it, removed it, and indicated by a shrug that his caller should proceed and elaborate upon the claim if she felt so inclined. It would also give him the breathing space he required. Edward Drannaghy was a most amenable young man but the handing over of the farm! Then there was the question of Mollie's definition of property and belongings! He leaned back in his chair and closed his eyes as though he were hearing confessions.

'Well Father it would be the Ram's moral duty to settle the land on my two little girls, a half for each, to be held in trust until the children came of age. It's no more than their right in the sight of God. It would be the wish of the Ram's brothers and they are the rightful owners of the land, God be good to them. The Ram has no claim as you know Father no more than me or you or a stranger walking the road. His share was to be his education and he has most of that got. The girls will provide the rest when the land is signed over and the stock, of course, and whatever else is part of the farm and they won't be mean for 'tis not in their nature to be mean Father.'

Mollie paused to light another cigarette and to hear what Father O'Connor might have to say. He sat unmoving, his eyes still closed, which led Mollie to believe that she was at liberty to proceed further.

'He'll have no need for the farm where he's going Father and if he's ever short of anything doesn't he know where to turn.'

Father O'Connor sat suddenly upright lest Mollie make further demands although he could think of nothing else.

'I'll speak to him,' Father O'Connor said wearily.

'It would want to be soon Father,' Mollie cautioned, 'and seeing as I told you so much I might as well tell you all.'

Father O'Connor sat back again and closed his eyes.

'The Stringer McCallum is free and single as you know Father and is as hard-working a man as ever wore shoe leather. He always had a longing for Kate and he won't see her short. She's the best of five months gone. Noreen is only four so there's no emergency there yet you might say.'

Father O'Connor wondered to what degree she might think he had committed himself when he promised to help.

'Of course, it would give the Stringer and Kate a great start if the Ram was to hand over the farm right away. Then the divide could be made and the Stringer could move in with Kate after you had them married, of course. That way the child would have a father and we wouldn't be giving the parish a bad name. Noreen isn't too pushed as yet but when she has the land there will be no shortage of good prospects.'

'I'll speak to Edward as promised,' Father O'Connor felt that Mollie's spiel needed to be terminated, 'but in the end he must make his own decision.'

'What other decision can he make in God's name!' Mollie expostulated loudly, 'unless he wants his own flesh and blood reared as bastards. He's their uncle. It's his responsibility to see that they are brought up legitimate. They are the rightful heirs to the farm. In God's eyes no one else has any claim and that's all that really matters.'

'In God's eyes yes but a courtroom is another proposition,' Father O'Connor reminded her. 'Even the Catholic Church which occupies a special place in the constitution has been pilloried in the courts. Irish judges seem to shed any merciful inclinations they might harbour when the Church is in court. It's as if they were trying to balance a redress.'

'I don't know anything about that Father,' Mollie interrupted, 'but I do know one thing and that is there will be hell to pay if these unborn babies are done out of their rights.'

Father O'Connor placed his pipe ceremonially on the mantelpiece to indicate that he had heard his fill. As he ushered Mollie to the door she thrust her hand into her handbag and withdrew two twenty pound notes.

'You'll say a Mass anyway Father,' she said as she thrust the money into his hand, 'that God's will might be done in this matter.'

'I will to be certain,' Father O'Connor assured her.

As Mollie left the presbytery she congratulated herself on a night's work well done. She'd set a few tongues awagging among her disciples in the village and countryside, tongues which because of their known virtue, would lay valid claim to the ear of the parish priest but there might be no need. If the Ram was as amenable as Father O'Connor believed then all Mollie's troubles were over. The Stringer, for all his leanness and angularity, was a sounder man and a more reliable worker than Will Drannaghy had ever been.

AS SHE NEARED THE supermarket on her way from the presbytery Mollie caught a glimpse of Mary Creel as she gazed at one of the well-stocked windows.

'More pinched by the hour,' Mollie observed. At Mollie's approach Mary had run off. Some days before Mollie had seen her engaged in conversation with Cha. Cha was a good businessman but he would be putty in the hands of a girl like that. There was no time to waste. She had seen the infatuated look on his face as he thrust an apple on her when he thought nobody was looking. There had been a few other times of late when she had observed him with a distant look in his eyes.

Mollie woke Tom to tell him all that happened when she arrived home.

'Another thing,' she nudged Tom before he drifted back into the uneasy sleep from which she had awakened him, 'is Cha.'

'What about Cha?' Tom asked.

'It's time he went out in the world.'

'Oh I couldn't do without Cha. Tom was adamant.

'Not for good silly,' Mollie assured him. 'He'll be taking over here one day and he'll want his wits about him.'

'He has his wits about him,' Tom argued.

'I know. I know,' Mollie went on patiently, 'but he'd want a year or two in a bigger establishment.'

'Good thinking,' Tom agreed. 'What would you say to Trallock?'

'Too near,' Mollie argued again, 'and too small. I was thinking of Cork or Dublin. You have the contacts. It shouldn't be any trouble to you to place him.'

'He might not come back,' Tom warned. 'He's a

good lad you know, an industrious lad and honest too. If I was his boss I wouldn't want to see him go.'

'He'll be back when he's ready, when he knows it's time for him to take over.'

Tom was forced to concede that there was much to what she had said. He promised to give the matter his most urgent consideration.

12

MOLLIE CRONANE'S PLOY TO use the intervention of Father O'Connor did not succeed.

'You will want to do the right thing in the sight of God,' the old priest counselled his protege.

'I will look after the Cronane girls in my own way Father,' the Ram explained.

'Does this mean you will not be handing over the land?' Father O'Connor's alarm disturbed the Ram.

'I will be making adequate provision for the Cronane girls,' the Ram was adamant. 'I intend to settle a substantial sum on each but the farm will remain in my hands.'

Father O'Connor made no effort to conceal his disappointment.

'I cannot believe my ears,' he said sadly. 'Here we have a situation which demands no great sacrifice on your part. You have a heaven-sent opportunity to prove yourself worthy in the sight of God.'

'I am satisfied in my conscience,' the Ram of God went on patiently, 'that I am doing the right thing. I am being more than generous.'

'But my son you must surely see,' Father O'Connor argued, 'what is expected of you here and that is nothing less than the maximum sacrifice.'

'I am making that sacrifice,' the Ram persisted. 'I will make available to the girls the proceeds of all the resources I own in this world except for the farm which I regard as a heritage to be cherished and preserved until such time as I am too old to perform my priestly duties satisfactorily.'

'You must ask yourself,' Father O'Connor was equally persistent, 'whether this obsession with your land and your vocation for the priesthood may go hand in hand.'

'It's not an obsession,' the Ram argued. 'I don't see how you can say that. Even priests are entitled to certain material comforts when they retire.'

'You speak of retirement,' Father O'Connor found himself laughing, 'and you have yet to wear the deacon's collar!'

At the end of their discourse nothing was resolved. Father O'Connor reported the unsatisfactory outcome to Mollie Cronane who professed tearfully to the disappointed parish priest that it must be a strange vocation indeed that could not see its way towards righting a natural wrong.

In the days following his confrontation with Father O'Connor the Ram had many an argument with himself in his efforts to justify his tenacity with regard to the land. He felt in his heart that it would be bordering on the sacriligeous to hand over to the Cronanes. They would use the land, exhaust it, demean it and he could not allow that to happen. The land was sacred; in a way it was as sacred as his vocation which was not threatened; of this he was convinced. His feelings about the land and the vocation were quite compatible. Father O'Connor did not understand. He was under somebody's influence, probably Mollie Cronane's. The Ram discussed the matter with Nonie Spillane.

'I knew priests that came into land,' she said, 'and it did not stop them from being priests.'

'What I feel for this land,' the Ram explained, 'has nothing to do with greed. It has more to do with love.'

'Of course it does,' Nonie could not get the

words out quickly enough to endorse his sentiments. Certain now in the knowledge that the farm would not go to the Cronanes and to the McCallums Nonie felt like celebrating.

She never said it to the Ram but she began to notice a certain air of proprietorship about him, about the way he walked the land and his hurry to be out and about in the fields as soon as his meals were concluded. What Nonie really hoped for was a day when he would no longer be able to reconcile his vocation with ownership of the farm. Then maybe he would cast about him for a suitable partner, somebody like Patricia Cahalane. He had, in her estimation, never looked like anything but a spoiled priest but now he was beginning to look more and more like a farmer.

Only a fortnight had passed since the burial of his brother Murt but it was not only the tragic drowning of the second twin which left the Ram so disordered and disturbed.

'We'll want help,' Nonie reminded him not for the first time since Murt's passing, 'the yard is getting the better of me. I'll need a woman two or three days in the week and you'll be needing a man full time.'

'It won't be for long more,' the Ram promised.

'And what's that supposed to mean?' Nonie asked as she caught the dropping ash in her palm.

'It means that I'll be getting rid of the cows and replacing them with dry cattle.' The Ram spoke with a finality which surprised him. The idea was at the back of his head but he had not made up his mind.

'I never heard of such a daft thing in all my days,' Nonie turned on him, 'getting rid of cows indeed and the yield never better and does this mean that you're still angling for that Roman collar?'

The Ram permitted himself a smile.

'You might say that,' he returned.

'In the name of Christ and His blessed Mother have you any idea what's at stake here?' Nonie rose from her chair and stood confronting him, hands on hips. 'When will you realise that you are now the owner of one of the finest farms in the country-side, with one of the cleanest herds to boot! You were never cut out to be a priest. You're a farmer but it might be too late before sense dawns on you. No one has a feel for the land like you. You're good to it and it's good to you. The land knows its own. And what do you think that round collar is going to do for you! Bring you peace and happiness! Well I can tell you you'll have no happiness until you put a young woman's legs under that table where you're now sitting and rear a family like God or-dained. You won't get a minute's peace from wom-en once that collar goes around your neck and you draw on the black clothes. You're a fine-looking man and there's plenty women around who spe-cialise in trapping innocent priests. 'Tis a way of life with them. Don't carry that natural love of women that's in you into the Church because it will come at you yet as sure as there's a God in His heaven.'

'I wish you wouldn't talk like that.' The Ram tried to conceal his mounting annoyance but Nonie was only beginning.

She was spitting out the words now realising that this was possibly the last chance she might ever have of trying to make him see sense. Let him be angry. Let him turn on her. She would have her say because it was her duty.

'You don't belong where you're going. Is it a man that mounted the cream of New York without having to ask!'

The Ram of God jumped suddenly upright but Nonie pushed him back on to his chair.

'Hear me out,' she begged, sorry for the crude way in which she had couched her last statement but determined to show him that he was doing the wrong thing. The Ram sat shocked in his chair at the violent upturn in the exchange.

'The good God meant you to be a ram not a lamb. Your brothers are dead and there's no Drannaghy left in Ballybobawn and there never will be another Drannaghy here if you have your way and you try to tell me that God wants that! God don't want nothing of the kind. God's will is done in the way things have turned out here. The curls on your head will never be seen again in this world if you enter the Church and what about your strength and your courage! Will you deprive your sons of these and sons you'll have in plenty if you drop this mad notion for good. Who's to inherit the gentleness of you and the kindness and the tenderness you've always shown to people no matter what their station! No one will because your seed will rot and God would agree with me that it isn't right or fair that you should allow this to happen.'

Spent and pale-faced Nonie Spillane's hands trembled as she endeavoured to light a fresh cigarette from the butt in her hand. Unable to do so she flung both cigarettes away from her in disgust and without another word went out of doors. Nonie was deeply affected after the outburst subsided. The truth was that she was the victim of a fatigue which was completely foreign to her. The delivery of her excoriation had left her in a state of near collapse. She did not feel ashamed. If she felt anything it was regret for not having expressed her

198

feelings earlier. She hoped that she had not spoken in vain. She honestly believed that he was not material for the priesthood. He was too sensitive and too soft and while these traits in themselves were commendable they needed to be compensated by a certain toughness and even ruthlessness which the Ram of God lacked. Nonie felt that he would make an excellent martyr with canonisation ultimately guaranteed but he would be altogether too naive for the devious challenges of a parish.

Before the Ram of God set out to see his solicitor in Trallock he traversed the High Meadow on the Ferguson. After a circuit and a half he alighted at the fields' most elevated point. The silvery-green aftergrass flickered and whispered in the light south-westerly breezes, strengthening with the advance of noon. Savouring the salty breeze-borne tang the Ram inhaled deeply, standing stock still with his uplifted face turned towards the distant sea. Along the hedgerows the creamy white of meadowsweet and the purple of blooming loosestrife blended immaculately to present an eye-catching display along each of the field's four headlands. The sound of chuckling waters meandering along their fern-covered, gravelly courses should have had a soothing effect on the last remaining member of the Ballybobawn Drannaghy's but this was far from being the case.

He remounted the Ferguson and as he drove downward he considered the implications of Nonie's outbursts. She would have him abandon his vocation altogether and throw it aside in tatters in exchange for material comforts and yet Nonie was no agent of Satan. He had never known her to be dishonest or sly in her outlook. Outspokenness had always been her strong point and yet his vocation was being threatened from this most un-likely of sources. He remembered what Father O'Connor said about the devil using innocent mediums for his foul purposes. He shook his head. Nonie would be proof against any diabolical infiltration. There was, of course, a certain amount of truth in what she said but it was not the truth as the Ram of God saw it.

ALFIE NESBITT SAT REGALLY in his specially raised chair which dominated the office in the great square of Trallock town. For some reason which he could never fathom Alfie liked to conduct business with his feet off the ground. The only excuse he could offer for this unprofessional behaviour was that it made him think more clearly. He shrewdly took appraisal of the Ram of God through his gold-rimmed spectacles. Educated, aristocratic, favouring his mother more than his father, priestly and yet there was a hint of sensuality. Handsome, in fact downright elegant! In selecting a sire for her offspring Lorraine Dupree had chosen well under the circumstances. Alfie Nesbitt had known the American woman although not to the degree that he would have liked.

'Sit down Edward my boy. It's been a long time.'

'It has indeed,' the Ram of God returned. 'I came in answer to your letter Alfie.'

'My letter!' The elderly solicitor seemed at first appearance to be an absent-minded sort of old gentleman, benign and amiable, which indeed he was until he entered a courtroom. He began a search through a rather bulky file. 'Here we are,' he said. 'Here is your father's last will and testament.'

He handed the document to the Ram of God. As the younger man perused the solitary sheet of paper Alfie was afforded a second and more lengthy opportunity to study the features before him. He liked what he saw. There was resolve and integrity but there was also a warmth and sensitivity which Alfie believed would disarm even the most redoubtable of females. Alfie, himself often referred to as a ladies' man, had no doubt that the Ram would have serious problems from the moment he placed a Roman collar around his neck. There was no granite in the make-up and granite was needed in the Church of Rome as it had never been needed before.

'Is this all there is?' The Ram's query cut in upon Alfie's musings.

'That's all,' Alfie confirmed.

The will, which the Ram of God returned to his counsellor, had little to say which, as Alfie endorsed, made it a good will in every sense of the word. The chief beneficiaries were the late, lamented twins but there was a clause which provided for the Ram's education as defined in a separate document by his parent and solicitor.

'What does this mean?' the Ram of God asked.

'What it means,' Alfie leaned back in his chair, 'and what you must already know full well is that since you are the next of kin all the worldly possessions of your two brothers are now lawfully yours, the farm, the dwelling-house and out-houses, the machinery, the stock and any and all monies, investments, personal effects, in fact every goddamned article from the milking machine to the family chamber pot!'

'Is there money?'

'Only five thousand pounds,' Alfie smiled, 'but

there's no debt and you are left at the end of the day with as choice and as valuable a going concern as could be found in this part of the world. By any standards you are a well-off man.'

'When do I come into possession of the land?' the Ram asked nervously.

'Almost immediately,' Alfie assured him. 'There are a few formalities. Administration will have to be taken out and, of course, the property transferred into your name. I presume you will be selling out before you leave for California.'

'That's not my intention,' the Ram of God spoke with the conviction of a man who had already made up his mind. 'I intend,' the Ram of God slowly unfolded his plan, 'to dispose of the milch cows but I would hope to hold on to the fat stock. There are twenty-eight two-year olds and yearlings and there are thirty-seven calves from this years' crop.'

The Ram of God paused expecting some comment from his solicitor. None was forthcoming. Alfie indicated with his hands that the full details should be disclosed.

'I propose to hold on to the land,' the Ram continued, 'until such time as I retire from my ministry. I would leave a caretaker in charge on a part-time basis for a trial period of a year or two and if things worked out I would stock the land to its fullest when I come home for a holiday, or whatever. If it doesn't work out then I'll sell the existing stock and let the land or rather you'll let the land for me on a yearly basis. That way the land will not be fallow when I retire.'

There followed a silence but still no word came from Alfie. His eyes had closed although not of their own volition as the Ram unfolded his carefully-wrought proposal.

'My main problem,' he continued, 'is that the two sisters my brothers intended to marry happen to be with child and it has been suggested to me that I should hand over the farm to them to be held in trust until the children come of age. I would rather not part with the farm as I would like to come home and live there in seclusion and, of course, raise cattle. You see I love that farm and I feel duty bound because of my father's love for it to keep it in the Drannaghy name. When I sell the herd it should realise about thirty-five thousand pounds. I would divide this money between the two Cronane girls on condition they gave up any right which they might feel they had for the farm. That's my story,' the Ram concluded. 'You are the only person to whom I have spoken and I would be most anxious to have your advice.'

'Before I do that,' Alfie returned, 'there are a few questions I would like to ask. First of all when you say you propose to retire from your ministry does it mean that you will remain in the service of God until your sixty-fifth year?'

After a moment's hesitation the Ram of God answered in the affirmative. 'Yes,' he said firmly, 'although not necessarily in California.'

'My second question,' Alfie crossed his feet beneath his chair, 'what proof have you that the unborn children of the Cronane sisters are your late brothers?'

'I heard them admit it before they died. In fact they used to boast about it.'

'Can you be certain that you will not change your mind about the priesthood before your ordination?'

'I believe that nothing except death alone will stop me from being a priest.'

In the Ram of God's reply was a conviction that impressed the older man and he would always be the first to admit that he was not easily impressed.

'Having heard you out,' Alfie leaned back on his chair a second time and looked his client in the eye, 'I would advise you to sell the farm and have done with it. The money from the sale will give you a decent income should you decide to quit the seminary.'

'I would rather sign the place over to the Cronane girls than do that,' the Ram sounded adamant.

'Letting a farm over a long period would give rise to all sorts of legal difficulties and it would be impossible to forecast what way the courts would decide should there be litigation. Thirty years is a long time my boy.'

'I will not sell,' the Ram sounded more determined than ever.

'Well if you will not sell I suggest that you sell off all your stock and let the farm for one year and then to somebody else for another. You will see then where you stand and some of the difficulties I warned about will start to surface.'

'Such as?'

'Such as a ring or cartel,' Alfie replied, 'where a few locals get together and intimidate outsiders. That way they pay the price they feel is right but not the market price and it will happen, especially in a close-knit farming community like Ballybobawn. As for letting the land, I must warn you that after several years of letting to the same interests your position could eventually become untenable. Let me be blunt my dear Edward. Your generosity towards the Cronane women, Christian and charitable as it is, is sure to be interpreted in that quarter as softness or a licence to impose further penalties on you for, as sure as shooting, nobody is going to bid against the man or men who will be filling the shoes of your twin brothers, who will be standing in as fathers for them and that is how the countryside will see them and although the law will be on your side there are times when the law is rendered powerless. You will also find yourself an extremely unpopular man. In effect you will be an absentee landlord and you will be seen as the cruel uncle who has deprived the true heirs of their estates. The vested interests in the community will perpetuate this image. I say all these things now so that you might know what you are letting yourself in for. If you decide to hold on to the farm I will, of course, be proud and honoured to protect your interests and I believe I can do exactly that to the bitter end but I am obliged to point out all the pitfalls. My advice, therefore, is sell the farm so that you may pursue your studies without pressure and so that you might come home to a welcome every summer. Try not to see the sale as a form of capitulation but as a means of making life easier for you.'

'Would I get a fair price if I were to sell?' the Ram asked.

'I'm sure you would,' Alfie said. 'The money you would settle on the Cronane sisters is quite substantial. Tom Cronane is a wealthy man and I'm pretty certain he would unloose the purse strings. As well as that the Stringer McCallum has a nice bit put aside for such a contingency. It's the answer to his prayers in fact. His brother Joe has been pulling and dragging for years on that holding of his but he's not short of money.'

'Wait a minute!' The Ram of God's surprise showed clearly on his face. 'I guessed that the

Stringer McCallum would resume his courtship of Kate Cronane as he is perfectly entitled to do without my leave or yours but where does Joe come in?'

'Where else but at the side of Noreen Cronane,' came the response, 'as she kneels at the altar in Ballybobawn to celebrate the double wedding and this last event my dear Edward, as the whole countryside knows, must take place sooner rather than later. Now when do you propose to settle this money on the sisters?'

'Immediately but of course they must relinquish any claim.'

'You can set your mind at ease on that point for they have no claim.'

'Are you sure?' The Ram of God sounded dubious.

'They have the same claim as that moth fluttering near the window which is no claim at all,' Alfie assured him, 'and which is more they are fully aware of this and you may be sure that Mollie Cronane has paid good money to the most astute senior counsel in the land in case there might be any flaw in the law in relation to the special position in which her daughters find themselves. When do you propose to sell the cows?'

'The representatives of Trallock Livestock Mart have offered me thirty-five thousand for the entire herd. I propose to accept and I can return here straightaway with the cheque.'

'I think,' Alfie eased himself sideways from his chair, 'that a settlement of say, ten thousand apiece would be more than generous. You are not obliged to part with a farthing but I do appreciate that you want to do the right thing by the girls.'

'You will send them each a cheque for seventeen and a half thousand pounds.' The Ram of God finalised the matter by rising too.

'You may be right,' Alfie, who was moved by no such generous motives, acquiesced. 'It will be seen by reasonable people as a more than liberal compensation and by those who are not so reasonable as a difficult gesture to brush aside.'

AS THE RAM OF God walked to his car to go home for the milking he ran into Patricia Cahalane. She was in the company of several other females of varying ages. The party was on its way at the time to the Trallock Arms. Involuntarily he raised a hand. Immediately she left the group and came towards him smiling. They shook hands. The Ram explained haltingly that it had been his intention on several occasions to call to the pub for a drink or two but he had been unable to shake off the suffocating lethargy brought on by the drowning until that very morning. Now that he found a true sense of reality returning to him, albeit slowly, he would drop in for a drink at the earliest opportunity.

'When are you leaving?' Patricia asked. She had heard from Nonie that his departure had been postponed.

'In a month or so,' the Ram of God replied. 'Oh by the way,' he asked anxiously, 'have you seen Mary Creel lately?'

'All I've caught of that girl are glimpses and those have been few and far between. Now that you mention it I'll make it a point to see her. I would have called to the house but her father does not encourage visitors and I have the feeling he might take it out on Mary and the other children if I persisted.'

There had followed a silence while each tried to

think of something to prolong the conversation.

'What brings you to town,' the Ram asked.

'There's a teachers' conference in the school. We've just finished so we're on our way to the hotel for something to eat. And what brings you?'

The Ram hesitated for a moment wondering whether he should take her into his confidence. He decided in favour. Hastily he outlined his visit to Alfie Nesbitt, his settling of the money on the Cronanes and his plans for the farm after he left the country.

'They're doing well,' Patricia spoke thoughtfully. 'There's many a girl got far less and most, unfortunately, get nothing at all.'

Another silence ensued during which Patricia imagined that people engaged in conversation in the street had them under close observation. She guessed correctly. She was a well-known figure in the town and he was, after all, the notorious Ram of God who, if accounts were true, had sired more ewes than he was ever likely to remember.

'They say,' a housewife who stood in a nearby doorway talking to a neighbour said, 'that he would mount a coarse brush.'

'He don't look it,' said the recipient of this salacious titbit. 'He looks downright holy if you ask me.'

'They're the worst,' said the other. 'They say he can accommodate women as fast as you'd pull them out from under him.'

Patricia decided it was time to take her leave. She had no desire to add fuel to any fire which might have been occasioned by their chance meeting.

'I'll see you then before you go,' she said.

'Oh yes,' the Ram of God answered enthusiastically.

'A farewell drink?' Patricia suggested.

'Yes,' he nodded eagerly, 'a farewell drink.'

'But not in Ballybobawn.'

'Not in Ballybobawn,' he affirmed readily.

'Perhaps here in Trallock?' Patricia's hazel eyes displayed no more than their usual calm.

'Yes, of course.'

'At the Arms?' Patricia hurried the words out, fully aware now that the onlookers would be guessing that the seeds of a tryst were being sown.

'The Arms would be fine,' the Ram agreed.

'The night before you leave?' Patricia proposed.

'Perfect,' came the response.

'About nine?' from Patricia.

'Nine would be fine,' from the Ram of God.

'That's grand then. 'Bye for the while.' She moved off gracefully in the direction of the hotel, nodding politely to the responsive onlookers.

WORD WAS RELAYED TO Mollie Cronane from one of her usually impeccable sources in the town of Trallock that the Ram of God was about to dispose of his dairy herd. It was the most shattering blow as far as Mollie was concerned since the drowning of Murt Drannaghy. It meant that the Ram had no notion of transferring the farm as a going concern to her daughters. Desperately she tried to think of some measure to forestall him. She dismissed the idea of a boycott. She would first appeal to his better nature. Joe McCallum was summoned into her presence; he and the Ram were neighbours and friends of long standing. He was presented with his brief. He was to ask first if the Ram was interested in Noreen. If he was, there would be advantages.

Subject to his agreement on a division of the farm as envisaged by the dead twins she would be prepared to settle ten thousand on her daughter.

'Suppose the Ram says no to my first question?' Joe had asked.

'Then your business there is finished. You come back here and tell me the outcome.'

'If he says no,' Joe hesitated before setting out his own proposal, 'I would be glad to take Noreen off your hands. She might be glad to have me in the heel of the hunt!'

'Where's the catch?' Mollie asked suspiciously.

'No catch,' Joe assured her, 'but between us all we could surely buy the farm from the Ram. What use can he have for it and he off to California? My own place would make a tidy sum if I were to put it up. And we could proceed as planned.'

'Do what you have to do first,' Mollie advised him. After he left she laughed at his opportunism.

AS THE RAM NEARED the farmhouse he noticed Joe McCallum's car parked on the driveway at the front. This was totally unprecedented. No farmer in the locality would leave his car parked at the front of the farmhouse. Always they would turn to the left immediately after the gable and park in the spacious yard at the rear. Let the priest and the doctor park by the front door or visitors from towns and cities who could not know any better but a farmer's place was in the yard. As the Ram drew to a halt he saw Joe standing impatiently in the front doorway. He was dressed in his Sunday best which, in Joe's case, meant that he had gone to the trouble of donning a collar and tie and discarded the wellingtons he normally wore in favour of shoes.

'I'd like a few words with you Ram,' Joe fingered the tie knot which had slipped inches below his Adam's apple.

'Fire away Joe,' the Ram drew off his shoes in the kitchen and drew on the wellingtons which Nonie Spillane handed to him.

'Not here for God's sake!' Joe lifted the tie knot up to his chin.

'Go on out then and I'll be out after you.' The Ram turned to Nonie expecting some sort of explanation after he had gone.

'I've thought about it and thought about it,' Nonie puckered up her nose as she took the ash-topped cigarette from her mouth, 'and all he reminds me of is two things. One of them is a scarecrow and the other is a matchmaker who came to my grandmother's house years ago looking for the pedigree of a man who needed a wife.'

Nonie's intuition was accurate.

'I'm a man of few words,' Joe opened, 'and you look like a man who wants to get on with his milking so here goes. Will you or will you not marry Noreen Cronane and be a father instead of an uncle?'

'Who sent you?' the Ram asked, scarcely able to believe his ears.

'Never mind who sent me. The thing is that she's willing if you are.'

'Did she send you?'

'Yes. She sent me,' Joe waited fingering his tie with one hand scratching his posterior with the other.

'I'm flattered,' the Ram of God answered, 'but she must know I have other plans.'

211

'Does that mean you won't marry her?' Joe asked, a beaming smile of hope appearing on his face.

'I won't marry her.' The Ram assured him.

'That's the best news that ever came my way,' Joe danced from one leg to another, 'because it clears the way for me. Beggars can't be choosers you know and that cuts both ways.' Whistling and clapping his hands together he trotted gamely round the gable, sat into his car and hooted the whole way down to the cross of Ballybobawn.

On Joe's return from his mission he made no attempt to conceal the triumphant grin which replaced his normal look of tormentation. Mollie Cronane wheeled around sharply to conceal her anger and frustration after hearing of the rejection.

13

AS LUKE HOLLY SAT on the wooden bench which he sometimes brought out of doors in fine weather he surveyed the empty street. At a rough estimate, the sergeant wagered, five pairs of eyes were fixed unblinkingly upon him from various vantage points downwards as far as the cross of Ballybobawn. Should he rise at any stage and proceed in any direction whatsoever that number would be doubled in a matter of moments and that was as it should be, Luke conceded. I am a public servant, he would often remind himself and I am, therefore, always open to inspection.

The sergeant was deeply perturbed. The deaths by misadventure of the Drannaghy twins had placed the village under a powerful spotlight and whenever this happened there was always the danger that hitherto concealed distortions and blemishes would also present themselves for scrutiny. There was the business of the pornographic videos. Father O'Connor, as mild-mannered as a man could be, had been adamant that unless action was taken the matter would go further. Luke had gone only the night before to the Load of S. He entered shortly before closing time without prior warning and in a thrice landed himself in the iniquitous den where the television set took pride of place. There were several viewers in the area all seemingly absorbed by a recital of chamber music on the second channel. He guessed rightly that somebody in the room had operated the remote control which could switch in an instant from video to live reception.

'By Jasus that's what you might call music sergeant!' Mickey Creel announced proudly as he closed off one nostril with his thumb and expelled a snot to the floor from the other in appreciation. The other patrons in the back room were teenagers, two of whom one male and one female, both under age, drank what appeared to be orange and coke. The sergeant dipped a finger in each glass and sampled the contents. He could not be certain. He could have confiscated the glasses and had the contents analysed. Instead he spoke to the young man behind the counter.

'I know you're showing dirty films here,' Luke deliberately kept his voice down so that nobody else might hear, 'and I hereby caution you that if you continue to do so you will be prosecuted under the act.'

Luke was not quite sure what act would cover the charge but the young man at the receiving end had turned pale and was obviously impressed.

'You will also be prosecuted and the licence will be endorsed and maybe even revoked if you persist in selling intoxicating drink to young people under the age of eighteen.'

Without another word Luke turned on his heel and departed the premises. He went straight to the barracks where he dialled the Trallock number of Willie Halvey. There followed a most unpleasant exchange during which Willie insisted that he would conduct the business of the Load of S without interference from priests or bishops. He went on to suggest that Luke might find more profitable ways of spending his time.

'I've sunk a fortune into that dive,' Willie fumed when Luke inferred that he would be obliged to take a closer look at the goings on in Ballybobawn's busiest hostelry. 'Those videos are part of the attraction and what the hell is it anyway but straight sex!' Willie grew angrier as he warmed to his task. 'It isn't as if there was violence or buggery going on. Sex, straight and wholesome, is what we serve up out there and what could be more natural than that I ask you.'

When Luke tried to explain the bishop's concern for the youth of Ballybobawn and the parish priest's revulsion Willie guffawed loud and long.

'The legal position,' Willie pointed out, 'is that neither the parish priest nor the bishop have any business telling me how to run the Load of S.'

'They have the right to protest against obscenity,' Luke insisted.

'Since when did straight screwing become obscenity?' Willie protested.

'I am not going to argue the rights and wrongs of it with you,' Luke evaded the question. 'All I will say is this Willie and you had better take note. A complaint has been made to me by the parish priest of Ballybobawn which leaves me with no option but to carry out searches of your premises on a regular basis.'

'If you do that,' Willie complained, 'the business will fall away as you well know. I would call that harassment and I will do all in my power to stop you.'

'I have a job to do,' Luke Holly reminded him. 'It's nothing personal Willie. All you have to do is stop showing videos.'

'I hope you won't take it as personal either Luke if I ask you do you like moorland scenery?' Willie's tone sounded menacing.

'I don't understand you,' Luke sounded puzzled.

'The reason I ask,' Willie let the words sink in,

'is that you might wind up somewhere in the arse-hole of Ireland in the middle of some bog.'

Luke recalled that Willie and a certain government minister were friends of long standing as well as belonging to the same political party. He wouldn't be the first sergeant to be uprooted and transferred by an irate minister. There would be talk of petitions for a while and there would be newspaper comment and the local member of the opposition would be unequivocal in his condemnation but when the initial rumpus subsided a new sergeant would take over and the old sergeant would be no more than a memory.

Luke had no wish to leave Ballybobawn. It had become his home and for some time he had been on the look-out for a modest house where he might spend his retirement. There was also the fact that in the village resided the one person who was rarely out of his thoughts. Despite his overtures on the night he had visited the premises with Thomas Connelly there had been no appreciable change in their relationship. He sensed that she would never re-marry. He had, more or less, decided that he would settle for the warm friendship which had developed between them over the years. There was a chasteness about the woman which, while not altogether forbidding, was almost nun-like. He simply could not visualise a situation whether married or otherwise which would see them in bed together.

Sadie Calahane would regard any form of close physical contact with a man as gross infidelity and this despite the fact that she had been a widow for almost as long as Luke could remember. She admitted privately to herself that the sergeant was a fine, decent man. She liked his presence in the community and even more so in the pub but she saw to it that the counter always remained between them. Neither did she entertain any fantasies about him and on the rare occasions when his face intruded she quickly entwined her Rosary beads around her fingers and prayed fervently and successfully for his eviction from her thoughts.

When Luke rose from his temporary seat he decided against a round of the village. There was something in the air which he found disturbing, an undefinable sense of foreboding which seemed to grow more tangible as the days went by. He grew even more apprehensive when he found himself indoors. It was as if there was no escape from the unavoidable and oncoming gloom. He feared not for himself but for more vulnerable parties yet to be identified by cruel circumstance. He decided to return to the outside and longed for nightfall when he might slip into the Widow's and partake of a pint with one of his farming friends. He would give the Load of S a miss for the present. He would play that particular business by ear and hope for the best.

On the roadway he encountered the Stringer McCallum. He was on his way, Luke guessed quite rightly, to the supermarket where top-secret negotiations must surely be taking place. The Stringer dismounted from his bicycle as he drew abreast of the sergeant.

'Tis horrible warm,' the Stringer opened.

'Tis all that surely,' Luke replied as he took stock of the Stringer out of the corner of his eye. He looked even more haggard than he normally did, if such a thing is possible, Luke told himself.

'Anything new?' Luke asked.

'Nothing much,' the Stringer responded lazily, 'except that Bob's Biddy is to be married to one of them Killillys from Galway. At least that's the news that's going around. The Monday after Puck fair they say. You might like to know that Bob's clan will be stopping over for a night or two in Ballybobawn when the wedding celebrations are over.'

'Oh dear, oh dear!' Luke shook his head. 'I could name certain people who won't like that.'

'One thing is sure,' the Stringer spoke with authority, 'and that is you'll have less grass after them than you had before.'

Everyone has his own trouble, Luke thought.

'Do you know what should be done to them?' the Stringer spoke without malice and without waiting for Luke to ask. 'One in every four of 'em should be shot and the rest castrated. That would be my remedy. That way they wouldn't hang around a place too long and the grass would get a chance to shoot.'

'You're sure of the marriage?' Luke asked.

'Sure as sure can be. The talk is that the money Bob's Katie stole from the Cronane's was stole from Bob Latty and he drunk and now he has to sell his horses and foals to pay for the wedding.'

'I hope there won't be any trouble when they arrive here afterwards.' Luke hoped that his wish would be interpreted as the warning it really was.

BOB LATTY'S HERD CONSISTED of two mares, two geldings, a sire and two foals, all of them skewbald and of chiefly Clydesdale strain, the mares and geldings showing fresh summer fat, the stallion less presentable, due no doubt, to the fact that he was the only source of service to the mares of the travelling people for miles around. A third mare had been killed instantly by an articulated lorry which failed to stop. The foals were both fillies and in this the first summer of their lives they displayed a rare fettle which would disappear forever after the hardship of the first winter without shelter or adequate fodder.

The lot of the travellers' herd was not a happy one. They were often required to travel prodigious distances from one fair to another. The Latty's had not yet risen to the price of a horse box and not one of the numerous bands of travelling folk in the south-west of the country was possessed of a cattle or horse truck. Grazing was always hard to come by. Some of the settled travellers often rented run-down pastures but such would be the state of these after the hooves of the giant skewbalds had finished with the rain-softened crust that a second tenure was rarely granted. In the first place the pasture would have to be of truly inferior quality before its owner would consider letting it to the travelling fraternity. Another disquieting feature of this type of rental was that the horses of the travellers had a habit of showing up quite mysteriously in greener fields close by. Consequently the proprietors of likely letting fields were actively discouraged from dealing with the travellers. Other sources of grazing were disused railway lines and the margins of by-roads as well as any and all land not properly enclosed.

Bob Latty could not remember how he came to be parted from his money. He had been drinking with his McMunley in-laws for two days when an overwhelming desire for sleep seized him. He fell to the ground near a deserted encampment and crawled under a pony cart where he fell into a deep sleep. The pressure of urine in his bladder awakened him after several hours and it was while he relieved himself by the side of the cart that he thought to ensure that the roll of notes was still intact in his breast pocket. There was nothing there, not even the safety pin which he used to close off the mouth of the pocket lest the money fall out.

'Thieves!' he cried out as soon as he verified that he had not transferred the money to another pocket. 'Robbing thieves that won't have a day's luck from here to the grave.'

His condemnation went unheard. There was nobody to be seen. The camp-site, abandoned but for the cart, was more than a mile from the town of Killorglin where the festivities were still in full swing. For a moment the thought struck him that he should visit the garda barracks and report the theft and theft it was for he remembered quite clearly checking the still substantial roll and the safety pin which closed the pocket just before he fell asleep. For all his weariness and drunkenness he had thoroughly secured the money. There was no doubt in Bob Latty's mind that the theft had been perpetrated by an old hand, a female most likely, who bided her time until the ever-adjusting body presented the required opening. He found his wife sitting on an upturned box at the bottom of the town. She was in the act of gorging herself with a double portion of French fries.

'Where were you, you bitch?' he screamed as he struck her with the flat of his hand across the face, knocking her off the box and sending the French fries flying around the street. It was certainly not the first time that Bob's Katie had shown her myst-ification after she had been at the receiving end of a husbandly wallop; but then Bob Latty never needed a reason for striking his wife. What was unusual in her eyes was that he struck her in public for all to see and in a town near where her brothers and sisters were encamped for the week. She struck back quickly as soon as she found herself erect. She landed two telling blows with her fist. It was the element of surprise that sent him reeling. He prepared for an all-out onslaught, clenching both his fists just as a member of the civic guards came into view.

Later when she discovered the cause of his wrath she set about consoling him. She plied him with large bottles of stout which she had purchased in the town. Out in the night after they had fully bemoaned their loss they concluded that there was no use in crying over spilled milk. There was no chance of recovering the money and he had, after all, been fair game and who was to say but he would not have done the same himself.

'The horses will have to go for the present.' There was resignation in Bob Latty's voice. It was the latter part of the statement which held the key to the banking system of the travellers. Horses, ponies and donkeys were no longer used for transporting carts and caravans. They were now a form of security, money on the hoof so to speak, only to be sold when age or disease made it a necessity or on very special occasions such as funerals and weddings when large sums would be needed to cover the heavy expenses involved.

It was after midnight in the brightly-lit, mid-Kerry town when Bob Latty and Katie discovered the man they were looking for. He was seated in the midst of a circle of inebriated cronies.

'That's far enough,' the woman behind the counter announced the moment the travellers appeared in the doorway.

"Tisn't for drink we're looking missus,' Bob's Katie assured her, 'all we want is a word with Mister Cone.'

'Stay there,' the woman issued the command firmly. 'I'll get him for you.'

Joe Cone was none too pleased as he made his way to the doorway. He knew straight off why the Latty's sought him out. Concealing his real feelings he shook hands with both and asked how he might be of assistance.

'I'm selling off the horses,' Bob Latty informed him.

'You hardly expect me to look them over this hour of the night!' Joe Cone told him.

'I wouldn't want you to do that,' said Bob Latty, 'the morning will do grand. The reason I came so late was that I thought you might be gone home, the fair being nearly over and all that.'

'I'll be out to see them some time around the noon of the day,' Joe promised.

'I'll be expecting you so,' Bob hung his head before making his second request.

'Is there 'ere a chance you'd call a drink for us Mister Cone?'

'I'll call all right,' Joe agreed, 'but will she serve!'

'Will you give this poor man and his wife a drink missus?' Joe called loudly to the woman behind the counter. The look he received by way of response suggested that he should have known better.

'What did I tell you,' Joe Cone turned and rejoined his friends.

'That it might scour you!' Bob's Katie called out to the barwoman as she followed her husband onto the street. The imprecation fell on deaf ears as did

222

the others which followed as she trailed her husband down the street.

'I'LL GIVE YOU TWO thousand for the lot.' Joe Cone made the offer as though he were indulging in an act of unparalleled munificence. The proposal was greeted with loud laughter. The travellers knew that another thousand would not be an overrated estimate of the herd's true worth.

'Laugh away,' Joe said haughtily before turning his back on the group and opening the door of the horse truck before entering the cabin. His left leg stalled as he pulled himself upward. He knew that he would be restrained as was the fashion and led back to the parley so that negotiations might be resumed. The itinerant group consisted of Bob Latty and his fifteen year old son Neddy, Bob's brothers-in-law Phelim, Joss and Jay McMunley and an elderly travelling man by the name of Sherbet with a good eye for horse flesh and a penchant for bargaining. If a deal was negotiated and money changed hands he would receive a small commission from both the vendor and the purchaser. It was he who prevented Joe from entering the cabin and it was he who outlined the merits of the animals for sale. Traditionally the womenfolk of the travellers were never allowed to participate in the bargaining. They might, at their own risk, watch from a respectful distance but if a deal fell through their presence in the vicinity might be called into account. When Sherbet finished Joe spoke and the travellers listened. They might not believe all he would say but Joe never failed to entertain and they were always intrigued and amused by his manner of saying it.

'I don't want the horses,' Joe began. 'I have too many horses already. Besides one of those geldings is on his last legs. Look at his eyes and they the colour of two gold sovereigns. We all know what that means.' Joe went immediately to the geldings head and rapped the animal's forehead with his knuckles. It was not a cruel blow. Rather was it a sharp rap which in normal circumstances would have no effect whatsoever on a shire-size gelding. On this occasion the gelding fell backward on its haunches, its flanks trembling, its eyes opening to reveal flashes of the sovereign yellow to which Joe had earlier alluded.

'Cirrhosis poor chap,' Joe concluded professionally as he commenced an examination of the other horses. Joe's diagnosis was correct. Cirrhosis was the most common of all maladies among the horses of the travellers. As the Lattys, father and son and their in-laws, assisted the gelding to its feet Joe announced that the creature would be lucky to survive the journey to the abattoir which was over fifty miles away. Here horses were slaughtered for export to the continent, particularly the countries of France and Belgium.

'We'll leave the invalid out of the reckoning,' Joe suggested, 'until he arrives in one piece at his destination.'

Joe approached the stallion with understandable caution. Faster men than he had been maimed by rogues of the species.

'What sort of manners has this fullball?'

'The same as a child Mister Cone,' Bob assured him.

'In that case,' said Joe, 'you hold him by the head while I look at his teeth.' The dental examination concluded, Joe's expert hands moved over the shoulders and withers, then over the back and croup, stopping at the fetlock which he gingerly lifted before conducting an examination of the hooves. The skilled palm moved along the flank and ribs before finally patting the twitching shoulder. The teeth had already told Joe most of what he wanted to know about the stallion but he liked to show his expertise in the handling of horses. The travellers would be the first to admit that Joe knew his business and would hardly be duped at this stage of his career. The mares came next. Hobbled and subdued they submitted themselves for examination, beginning with the teeth and this time followed by a lifting of the tails. Satisfied, Joe suddenly turned and clapped his hands. The fillies, startled by the unexpected report, galloped over the roadway, their movements free and fluent.

Satisfied that they were without blemish Joe grinned and extracted his upper set of dentures. He returned them immediately before frowning and covering his face with his hands. It was obvious to the onlookers that bewildering calculations were taking place inside his head.

'Twenty-two hundred pounds,' Joe announced the result of the mental arithmetic with outstretched hands.

'Twenty-five hundred,' Sherbet took Joe's right hand and slapped it with his own.

'Can't be done,' Joe shook his head. 'Remember the invalid is not included.'

'Then include the invalid.' It was the first time Bob Latty spoke, 'for he's no use to me.'

'Right,' Joe's face assumed the same aura of munificence as when he made the first offer.

'Twenty-five hundred for the lot.'

'Twenty-eight,' from Sherbet.

'Twenty-six,' from Joe, 'and that's it for good and glory. Remember,' here Joe's voice assumed a deadly earnestness, 'this is holiday time in France and all the boarding schools are locked up. There's no demand for horsemeat or donkey meat or pony meat or any kind of nag meat. I'll have to feed these animals till the October fair bar the invalid who's for straightaway slaughter if he lives through the journey.'

'Twenty-seven hundred,' the plea came from Sherbet.

'You're out of your mind,' Joe told him. Then extending his hands in a plea for understanding, he listed the costs of the varying grazing and fodders which went into the feeding of horses.

'Do you know what they're charging for bed and breakfast in the pound in Tralee town?' Joe asked.

Sherbet shook his head, already partly mesmerised by the trader's free-flowing lingo.

'Thirty pounds and there's no extras included in that. You know what a veterinary charges these days and you ask me to fork out twenty-seven hundred for half a lorry load of horseflesh!'

'Twenty-six and a half hundred,' Sherbet relented.

'I have to go,' Joe opened the cab door for the second time. 'I'm a busy man and I've wasted a morning for nothing.'

'Twenty-six hundred it is then,' Bob called out.

Joe turned and from an inside pocket produced a wad of bank notes several inches thick. As he peeled off the hundred pound notes the travellers gathered round whistling their admiration at the unprecedented display. The transfer finished, Joe's assistant, a burly-looking man in his twenties, nicknamed the Pony Corgan, came down from the cab to help with the loading. Only then did Bob's Katie and Bob's Biddy present themselves.

'Where's my luck money?' Joe demanded.

Bob Latty handed over a twenty pound note.

'There's many might say a hundred would be a fairer figure,' Joe pouted.

'Something for the daughter Mister Cone! She's getting married in two days time!' Bob's Katie pushed the blushing teenager into the limelight. After a brief inspection Joe favoured her with a look of approval.

'She'll carry well,' he announced, 'that's if she's not carrying already.' He handed her the twenty pound note which Bob had given him and withdrew another from his pocket.

'Take that,' he said with a smile, 'and don't ever let a day come when you have to sell your horses.'

Bob's Biddy smiled her gratitude.

'What a charming girl,' Joe thought, 'but already with a price on her head so to speak through no fault of her own.'

'Come for a drink,' Bob invited, 'the night of the wedding.'

'I could do worse!' Joe returned although it was the farthest notion from his head. Knowing the Lattys and their present in-laws not to mention the new in-laws, Joe Cone decided that it would not be in the best interests of a wily horse-blocker to attend the festivities.

Pony Corgan often spied on the travellers from the shelter of the dense alder groves which overlooked the Ogle river. It was from such a vantage point that he watched Bob's Biddy dance in the moonlight a few weeks before. He was quite overcome by the suppleness of limb and perfection of form but if he had eyes for the young travelling girl

227

her eyes were directed elsewere and her performance was geared to impress one person more than any other. That person was young Red Killilly, an eighteen-year-old and the oldest boy of his approving parents.

Pony was a man well-versed in the lore of the travelling folk and a man intimately acquainted with their comings and goings, particularly the Latty clan for whom he cherished a consuming hatred. The Pony's aversion was born of rebuff. When he let it be known to Joe Cone that he might be disposed towards a union between himself and Bob's Biddy provided that she would come and reside with himself and his ageing mother in their cottage on the Cork road a mile beyond the suburbs of Trallock Joe passed on word of his assistant's amorous intent.

The disclosure occasioned much laughter in the Latty family. Apart from the normal reluctance to marry outside the travelling fraternity it was felt that Pony Corgan was less than human. Certainly his barrel-chested upper regions and his bandy legs were hardly likely to appeal to a teenage girl. His mouthful of discoloured teeth were no advantage either but worst of all was the fact that he had been rejected outright by every available girl in the settled community. This was well-known to the Latty parents who were not unaware of the Pony's attentiveness. Still in the best interests of the young lady in question it was felt that she should be acquainted with the Pony's proposal. Typically she sat down and considered the advantages and disadvantages and in the end came forward with an emphatic negative. Pony had the reputation of being a bully boy and something of a scourge when under the influence of alcohol which was more often than not.

'Tell him,' Bob's Katie informed Joe Cone, mustering all of her customary malice, 'to go and get himself gelded for 'tis certain he'll not rear up on any travelling girl and you can tell him 'twas me said it!'

Joe Cone brought the bad news to the Pony, mentioning merely that the girl was not interested and was, most likely, promised to one of her own kind. Joe could not recall a single occasion where a girl from the travelling people had married a man from the traditionally settled community. Under pressure from the Pony he revealed the full text of the response from Bob's Katie. Instantly he regretted the decision. There appeared on the Pony Corgan's face a frightening look of intense hatred. The only sound that came from between his bared black teeth was a squeal of unsuppressed savagery.

14

AS THE RAM SAT in the kitchen reading the day's paper he was surprised to hear a car draw up at the front door. Nonie had departed for Trallock that evening on a Bingo bus and would not return until midnight.

'Come in!' the Ram called, lowering his paper wondering who his caller might be. He was astonished to behold the chubby but commanding figure of Mollie Cronane. She cut a striking pose clad as she was in a simple black frock without jewellery of any kind. She carried a matching handbag.

'I have never been alone with this woman,' the Ram of God told himself, 'and I'm glad because there is something positively sinister about her.'

The hairs tingled on his scalp as she closed the door behind her.

The Ram rose and offered her a seat. She declined stating that her business would be brief.

'I have come,' Mollie came quickly to the point, 'to ask you to put a price on the farm.'

Earlier that day she had received the cheque from Alfie Nesbitt. The Ram of God wished with all the fervour he could muster that somebody would knock at the door or that Nonie might return prematurely or for any form of interference that might in some way counteract the stunning power of her presence.

'The farm is not for sale,' he replied in what he hoped was an unequivocal manner. There could be no temporising with a woman as forceful as this.

'I have here in my purse your cheque which I received this morning.'

Mollie's tone had a shattering effect on the Ram. He found himself shaking. He laid a steadying hand on the back of the chair from which he had risen. He sensed the presence of evil in the kitchen. He was tempted for a moment to run towards the holy water font and cast its contents on this terrifying intruder.

Mollie continued in chilling tones. 'I have my husband's cheque for twenty-five thousand. That's a total of sixty thousand. Between them the McCallums will give you thirty-five thousand more. You will be ninety-five thousand pounds the richer and you will have the satisfaction of knowing that your nieces or nephews or whatever will never know want. Now what have you to say to that?'

She advanced a step. The Ram stood anchored to his chair, his palms clammy now, a cold sweat on his forehead.

'Don't tell me another time that the farm is not for sale,' Mollie cautioned with devastating earnestness, 'because I won't like that one bit.'

Unable to reply the Ram stood paralysed. 'This is the worst experience of my entire life,' he told himself.

'What sort of a bastard are you at all,' Mollie screamed, 'to deny your own flesh and blood the respectability that's their right? Do you think I'm going to stand aside and watch my grandchildren deprived of what is theirs by every natural law! Sweet Jesus man I'll give you this handbag across the mouth, buckle and all, if you give me any more guff about no sale. You give me the scour you do with your notions and you nothing but a common ram! How can you blame your brothers you moryah man of God when you sired before either of them knew what an erection was. You set them the example, you that mounted that Yankee woman and God alone knows how many more. Do you think that you're going to dictate to me with my daughters up the pole by your dead brothers? I'm warning you now Ram that I'll swing for you if you don't climb down.'

Try as he might the words refused to formulate in his mouth. He was convinced that she was the devil incarnate and there was in him, although deeply suppressed, a long-time fear that he would one day encounter the Prince of Darkness in some shape or form. He was right. The visitation was taking place. The heaving breasts and flashing eyes repelled him. He collapsed on to his chair, unable to utter a single word. He fumbled in his pockets for his Rosary beads but they were nowhere to be found on his person. Fearfully he recalled that he had left them in the bedroom that very morning after he had offered prayers for the repose of the souls of his brothers. Weakly he raised his right hand and made the sign of the cross. The creature who now towered over him seemed not to notice. She was belching forth words of fire once more.

'I don't want your money and I don't want your blessings and I don't want your sympathy. All I want is what is mine. Now like a good man you'll accept my offer and we'll depart friends.'

'No!' The Ram of God never knew where the word came from. Maybe it was his guardian angel who imparted it through the medium of God to his lips. Whoever or whatever it was it had not surfaced naturally. The solitary negative seemed altogether to inflame the dancing demon who seemed to grow in stature every time she opened her mouth. He found the spittle of her vehemence striking his face like the warm spume of a suddenly disturbed summer sea. Like the very tide of that same sea she seemed to assume a superhuman force. Suddenly her tone dropped. She was hoarse now with a depth that seemed to come from her very core.

'Or do you want me to take off my knickers Ram. Is that it? Would that swing the issue Ram? Is that what you're holding out for? You can answer me Ram. You won't find me unwilling.'

Slowly she unbuttoned her dress to reveal a surprisingly attractive body. She wore no underclothes. Her skin was sallow, her breasts full and still possessed of the trembling agitation she had once used with such powerful effect on Tom Cronane. As the dress fell to the floor she turned, full circle, addressing him with dark eyes filled with lustful invitation.

'I've always had a secret yen for you,' she whispered throatily. She held her palms over the inviting breasts. Suddenly the Ram of God came to life but not in the way that Mollie anticipated. He pushed her to one side with a despairing cry and was gone through the front door before she could stop him. Behind him he could hear her screams of rage, her litany of profanities infinitely more devastating than anything Bob's Katie could ever hope to devise. The Ram vanished through a gap in the hawthorn hedge which skirted the roadway before she emerged from the house. He ran for all he was worth until her voice was rendered silent by the distance he put between them. He found himself, eventually, at the High Meadow. He vaulted the iron gate startling the calves and yearlings as they lay in their nocturnal retirement. For the first time

233

he walked. Turning, he could see below him in the moonlight the outline of the house. Then he heard a car splutter and start. The headlights came on and the vehicle sped down the incline which led to the cross of Ballybobawn. The Ram experienced a relief that was blessed in its salving mercy. He stayed put until he saw the lamp of Nonie's bicycle as she cycled uphill from the cross.

THE MORNING AFTER MOLLIE Cronane's invasion the Ram of God had another visitor.

'I came,' Father Harry Hehir explained after he had taken a seat, 'because I feel you are doing the wrong thing by the Cronane girls. I'm no diplomat. Like Caesar I am a plain, blunt man. I am not here solely of my own accord. Father O'Connor suggested that you and I might have more in common, being of the same age and all that! I am simply asking you to see reason Edward. There is a growing feeling of ill-will in the parish.'

'And I know who's responsible,' the Ram of God interrupted, 'none other than Mollie Cronane. She came here last night and offered me her body if I would relent. I tell you this because I know it will go no further but I want you to know the type of woman she is.'

'The poor creature is in desperate straits. She would never do such a thing but for being driven to it. I'm sure you'll hear no more from her. You must understand Edward that a mother will do anything to protect her young.'

'Of course,' the Ram of God agreed, 'but I must also protect myself and that is why I visited Alfie Nesbitt this morning and instructed him to draft a letter to Mollie Cronane. If she interferes with me in any way ever again she will answer in a court-room.'

'You've changed Edward. You are no longer a man of God. You are a man of property first.'

'Not so,' the Ram replied. 'If I were to part with the land it would be violating a trust. I believe it is the will of God that led to the events which left me with the land in the first place. I am convinced that I was destined to own that land. It is a most precious property and not because of the cows it maintains or the cattle it fattens. It is a special place to me and the High Meadow is a sacred place, sacred to the memory of my mother who loved to walk there. It is my mother's shrine. I will not have it defiled. The Cronane sisters have been treated generously and I have no more to say on the matter.'

'And you think you have the strength of character and mind to become a priest?' Harry Hehir raised his voice, 'when you will renege on your moral duty. For heaven's sake man give the land to those who are entitled to it. It's not as if they wanted it for nothing. You will be well remunerated.'

In spite of himself the Ram found that he also raised his voice. 'I don't see what business it is of yours!' he declared.

'These girls are my parishioners,' Harry Hehir shouted back. 'I have a scared duty to see to it that their children are born in wedlock. I am entrusted with their moral well-being as I am with yours and with every other person's living in this parish. I am obliged, therefore, to point out to you that what you are doing here is a dereliction of your moral obligations. If I failed to do this I would be abro-gating my priestly responsibility. I thought you, of all people, should understand this! The Church cannot remain inactive in a matter like this. The future of innocent children is at stake here.'

'You are exceeding yourself,' the Ram of God hurled the words at the curate. 'I have discharged my moral obligations fully. If you listen you will hear the cattle trucks outside this very window. I have sold the entire dairy herd in order to discharge those obligations and you now come here and tell me that I should give more!'

'Boys! Boys!' It was the voice of Nonie who was listening from the kitchen. 'Lower your voices or the pair of you will be the talk of the parish. There's cattle trucks ouside and there's cars and this is just the sort of thing that's needed to get things going.'

'I have no reason to be silent,' Harry Hehir announced in greatly modified tone. 'I have nothing to be ashamed of.'

Still expostulating for the benefit of those outside he joined a group who had gathered in front of the leading cattle truck. It was immediately clear to the Ram of God that the aim of this group was to prevent the loading of the milch cows which were herded together in the yard at the rear of the house.

Tom Cronane was the most vocal of the group. Willie Halvey stood by his side. The Ram was surprised to see Joe McCallum prominently figuring. The Stringer stood with Tomboy Cronane. Tomboy worked full-time in the supermarket since Cha's departure. There were several other farmers. These avoided the Ram's searching eyes and began to closely inspect their boots and shoes. As the trucks moved at snail's pace into the yard there was loud shouting. This was orchestrated by Tom Cronane who warned the drivers that they would be taking their lives in their hands should they leave their vehicles. An hour passed then another. The drivers sat impassively in their cabs. The protestors sat on hay bales, determined to hold out until the empty trucks left the yard.

Two hours would pass before Alfie Nesbitt arrived in answer to the Ram of God's phone call. Standing on a hay bale he addressed the protestors.

'You are all breaking the law,' he informed his listeners. 'In the first place you are trespassing on private property and secondly you are causing an obstruction. I must now ask you to leave peacefully. Otherwise I will be obliged to have you removed forcibly by the civic guards.'

The farmers in the group exchanged uneasy glances. The McCallums looked to Tom Cronane for direction.

Alfie stepped down from the hay bale and intimated to Tom that he wished to have words with him. Both men moved to the front of the house.

'Why should you cut your own throat Cronane?' Alfie asked when he was sure they were out of earshot of the others. 'I thought that at least you would have more sense.'

Tom looked uncomprehendingly at the smaller man.

'If,' Alfie raised an admonishing finger, 'those cattle do not arrive at the mart in Trallock this evening, that cheque I sent you will be worthless. If you want to see thirty-five thousand pounds go down the drain that's your business. The way you're going about things now you'll wind up with nothing!'

Tom considered the lawyer's proposal. There

was merit in what he said. Tom stood undecided for awhile, still considering.

'There won't be any loss of face,' Alfie assured him. 'Just walk back there and call it off.'

'Easily said,' Tom thrust his hands into his trouser pockets dejectedly. 'The future of my daughters and my grandchildren is at stake here Nesbitt.'

'Your concern is understandable Tom,' Alfie was at his most placatory, 'but thirty-five thousand pounds in the hand is worth more than a farm of land to which you have no legal claim. Go on back there and do the right thing. Confrontation with Edward Drannaghy will get you nowhere. He has the law firmly on his side.'

'It's not over yet,' Tom warned as he moved to the rear of the house.

That night he sat in the kitchen of the supermarket with his wife Mollie, his daughters Kate and Noreen and his most recently acquired allies the Stringer and Joe McCallum. The remaining members of the family Sammie, Donie and Tomboy were sent off about their business earlier in the night. Tomboy had managed to misappropriate the sum of thirty pounds during his first week in the supermarket and this was why the happy trio sat contentedly, sipping from pints of cider, in the sanctum of the Load of S. There were serveral teenagers from the district also present. Some new films arrived that morning and the first of these was now on show. It consisted of a medley of contrasting systems of sexual intercourse often involving several participants. The climax of each performance was greeted with derisory hoots and bawdy cheers.

Mollie sat at the head of the table, a sheet of

foolscap in her hand. Already on the table were three such sheets, filled from top to bottom with the names and addresses of nearly three hundred people. Everybody who was anybody or even remotely approaching anybody in the parish of Ballybobawn figured in the invitations. Mollie decided on the extra guests for a number of reasons. She would need all the available goodwill in the district in the coming weeks and now that they had decided to accept the Ram of God's cheque they would celebrate by way of a bigger and better splurge. The proceedings came to a sudden halt when Noreen, unexpectedly, asked if it was her parents' intention to invite the Ram of God to the wedding. The question hung in the air for a long time.

'Why not?' Tom eventually asked.

'He wouldn't come,' Mollie toyed with her biro.

'How do you know?' Noreen asked.

'It's like a thing the bastard would do,' Kate came to her aid.

'Put his name down,' Tom dismissed the matter with an expansive wave of the hand. Laboriously Mollie wrote the name and address on the foolscap under her hand.

'What about the sergeant?' the Stringer asked innocently.

'I'd invite the devil first!' Mollie retorted viciously.

'We could invite Garda Connelly,' Tom suggested, 'He's a harmless sort and that way we would be recognising the law.'

'Better on our side than not,' the Stringer approved.

'And it would be a nice kick in the arse to Holly,' Mollie agreed as she added Thomas Connelly's name to the lengthening list.

In the street ouside Luke Holly stood with his back against the lamp-post. He saw the McCallums enter the supermarket and the sons of the house of Cronane enter the Load of S. The street was its quiet self with not a soul abroad. The only creature stirring was a black cat which furtively crossed from one side of the street to the other before disappearing into an alleyway where his arrival was greeted by the seductive mewing of an unseen she-cat.

Luke braced himself, no longer undecided. Routinely he walked past the Load of S but then turned suddenly and burst through the front door and was in the parlour of ecstasy before the barman had a chance to change from the video to one of the channels.

'Stay as you are!' he commanded, as the Cronane brothers tried to rush past him to freedom.

'I'll have that,' Luke indicated the film being shown. Luke had never seen a blue movie. He was horrified by the sheer abandon of the nude performers, the degradation and shameful exposition of the human form but most of all by the awesome prospect of its perverting influences. He pocketed the cassette which the barman handed to him.

'Now I'll have the others,' he said coldly. When he was certain that all the tapes were acounted for he sampled the contents of the glasses which were still partly filled all around.

'You agree that this is cider,' he addressed himself to the barman.

There came a frightened nodding of the head by way of response.

'You must be aware that these people are under the age limit?'

To this there came no reply.

'The premises will be prosecuted for serving intoxicating drink to minors and if I ever catch you serving another teenager or showing another of these vile cassettes I will personally break your jaw and to hell with my job!'

As the cider was being emptied Luke turned on the Cronanes and the several other under-age drinkers who occupied 'the parlour of ecstasy' as one local wag called it.

'Go on home,' he said quietly, 'and don't ever darken the door of these premises again. If I see any one of you come through that door I will go immediately to your parents and your teachers and inform them of this whole sordid business.'

Sheepishly they filed out into the night. Luke was gratified to note that there were no covert verbal exchanges and no sniggering. A summons would be served on Willie Halvey, the proprietor, for permitting minors to be served on his premises. For the sake of the young people, and the parish as a whole, Luke would overlook the showing of the pornographic films. These he would hand over to Father O'Connor who could consult with his bishop.

The McCallum brothers and the Cronane sisters repaired to Tom's Tavern after the invitations had been finalised. The girls sat together in one of the four musty alcoves which had once been the talk of Ballybobawn but which had now faded into a declining second place after the renovations to the Load of S. Musty the plush alcoves might be, but the bar was clean and bright and Tom, the proprietor, was as genial a fellow as one would meet in a day's walk.

While the Stringer called the drinks his brother Joe stood by his side at the bar counter. Joe felt

241

that he was not yet sufficiently acquainted with Noreen to talk directly to her without the aid of his brother who had known Kate for years.

The Cronane sisters stretched their bodies and spread their legs in the alcove. They indulged in a bout of tittering induced by the ungainly stances of the brothers and Joe's reluctance to face the women without the support of his brother. The drink consisted of two half-pints of lager for the ladies and two half-pints of stout for the men. Tom Dudley could recall a time when the Cronane sisters, between them, would have little difficulty in downing a dozen pints of lager in the round of a night. They had sobered in the interim in every sense of the word. They had fallen upon hard times in Tom's eyes. The McCallums were regarded as nothing other than the bottom of the barrel in the marriage stakes. In truth, however, the sisters did not see them in this light. They were manageable men. Land would improve their looks and land they would have one way or the other before long.

When the brothers joined them Kate broke the ice by remarking what a fine man was Harry Hehir, the live-wire curate of Ballybobawn. Her sister enthusiastically agreed. Father Harry had ranged himself on the side of the Cronanes with the approval of his parish priest and for once with the approval of his bishop who saw the Cronane girls' determination to have their babies at home in their own village as an act of hallmarked Catholicism. They might quite easily and with the Church's approval have gone away and had their babies in a nursing home run by a religious order and then handed over the babies for adoption but no! They had faced up to the challenge and they had not been found wanting. They might have, at an earlier

242

stage in their pregnancies, taken a plane to London and availed of any one of the medically approved abortion clinics in which the city abounded. It was the fashionable thing in recent times, a trend which outraged the bishop although Harry Hehir had more modified views on the subject. In this instance, however, he was one-hundred-per-cent on the side of the sisters and could not praise their decision highly enough.

'It's a heartening sign in these evil times,' the bishop told the curate.

'It is my Lord,' Harry Hehir, with a view towards a transfer to a more populous town, most fervently concurred.

'Is there do you think,' the bishop asked, 'a possibility that the action of these girls might help reverse the terrible trend towards abortion?'

'I have no doubt about it my Lord, no doubt whatsoever.'

Some parish with a good golf course would be the answer to his prayers. Work he would not mind so long as the course was a challenge.

'Then stand fast with the girls,' the bishop urged.

'I'll stand fast my Lord. Have no doubt about that.' The interview terminated after Father Hehir promised that he would pay a second visit to the Ram of God.

'You might intimate to him in the nicest possible terms that I cannot any longer offer my patronage to a man who places material things before his vocation. I will not stand in his way. Let that be clear but I cannot be associated with a person who observes double standards. Be discreet! This is a delicate business. There is much more here than meets the eye. The stakes are high.'

Joe McCallum found himself boasting about the prime condition of his weanlings which in turn prompted the Stringer to delcare that if meadows were properly manured after cutting, the fattening power of the aftergrass could not be surpassed. The Cronane sisters remained dutifully serious at these and other equally perceptive disclosures. The girls swapped looks from time to time but it wasn't until Joe announced in passing that natural dung was preferable to factory fertilisers that the girls surrendered their restraint and burst out into peals of laughter. The brothers' faces registered unconcealed alarm but they quickly entered into the spirit of the thing when Kate conspiratorially elbowed the Stringer in the ribs and Noreen slapped Joe on the thigh.

15

THE CREEL CHILDREN, SIX in number, ranged in ages from sixteen downwards to four. There had been three miscarriages and there would have been more children but a hysterectomy had dramatically terminated Maggie Creel's years of fecundity. Mickey Creel was recognised by all as a good-for-nothing although his worst enemies would agree that he was good for fathering children and for wheedling drinks.

In the latter art he had acquired a proficiency which was one of the great boasts of the country-side. Strangers who included him in rounds felt inexplicably that it was they who were being accorded the favour. He was attentive, respectful and worshipful to whomsoever might offer him a drink. At home he was a tyrant who imposed a never ending reign of terror on his wife and children.

Once, after her fourth child, Maggie found that she was unable to take any more. With her family in tow she set out for her mother's home in the mountains, several miles away. She was coolly received but bedded down with her children for the night and incontrovertibly returned home by pony and cart before noon of the following day. She was cautioned she was never to leave home again, sentiments heartily endorsed by Mickey who, to make sure she observed her parents injunction, administered the severest beating up until that time when he returned from Tom's Tavern.

Mary was the eldest child. Her father's initial

disappointment that she had not been born a boy was soured still further when a second baby girl followed. In her life there were three periods of happiness. The first was when she was seven years of age. Her grandparents invited her to spend the summer in their home in the hills. She grew to love the old couple. Her grandfather quickly became the centre of her life. When he died suddenly the year following that first holiday Mary was heartbroken. Her grandmother pined after her partner of a lifetime and died in her sleep after a period of decline towards the end of the same year.

Mary's second encounter with happiness began the Easter Nonie Spillane invited her to help out around the farmhouse. The insecurity and humiliation which had confounded her all her life seemed to dissolve in the gentle and compassionate presence of the Ram of God. She found Nonie a rare tonic. The teenager began to experience life in a world where humour and goodness and a sense of loyalty seemed to be the essentials. The isolated incident, so totally at variance with life on the farm, slipped her mind less than a week after its occurrence. She never once thought of it afterwards and her relationship with both twins had grown into something which the rough and ready pair would quietly acknowledge was not without affection.

Her third period of happiness began after she encountered Tomboy Cronane on several different occasions as she walked to the cross of Ballybobawn swinging the gallon of milk which the Ram of God filled for her every evening. At first his presence was concealed by the roadside hedge but she knew he was at the other side and that he would accompany her unseen to the bottom of the long field which ended at the crossroads. Eventually he revealed himself and as the spring days lengthened he met her nearer the farmhouse and relieved her of the milk gallon but under no circumstances would he carry it further than the cross of Bally-bobawn. To do so would have been to invite ridicule from his friends and brothers.

In the warmth of April they began to meet after dark and on the fourth night of that month they exchanged their first kisses under a full moon. A week later under the influence of cider and hardly knowing how it had come about Mary found herself unable to resist the intimate advances of Tomboy. It happened in the darkness of the store at the rear of the supermarket. At another later date, also induced by cider, Mary yielded to impulses she could not fully comprehend. However, after she began to realise the folly of what she was doing, not to mention the risks involved, she refused to countenance any further intimacies. Tomboy threatened he would never speak to her again and, foolishly, as she found out to her cost, she relented.

By that time it was too late. In the parlance of the older women of the village she had the poison taken. Her fleeting days of happiness came to an end forever. She became a martyr to intolerable feelings of shame.

It was, however, the vicious verbal attack by Mollie Cronane that fully brought home the unworthiness she felt. When, without any warning, Tomboy stopped seeing her she gave him the benefit of the doubt and was prepared to believe that he was merely avoiding temptation.

As the summer days went by and she found herself advancing in pregnancy with nothing to do except to steer clear of her father, she began to look around her objectively at other girls in the village and its surrounds.

'It was inevitable,' she told herself, 'that this would happen to the likes of me. I have the right address, the right background and I come from the right kind of parents. It comes as a surprise to the respectable matrons of places like this if I manage to keep myself intact. I have done what was expected of me and the awful thing is that I am becoming resigned to it because, since it is expected of me, I am free to sit and wait.'

She felt too that she betrayed the people to whom she might turn. In her eyes they were the good and the pure and she would do anything rather than call upon Nonie Spillane or Patricia Cahalane or the Ram of God. There had been a long night when she waited for the Ram on the boithrin which ran from the cross of Ballybobawn to the house and beyond but he had not appeared on the roadway. She had peeped in the window of the kitchen and she saw Nonie fussing about with an extinguished cigarette butt between her lips. There was an instant while Nonie was expelling the butt from her mouth before replacing it with a whole cigarette. Nonie looked perplexedly towards the window but it was obvious from the expression on her face that she saw nothing. Mary was tempted to rush into the kitchen but her shame got the better of her and the urge was suppressed. She felt like crying out and waiting for Nonie to come out to see who was there. Instead she cried silently to herself and hurried back the way she had come.

Then she fleetingly and unintentionally caught her father's eye one morning. His glance frightened her, brief as it had been. There was a skulkiness about him which led her to suspect that he might conduct an interrogation at any moment.

Since all his investigations began with a physical assault which rendered his victims incapable of any response other than blurting out the truth to stave off further punishment Mary decided to remove herself from his vicinity.

He sat, after that first glance, at the head of the table moistening his lips and casting hostile looks in her direction. Maggie Creel, sensing that he was whipping up sufficient frenzy for what might be a savage physical assault, announced that she saw a party of tourists alighting from a bus outside the Load of S. The desire for drink overcame the growing suspicions he harboured about his first-born and, anyway, he could deal with her later. He quickly rose and went out into the street. He would return at once to nail his wife's fabrication.

Seizing her opportunity Mary made her escape through the back door and ran through the narrow laneway until she reached a side-track which led her to the banks of the Ogle river and the cover of the groves which abounded there. Unfortunately, the rain which started several hours before was now at its heaviest. Still, anything was preferable to a confrontation with her father.

Drenched to the skin Mary sat huddled above the river while the rain-whipped surface steadily rose under the persistent downpour. She remained in the same contracted position allowing the rain to run down her face over her clothes, until eventually she was soaked to the skin. The rain was warm. The air, what little there was, had grown humid. No breeze disturbed the shining raindrops which rested on the broad leaves of chestnut and sycamore but trickling streams began to form at Mary's feet. She thought of postponing any positive decision about herself and the baby's future until after the results of the Intermediate examination were known but nova circumstances ordained otherwise.

Absently she blessed herself as the slow, sad pealing of the Angelus bell solidly impressed itself on flowing river and leafy groves. Mary found the drifting tones sepulchral and depressing. Unable to concentrate she abandoned all attempts to recite the prayers of veneration and returned instead to her own condition. She would not wallow in self-pity. There was no need. Were not the searing facts adequate testimony to her unshared misery! As she grieved over her lot a tiny rabbit appeared suddenly on the narrow pathway which skirted the river-bank. Halting for an instant it turned its terror-filled eyes on the creature overhead. Scurrying beneath a briar patch it disappeared from view. An oppressive silence hung over the glade after its departure. Then came a stoat, erect of head, sleek of frame. It paused too for an instant, raising a foreleg like a setter, quickly determining the intent of the creature overhead before dismissing any threat that might exist. Diabolical of mien, deadly of eye, it continued with its unthwartable pursuit. Mary looked round for a stone which she might fling after this loathsome intruder but there was none.

'I too know what it is to be hunted,' Mary Creel expressed herself aloud knowing that there would be nobody within earshot to convey her tale of woe to the people of the parish, most of them ravenous for any kind of bad news, true or false. 'I know it only too well,' she addressed herself to the scene all around, 'for I have been hunted now this long while. I'm only sixteen and nobody knows better than me what it's like to be out on a limb. I should be out and about with other girls of my age and I

250

should be free and unfettered. I know what it is to be hungry and I don't think anybody in the whole wide world knows better than I what it is to crave for a bit of style to put on my back.

'I know what it is to be molested and degraded and I know what it is to be used and I know what it is to lose faith. Oh God!' Mary spoke in chastening tones now, 'what if somebody heard me!' A gust of wind suddenly rustled the leaves in a nearby grove. Mary imagined it to be the reproachful breath intake of a scandalised parish.

She began to cry to herself as she saw nothing but hopelessness looming out of the future. So taken up was she with her own thoughts that she missed the death cry of the tiny rabbit who met with the piercing nippers of its executioner in the dark shade of a towering elm not twenty yards from where she sat.

Mary's decision to submit herself to the floodwaters of the Ogle River was made hastily in the end. One minute she was sitting on the little knoll above the Ogle River and the next she was being swept along by the surging floodwaters. The volition which dispatched her downwards was her own and yet she did not fully commit herself. She guessed that if she did not personally precipitate some action, however minor, that nothing whatsoever would happen. That was why she stood up and looked at the river as though it was about to befriend her in her hour of need. Then came the sudden conviction that what she really needed was oblivion.

When she found herself sliding down the slippery slope of the knoll she was tempted to cry out but a new and welcome passiveness absorbed any outcry she might make. As the river waters drew

near it seemed for a moment that she was participating in a game. It wasn't until she struck the
water that the shock alerted her to the awfulness of
the deed she was about to perpetrate on herself.
She was assailed by a chilling fear which she had
never before experienced. An agonising scream
escaped her trembling lips. As the flood swept her
along on its bosom she clawed vainly for a hold
which would bring her to safety.

'Oh Jesus I didn't mean it!' she called out but
there was no response, nothing save the deep
chuckle of the loam-rich flood. There were to be no
more words, splutterings and gaspings yes. And
then silence as the Ogle River bore her to the sea.

MARY WAS MISSING FOR six days but it wasn't until
her second night away from home that any sort of
alarm was raised. Even then there was no real
feeling of apprehension among the neighbours. In
recent times she displayed a tendency towards
moping and her brothers and sisters verified that
she spent most of her time out of doors in quiet
backwaters and seemed to have become altogether
addicted to seclusion. On the third day the villagers became uneasy when her brothers, Jonathan and Mícheál and her sister Susie, freely admitted to friends that she confided to them her intention of leaving home. She asked them to pray for
her but not to tell her parents. She promised to
keep in touch and to tell them of her whereabouts
when she eventually arrived at her destination.

The body was in the water for six days, surfacing at the end of the third and allowing itself to
be borne landwards and seawards at the whim of
the tides. It was discovered by the net fishermen of

the Ogle River estuary on the final day of their four-month-long season.

'THAT'S THE END OF it now please God!' Tom Cronane spoke with conviction when news of the tragedy reached him as he sat reading the *Independent* in his sitting-room. What Tom inferred to the Stringer McCallum who brought him the news was that the tragic cycle to which he ominously referred after Murt Drannaghy's funeral had now symbolically exhausted itself with the demise of the third victim.

'They go in threes,' he explained to the Stringer.

'Who found the body?' he asked.

'Ned Barber the fisherman was the first to sight it at the end of a haul. Himself and his son Mocky brought it ashore.'

'Do you know by any chance where it is now?' Tom asked.

'In Trallock General Hospital,' the Stringer informed him, 'and there it will stay until after the what-you-call?'

'The post mortem,' Tom suggested.

'That's the very thing,' the Stringer confirmed.

'Sacred heart of Jesus,' Mollie made the sign of the cross as she entered the sitting-room, ''tis a black day for Ballybobawn.

'Black as the ace of spades,' the Stringer agreed.

'And if there isn't a certain man's conscience troubling him this day,' Mollie lifted her dark eyes heavenwards, 'then there's no God there! That's all I have to say.'

'What are you talking about woman?' her husband asked in puzzlement.

'They say the poor creature was with child,' Mollie made the announcement with the assurance of a woman who was privy to this gruesome fact all along. She stood with hands folded, looking every inch the repository of even darker secrets but waiting to be asked and asked formally at that before yielding more precious gems from her store.

'And who do they say is the father of the child? Tom asked.

'Who else could it be but the Ram?' Mollie fairly hugged herself as she made the triumphant disclosure.

'Ah missus,' the Stringer found himself taking the Ram's side, 'that wouldn't be the man's style at all.'

'I'm not talking about style,' Mollie shrieked back at him. 'I'm talking about a Ram.'

The Stringer decided there and then that it was in his best interest to remain silent.

While Sergeant Holly and Guard Connelly stood awaiting the arrival of the ambulance from Trallock Superintendent Chaney arrived at the estuary. He motioned to the sergeant that he should join him in his car. Luke, in answer to the superintendent's request for a progress report, informed his superior that he had taken statements from the fishermen who had discovered the body, and that he had notified the coroner.

'What in the name of Christ is happening here at all Luke? Have you any idea? This is the third death by misadventure in three months in a village the size of a shagging shirt button.'

'Just coincidence,' Luke answered calmly, too calmly for the superintendent's liking.

'This is the third spotlight in my bailiwick inside twelve weeks. Spotlights I don't want Luke.

254

Spotlights show up cracks and we have a few cracks haven't we?'

'I'm sure I don't know what you mean,' Luke sounded perplexed.

'This business about your confiscating films at the Load of S and threatening the manager with all sorts of crucifixion.'

'Purely in the line of duty,' Luke tried to sound matter of fact.

'And are you going ahead with the summons?' Superintendent Chaney asked.

'I have no choice,' Luke replied.

'You know what you're starting here Luke?'

'No!' Luke looked directly at the superintendent for the first time.

'Willie Halvey and the minister are inseparable,' the superintendent informed him.

'Everybody knows that', Luke returned.

'You give me those tapes and there will be no more about them and for the present keep away from the Load of S.'

'I can't do that,' Luke replied coldly.

'You keep a low profile for a while,' the superintendent spoke in hoarse tones, 'or we're all going to find ourselves in trouble.'

'I have nothing to hide,' Luke realised after he spoke that he must have sounded smug, too smug for the preservation of the calm the superintendent was struggling to maintain.

'I want none of your bloody heroics Holly,' the superintendent unleashed his fury on the sergeant. 'I have two sons attending university and I'll have a daughter attending next year with God's help. I need my job but even more than that I happen to need promotion if I'm going to make ends meet and give my children the education they deserve and

255

what do I find? I'll tell you what I find. I find one of my shagging sergeants bullshitting me about having nothing to hide as if the hoor was our Lord Jesus Christ. Listen to me now Holly, you son of a bitch and listen good. You haven't chick nor child and you may think you can afford to be cocky but you make one false move until the smoke from this latest fiasco blows over and you'll find yourself on the Saltee Islands knocking off seagulls instead of widows!'

'I resent that,' Luke raised his voice for the first time.

'Even if it isn't true it is what certain people believe and that is what concerns me,' the superintendent told him. 'I have a complaint that you drink in the Widow Cahalane's after hours and that there are far worse excesses going on there than in the Load of S. My informant is a respectable citizen and her information cannot be ignored.'

'Mollie Cronane again!' Luke shook his head in contempt.

'Just remember to walk on the balls of your toes for now,' the superintendent opened the door of his car, 'you can start making arrangements for a transfer from Ballybobawn. You should know by now that there has to be give and take in this game. I'll collect the tapes on my way back to Trallock. I don't expect to be here too long more. Let whoever comes after me mount a crusade. I'll brief him well.'

Doctor Billy O'Dell, bag slung across shoulder, was on his way from his Hillside Row home in Trallock to the golf course nearby when he was summoned by Superintendent Chaney. His afternoon surgery finished a quarter of an hour before. His wife who was also a doctor volunteered to

256

stand in for him until his return. All through the day he had looked forward to the eighteen-hole session in which he indulged, regardless of weather, three times a week. What now, he asked as the superintendent closed the car door behind him and advanced across the roadway.

'Can't it wait?' he asked when the burly police chief announced that his services were required at the hospital.

'Not this time,' the superintendent shook his head gravely. 'You know me well enough to know that the last thing I want is to interrupt a man on his way to the golf course.'

In the car there was silence for a few moments as they drove towards the hospital.

'What's so bad that it should come between a man and his golf?' Billy asked.

'There's been a drowning,' Joe changed gears as they drove through the town square. 'The body's in the morgue awaiting your arrival. The priest has come and gone.'

'I'll need a technician,' Billy suppressed a yawn.

'He's been alerted,' Joe informed him, 'he should be there before us.'

'Who's the victim anyway?' Billy tried to sound casual.

'A young girl from Ballybobawn, name of Creel.'

'Mary Creel?'

'Yes. I believe Mary was her name. Do you know her?'

'Yes. She's in the same class as my daughter at the convent. I met her once or twice. A pretty little thing.'

'She's not so pretty now I'm afraid.'

'How long has she been missing? Billy asked.

'Six days,' came the response.

'After six days she wouldn't be particularly pretty.' The casual exchanges helped steady him down. The cold truth was that he did not relish performing the post-mortem examination. He had only performed seven of the kind required now in twelve years. He would never get used to it. He had been a doctor for almost ten years when his wife suggested that he do a post-graduate course in pathology. It seemed logical enough at the time especially with the residency of Trallock General about to become vacant. The exam had presented no problem and the extra qualification proved to be the decisive factor when he found himself on a shortlist out of a large field for the Trallock residency.

The technician at Trallock General was an elderly fellow by the name of Digby Patton. A Londoner by birth he had come to Ireland after marrying a girl from the northern suburbs of Trallock. After a score of years in one of Dublin's busiest hospitals his wife spotted an advertisement in a weekly paper for a technician at Trallock General. Digby had, in his time, prepared hundreds of cadavers, mostly drowning casualties.

'Business is pickin' up mate,' he announced to Billy O'Dell as the latter donned his mask and gown.

'Anything unusual?' Billy asked.

'Naw! Nothing out of the ordinary 'cept maybe she's pregnant,' Digby informed him.

'How pregnant would you say she is?' Billy asked the question not out of curiosity but rather to test Digby's uncanny powers of detection. He had never known him to be wrong.

'Dunno for sure,' the technician replied as he surveyed the body, 'but I reckon she's four maybe

258

five months gone. Four I'd reckon.'

Billy knew that the Londoner had already made his own examination, far more comprehensive and revealing than any the doctor might make. Nothing escaped him.

'What the hell am I going to do when you retire Digby?' It wasn't the first time the question was posed.

'You'll know it all then mate won't you!' was the standard reply. The pair got on well. They made an efficient team.

'I'd better open the chest wall.' Billy prayed silently as he made the incision. It seemed a routine drowning. There was water in the lungs and that would have been that but for the pregnancy. As usual Digby was on target. There was the unmistakable darkening of the nipples. The increased pigmentation of the anatomy as a whole confirmed the findings of Digby.

'I'll have to open the stomach.' Billy grinned his dislike of the task ahead.

"Sawright mate you 'aven't 'ad supper yet!' Digby consoled.

Billy hesitated before making the second incision.

'Four months,' Digby's estimation of the age of the exposed foetus was exact as usual.

'You go on,' he said, 'law's waitin' for you. I'll zip 'er up.'

'Anything for me?' Joe Chaney asked as soon as the doctor appeared in the corridor. Silently intimating that the superintendent should follow him Billy headed straight for his office, opened a small cabinet and withdrew a bottle of Powers Gold Label and two glasses. He poured liberally into both and was half-way down his own before the superintendent had time to wish him sláinte. After a decent interval Joe Chaney spoke.

'Have you established the cause of death?' he asked.

'She died from drowning. There's no question about that but she was carrying a four month old foetus at the time so the matter doesn't end here.'

'Any marks on the body?' Joe rose and turned on a tap in the washbasin. He filled his glass with water and returned to his seat.

'There were no marks,' Billy's composure returned, 'not even a scratch. Certainly there was no struggle. There would be something to show for it if there was.'

'If she had been pushed unexpectedly from behind,' Joe suggested, 'there would be no mark.'

'True,' Billy agreed. 'All I can do, however, is inform the coroner and arrange a time for the inquest. No doubt you'll be making some kind of an investigation?'

'A discreet one but if you ask me it's just another pregnant girl who decided to end it all. There's only one man sweating over this and that's the father of that foetus or maybe there's more than one man sweating.'

Tomboy Cronane heard the news of the drowning from his father. At the time he was stocking empty shelves at his mother's behest. His worst fears were realised. He prayed silently that Mary had told nobody about their intimacies. He consoled himself with the thought that she wasn't the type of girl who would blab about such a relationship and in this he was correct.

She had never mentioned his name to anybody save herself and she had done this repeatedly up until the time she had kept her appointment with the Ogle River. It was to the same destination Tomboy betook himself after supper that evening but with far different intent. There was a possibility that he would be asked questions. He needed a place where his thinking would be uninterrupted and such a place was the bank of the Ogle River. For a moment as he stood on the knoll, where his former lover had sat in agonising loneliness, he was seized by an impulse to run for all he was worth, to crash through the undergrowth, to leap the tiny streams that fed the river, screaming and shouting at the top of his voice but someone would be sure to see and someone would be sure to hear. Instead he sat on the knoll and composed himself for the personal ordeal which was to come.

THE DEATH OF MARY Creel was the turning point in the community's attitude towards Mollie Cronane. She was now the recipient of unbegrudging sympathy whereas the Ram of God was fast becoming the most despised figure in the community. With such a record as his there now seemed to be no doubt in anybody's mind but that he had taken advantage of the Creel girl, had availed of her background and innocence to seduce her. The loudest outcry of all came only a week after the drowning when the results of the Intermediate Examination were announced. Mary received high honours in all of the eight subjects.

'And to think,' Mollie Cronane whispered to a crony as she left the church after Sunday's morning Mass, 'that she might have any job she wanted but for a certain gentleman up on the hill.'

The Ram once regarded as a sort of harmless eccentric and even a romantic found few voices to speak out on his behalf. Luke Holly would never believe that he ever laid a hand on Mary. Luke was well aware of the absolute trust the young girl placed in him. Thomas Connelly was less sure after the double wedding where there had been unanimous condemnation of the Ram, all orchestrated, unknown to Thomas, by Mollie Cronane who seized every opportunity during the celebrations to further downgrade her arch-enemy in the eyes of the countryside.

Patricia Cahalane would swear to the Ram's innocence although she would never permit herself to enter the controversy which had now turned almost unanimously against the would-be cleric, isolated on his hill farm, unwelcome in the village and in the countryside and even in the town of Trallock where word of his unspeakable fornication was quickly spreading.

16

UPWARDS OF FORTY HIACE vans showed up for the Latty and Killilly wedding. The reception was held at the Trallock Arms Hotel with the stipulation that the entire party would evacuate the premises on the stroke of eight the same day and continue with the celebrations out of sight and sound of the townspeople. The continuation took place at a venue beloved of itinerants, the clearing over the Ogle River to the north of Ballybobawn. Not until dawn's badger-grey streaks began to illuminate the nearby mountains did the last of the revellers leave the encampment and only then to seek out more liquor on their numerous roads home. The wedding, by travellers' standards, was successful enough. There was a fierce but short-lived row after which two alcoholically-inflamed bucks were transferred by ambulance to Trallock General hospital. One was detained suffering from superficial injuries but another, with a serious head wound, was transferred to Cork where his condition, after the insertion of twenty-two stitches, was said by the hospital spokesman to be comfortable.

After the dawn departure of the bride and groom in a second-hand Hiace, a gift from the groom's parents, the Lattys and their old in-laws the McMunleys turned in for a richly deserved sleep in their Hiaces and caravans. They slept the sleep of the just.

TOM CRONANE SAT AT the head of the table. His wife Mollie sat facing him at the other end. At one side sat the brothers McCallum, Joe and the Stringer. At the other sat Joe Cone's rough and ready assistant, the Pony Corgan. The man who sat next to the Pony at the Cronane convocation was a strong farmer by the name of Padge Keelsy from the south of Ballybobawn. His fields had played host, on many an occasion, to the Latty horses. Despite the most careful and elaborate fencing the insatiable skewbalds always managed to gain entry to his pastures.

'How many men can you count on?' The question was posed by Tom, a new and fresher Tom with a crispness about him. It was several weeks since he last indulged in a shaughraun. He had, he was obliged to confess to himself, never felt better.

'There's only myself,' the Pony Corgan admitted.

'And you?' Tom addressed Padge.

'There's myself, of course, makes one,' Padge answered, 'and there's my two neighbours, two able men as good as four ordinary men and there's the two Cooley's out near the verge of the bog. That's five for sure and by the time we're ready to march I think I'll be able to guarantee two or three more.'

'Let's stick to certainties!' Tom spoke sharply.

'Stringer?'

'There's myself and Joe and I can assure you of eight more on the night, solid men every one and not one of 'em that hasn't contributed grass and better to the Latty horses. They'll be anxious to settle their accounts!'

'Good!' Tom stroked his chin. 'Now!' he summed up authoratively, 'that gives us a grand total of eighteen, including Tomboy and myself. Cha would be a better man but he's in Dublin learning his business. Now Pony, you are our intelligence officer.'

Pony Corgan bent his uncombed head modestly at the unexpected commission. His stock had never been so low. To have his suit rejected by a girl of the locality meant no loss of face although there might be a limited element of ridicule but to have it rejected by a travelling girl turned him into the laughing stock of the countryside or so he believed. His hatred was not directed at Bob's Biddy. He did not believe that she rejected him of her own accord. In his eyes, her mother, Bob's Katie was the sole architect of his degradation.

'They'll be staying on,' he informed Tom, 'for only a night after the wedding and then it's back across the Shannon with them for the winter. We won't see hide nor light of them till the run up to Puck next year unless there's a funeral or another wedding.'

'How many able-bodied men will be in the encampment?' Tom asked.

The Pony joined his hands together like a schoolboy who knew the answer to only one question after that question had unexpectedly come up. 'There will be Bob Latty himself and his son Bob's Neddy.'

'He's only a garsún,' the Stringer protested.

'Maybe,' Tom admitted with a grim smile, 'but on such a night a garsún could grow into a man.'

'There will be the three McMunley families, Phelim's, Joss's and Jay's. There will be a scrap party but that will finish by midnight. Our way should be clear after that.'

'So!' Tom pursed his lips together, 'we have five able-bodied men to contend with and we number eighteen. The odds would be very much in our favour were it not for the women. How many Pony?'

The Pony Corgan's face reflected his delight. The question was child's play to him.

'All the women that will be there,' he answered, 'is Bob's Katie and the three wives of the McMunleys.'

'And children?'

'Not many,' came the prompt reply, 'all of the McMunley brood are married and scalded and there's only two of the Latty brood left, Neddy and Maggie, a blondie twelve year old. She's dangerous!'

'We will not settle on any fixed plan,' Tom, in his role of commander-in-chief, announced to his lieutenants. 'We don' know what kind of a night it will be so I propose that we meet here, using the back entrance and making sure that nobody sees us. There will be no knives and no guns. I will bring along a shotgun. The shock of a few salvoes at one or two in the morning should demoralise the thieves.'

'Would it be all right to bring sticks?' The question came from the Stringer.

'No harm in sticks,' Mollie provided the answer, 'so long as they're good and stout and laid on with plenty force.'

'Sticks should be all right,' Tom nodded his approval, 'but we don't want to overdo it! Remember we have here the greatest collection of perverts in the country. 'Tis known they have robbed the elderly and the poor not to mention ourselves but we must still remember we're civilised people. If the law was any good we need not bother ourselves but the law is clearly on their side and if their horses trespass on your fields it's against the law to put them out even if they are in the process of eating you out of house and home. We'll adjourn then until tonight.'

'I'll see to it,' Mollie promised, 'that every man is well primed before the fireworks begin. There will be whiskey galore and whatever else is requir-ed.'

THE PONY CORGAN WAS the first to arrive at the supermarket, using the rear entrance as planned. He was welcomed by Tom who issued instructions that a glass of whiskey be poured for the visitor. In other circumstances Mollie might have been reluc-tant to ply the Pony with whiskey. Whiskey never failed to unsettle him, as the entire parish knew only too well whereas beer or stout made him sleepy and anxious for bed. None of the hostelries in Trallock or Ballybobawn would knowingly sup-ply the Pony Corgan with short drinks of any den-omination.

Mollie felt totally justified as she poured a second glass for her guest. Her hatred of the Lattys, particularly Bob's Katie, superseded all others save the Ram of God. When quizzed by Joe McCallum about the advisability of engaging a man of the Pony's unstable temperament for such an under-taking, she replied brusquely that he was to be given free reign on the grounds that the Lattys had it coming to them!

Mollie would have cheerfully put a gun to Bob's Katie's head and pulled the trigger if she thought she would escape without retribution. With equal cheer she would have watched the extermination of the rest of the tribe by whatever means might occur to their executioners. The Pony Corgan endorsed Mollie's viewpoint and while Tom would not agree with extermination he would certainly settle for physical punishment without too much limitation.

Next to appear were the McCallums and one by one the remainder of the ambush party arrived by the back entrance. All were warmly greeted but none more so than Willie Halvey who had been informed of the raid at the last minute by Mollie. The millionaire had his own scores to settle. His extensive pastures had been frequently eaten into by the trespassing skewbalds. Willie's arrival greatly encouraged the landowners present. After all he was a friend of the minister's. He was also a man of great wealth and property, all hard-earned. If some of his activities were questionable it would have to be argued in his favour that he was a fair employer and an asset, because of his standing with the authorities, to any undertaking.

Last to arrive were the Coolie brothers from the verge of the bog. They were accompanied by three neighbours. This group, more than any, because of their proximity to the bogland which was regarded as virtual commonage by the travelling folk, had suffered most from the frequent incursions of the skewbald menace.

Shortly before midnight the Pony Corgan and Tomboy returned from a scouting mission on which they had embarked after the full contingent of Tom's punitive expedition gathered in the kitchen and sitting-room of the supermarket. Their report was accorded respectful silence.

The travellers were fast asleep, each and every one. All the males including Bob's Neddy seemed to be in a drunken condition as they retired for the night. The encampment was littered with empty bottles and cartons, bones, scraps and discarded garments as well as the remains of two turf fires whose ashes had whitened the area all around so that, under the light of the full moon, it looked as if snow had fallen earlier in the night.

As the Pony neared the end of his recital Willie Halvey arrived from the Load of S with a case of whiskey and two cases of stout. Mollie's supplies of hard liquor had just run out and there was nothing but tea to wash down the heaped plates of sandwiches and cocktail sausages which were specially prepared for the occasion. There was a decidedly festive air about the gathering and Mollie used the opportunity to bring the Ram of God into further disrepute.

Willie Halvey had nothing against the Ram of God nor did he believe that he was the father of the dead foetus but he kept his counsel. This was not a time for division he told himself. First things first! Every other man in the room firmly believed that the Ram of God was the father of the unborn child which the drowned girl was carrying. All the evidence pointed in that direction despite assurances from Sergeant Luke Holly that there was no evidence whatsoever to connect the Ram with such a gross violation.

'He's nothing but a land grabber,' Mollie told Padge Keelsy making sure that the Coolie brothers and their friends were within earshot.

'A land grabber and a seducer of children,' Mollie continued as she pressed sausage and sandwich upon her avid listeners.

'Maybe,' said Padge, 'we're going to the wrong place this night?'

'Hush man dear!' Mollie cautioned, 'the walls
269

have ears and besides there will be other nights.'

'There will indeed,' said Padge, 'and there will be darker nights.'

'He's a hard man surely,' said the more vocal of the Coolie brothers who was greatly impressed by the apparent genuineness of Mollie's welcome and latterly by her liberal hand as she repeatedly filled his glass. He had no previous dealings with Mollie although he had heard his wife to say that she was tight-fisted in her ways. No sign of tightness to-night. Mollie could always count on his services and the services of his brother. There can't be much wrong with a woman, he told himself, who pours out whiskey and lashes out grub the way she does.

'Boys!' Tom raised a hand for silence, 'we will all now blacken our faces with polish and pull our caps and hats firmly down over our foreheads. Let there be no talk. We will split into two parties. One half, under my command, will meet at the entrance to the encampment. The other half under the command of Willie Halvey will go by the river. At the sound of my shotgun we will attack simultaneously. There must be no loss of life. A good hiding should do the job. Now on your way in ones and twos until we meet for our night's work in earnest.'

Silently they trooped out into the night breaking up into pairs and threesomes but not before Mollie issued instructions to her daughter Kate that the Lourdes water was to be brought down from her room. There was a time-honoured silence as Mollie made known her intention of sprinkling all engaged in the enterprise with the imported waters of purification. Caps and hats were instantly swept from tousled heads and the sign of the cross was reverentially executed as the water drops

270

fell profusely on the bent heads of the transformed assembly. Noreen and Kate found the scene quite touching as they surveyed the hardened faces softening temporarily under the influence of the whispered words which accompanied the sign of the cross. Willie Halvey thought he never witnessed anything so macabre in all his born days!

For many of those present a new meaning was invested in the proceedings. Any qualms of conscience, however minor, which existed up until the sprinkling of the water now vanished altogether and a new determination fired by the spirit of righteousness dominated the feelings of the less intrepid members of the force. All were now united as they never before had been. When Tom issued further orders there were respectful salutes as exact as any which might be proferred by the most professional of soldiers. Mollie smiled grimly as she emptied the contents of the bottle.

'She was like Brian Boru before Clontarf,' Joe McCallum would declare later.

'God bless the work!' she called out as the freshly-anointed volunteers made their ways through fields and by-ways to the encampment of the travelling folk.

With Tom were the McCallum brothers, his son Tomboy, Padge Keelsy and his neighbours the Coolies, the Pony Corgan and three smallholders who happened to be neighbours of the McCallums. The group stood silently at the entrance to the encampment. There were no lights to be seen in any of the caravans. Nothing stirred in the vicinity. Motioning for absolute silence Tom placed a finger on his lips before locating a cartridge in his coat pocket. Loading the shotgun he advanced furtively followed by his silent subordinates.

As they neared the caravans the Pony Corgan drew abreast of the leader and whispered in his ear that the smallest of the habitats on view happened to be the dwelling quarters of the Lattys. Tom nodded gratefully and again motioning for absolute silence advanced to the side window. Aiming his shotgun in the direction of the sky overhead he waited a while listening to the deep snoring which came from the interior. Newly-arrived clouds obscured the twinkling stars and the full moon which had been the main features of the cloudless heavens throughout the earlier part of the night.

A light rain began to fall. Gently it pattered against the window pane where Tom stood, his shotgun cocked. His finger closed on the trigger, then squeezed. The explosive sound which followed shattered the quiet of the travellers' glade. A pheasant broke instantly from where it roosted peacefully on the branch of a nearby sycamore. Shouts and screams erupted from the caravans. Tom's next act was to smash the caravan window with the stock of his shotgun. The shattering glass added to the confusion.

Bob Latty streaked from his caravan, clad only in his everyday shirt. He took one look at the blackened faces, hesitated for the barest fraction of a second and disappeared from the scene so swiftly that he was destined to escape all retribution. He ran till he was exhausted. He might have shouted a warning to his son Neddy who emerged soon after pulling on his trousers but Bob Latty was so concerned for his own safety that he did not even consider his family.

The McMunleys emerged from their caravans at precisely the same time as Bob's Neddy. Experienced fighting men they took hasty stock of the odds and were not unduly alarmed. Their opponents or so they guessed would be country folk, small farmers more than likely, strong and tough no doubt but unskilled in the use of fist and boot and, with rare exceptions, seriously restricted by lack of agility. The thing was to avoid close bodily contact such as wrestling or mauling and concentrate on the landing of telling blows. As soon as Bob's Neddy alighted from the caravan the Pony Corgan attempted to maim him with a swinging body blow into which the burly, bandy-legged horse blocker concentrated all his strength. He was well wide of his target.

Bob's Neddy gratefully accepted the eighteen inch long iron bar which his mother thrust into his hand. In the face of this formidable weapon the Pony retreated awaiting the opportunity to seize the youngster in his brawny arms and render him ineffective. He was forced to move swiftly in order to avoid the murderous flaying of the young itinerant who sought to join up with his three uncles, Phelm, Joss and Jay McMunley, who, aided by their womenfolk, were fighting like madmen and must have caused serious concern to Tom's command but for the arrival of the riverside reinforcements under the command of Willie Halvey. In a few short moments the travellers were beaten senseless and their womenfolk forced to seek the shelter of the nearest caravan.

The Pony Corgan succeeded in seizing Bob's Neddy from behind and had little difficulty in prising the iron bar from his hand. Flinging the bar aside he held the fair-haired youth at arm's length by the throat, a mocking grin on his face.

'That's enough!' Tom called out sharply, fearing for the youth's life. No sooner had he given the command than Bob's Katie appeared at the door of the caravan from which she emerged screaming, followed by her twelve year old daughter Maggie. The latter was armed with a hatchet. Like tigresses Bob's Katie and Bob's Maggie flung themselves upon the Pony Corgan. For his part he immediately released his hold on Bob's Neddy and struck him on the jaw, knocking him unconscious, thus enabling him to meet the challenge of mother and daughter. Of the two the daughter was the more dangerous. She moved with bewildering speed, all the time manoeuvring herself to that she could fling the hatchet if need be.

'Split the bastard!' Bob's Katie screamed but her young, offspring seemed not to heed. Continually moving she never took her eyes from the Pony Corgan's face. Several times he lunged forward but she evaded him easily, all the time awaiting an opening. Tom's entire command stood spellbound, none willing to interfere in what seemed set to be the makings of an outstanding contest. Its very novelty appealed to their sense of the incongruous as the Pony managed to seize Bob's Katie by the hair. His inflamed eyes still trailing the daughter's every move as he secured the tightest possible grip and slowly forced Bob's Katie to her knees. Such was the effort required that the Pony momentarily lost his concentration. Hatchet upraised Bob's Maggie dashed under his free hand and struck but, unfortunately for her, her bare feet lost purchase on ground made slippery by the ever-increasing rain. The hatchet flew from her hand narrowly missing the Pony Corgan's temple, its shaft glancing off the side of his head to no effect. Effortlessly he stunned her with a backhander which might have been more lethal but for the struggle being put up by Bob's Katie.

'Let her go this instant!' Willie Halvey called out.

'Enough is enough!' Joe McCallum urged but Bob's Katie had now seized the Pony's free wrist with her teeth and was holding fast to her grip.

'Let go you bitch!' the Pony screamed as he forced her to the ground a second time. He scream-ed in anguish as her teeth bit deeper. Suddenly before anybody present could restrain him he bent her body till it was almost doubled and then he kicked her with his booted right foot into her bulging midriff. It was the force of the kick which shocked the onlookers. The Pony was seized by rough arms lest he use the boot a second time.

'There was no call for that man!' Joe McCallum raised a fist as though he would strike him but in turn was restrained by his brother.

'She's all right,' the Stringer conveyed the tid-ings as Bob's Katie managed to rise to her feet holding her stomach and mouthing the most diabolical obscenities.

'Time to go!' The command came from Tom. In an instant the glade was deserted save for the travelling folk.

After the raiding party broke up the Pony Corgan and Tomboy hid in a nearby grove and watched as the travelling folk saw to each other's needs. They remained only long enough to ascer-tain that nobody was seriously injured.

'I'd swear that it's not in the power of man to kill them,' Tomboy had whispered.

'Oh 'tis within my power all right,' the Pony retorted, 'but I would have to be given leave.'

When they returned to the supermarket they found a greatly subdued Tom. He received a thorough wetting and complained of a burning in his chest.

'Your hands!' Mollie uttered the words with revulsion upon beholding the marks left by the teeth of Bob's Katie on the Pony's hand. Puzzled she looked at the other hand around which was entwined a heavy bloodstained tress of blonde hair, clinging to which were several small gobbets of flesh.

'What in God's name!' Mollie covered her open mouth with her hands.

'It's hair,' the Pony answered unabashed.

'Why didn't you leave it?' Mollie shouted.

'Because woman,' the Pony replied, 'I didn't notice the damned thing until now!'

A horrified look had appeared on Tomboy's face.

'It's off her head all right,' he confirmed with trembling voice.

'I declare to God,' Tom laughed nervously and shrilly, 'but you've taken her scalp Pony.'

'Better you took the whole head,' Mollie turned her face away as the Pony Corgan began to unravel the strands, assisted by Tomboy.

'I didn't think their hair would come away as easy as that,' the Pony's fingers, chubby and grimy, were hardly the ideal instruments for the delicate work in hand.

'A scalp!' Tom chuckled to himself. 'Did I ever think I'd see the day when there would be a scalp laid out on my table.'

'Should we hang it up somewhere?' the Pony asked, 'where all could see it?'

'Get it out of my sight,' Mollie shrieked, 'flush it away somewhere.'

Dutifully Tomboy seized the offending trophy

and hurried to the bathroom.

'My chest!' Tom wheezed, 'it's like I'd be after breaking a rib.'

'It's nothing but a cold,' Mollie assured him. 'Go on away to your bed and I'll bring you up a hot water bottle.'

Tom's uneasy sleep was be disturbed by a succession of nightmares in which blood, mayhem and scalp-lifting abounded. Later in the morning when Mollie summoned Doctor O'Dell Tom was engaged in a hand to hand struggle with a hatchet-wielding squaw-cum-traveller who would maim his beloved Madeleine.

'I'm afraid it's pneumonia.' Dr O'Dell's diagnosis did not surprise Mollie. Although Tom did not take part in the fighting during the raid, as befitted his rank on the occasion, he had supervised the action from nearby. When he left the supermarket there was no indication of the unexpected downpour which coincided with their arrival at the scene of the action.

All the travellers were on their feet shortly after the departure of the raiding party. Most were groggy and bleeding but there had been no serious injury although Bob's Katie complained of stomach pains. They decided, because of the early hour, to lick their wounds and bide their time until morning when they would present themselves at Doctor O'Dell's surgery in Trallock.

A quarter of an hour passed before Bob Latty returned to the encampment. Without a word as to anyone's welfare he made straight for the caravan where he immediately bunked his shivering body having thrown his wet shirt to the floor.

A large red weal showed on Bob's Katie's poll. It was first noticed by her daughter. Immediately

Bob's Katie placed a hand on the afflicted area. Her fingers were bloodied when she drew away the hand although there was no incision or fracture as such on the skull. It was simply that a large portion of her hair had come away and with it some of the skin beneath. Bob's Katie expressed no concern. Her only thought was for the creature in her womb and in this respect she feared the worst.

No mention was made of Bob Latty's flight. The McMunleys remained silent out of respect to Bob's Katie and Katie herself dared not mention her mate's cowardly conduct for fear of reprisal later on.

LUKE HOLLY, TOTALLY UNAWARE of the happenings in his bailiwick, supped a pint of stout in the Widow Cahalane's. Thomas Connelly sat in his car on the outskirts of Trallock. By his side sat a young lady who had captured his attention some nights earlier as she cycled homewards without the benefit of front light or tail light.

Thomas cautioned her about the dangers of cycling after dark without adequate lighting. Moved by the contrite look on her attractive face he there and then escorted her home by the simple expedient of driving his car a few yards ahead of her. She had invited him in for a mouthful of tea as she put it and a date for a future meeting was negotiated.

Both policemen were, in fact, off duty on the occasion of the raid but both would have willingly forfeited their entire year's leave to have aided the travellers.

Luke and Thomas presented themselves at the encampment bright and early. They were notified of the raid by an infuriated Tom Pearson who heard of the affair on the rural grapevine. He demanded action.

'What action can I take,' Luke asked him, 'when not a single one of the victims is willing to make a statement or give me the slighest clue who their attackers were and all this in spite of the fact that Bob's Katie has lost the babby she was carrying?'

In the simplest medical terms Dr O'Dell explained that the afterbirth had been cut off from the wall of the uterus and the foetus expired for want of sustenance.

'You could call it murder,' Luke suggested.

'You could,' Billy O'Dell agreed, 'but you'lll never get a conviction because that's the end of it as far as the travellers are concerned.'

Luke was not content to let the matter rest. He had a fair idea of who the raiders were although Tom Cronane was not among those he suspected. He questioned several people unsuccessfully. In the hope of panicking some of the participants he also leaked the story to the national press but the incident never became anything more important than a nine-day wonder.

The stock of the itinerants rose considerably when word went out among their attackers that no representations had been made to the authorities.

On the Sunday following the raid Father O'Connor and Father Hehir devoted their sermons to the raid, remarking on the brutality and lack of christianity displayed by the guilty parties. At the conclusion they asked for prayers so that the attackers might be forgiven their iniquities. The reaction of the mass-goers was one of dissent. Many felt that the travelling folk had been given their just desserts, that there had been no loss of life. When somebody later protested in the Load of S that Bob's Katie suffered a miscarriage Mickey Creel suggested that it wasn't as if an ordinary christian had incurred the loss. His remarks were greeted with laughter.

'Give the cadger a pint of stout,' Padge Keelsy, who savoured the comment more than anybody, instructed the barman.

Mickey Creel who recognised a genuine source when he saw one advanced a step and taking Padge's hand drew him out of earshot of the others.

'A great night's work!' He shook his head in admiration as he pumped his benefactor's hand.

17

TOM CRONANE MANAGED TO survive the pneumonia to which he fell prey shortly after the raid on the encampment. 'To be candid,' Billy O'Dell confided to Mollie, 'I didn't think he'd pull through. If he stays away from the booze now he should be all right.'

Somehow he managed to elude the family custodian assigned by Mollie. Under no circumstances was he to be allowed out of doors. During Tomboy's watch in the early afternoon of the third day of his convalescence he made his move.

'A cup of tea Tomboy like a good man!' The request was routine. Tomboy went to the kitchen. When he returned there was no trace of his father.

Thinking he might have made his way into the shop Tomboy hurried to where his mother was talking to a customer.

'Is he here?' Tomboy asked.

Silently Mollie steered him back into the room he had just left.

'Don't you know better,' she hissed, 'than to discuss family business in public. Try upstairs. Hurry!'

There was no sign of Tom in any of the overhead rooms. Later that day he was brought home in a state bordering on the insensible from Tom's Tavern. The latter was surprised when Tom slumped to the floor in one of the alcoves after no more than three whiskies. He sent immediately for Mollie. Between them they lifted him to the rear of the premises and into the back seat of Tom's dilapidated Ford. They took him on an out of the way route along one of the village's many back roads before depositing the now inert cargo at his normal place of residence.

When Mollie bitterly upbraided her son Tomboy for his negligence Tom Dudley came instantly to his aid.

'Now, now Mollie,' he chided her pleasantly, ''tis easier juggle with quicksilver than mind a man with a desire like Tom's.'

Tom endured three nights in a semi-comatose condition when Billy O'Dell declared that he might be nearing the end.

'Will I send for Cha?' Mollie asked anxiously.

'I think that would be best,' Billy counselled.

'What exactly is it?' Mollie had asked.

Dr O'Dell hesitated before answering. He wasn't one hundred per cent sure himself but all the indications were that Tom was declining rapidly.

'A number of things,' he informed her. 'He's senile you know and that last outbreak, short as it was, didn't do him any good. The worst part is that he's disorientated. He knows he's dying but he doesn't care. It's as if he had decided to have done with the whole business of living and that could be because he just doesn't have the strength to go on. Try to keep him comfortable.'

When Tom awakened from his dream-disturbed sleep he saw his wife peering down at him from what seemed an enormous distance.

'That's some nightmare you've been having,' she told him.

'Where is she?' Tom asked, countering his wife's enquiry as to whether he was fit to get up.

'Your temperature is normal,' she informed him, ignoring his query. 'Doctor O'Dell says you

282

can get up and convalesce in the sitting-room or I can bring you breakfast right here.'

'No need,' he responded peevishly, 'I'll get up.'

'Suit yourself!' came the reply as his wife silently closed the door behind her.

He eased himself out of the bed and looked around for Madeleine Monterros. He knelt by the bedside and started to whimper. His heart ached as though it would break. His anguish exceeded anything he had ever previously felt. He buried his head in his hands, his body shaking with the overpowering grief. He looked in the wardrobe and under the bed, vainly calling her name.

'I never realised it would be as bad as this,' he told himself between sobs. He sat on the bed for over an hour until his wife returned to tell him that the girls were back from their honeymoons and were anxious to see him.

'Not yet,' he told her, 'not while I'm like this. Give me a few minutes and I'll be down.'

Wondering at his woebegone state she asked if he felt all right.

'How would I feel!' he cried out in lamentation, 'when she's gone.'

Mollie stood in the doorway, an incomprehensible look on her face.

'But I won't be long after her,' her husband said.

Later, as the entire family sat in the sitting-room the Stringer McCallum provided an hilarious account of their week-long honeymoons which the foursome had spent together in Galway. The Stringer was impressed by the quality of the pasture lands in the vicinity of the city.

'They turn out a good quality bullock there,' he told Tom and when that failed to excite the older man's interest, he launched into a hair-raising recollection of the morning they had spent near the cliffs of Moher. Tom sat unimpressed, a glum look on his face, his eyes fixed on the floor.

Joe reminded his erstwhile honeymoon companions of their bafflement upon hearing a group of Connemara people speaking in their native Irish in the bar of a city hotel.

'For all we know,' said Joe, 'they might have been talking about ourselves.'

'Sure they could be saying anything!' the Stringer opinioned.

'Oh from the sound of it 'twas nothing good to be sure,' his brother Joe agreed.

Under different circumstances Tom would have encouraged the brothers, egged them on for further recollections of their travels in the west of Ireland. Instead he sat, listlessly, with bent head even when Mollie invited the brothers to partake of a glass of wine.

While the drink was being poured Tom stirred himself and announced, in feeble tones, that he wished to go to bed. Filled with concern and sensing that he might be at the end of his tether the newly married daughters undertook to convey him upstairs to his room. He voiced no objection nor did he answer when Mollie asked if he might care for tea or coffee or any beverage to his liking.

'That man isn't well at all,' Joe announced after the group had departed.

Tom never again, of his own volition, left the bedroom where his daughters left him. Theirs had never been a loving relationship. For his part Tom felt that they never quite grew out of their teenage tomboyishness with the result that he was often quite revolted by their crudeness and by their indifference to the finer things in life. For their part they thought him distant and, more often than not, irritable. They never saw him as a figure in which they could confide and for a number of years before their eventual unions with the McCallums, he held no special status for them. Rather was he another member of the household, recognisable for what he was but somewhat inconspicuous as far as they were concerned.

The following evening Tom was discovered by Tomboy in a comatose condition from which he never fully emerged, except for a brief moment at the very end, but it was clear from the twitchings of his face and the excessive perspiration which necessitated a change of vest and pyjamas every few hours that he was undergoing considerable physical and mental anguish. When his condition remained unchanged, Father O'Connor was sent for and Tom was anointed for the first time in his life. Father O'Connor remained on after the ceremony to express his sorrow and concern at the obvious decline of such an admirable church-goer and devout Catholic.

'He had more than his share of troubles,' Mollie confided to her parish priest as they sat afterwards in the kitchen drinking the tea which Mollie had insisted was brewing anyway and would only be going to waste if Father O'Connor persisted in refusing it.

'His only concern, the poor man,' Mollie began to sob, 'was the welfare of his daughters.' Father O'Connor nodded in agreement but was careful not to voice any sentiment. Much as he might admire Mollie's generosity, her exemplary husbandry and capacity for hard work he suspected that were he to make any careless pronouncement its confidentiality was not likely to be guaranteed. He risked the occasional platitude which could not possibly be taken as approval or disapproval of whatever statements Mollie was likely to make in her own interest. The slightest confirmation was all she needed to show that her aspirations were stamped with the parochial seal.

'I'll mention no names,' she issued the solemn announcement as he rose to take his leave, 'but may God forgive that spoiled priest up on the hill that has my poor husband the way he is this night. May God forgive him. That's all I have to say.'

From midnight onwards Tom grew more delirious and feverish. At all times throughout the night and early morning one of the family was in attendance at the bedside. At rare intervals he opened his eyes but try as he might he could never focus them for more than a moment on any single one of his ministering flock. Towards dawn Cha vacated his chair in the sick room and gently roused his mother who, despite her best efforts to stay awake, had fallen into a deep sleep.

'I think he's going mother,' Cha announced gently as soon as she was fully awake.

'Call the others,' Mollie said.

When Mollie arrived at the sick room shortly after Cha's summons the entire family were gathered around the bed. Cha stood at the top, the damp cloth in his hand pressed to his father's forehead. Mollie concurred with Cha's findings. The restlessness and the fidgeting and the feverishness seemed to have abated.

Shortly before he expired a deep and blissful tranquillity seemed to settle on Tom. His eyes flickered in recognition of some presence beyond the confines of the room. His once troubled features grew more relaxed and composed. His whole body seemed to surrender to some benign and powerful influence.

'Tomasso!' Tom heard a female voice call.

'Tomasso!' it called again, 'I have come for you.'

With a cry of delight Tom managed to raise his head and call her name.

All save Cha, who stood mopping his father's brow, knelt around the bed but before Mollie had a chance to deliver a single prayer Tom Cronane's head fell back on his pillows. On his face was a joyful smile, on his lips the name of his Mexican paramour.

His listeners were not certain about the nature of the final word to leave his lips. Cha who was the nearest thought it sounded like Madeleine. As far as he was concerned Madeleine was a saint or holy soul whose intercession his father was invoking against the powers of darkness.

Lovingly Cha closed his father's eyes and smoothed back the tousled wisps remaining on his balding head. One by one the family kissed him on lips and forehead before rejoining their mother who promptly despatched young Donie for the priest. When the Rosary was recited she rang Doctor O'Dell. There was the matter of a death certificate.

Mollie could not bring herself to shed a tear. She would miss his company. He had a good head on his shoulders for all his drinking but there had been nothing between them for years, none of the cosy intimacies or mature affection which was the expectancy of couples who spent so much time together. In the latter years his sexual ardour declined and eventually disappeared until there came a time when not even a kiss was exchanged. Eventually an amiable tolerance of each other became the sole bulwark of the marriage. Mollie consoled herself with the thought that it might have been worse.

Mollie often longed for a man's arms but her only incursion to the heady realms of seduction had been her practical but abortive onslaught on the Ram of God. She admitted to herself that it was one of the few enterprises which she had mismanaged. She failed to take his moral sensibility into account. Her timing was also wrong. Basically the Ram of God was a man like any other with the same weaknesses and the same capacity for debauchery. He might not be the libertine people made him out to be but he was fit and under forty and he had already known one woman as intimately as any man might know her. Given the right circumstances he was there, like any other man, for the taking.

'If,' Mollie surmised, as she lay on her bed one morning, 'I had waited until the first light and stole to him in his bed without shoe, stocking or shift, I would have made a better fist of it and that's for sure. I never took his temperament into the reckoning. Sure isn't he nearly the same as a monk or a priest although not quite. All would have been surmounted if I had slipped under his quilt in my pelt. There's no way he would have got himself out of that one.'

NONIE KNEW OF MOLLIE Cronane's visit and quite rightly guessed its seductionary nature.

'No blame to her,' Nonie had told herself, 'if "twas a man she wanted. God knows poor Tom was too feeble to be any good to a lively woman like Mollie. A man don't need cause to wander but a

288

woman does so no blame to her but Mollie wanted more than just a man. If she had succeeded in seducing him it would have strengthened her hand because the Ram is a conscientious man and he would feel seriously obliged to her unlike the run-of-the-mill adulterer who would just take what was available and run.'

Nonie had a very poor opinion of Mollie and not just because of her designs on the Ram of God and the farm. 'She has no class,' she informed the Ram, 'Bob's Katie is a saint by comparison.'

'I liked him,' Nonie said after the Ram informed her of Tom's death, 'a bit grand maybe and grandeur is a bad disease but I liked him for all that even though he was one of the ringleaders behind the plot to oust you. Where Tom took the wrong turning was when he married beneath himself. There was no way back for him after that. He must be forgiven a lot on that account.'

'I always liked him.' The Ram of God recalled that the older man always treated him civilly and respectfully, especially during those first crucial weeks after he had been forced to leave the seminary. To Tom's credit he refused to involve himself in the public house banter which arose from exaggerated accounts of the Ram's downfall.

'I'm sure he's gone to heaven,' the Ram said after he paused for a few moments to estimate the dead man's chances of admission to that cherished clime beyond the grave.

''Twill take the pressure from us for a while if nothing else.' Nonie with her ever practical attitude to matters that affected her master was quick to see the advantageous aspects of the situation. 'There will be peace for a few days. After that we can be preparing ourselves for anything.'

'I'll be gone,' the Ram of God spoke as if he was on his way to the plane, 'and you'll be in your cottage and there's nothing anyone can do about that.'

'You won't be gone,' Nonie scoffed. 'There's something always coming between you and that Roman collar you're so anxious to tie around your neck. Can't you see it's God's will that's coming in the way.'

The Ram opened his mouth to speak but wisely refrained.

'I've never won an argument with this woman,' he told himself, 'and it looks like I never will.' Hands in trousers pockets he moved towards the doorway where he stood framed, surveying the placid scene outside. Slowly he moved away from the door.

'Watch out for yourself!' Nonie called after him, 'or better still take a weapon with you.'

Nonie's cautionary note was due to the increasing number of trespasses by the insatiable in-calf heifers from the over-grazed pastures of their near neighbour Joe McCallum.

'Joe used to be a grand oul' fellow,' Nonie mused, 'until he met up with them Cronanes.'

As the Ram directed his footsteps towards the High Meadow the first of the stars began to flicker in the clear skies which stretched without vestige of cloud to the farthest horizons.

He decided to take a turn around the meadow before retiring for the night. The fields were strangely quiet without the presence of cattle. He had sold everything on the advice of Alfie Nesbitt.

'Convert every living thing bar Nonie Spillane into hard cash as soon as you can,' was the wily old lawyers advice. 'That will foil them for a bit. They can't damage the land and they can't steal it.

When their cattle trespass let them trespass. You have nothing to lose but a few blades of grass at this point in time.'

He disposed of everything, calves, yearlings, bullocks, prime and otherwise, as well as heifers. For the fifty head he received a cheque for twenty-one thousand pounds.

'You're stark, raving mad!' Nonie flung the accusation at him when she heard the news. 'How in the face of the crucified Christ are you ever going to stock that land again?'

Patiently he explained that he was acting on the advice of Alfie Nesbitt, that, in in his absence in California, Nesbitt would be acting as his agent and would let the land to Trallock corn contractors who would see to their own interests with a ruthlessness that even Mollie Cronane could not match. Apart from a mild curiosity the people of Trallock had little interest in the feuding of their Ballybobawn neighbours. To them Ballybobawn was country, a place to be tolerated and kept firmly in its place. It was peopled by rustics and that explained the present trouble as it had all the troubles over land in the past.

The most hurtful feature of the village's hostility as far as the Ram of God was concerned was the continuing refusal by supermarket and shopkeepers to provide the supplies which Nonie was in the habit of purchasing every Friday which was the day on which she collected her old-age pension.

'I won't put any curse on you like the tinker woman,' she informed Tomboy, 'for the likes of you aren't worth cursing.'

Rather than have the Ram drive her to Trallock she handed in a provisions list to Patricia Cahalane on the Thursday night and collected the supplies on Friday evening. The Ram knew nothing of the arrangement.

'Why the hell don't you drive up with them?' Nonie suggested as she transferred plastic bags to carrier and handlebars.

'You know as well as I do,' Patricia responded, 'that I'm not wanted up there. He knows where I am.'

'In that case,' Nonie had countered, 'you'll be down here till you have whiskers on your chin and a walking stick in your hand.'

'Better that,' Patricia had hit back, 'than be where I'm not wanted.'

'If I was you Miss,' Nonie had informed her after the groceries were safely transferred, 'I would put my pride under my oxter and climb the hill.

'Goddam you for a gutless oul' maid!' Nonie stung her with the words, 'you'll get nothing down here but cold sheets and a cold bed and the Rosary round your fingers in time like your mother. Is that what you want?' Nonie flung the question at her.

As ever the reply had been the same. 'If he wants me he knows where to find me.'

She gave more careful consideration than she pretended to Nonie's proddings. She was tempted but it had ended there.

'For a woman of my background and upbringing to do such a thing,' Patricia told herself, 'would be to break the mould completely and to renege on everything I ever cherished or am supposed to cherish.'

She pondered on her virginity and often she asked herself, 'why am I holding on to it? For what and for whom?'

Yet she could not and would not willingly surrender. She was the prisoner of the same traditions and precepts as her mother and unwillingly she had come to realise the fact. She found a measure of consolation in telling herself that, at least, she faced up to the truth of her situation.

'Even if I were to give myself to a man,' Patricia confessed, 'I would reserve some thing or some part of me which I believe is not mine to give.

'The Church might say that it exercised no influence over the vast majority of its female members but the grip of the Church was as firm and unyielding as ever and the trouble is that the majority of the women of Ireland seem to need to be held fast by some sort of authority.'

18

'WHAT ABOUT THE RAM of God?' Mollie asked the Stringer

'Some night this week for sure,' he assured her.

'What will you do?' Mollie asked, an excited tremor in her voice.

'A hiding might not work,' Joe McCallum replied thoughtfully, 'he's strong and fast and apart from that there's the danger some of us would be identified.'

'Then it will have to be the double barrel. Did you see the way it worked with the tinkers?'

The Stringer shook his head in admiration of the twin-barrelled fowling piece, so common to every farmhouse in the district. Nearly always it was prominently displayed over the kitchen fireplace as a deterrent to would-be raiders or wilful trespassers. A shot in the air was nearly always sufficient to make clear the intent of the property owner. In serious land disputes the gun was sometimes brought into play but chiefly as a means of intimidating land grabbers and other usurpers. Only rarely was it used to do the work for which it was designed, that of legitimate fowling and vermin extermination. No other make of firearm, single shotguns excepted, existed in the countryside.

'We don't want to maim or kill him,' Mollie cautioned, 'just something to let him see that he had better get out.'

'I hear tell he inspects his fences every evening before dark,' the Stringer revealed, 'and if there happened to be someone behind a well-stitched hedge in the next field who might let go a shot in the air and then when he took to his heels to let go the second barrel in the direction of them very same heels. If he picked up a pellet or two in the process there would be no great harm done.'

'That would put him thinking all right,' Joe smiled grimly, 'and the Stringer here has an aim that would take the heels from his shoes.'

'Say no more!' Mollie busied herself with the transfer of cups and saucers from cupboard to table as she heard her daughters come in

THE RAM OF GOD, clear in his conscience and un-yielding in his determination to arrive at Saint Rowland's for the beginning of the second term, sat on his Ferguson, his eyes fixed on the night time sheen of the distant sea, his lips moving in silent prayer. Earlier as he alighted from the tractor to open the gate which provided access to the High Meadow he counted seven in-calf heifers grazing contentedly near the corner which bounded the outmost grass-denuded field of Joe McCallum's limited acreage. He decided to ignore the intrusion but he would have much preferred if Joe had asked his permission. Certainly the scrawny creatures, due to calve in the early spring, needed the grass, 'but then,' the Ram reminded himself, 'didn't each and every head of the McCallum stock need grass whether bullock, in-calf heifer or milch cow reg-ardless of the time of year.' Even in the lush days of summer they would raise their heads and longing-ly survey the richer pastures of the Drannaghy farm.

The Ram of God alighted from the Ferguson and walked uphill to the knoll which provided a full view of the distant sea and the farmlands in between. He always found it to be an inspiring vista. As he watched, the crimson sun sank slowly into a blushing horizon.

'Surely a time and a place for prayer,' the Ram of God thought as he endeavoured to dismiss the hazel eyes of Patricia Cahalane from his mind. He decided to break his promise and to forego the farewell meeting which they planned the day they met in Trallock. He would drop her a line expressing his regret. In a little more than forty-eight hours he would be on his way to California. He would be relieved when he found himself aboard the plane. He found thinking of her disquieting. She had, since their meeting on the street in Trallock, become the major threat to his vocation. He felt with justification that if God wished him to make a personal goodbye the Creator would have impelled him to move irresistibly down to the village to do so.

While he might feel some form of obligation to meet her as promised he also felt that his vocation had withstood as much as it was going to withstand. He doubted very much if there was ever a vocation which stood so fast in the face of so much over so long a period. It had, therefore, to be a vocation of the most sublime and yet steely character. It was a vocation of which he was proud. It had survived everything and here he was on the point of departing to a place where it would be fully realised at long last.

Although he convinced himself that he had dismissed Patricia from his mind she nevertheless, regularly interrupted his prayers by making brief incursions into his thoughts. As he turned his back on the sunset and descended the High Meadow he brought all his powers of concentration to the Sacred Litany which he always found to be proof against all distractions, no matter how vocation-sapping their form. He was not aware that his every move was being faithfully measured by two pairs of eyes, those of Joe McCallum and his brother the Stringer. They were carefully conceal-ed from the Ram's view by the density of the white-thorn bushes which formed the hedge between both properties. Head bent, as he totally concerned him-self with the Sacred Litany, the Ram of God loving-ly intoned the precious lines:

> *All ye holy Apostles and Evangelists,*
> *All ye holy disciples of our Lord,*
> *All ye holy Innocents,*
> *Saint Stephen, Saint Lawrence and Saint Vincent,*
> *Saints Fabian and Sebastian,*
> *Saints John and Paul.*

'What in the name of Jasus is he on about?' the Stringer whispered. 'Who are all them chaps he's talking about?'

'Cattle jobbers,' his brother Joe replied, 'from the midlands I'll wager.'

'Saints Cosmas and Damian,' the Ram of God continued as he turned and made his way uphill towards his tractor and the fading sunlight, which had by now, all but surrendered to darkness.

> *Saints Gervase and Protase and all ye holy*
> *Martyrs,*
> *Saint Gregory, Saint Ambrose and Saint*
> *Augustine,*

Saint Jerome, Saint Martin and Saint Nicholas.

'Here goes!' the Stringer whispered as he raised the shotgun and took aim. He squeezed upon the trigger and fired. The Ram of God was on the point of invoking the aid of the holy Bishops and Confessors when the pellets ripped through his trousers and embedded themselves in his thigh and calf. He leaped three feet off the ground screaming in agony. Overcome by shock and surprise he hopped first on one foot, then the other, as the searing pain almost sent him off into a shortlived faint. Recovering quickly he jumped on to the tractor and careered downhill, crashing through the gate, furious now and hell-bent on retribution, the soothing lines of the Sacred Litany gone altogether from his mind. What really enraged him was the prospect of being hospitalised. His departure might be delayed once more.

Without lights he drove at breakneck speed to the cross of Ballybobawn. On his way he met Nonie Spillane, hurrying uphill, bearing a storm lantern in one hand and a flashlamp in the other.

'I heard a shot!' she called after him.

At the cross the Ram of God turned into the main road and left it after a hundred yards to venture into a narrow laneway. Slowly now, almost noiselessly, he drove towards the McCallum farmhouse but stopped at a gateway some distance from the house itself. He had not long to wait. Wincing with pain he alighted from the tractor and stood, motionless, at one side of a gate pillar.

Joe McCallum easily vaulted the five-bar gate and was met with a stunning right fist before his feet touched the ground. The Stringer, gun in hand, lacked the athletic prowess of his brother and so

had to content himself with merely climbing the
gate. The Ram caught him fairly and squarely on
the jaw. He fell backwards, the gun falling from his
hands, not so much as a lisp escaping his lips. Still
hobbling the Ram of God opened the gate and lifted
the Stringer from the ground. He held him firmly
by the shirt front and landed three savage left-
handed blows to the face. The Stringer fell away
from his grasp, senseless and bleeding from three
different wounds. Joe rose in time to see an outsize
fist coming his way. Too dazed to duck he closed
his eyes and fervently prayed that the fist would be
wide of its target. His prayers were in vain. The
Ram did not strike Joe a third time. In the first
place there was no need and in the second place he
quite rightly deduced that it was not Joe who pulled
the trigger.

'HOW DID IT HAPPEN?' Billy O'Dell asked after a
preliminary examination.

'Accident,' the Ram answered.

'What sort of accident?'

'Just a few stray pellets,' the Ram replied
casually. 'There was a fowler somewhere in the
vicinity and visibility was restricted.'

'And you have no idea who it was?' Billy asked
suspiciously.

'Not a clue,' the Ram of God found lying less difficult than he imagined it would be.

'Problem is,' Billy informed him, 'that I will be
obliged to report the matter to the civic guards.'

'But if it's only an accident why bother?'

'Because it's standard practice,' Billy would
like to believe that the wounds were accidental but
he was only too well aware that it was a tension-

filled time in the district.

'When do you propose to remove the pellets?' the Ram of God asked.

'First there will have to be an x-ray to find out where the pellets are deposited. From my preliminary examination I don't foresee any problem. Let's go to the hospital right away. The x-ray shouldn't take long. With any luck the whole thing should be over in a few hours. A local anaesthetic should be sufficient.'

'Will I be detained?' the Ram asked.

'It's not absolutely necessary,' Billy replied, 'but I would recommend that you stay overnight.'

Later, after the pellets had been removed, the Ram of God insisted that he be permitted to return home.

'In that case,' Billy informed him, 'we had better put a plaster on to support the muscles.'

'In less than forty-eight hours,' the Ram spoke hesitantly, 'I hope to be on my way to California.'

'I know all about that,' Billy waited for further developments in the conversation.

'If you report the matter to the civic guards,' the Ram went on, 'what with red tape and heaven knows what else I might be obliged to postpone the flight indefinitely and if that happens I will miss the opening of the second term. I have already missed the first through no fault of my own. If I were to miss the second my place in the seminary would be in jeopardy.'

Billy pondered the proposition for a full minute before replying.

'You're sure it was an accident?' he said.

'It was an accident,' the Ram of God lied.

'Very well,' Billy smiled. 'I'd hate to be the man to come between you and your destiny at this stage

300

in your life. I wish you luck. Maybe you'll shrive me of my sins one day!'

Neither Joe nor his brother the Stringer availed themselves of medical attention. Their womenfolk saw to their wounds. The Stringer sported two black eyes which promised to be the focus of much curiosity as soon as full-scale discoloration, in its many stages, began to show. Apart from a swollen jaw and a few loose teeth Joe was none the worse for wear. When his wife expressed fears that the Ram might notify Luke Holly, Joe explained that this was most unlikely.

'He would have gone to Holly in the first place if that was his intention,' Joe explained. 'He ruined his case by attacking us and I think he knows that. Anyway he'll be wanting no truck with the law if he ever wants to see California.'

19

'IT'S AS IF YOU were deliberately trying to thwart me,' Superintendent Joe Chaney rose from his chair and moved towards the window which looked out on to the village street, 'this goddamned division had everything going for it until you crossed Willie Halvey.'

'I didn't cross him,' Luke Holly denied the allegation. 'I merely did my duty.'

'I hear you're very slow to do your duty in respect of a certain Edward Drannaghy commonly known as the Ram of God,' Joe Chaney made the charge heatedly, 'whereas you persist in harassing every second farmer in Ballybobawn just because a few itinerants got their come-uppance!'

'One of the victims of that attack had a miscarriage.'

'And how many unfortunate women in the settled community have miscarriages every other day for one reason or another?' Joe Chaney struck the wooden table with his fist and sat again on the chair he had just vacated.

'The priests of the parish are taking it very seriously,' Luke answered calmly, 'they referred to the matter again last Sunday in fact. The parish priest wanted to know if travellers had the same rights as settled people or did the law favour one before the other?'

'The priests of the parish can kiss my royal Irish arse,' Joe shot back. 'I have a government minister breathing down the back of my neck, a minister with close friends and sympathisers in this neck of the woods. You may have managed to sink your own ship sergeant but you're not going to sink mine.'

'What about the films?' Luke spoke accusingly.

'I gave them back to their rightful owner for private viewing only,' Joe returned 'because I don't want a senior counsel making me look foolish in court. Do you know anything about obscenity laws or copyright laws Holly?'

'Nothing I'm afraid,' Luke replied coldly.

'Very well,' the superintendent seemed to grow somewhat mollified, 'and until such time as you have enough knowledge on those subjects to take on a senior counsel you say no more about confiscation of films.'

'You said there a moment ago that I managed to sink my own ship. Might I ask what that's supposed to mean?' Luke asked anxiously.

'What it means,' Joe deliberately averted his gaze as he answered, 'is that you will be transferred to a station in Donegal.'

'Donegal!' Luke echoed the word with disbelief. 'Where in Donegal?' he asked as if the whole business was a crude joke.

'Some village or other. I never heard of it before. I've forgotten the name.'

'But why?' Luke Holly asked.

'Too many complaints. For instance you would persist in drinking after hours at the Widow Cahalane's which weakens my hand considerably whenever I mount a campaign against after-hours premises in Trallock or elsewhere. They say it's all right for the guards to drink after-hours but not for the man on the street. You've embarrassed me long enough Holly. You're a bloody Jonah and that's all I'm prepared to say about the matter.'

'I'm not going to take this lying down!' Luke tried to sound convincing.

'Let me tell you something for nothing Holly. Do you ever remember an instance where a guard or a sergeant won out over a superintendent? Of course you don't and you never will.'

Joe slowly closed one hand over the other. 'I found it very hard to become a superintendent Holly and I'm well on my way towards becoming chief. Don't make things difficult for me or I'll go for your jugular. I have the full backing of the minister. The locals are also growing tired of your carry-on. If the chips are down you won't have a leg to stand on. You are supposed to protect people, not harass them. You are duty bound to uphold the laws, not ignore them. Your moral principles are all screwed up. You impose one set on the Load of S and another on the Widow Cahalane's.'

'I resent that,' Luke found himself trapped. It mattered not that his relationship with the Widow Cahalane was innocent or that she was pure as the driven snow. He was guilty of drinking after hours and if the truth were known he was obsessed with the woman.

'You could always retire,' Joe suggested as he rose to leave.

'I'm too young to retire,' came the indignant reply, 'what would I do with my time?'

'You could take on with your widow,' Joe Chaney decided to wear his human hat for a moment. It wouldn't cost him anything. Luke did not bother to inform his superior that the widow was not the marrying sort, that she was still one-hundred-per-cent faithful to the memory of her late husband and that she would never consider any form of illicit relationship. He did not explain that she was a victim of local tradition, that she had, like so many of her kind, strangled the cry of flesh and blood with her Rosary beads and killed it off before it assumed proportions capable of challenging her fast held tenets of piety and chastity. Luke Holly would swear that she was a good woman in every sense of the word, a nun-like woman. He wished fervently and futilely that she was made of softer clay.

At the doorway Joe extended a hand.

'No hard feelings,' he suggested hopefully.

Luke surveyed the extended palm with mixed feelings. 'If I shake it,' he told himself 'I'll be a hypocrite just like he is and if I don't I will, all of a sudden, betray a lifetime of good manners.'

He shook the superintendent's hand.

Patricia heard with regret of Luke's transfer and greatly regretted his rejection by her mother. He waited until all the other customers left the bar.

'You better listen to this too,' he insisted when Patricia expressed her intention of retiring for the night. 'If,' said Luke to the bewildered Widow, 'I thought you would marry me I would retire from the force and settle down here with you. It's up to you. If you say no I'll accept this transfer to Donegal. If you say yes I'll give you a good life. I'll love you till my last breath and I'll always take care of you.'

Patricia listened silently while her mother stood, head bent, unmoving after Luke's desperate plea.

'I'm sorry,' Sadie Cahalane never raised her head, 'I'm really sorry.' Slowly without a glance at either her daughter or the sergeant she noiselessly vacated the bar leaving a chill silence behind her.

'She's in bondage,' Patricia tried to explain, 'to
305

her religion and to her past and to the restraints she has imposed upon herself. Even if she cared for you she would never admit to it because that's the way of her kind.'

Before he left there was one other thing Luke Holly wanted to accomplish. He commissioned Mícheál and Jonathan Creel with the whitewashing of the stone walls which surrounded the barracks. It was part of a general tidying up which he undertook before handing over to his successor.

When Mícheál and Jonathan joined him in the dayroom, for tea and sandwiches and a settlement of accounts he had asked the brothers if they had any interest in boxing. In no time he had them sparring, enjoining them beforehand that under no circumstances were knuckles to be brought into play. Now and then he intervened to point out the advantages of a straight left or a right cross and when opportunity presented itself he indicated the locations of such vulnerable areas as the solar plexus.

'You know what gentlemen!' he declared at the end of the session, 'but either one of you would give a grown man a run for his money, and,' he paused meaningfully, 'a small fat man would have no chance at all against the pair of you.'

He informed nobody of the exact date of his departure, intimating to the curious that it would not be for some time yet. If he felt anything about leaving it was resignation rather than bitterness. When the station sergeant in Trallock suggested over the phone that the customary farewell party should take place in the Trallock Arms Luke informed him he would much prefer if his leave-taking went unnoticed.

'But there's always a presentation on such occasions,' the station sergeant reminded him.

'Not this time,' Luke countered.

'But why not?' the station sergeant asked, perplexed at Luke's unprecedented departure from the norm.

'Because I am not taking my leave voluntarily,' Luke replied. 'I'm being transferred without ceremony so let there be no more about it.'

'It's your party Luke,' the station sergeant concluded without rancour.

Luke Holly departed the village of Ballybobawn at 11.30am on 25 October. He shook hands with a confused Thomas Connelly at eleven twenty-five that morning and then loaded his belongings in the boot of his venerable car.

'I'm off Thomas,' he extended a hand to the younger man. Words came to Thomas' lips but they travelled no further. Futilely he searched for something to say but Luke was gone, closing the barrack door quietly behind him.

Later in the day Superintendent Chaney arrived having been informed earlier by his station sergeant that Luke insisted on foregoing both farewell party and presentation. Joe Chaney made the call in the hope of making the Ballybobawn sergeant see reason. He expressed his annoyance on finding that the sergeant had gone.

'This won't look good,' he thought, 'even to the very last the bastard embarrasses me!

'Strange fish!' he threw a glance at Thomas, expecting him to concur dutifully.

'He was one of the few straight men I ever met,' Thomas looked his superintendent in the eye, 'and, furthermore, having served under him, I hope to be like him one day.'

'When I want opinions from you I'll ask for

them, all right!'

'Sure,' Thomas returned to the report he had been writing before the superintendent's arrival.

Joe Chaney was about to say more but changed his mind.

Luke never again sojourned in the Widow Cahalane's after the night of his rejection but on his way through Trallock he stopped off, briefly, at the Presentation Convent.

'I'll miss you,' Patricia felt the tears welling in her eyes as he held her hand, 'and she'll miss you too Luke, far more than you would ever believe and far more than she would ever be capable of saying.'

'Give Edward my regards!' Luke held her gently in his arms. 'I know you two will make out.' Without another word he was on his way.

AS THE RAM OF God surveyed the setting sun he thought of Mary Creel. He had wanted to lay a wreath on her grave before he departed for California. He could not bring himself to attend her funeral.

He still felt an intense guilt about her.

'She is without doubt in heaven the poor girl,' he told Nonie after she asked him if her suicide might militate against her paradisian prospects.

'Be sure,' the Ram responded as though he were speaking *Ex Cathedra*, 'that we have a true friend in heaven.'

Neither did he attend the wedding of the Cronane sisters to the McCallums. He wrote a note of thanks and sent a gift of cut glass decanters to both parties. He also avoided Tom's funeral. He felt that because he was in such bad odour with the majority of the community his presence might offend both family and community.

Dusk was falling as the Ram of God entered the graveyard of Ballybobawn. Silence was everywhere except for the final flourishes of bird song which the Ram always associated with his mother's burial place. Briefly he prayed over the family plot. The mounds which covered the recently-buried twins had subsided but little. Nonie informed him that Mary Creel lay buried in the right-hand corner furthest from the main entrance. He hastened to the spot without delay silently praying that his visit would go unnoticed. There were but two wreaths on the freshly made grave. One came from her schoolmates and the other from Patricia Cahalane. He laid his at the foot of the grave and knelt in prayer until darkness enveloped the tiny cemetery. As he rose to leave he heard his name being called. His scalp tingled as he turned to see the seated figure of Cha Cronane.

'I would have made myself known earlier,' Cha explained, 'but I knew you wanted to pray.'

'Sorry about your father,' the Ram of God extended a hand to express his condolences. Cha returned the handshake.

'I've heard what they say about you,' he said.

'Surely you don't believe such an awful thing of me?' the Ram of God pleaded his innocence.

'I don't believe it,' Cha bent his head, 'because I know that you are not the guilty party.'

'Then in God's name clear me, and take away this cloud of shame that's been over my head since she drowned. You don't know what it's like Cha to be innocent and yet have every man's hand turned against you! You're the only person who can help me clear my name before I leave. I'm going the day after tomorrow.'

'And I'm going the day after tomorrow.' Cha walked by the side of the Ram of God as they made their way to the main entrance.

'That doesn't leave you much time,' the Ram lay a hand on the younger man's shoulder, forcing him to stop.

'I've thought it out carefully and I know what I must do,' Cha extended his palm to the Ram of God. They shook hands warmly.

'You go on home,' Cha said, 'and I'll do what I have to do.'

20

AFTER CHA TOOK HIS leave of the Ram at the graveyard entrance he returned home and bided his time
until Tomboy took it into his head to visit the Load
of S with Sammie and Donie in tow. Mollie Cronane
was absent and would be until midnight. She accompanied her daughters to the city of Cork where
they had an appointment with a gynaecologist and
where they needed to make a provisional booking
for their confinements at the Bon Secours mater-
nity unit. Mollie phoned to say that it would be late
by the time they arrived home. She spoke of a
chance meeting with Willie Halvey on Patrick
Street. It transpired that he was in Cork on business and insisted that the trio join him for dinner
at Jury's Hotel. Fearing that such a sensitive soul
would be offended if his generous invitation was refused Mollie accepted on behalf of herself and her
daughters.

As Tomboy transferred the day's takings from
the till to the safe in his mother's room, now permanently under lock and key, he secreted twenty
pounds in his trousers pocket. It never occurred to
Tomboy that his mother could estimate a day's
takings, give or take a pound or two, as accurately
as any till sheet; so for that matter could Cha
although he did not find out about his younger
brother's lavish spending habits until he surprised
him in the television lounge of the Load of S where
he was the centre-piece of a group who were viewing, somewhat detachedly, a film which dealt with
the seduction of a cherub-faced schoolboy by a

middle-aged, suburban housewife of surprising agility. Cha did not know, that for all their tender years, the watching group were now old hands in the scanning of erotica and if their interest was to be aroused and maintained for any length of time, a film of astounding and hitherto unreleased sexual perversion would be required.

Mickey Creel sat on his own in a corner. Some moments passed before he recognised Cha. Instantly he was at his side, shaking his hand, commenting on how well he looked and how the village had not been the same since he had departed for the metropolis. Cha ignored him and turned his attention to his brothers. Sammie and Donie were the first to see him. Alarmed, they rose from their seats, hangdog looks on their surprised faces. He was the last person they expected to see in the viewing room of the Load of S.

'Have a drink Cha?' The invitation came from a surprised Tomboy.

'Sure,' Cha replied, not seeming to notice the figures on the screen or the drinks which his brothers had speedily discarded.

'What'll it be Cha?' Tomboy made his way to the bar counter with a show of assurance he did not feel.

'Not here,' Cha's voice showed no trace of emotion. 'Let's move up the street to Tom's Tavern. There isn't any television. It'll give us a chance to talk!'

Sammie who was nearer to Cha in age knew his brother's moods better than the others. He felt a vague uneasiness which he could not explain. This was a different Cha, a cooler, more controlled Cha. He felt as though he was in the presence of an older man, a mature and highly capable man in

312

whose make-up no vestige of boyhood had been retained.

Tom Dudley set about dispensing Tomboy's order with some misgivings. Tomboy was under age. He could not be sure about Sammie. He gave him the benefit of the doubt. Cha was nineteen if he was a day and Donie a year younger. It was Cha's presence which decided him.

'He's as sound as bell metal,' Tom told himself, 'and wasn't he always a solid rock of a lad, pleasant and even-tempered like his grandfather Charlie Cronane.'

The brothers sat in the alcove farthest away from the main entrance. An uneasy silence ensued after the drink, four pints of stout, had been served by Tom and paid for by Tomboy. Tom discreetly withdrew to the rear of the premises although, unknown to the brothers, he would be privy to any exchanges, whispering apart, which took place. Not normally given to eavesdropping, Tom was curious. It was always refreshing and heartening to see family groups drinking together on occasion. The Cronanes were decent enough lads except maybe Tomboy.

'Something about him I don't quite trust,' Tom thought. 'Cha now, Cha was different. Cha was the type of young man that Ballybobawn could ill afford to lose. A village needed young men like him, young men you could turn to in emergency, men who had the respect of the people. There is something different about him tonight though, a trace of menace, maybe a score to settle!'

Tom busied himself with the reading of a newspaper but his ears remained cocked.

'Now,' Cha opened the proceedings after he had tasted his pint and toasted his brothers, 'let us get down to cases.'

Donie cleared his throat and fondly wished he was somewhere else. Sammie hurriedly searched his memory for any recent transgressions for which he might be held accountable. Tomboy sat tense and silent, his pint of stout still untouched.

'This business of the Ram of God,' Cha went on, 'we all know don't we that he is entirely innocent of any misbehaviour towards poor Mary Creel. Once the four of us accept that we can go on from there. You surely don't believe Donie,' Cha was at his most reasonable, 'that his relationship with Mary was anything but honourable? You know the Ram Sammie. He was never that kind of man. Look me in the face Sammie and tell me that the Ram is guilty.'

Sammie, the least intelligent of the family, shook his head.

'And you Donie? Are you going to tell me that the Ram was the father of Mary's child?'

'I never pointed the finger at him,' Donie, blustery and evasive when faced with any form of dilemma, hung his head as he spoke.

'I have to go,' Sammie bolted his pint and rose to his feet.

'Me too,' his brother Donie eased himself out of his seat.

'Sit down!' Cha held his eyes firmly on Tomboy as he issued the order to Donie and Sammie. They sat instantly, if reluctantly, unwilling to be party to the awful proceedings which all their instincts warned them were about to follow.

'Tomboy!' Cha paused before posing the question, 'you surely don't believe that about the Ram?'

With a shaking hand Tomboy raised his glass but removed it at once from his lips, unable to swallow.

'Come on Tomboy. Answer the question.'

Tomboy returned his pint to the table, his face deathly pale, his breathing heavy. Tom sat riveted to his seat, afraid to move, even to breathe lest his least action obstruct the course of the justice which he now knew for a certainty would clear the Ram of God. He had always been extremely doubtful of the Ram's involvement with the Creel girl but the evidence had been overwhelming.

'All I want to hear from you Tomboy,' Cha relentlessly goaded his younger brother into replying, 'is a yes or a no!'

The silence was now demoralising. Cha made the most of it. He would get the answer he wanted, sooner or later.

'You can't answer Tomboy can you? You're the man aren't you Tomboy! You're the man who bought the cider and made her drunk! She did it because she loved you Tomboy. I know because I know what love is Tomboy. I loved Mary Creel and even when it dawned on me that you were having your way with her I still loved her because she couldn't help herself. That was because she loved you so much Tomboy.'

The anguish in Cha's voice brought a tear to Tom Dudley's eye. It brought back memories of the wife he loved, who now lay buried in the graveyard of Ballybobawn.

'I loved her,' Cha was crying now, 'even though you soiled her I still loved her. She was an innocent little girl and where could she turn when she found out about her condition? Her father would probably have beaten her half to death. Her mother closed her eyes and ears. She couldn't go to the Ram because in her eyes he was a man of God and she couldn't tell me because she was ashamed of what she had done. Well she could have told me Tomboy,' Cha's voice was breaking now, 'because I would have died for her and there isn't a day or an hour since she drowned that I don't think of her. She'll haunt me till the day I die!'

Tom Dudley was tempted to rise and place a hand around Cha's shoulder but that would show that he was eavesdropping. He wanted to tell him that all was not lost, that he, Tom had also felt like Cha but that Cha was young and there was a whole life stretching before him, a life where he would surely meet the girl he so richly deserved.

His composure regained Cha dried his eyes.

'You know what you have to do don't you Tomboy?'

Tomboy nodded.

'The new sergeant will be expecting you. You just tell him the truth and there won't be another word. You'll be a new man Tomboy and you'll have cleared the Ram. God knows he's been on the rack but that's all over now. We'll go to the barracks with you,' Cha rose manfully, 'won't we boys?'

'Sure we will,' Donie placed a hand around Tomboy's shoulder.

'The four of us together,' Sammie circled the other shoulder.

Tom emerged as they were about to depart. His eyes met Cha's.

'You fellows will be all right,' he placed a bony hand on each of Cha's shoulders. 'You fellows can't go wrong as long as you stick together. When you do what you have to do be sure to come back here and there will be a drink on the house.'

Tomboy had made a voluntary statement to the sergeant. It was agreed that Tomboy would return to the city with Cha and that he would remain there until the dust had settled after his admission.

'It will be all over in a few weeks,' Tom Dudley assured them as they sat drinking the pints which he so generously donated.

'Mark my words,' he went on, 'but you'll hear of a chicken with three legs being born in Tubbertooviskey any day now or if it isn't a chicken it will be a calf with two heads over in Ballygorm. That's the way with the world boys. One wonder is hardly done with when there's another emerging out of nowhere. Wait now for a week or two and we'll be hearing tidings of mighty import. You boys will remember me when these events take place.'

Tom Dudley winked knowingly at Cha as he helped himself to a swallow from the double whiskey he had filled for himself.

CHA CRONANE ARRIVED AT the Ram of God's at eight o'clock in the evening. He was warmly received by Nonie. At her insistence, Cha agreed to accept the tea which she had offered him as soon as he stepped inside the door.

'He'll be back any minute,' she told him after he had enquired about the whereabouts of the Ram of God.

'Is it urgent?' she asked hoping that he might divulge the nature of his business.

'It'll keep,' Cha responded.

'He's off tomorrow God help him!' The wistful reminder was followed immediately by a flood of tears.

'Now, now, now,' Cha comforted, 'it's what he wants.'

'He doesn't know what he wants,' was Nonie's

317

bitter response as she wiped her eyes with the handkerchief which Cha tendered to her.

'Why is he going then?' Cha asked.

'I don't know but I know in my heart it's a small thing that would turn him. Maybe, maybe,' Nonie weighed him off with eyes that were full of speculation, 'you might be the very man. All he's waiting for is a sign. If we could get it into his head that it was God sent you here this night. If he could only see you as some form of divine intervention it might open his eyes to his real obligations.'

'I don't follow you,' Cha sat back in his chair as she poured the tea.

'Then don't try,' Nonie advised him as she unloaded her stratagem. 'When your business is finished invite him down to the village for a farewell drink. Insist on the Widow Cahalane's. I don't care how you do it but get him in there. Get him to the village first and when you come to the cross walk ahead of him until you come to the Widow's.'

'Patricia!' Cha thought, a smile of enlightenment appearing on his face.

'Promise me now.' There was no denying the desperation in Nonie's entreaty.

'I promise.' Cha always looked upon Nonie Spillane as a simple-minded if somewhat roguish menial.

'It's a lesson to me,' he reflected as he swallowed the first mouthful of tea, 'that one should never judge a woman by her station or appearance.'

'This will be him now,' Nonie's whispered alarm still retained the elements of conspiracy.

'I must go down to Cahalane's,' she explained as the door opened, 'to collect the groceries.'

'That's another thing,' Cha put in.

'What's another thing?' Nonie asked.

'That embargo is lifted. There will be a welcome in the village for both of you from now on.' Cha rose from his chair as the Ram of God entered, 'and the village knows now,' he went on for Nonie's benefit as well as the Ram's, 'who was the father of Mary Creel's child.'

A long silence followed which the kitchen's three occupants savoured to the full.

'I have business to attend to,' Nonie caught Cha's eye as she prepared to exit, her eyes once again, expressly reiterating her earlier injunction about the visit to the Widow Cahalane's. With a flicker of eyebrows Cha indicated that he had not forgotten.

The exchanges escaped the notice of the Ram of God. His gnarly right fist struck his left palm in appreciation of his acquittal. He could walk through the village again. Nonie could shop at will. The McCallums would now be without any form of justification for their excessive trespassing. The sympathy of the parish would be withdrawn and the Ram of God could pursue his vocation clearly vindicated in the eyes of God and man. It would mean too that he could make his goodbyes to Fathers O'Connor and Hehir without a cloud over his head and that they must surely now recognise the real villain of the piece.

When Nonie collected the groceries from Patricia Cahalane she asked the younger woman if she intended going out that night.

'Yes,' Patricia answered primly, 'some friends are calling for me and we're going to a flower arrangement class in Trallock.'

'Well!' Nonie folded her arms, 'if that's the way then there's no point in telling you to stay at home.'

'And why would I want to do that?' Patricia

asked.

'Because it might be in you best interest!' Nonie returned testily.

'Could you elaborate?' Patricia asked, trying to conceal the excitement in her voice.

'Just do what I tell you and it might pay you a damned sight better than flower arranging.'

Nonie stood leaning on her bicycle in the shadow of Ballybobawn parish church. Slung from the handlebars was a satchel of groceries. Cigarette in mouth she waited. Finally, she saw what she wanted to see. She had no difficulty in identifying the two figures who appeared together at the cross of Ballybobawn, the Ram of God tall, lean and angular, Cha Cronane stubbier and more portly.

'The devil take him now if he doesn't do what I told him!' She addressed the words to herself, silently praying that Cha would lead the way as he had suggested, towards the licensed premises of the Widow Cahalane's. True to his word and seemingly without deferring to his partner Cha made his way past the Load of S and Tom's Tavern. Nonie triumphantly expelled the cigarette end from her mouth and mounted her bicycle. Slowly she cycled in the direction of the cross unseen by the pair in front. Cha still led the way, the Ram some distance behind. When Cha stopped outside the Widow's the Ram of God also drew to a halt. It was as though he could not make up his mind whether to follow his friend or not. When Cha entered the Widow's the Ram hesitated for a moment, then followed suit.

Cha opened the door and made his way to the bar counter behind which stood Patricia Cahalane, hair neatly arranged, freshly applied lipstick glistening on her lips, eyes sparkling, her smart frock of turquoise blue matching her eye shadow.

'There's somebody with me,' Cha explained as he awaited the arrival of the Ram of God.

'I didn't realise you were so beautiful!' the words were out before Cha realised it.

'Why thank you Cha!' Patricia replied, her heart missing a beat as the Ram of God entered. After Nonie's departure she spent a half-hour preparing herself. Satisfied that there was nothing further she could to to enhance her looks she insisted that her mother take the night off.

'You look tired,' Patricia told her, 'I think you should go to bed.'

Sadie Cahalane agreed, confessing that she had been feeling a little out of sorts all day. When the bar was free of customers she invariably produced her beads and prayed for her late husband's soul. Lately she had added another to her list. Each night she recited a rosary for the well-being of Luke Holly. It was, she felt, an appropriate atonement for having turned him down. It was the least she could do for him.

Cha and the Ram of God sat on two high stools exchanging snippets of harmless gossip with Patricia. At closing time, as the other customers made their farewells, Cha suddenly announced that he had an appointment with his mother concerning some pressing business matters. He followed the others into the street, closing the door behind him.

'I'll have that farewell drink now,' Patricia pressed her glass against the Vodka optic and waited as the trickle settled in. She added a white lemonade and sat on the stool vacated by Cha.

'What time are you leaving tomorrow?' she asked solemnly, allowing the full force of her hazel eyes to focus on his.

The Ram of God did not reply to her question. Now that he was within range of those devastating orbs he found himself bereft of all speech. If she had not smiled he might have recovered sufficiently to manage some form of reply but such was the beaming clarity of the smiling radiance that he found himself totally incapacitated. They sat thus, silently, the only sound the gentle ticking of the bar clock.

'We're alone,' Patricia broke the silence as she brought her delicate profile into play. 'My mother went to bed early,' she felt obliged to carry the conversation since her partner seemed incapable of uttering a single word.

When she rose to replenish their glasses he also rose and looked steadfastly into her eyes. Without a word he took the glass from her hand and placed it on the counter. He took her hand and pressed it to his lips. Her face was serious, her eyes calm and fixed on his.

'I won't be going anywhere tomorrow,' he said, 'if that's what you want!'

'That's what I want,' Patricia replied as she placed her arms around his neck.

21

THE CREEL FAMILY SPENT the afternoon in the graveyard of Ballybobawn. For once Maggie Creel faced up to her husband and suggested that he should visit the graveyard with the rest of the family. For a while it seemed as though he were considering her suggestion seriously. Then there came the all-too-familiar eruption during which he showered abuse on her and cuffed the child nearest to him which happened to be his youngest daughter, Livvy. Her brothers, Jonathan and Mícheál, aged thirteen and fourteen, respectively, exchanged silent looks from where they stood near the doorway. Deep feelings of revolt had been simmering in both for a while. It was then that the same thought occurred to the brothers. They looked at each other speculatively. In that look it was decided that the inevitable was almost upon them.

Despite the loss of Mary the Creel family were as happy as they could be. They had recited the Rosary over her grave and, through the tears and heartbreak, supported each other. Then came the surprise. Mícheál and Jonathan announced that they were inviting the entire party to Tom's Tavern where, with the earnings from their half-day's whitewashing, they intended to treat the whole family to cokes and crisps and last, but not least, to provide a brandy and ginger ale for Maggie their mother.

The Creels never knew the identity of the mischievous creature who let it be known to their father that they were gratifying themselves, without his knowledge or approval, at Tom's Tavern, instead of grovelling dutifully, as was expected of them, in the famished kitchen until such time as their tyrannical overlord saw fit to return from his wanderings. In Mickey's mind there were only two kinds, those who bought him drink and those who did not. It was unthinkable that his family should have the gall to enter a public house without his approval. Hastily he finished off the remains of the pint which he had been carefully nursing for almost an hour in the forlorn hope of being presented with another. Even forlorn hopes had a habit of materialising in public houses where the scene might dramatically change from one minute to the next. Only those with money to spend, himself and his ilk excepted, frequented the hostelries of Ballybobawn and those with money to spend often spent indiscriminately when the drink took its toll of their natural caution.

As he hurried to Tom's Tavern it occurred to him that he might be the victim of a hoax. He dismissed the thought. His instincts told him that something was afoot. The glasses all but fell from the hands of his offspring when they beheld him at the doorway. Their first instincts told them to evacuate the premises while they were able to do so. The younger members rose, uncertainly, preparatory to flight.

'Stay put!' The command came from Mícheál. Those who had risen sat down at once. Mickey advanced and snatching his wife's glass sniffed its contents.

'Brandy!' He uttered the word mistrustfully, sniffing secondly and tasting. 'Who bought this?' he asked innocently.

'We did, Mícheál and me.' The answer came

from Jonathan.

Mickey handed the glass back to his wife who sat trembling, not knowing what the final outcome of her husband's interrogation would be.

'Where did you get the money?' Mickey asked as he advanced upon his second son.

'We earned it,' Mícheál replied.

'Buy me a drink.' A chilling coldness entered Mickey's voice.

'No!' the answer came from Mícheál.

'No!' his brother Jonathan echoed.

'Don't provoke me,' froth began to appear at the sides of Mickey's porter-stained mouth, 'don't provoke me or I'll kick the stuffing out of the pair o' you. Now buy me that drink!'

Two emphatic negatives sent the blood surging to his head.

'Get up,' he shouted, 'get up you dirty rotten bastards!'

'Don't raise your voice here,' the command came from Tom Dudley who suddenly presented himself at the bar counter.

'Sorry Tom, sorry boy.' Mickey's tone changed instantly. He lifted a deferential hand and apologised more profusely.

'Family business,' he explained after he made the most abject of apologies. Tom stood unmoving and unimpressed. Suddenly and shiftily Mickey turned and seized his son Mícheál by the hair of the head. He dragged him into the deserted byway which offered a discreet entrance to the Tavern before Tom could stop him.

Flaying wildly Mícheál sought to break free from the grimy hand which held him fast. Mickey landed several solid slaps across the face and head of his son before Jonathan was able to muster the courage to come to his brother's aid.

'Go on man!' Tom Dudley urged in a frantic whisper. Jonathan needed no further urging. He charged. It was an onslaught with too little thought and too much abandon. He succeeded, however, in securing his brother's release. Mícheál fell whimpering to the ground, his face bloodied and bruised while Jonathan bravely took the fight to his father. Again Mickey managed to secure a grip on his younger son's hair. He held him vice-like. It was fortunate that he had drunk only one and a half pints of stout. If it was night time he would have been half drunk at least and would surely be on the flat of his back by now. He brought his fist into play for the first time, catching a surprised Jonathan on the right cheek bone and then on the left as he released his hold. Jonathan fell semi-senseless to the ground. Mickey drew back his shoe but Mícheál was upon him before he could do further damage. Mickey was shocked and amazed at the tenacity and resilience of his oldest son. He could recall felling him, in recent times, and that had been that but here was a different proposition altogether. Gone was the cowering child so easily put down and in his place an undaunted youth who must not be given the slightest opening.

It seemed certain now that the day was lost, that the old dictatorial regime would not be overthrown. With Jonathan lying helpless on the ground Mícheál's courage was beginning to ebb.

'No matter what,' he told himself resolutely as he found himself unable to lift his aching arms in defence, 'I will not back off, not while Jonathan is down.'

Sensing that his son was weakening Mickey deemed that the hold on his hair was no longer necessary. He released him and instigated an all-out, two-handed attack. He stood, tongue extended, hands clenched by his sides, the panic on his face replaced by cunning as he surveyed his victim in an effort to determine where he would land his first blow. Sure now of his ground he advanced and was deeply gratified as his left fist made contact with Mícheál's jaw.

Then, with an inhuman scream, Maggie Creel threw her tattered headgear to the floor and leaped forward to the aid of her young. It was the unexpectedness of the assault, apart altogether from its ferocity, that turned the tide. Latent for years, Maggie's spirit erupted into a vehemence so ferocious that even Tom Dudley grew fearful. She charged her husband from the side just as Mícheál recovered in time to begin a despairing offensive from the front. Heartened by the providential intervention of this new and powerful ally Mícheál weighed the situation for what it was worth for the first time. He took careful measure of his now bewildered adversary. With a coolness and confidence far beyond his years he stepped inside his father's defence and delivered a right hand to the solar plexus. It was a blow with little power but it was sufficient to make Mickey drop his guard and clutch his midriff. His wife took advantage of his discomfiture to butt him again, this time into the ribs and with greater force. He staggered backwards, surprised by the speed and fury of his wife's onslaught. Uncertainty now began to cloud his face as he turned to ward off this latest threat and to raise a clenched fist to demolish this oft-defeated assailant. This was the signal for the remainder of the family to enter the fray. Jonathan also managed to drag himself from the ground.

Tom stood in the side door of his premises shouting encouragement. He was sorely tempted, during the crucial part of the engagement, after Jonathan's knock-down, to intervene but he had second thoughts.

'All is not yet lost,' he told himself. He would not be found wanting if matters got out of hand. He would not take sides. He would simply step in and stop it.

'The Creels,' he told himself, 'will have to win this one on their own.'

The family seemed to realise that it was now or never. Each and every one played a part from Maggie the mother, to Livvy the youngest. No single blow in itself was enough to incapacitate Mickey Creel but it was obvious that he had lost the initiative. He was now content to shield himself from the blows which came fast and furious from every quarter. Micheál's straight lefts were of the text book variety. Every second one landed with painful accuracy on Mickey's nose and mouth. He began an undignified retreat down the byway to where the open countryside stretched for miles to the gently sloping mountains

Two of the girls impeded his retreat by holding fast to his trouser legs. Kicking and swearing he managed to free himself and then he fled, unashamedly, out of the byway and into the fields hotly pursued by his entire family.

He galloped rather than ran across the fields, barely managing to stay ahead of his pursuers. He crashed through a whitethorn hedge as though it didn't exist, the pricking thorns tearing at his face and clothes. Unable to follow, his pursuers ran along the hedge looking for an opening. It was just as well, Tom Dudley thought, that they didn't find one. He became anxious about the well-being of Mickey long before the exhausted man took to his heels. Breathless, the avenging army returned to Tom's Tavern.

'We'll be disgraced entirely after this,' Maggie moaned.

'No you won't,' Tom assured her. 'There were no witnesses apart from myself and you won't catch me telling anybody. Keep your own counsel on the matter and that's as far as it will go.'

Long after the last of the regulars had departed the Load of S a lone figure, bedraggled and furtive, made its way from a byroad to the cross of Ballybobawn and thence to the abode of the Creels and knocked gently on the door. He knocked again and again as gently as though the door were made of wafer. When it eventually opened he straightened himself smartly, emitted a shrill cry and ran headlong down the street followed by two youths clad only in shirts. During the chase, shirt tails flying behind, they threw kicks and blows from every conceivable angle at the darting figure until he vanished into the byway from which he had earlier emerged. No other sound was uttered during this engagement unless the panting of the fugitive could be described as such. There was no witness to the extraordinary spectacle save for a solitary tomcat who hunched himself in a convenient doorway in fear of his life.

Days and nights would pass before Father Mortimer O'Conner, the parish priest of Ballybobawn, made representations on Mickey Creel's behalf. These were fruitless in the beginning but with the passage of time Maggie Creel relented and as the winter winds strengthened and the hailstorms beat their noisy tattoos all around so did her daughters. Mícheál and Jonathan were the last to give in and only then provided certain conditions were fulfilled. Tom Dudley it was who drew them up at the request of the brothers.

Mickey would never again indulge in strong drink. He would find a job and provide for his wife and family. He would never raise a hand to his wife or any of his offspring ever again and should he renege on any one of these conditions he would be taken from his abode, a block of limestone tied to his neck and from the loftiest cliff-bank on the Ogle River he would be cast without ceremony unto the deepest hole, there to disintegrate until the day of judgement when the angel Gabriel would blow his horn to summon the living and the dead.

Mickey observed the conditions and although the people of Ballybobawn marvelled at the transformation that took place they never knew the why and the whereof except that Mickey took to polishing his shoes and wearing clean shirts as well as being civil to his neighbours, loving to his wife and family and living in the fear of God, late in the day though this might be.

When word of the miraculous change reached the ears of Luke Holly in his faraway station amid the friendly folk of Donegal he smiled to himself, glad that the seed he had sown had sprung and yielded such a glorious harvest.

22

DURING THE LONG NIGHT after Tom's burial,
Mollie had cast her mind's eye about for a worthy
replacement, in a desperate exercise, she told herself, to induce badly-needed sleep. The judicious
eye alighted on the most eligible male not just in
Ballybobawn and vicinity but in the town of Trallock itself and for a radius of ten miles all around.
It was precisely on the morning of the Month's
Mind, shortly after the Commemorative Mass,
that Mollie began to spin the first delicate strands
of the web which would ultimately and inextricably enmesh her prey.

Mollie was certain that Willie Halvey was there
for the taking if one was prepared to make the necessary physical sacrifices and organise the requi-
site plans. After the Mass for the Month's Mind he
sympathised with her although condolences were
never tendered on such occasions unless the party
in sympathy was not present at the original obsequies.

As the owner of the undertaker's parlour where
Tom Cronane lay in state and from which he was
subsequently removed to Ballybobawn parish
church, Willie Halvey would be expected to show a
professional interest. Instead he had seen to the removal of the remains himself, a chore normally
undertaken by members of his workforce. All
through the various ceremonies from the laying
out of the cadaver to the sad finale he had been the
very epitome of attentiveness. Even the members
of the family, Mollie apart, remarked afterwards

about how helpful and genuinely concerned Willie was, humbling himself like any ordinary grave-digger, muddying his hands and expensive suede shoes and throwing off his hand-stitched short-coat to assist with the lowering of the coffin into its final resting place. The family appreciated the fact that his services were above and beyond the call of normal duty. He even wiped the makings of a tear from his eye the moment Mollie initiated the graveside lamentations with a weeping and a wail-ing that was matched only by the absolute hysteria of her daughters. Nonie who stood on the base of an outsize Celtic Cross, her hands entwined around the column for support, admitted, grudgingly that the Cronane females had put on a most convincing show.

During the weeks which followed Willie was a constant caller at the supermarket. He pooh-poohed Mollie's offer of immediate payment, sug-gesting that there was no need to settle the account until a fitting monument was erected to the mem-ory of Tom after the customary lapse of time.

'I don't know where I'd be only for you,' Mollie confided to him on more than one occasion as she squeezed a hand or fleetingly touched his face dur-ing the course of her tearful acknowledgements.

In mid-autumn, after the Month's Mind of her husband, Mollie embarked upon a puritanical regi-men to restore the figure which once captivated Tom Cronane and tantalised hundreds of others from drooling locals to visiting commercials. She began by having her hair cut and styled in the most up-to-date mode and by setting a date before which she hoped to reach her objective. Her aim was to shed seventeen pounds of excess flab between the sixteenth of September and Halloween. Ostensibly the daunting exercise was to atone for the sins, if any, of her late lamented husband. She hoped to achieve her ambition on the eve of All Saints' Day, the beginning of the month of mourning approved by the Church. Privately Mollie entertained thoughts which were far less devotional but she kept these to herself.

Since the instigation of her plan she firmly told herself if there was a hereafter, which she very much doubted, that Tom would find his way there sooner rather than later. God would surely approve of the manner in which he conducted the raid on the travellers' encampment. If Mollie had any influence over God she would have broached the subject of canonisation for Tom on the strength of that outstanding single achievement.

As the time passed and the flab began to melt under the rigorous onslaught of self-denial, Willie began to notice the emergence of a different and highly desirable Mollie. There were times when his heart raced as they sat drinking tea in the kitchen and there were times as she moved from table to sink or from kitchen to shop and back that he found it difficult to restrain himself. There were occasions when he painfully tore himself away from the kitchen confines out of respect to her bereavement.

Mollie, for her part, was in total control of a situation which was proceeding according to plan. Once as they stood side by side at the kitchen table, their bodies touching while they examined a selection of monumental designs, he brushed slowly against her rear as he moved to the other side. Brief as the contact was Mollie knew that she need never entertain any doubts about Willie's ability to satisfy any of the cravings which she experienced from time to time. When he placed a hand around her waist, a hand with a tendency to drift downwards, she did not remonstrate. Rather she said in the gentlest tones, 'Not here Willie and not now.'

It was the conspiratorial intimacy of her voice which decided Willie against any further gravitation downwards. Her tone unmistakeably suggested that if he maintained temporary control all would be his in the course of time.

Later in bed Mollie Cronane congratulated herself on her good sense in having opted for the biggest fish in the pond. She reviewed her position in the light of this new, although hardly unexpected development. Tom left her everything that was his to leave by agreement although the supermarket, for tax purposes, had long since been signed over to her eldest son.

Mollie knew for some time that Tomboy was thieving to augment the not ungenerous wage which he was already being paid. Cha never, and she would swear to this on a stack of Bibles, misappropriated as much as a solitary halfpenny during his years in the business. There was in Cha, Mollie had known for years, a righteousness and a sense of purpose to be found in no other member of the family. Cha had integrity and he was honorable. He did not bring these qualities from her side of the family and he did not bring them from his father. He had a way of looking at Mollie during confrontations which reminded her of the photograph on the mantelpiece of old Charlie Cronane. In her eyes Cha was incorruptible. She felt at ease when he was around. His brothers and sisters respected him. In their eyes Cha had always been special. He listened and was reasonable. He made no demands. Mollie knew that the business would always prosper while Cha was in charge.

The following night, certain in the knowledge that they had the house to themselves, Mollie and Willie held hands and kissed but they limited themselves to cuddlesome rather than passionate exchanges by mutual consent, Mollie expressing the view that it would be unseemly to go any further in the house where her late husband spent his life upon earth.

They agreed, instead, to meet at the cemetery the following afternoon at four o'clock when dusk would be falling and the prevailing mists sure to conceal them. From there they would proceed to the city of Cork where she would choose an engagement ring.

ALL SAINTS' DAY IN the month of the Holy Souls was a sombre occasion. Grave of face and slow of step the more elderly of the parishioners made their prayerful rounds in memory of the faithful departed, stopping occasionally, before exiting so that they might return again and resume their efforts to redeem the souls of friends and kinfolk. Every individual visit merited substantial indulgences for those so near but yet so far from the lustrous threshold of heaven.

Father O'Connor, in a wide-ranging sermon on the concept of salvation, likened the purgatorial exiles to lost wayfarers up to their waists in impassable wallows waiting only for the hand of a well-disposed passer-by to drag them from the depths and place them on the road to salvation.

'Each visit,' Father O'Connor explained to those who might be ignorant of the prevailing indulgences, 'to a consecrated place means that another soul has been saved from further anxieties and tribulations in his place of unwanted exclusion.'

Few, if any, farmers in the parish of Ballybobawn heeded his dictates. It wasn't that they might discount their parish priest's perception of Purgatory but rather did they feel that the observance of All Saints' Day and the practice of November visitations was the province of their wives. Since nearly all farmers in the district were in the habit of expiring several years before their spouses it would fall, naturally, to the wives to redeem them from Purgatory through the medium of inexpensive indulgences. Wives, as it was well known, specialised in that sort of thing and anyway it was traditionally taken for granted in the farming community that a wife would be responsible for the salvation of two rather than one. Farmers firmly believed that all religious matters were best left in wifely hands.

The Ram of God and Patricia Cahalane entered the cemetery of Ballybobawn on All Saints' Day. They spent lengthy periods praying by the gravesides of the Ram's parents and brothers, Patricia's father and Mary Creel. She could not remember her father as vividly as the Ram remembered the twins. Even now he smiled as he recalled their childish pranks and colossal drinking bouts.

'If they are anywhere in the vicinity,' he whispered to Patricia, 'they'll surely pelt me with clods just for the joy of it!'

'Let's take a stroll in the High Meadow,' Patricia suggested at the completion of their supplications. Hand in hand they made their way to the main entrance. A small slight figure appeared out of the mist as they were about to exit.

'She's like a young girl,' Patricia stepped to one side as Mollie in blue and white chequered head-scarf and smartly-tailored, navy-blue raincoat tripped past.

The Ram of God crossed himself fearfully. It would not surprise him if she had used her diabolical powers to shed the years for which there now seemed to be no accounting. As she swished past into the mist the fragrance of an exotic perfume lingered in her wake.

'She's never looked so radiant!' Patricia spoke in low tones. When no comment seemed to be forthcoming from her partner she looked quizzically upwards into his face.

'Don't you think she looks beautiful?' she asked. She instantly regretted having spoken. Noticing the look of genuine revulsion on his face she recalled the havoc which the rejuvenated widow had wrought upon the man in her life. She vowed not to mention the creature's name ever again, at least not in his presence.

'I may have come between him and his imagined vocation,' she thought, 'but he is still a holy man and the fact that we will soon be lovers will not make him any the less holy!'

As they entered the byroad which would take them past the Drannaghy farmhouse to the High Meadow he placed a hand across her shoulders.

'That's more like it!' Patricia addressed the sentiment to herself. She responded by leaning as close to him as their gait would allow.

FRESHLY SHAVED AND SHOWERED, garbed in a beautifully tailored tweed suit of gunmetal grey and shod in neutralising moccasins of taupe suede,

Willie Halvey withdrew his pocket comb for the third time since his arrival at the graveyard and proceeded to smooth his lank brown hair backwards from his forehead. Combing completed he used the long and index fingers of his right hand in a series of scissors-like snips to indent the several artificial waves which were frequently visible on the crown of his head. It did not matter that the lifetime of the waves would be of short duration. What mattered was that they would be in place when Mollie arrived at the graveside of her dear, departed husband. Now, of all times, he wished more than anything else to look youthful and presentable.

He glanced at his watch and saw that it was two minutes past four. He smiled as he dried his slightly-oiled hands on his handkerchief. She wouldn't be much of a woman if she wasn't late and what a woman she had turned out to be during the previous weeks! There was now no trace of the double chin which once seemed so pronounced whenever she bent her head. Her bra-less breasts now thrust themselves surgingly outward, with a greater urgency than ever before against the light fabric of the bright jumpers she had taken to wearing of late. He noticed too how her buttocks grew more tastefully and deliciously defined as the cushions of fat dropped away from her abdomen and over-endowed hips.

Mollie let him see too that the successful efforts at restoring her once seductive figure were solely for his benefit. A tremor ran through his body as he dared to anticipate the passion-filled encounter which lay ahead. Vainly he tried to dismiss her freshly-transformed body from his mind and, failing, surrendered himself to the prospect of frenzied entanglements and other indescribable delights.

Five past four and yet no sign of the rejuvenated enchantress who had utterly changed his life.
He dared to hope that the delay was designed to
titillate him but apart from all that he conceded
that he had not expected her to be on time. What
woman worthy of the name of woman ever was!
Then came the distant sound of tripping heels. He
peered into the mist, waiting for his loved one to
emerge. Reluctantly, slowly, the mist surrendered
her. In a thrice she was by his side, her arms
around his neck, her warm breath fanning his
cheek, her presence accentuated by the scent of her
perfume which induced a lightheadedness that
made him want to sit down. For a moment they
clung to each other. She drew away sharply as an
elderly couple emerged arm in arm out of the
cloying November vapour.

'I think,' Mollie was now speaking in the most
businesslike manner, 'he would like a Celtic Cross.
I once heard him say that it was his favourite type
of memorial.'

'A Celtic Cross it shall be missus,' Willie consented in stentorian tones and adapted one of his
more professional stances. When the elderly couple
vanished once more into the mist they both
laughed.

'Seriously Willie,' Mollie allowed her smile to
recede for a moment, 'do you think you could really
manage a Celtic Cross, something near enough to
the same shape and size as his mother's and
father's?'

'Now that's something I cannot understand,'
Willie sounded puzzled. 'Why in God's name didn't
he ask to be buried with them and even if he didn't
ask why didn't you opt for it and spare yourself the

339

cost of a new cross?'

'Because silly,' Mollie took him by the arm again, 'he always said that he and I would be buried together.'

They had both found it difficult to contain the laughter.

'We'll see about that,' Willie whispered proprietorially and with a fierce determination as they both looked down at the mound which covered the mortal remains of Tom Cronane.

Immediately, after a brief prayer at the graveside Willie informed her that he had booked a double room at Jury's Hotel. Before she could protest, although he was delighted to see that no protest seemed to be forthcoming, he informed her that he had made an appointment with a leading jeweller in the city to meet them in the aforementioned bedroom where Mollie might avail of the privacy to choose from a selection of engagement rings which ranged from three thousand to ten thousand pounds in price.

It was this revelation which prompted Mollie to opt for a January wedding rather than the late spring nuptials which they discussed earlier. Any man who had the foresight and generosity to make the arrangements which Willie so apologetically and informally divulged should not and must not be allowed to remain in a single state any longer than was strictly necessary. It gave her all she could do to stop joining her hands together and gloating unashamedly over her prospects. She already had an engagement ring, but it would be no more than a mere bauble when compared to the array which would soon confront her in the city of Cork.

She also resolved, there and then, that her gratitude would be at least commensurate with the amount expended on the engagement ring the very moment the purveyor departed the room. She intimated as much to a trembling Willie.

They embraced and kissed passionately.

'It's unseemly here,' Mollie was the first to draw away, her face exhibiting a newly found veneration for the consecrated ground on which they stood.

'If we are to be there ahead of time,' Willie took her by the shoulders and looked into her dark eyes, 'we would want to be getting a move on because if that fog doesn't lift it's going to add another hour to our journey.'

As they moved swiftly towards the rear entrance and the waiting Mercedes Willie remarked on how he had seen the Ram of God and Patricia Cahalane visiting the graveyard a short while before. Mollie's face clouded as it always did whenever she thought of the Ram of God. She was careful not to show her annoyance. The more she considered their relationship the more her fury mounted. She was always fond of saying that there was a fly in every ointment no matter how settled the scene. There was always one hitch and the Ram of God was hers. Somehow, in the course of time, she would bring him down. There was no doubt whatsoever about that in her mind. She would use the man by her side and his powerful connections, unkown to either, but use them she would in the pursuance of her steely determination to ruin the one man who had so far proved to be invincible as far as Mollie was concerned. She would find a way. She tried in vain to subjugate the intense annoyance which the mention of his name always seemed to stimulate and to think that if she had waited until now, for instance, she might have by the simple exercise of her womanly wiles brought him to his knees.

'As sure as Tom is in his grave this day,' she made the vow as she exited through the rear gate, 'I'll even the score with the Ram of God and he'll rue the day he crossed swords with Mollie Cronane.'

They had never before driven together in the white Mercedes. Gallantly he opened her door bowing with exaggerated courtesy as he did so. Soon they were cruising along the misty road that led to the city of Cork.

THE RAM OF GOD and Patricia stood on the knoll which always afforded such an excellent vista of sky and sea. The mist which obscured even the contiguous hedgerows as they climbed upwards began slowly to lighten as the November darkness began to fall. The clearance started after a freshly-risen westerly wind began to dispel the hanging fog bank out to sea. Even now the twinkling stars and crescent moon were visible in the distance where the clearance was absolute over the distant ocean. Gratefully the Ram of God drew the salt air upwards through his hair-bedecked nostrils and expelled it after a while with an appreciative sigh. He turned and looked down into the hazel eyes of his bride-to-be as though he was searching for a hidden commodity which had never before been found. Gently he placed his gnarly hands on her waist and lifted her, effortlessly, from the ground, his eyes still on hers as he held her at a distance. Having found the secret element for which he had been searching he allowed himself the broadest of smiles. Placing her on the ground once more he kissed her on the face and lips. Her response, warm and fragrant, made him want to cry out to the star-filled heavens as he felt the powerful stirrings take hold of his being.

They walked downwards, hand in hand, through the fields to the cross of Ballybobawn where groups of excited villagers, including Nonie, had gathered. A siren sounded in the distance and in the space of a few moments an ambulance, its blue warning lights flashing, sped by in the direction of Trallock.

'What's happened?' the Ram of God put the question to Tom Dudley who stood, hands behind his back, his eyes dolefully fixed on the ground.

He did not answer at once.

'There was a crash,' he said after a while. 'It was all the fault of that bloody fog.'

'Bad?' the Ram of God asked.

'I believe the occupants of the car were killed instantly,' Tom's gaze returned to the ground.

'Anybody we know?' Patricia asked.

'A man and woman,' Tom replied knowingly, 'in a white Mercedes. May God have mercy on their souls.'

'Amen!' came the sanction from Nonie.

Instinctively the Ram of God took the arm of Patricia and directed her to the church to pray for the repose of the souls of the couple who died. He guessed their identities as had Patricia. Nonie found herself with no option other than to accompany them. She could not very well give it to say to her new mistress that she might be lacking in charity. She followed dutifully behind, wheeling her ancient bicycle, nodding to passers-by who were too concerned with the congregation at the cross to pay any attention to the unlikely trio on their way to prayer. Nonie shook her head at the folly of the world and particularly at the folly of the pair who had so recently died.

'God have mercy on them is right!' she thought. 'He'll want to be every bit as merciful as they say He is if that pair is ever to see the insides of Heaven.'

More Interesting Books

DURANGO

JOHN B. KEANE

Danny Binge peered into the distance and slowly spelled out the letters inscribed on the great sign in glaring red capitals:

'DURANGO,' he read.

'That is our destination,' the Rector informed his friend. 'I'm well known here. These people are my friends and before the night is over they shall be your friends too.'

The friends in question are the Carabim girls: Dell, aged seventy-one and her younger sister, seventy-year-old Lily. Generous, impulsive and warm-hearted, they wine, dine and entertain able-bodied country boys free of charge – they will have nothing to do with the young men of the town or indeed any town ...

Durango is an adventure story about life in rural Ireland during the Second World War. It is a story set in an Ireland that is fast dying but John B. Keane, with his wonderful skill and humour, brings it to life, rekindling in the reader memories of a time never to be quite forgotten ...

THE CONTRACTORS

JOHN B. KEANE

Tom Reicey was the labourers' father figure and their fixer. He knew the high-ups in the police force. He went on holidays with chief superintendents and even a member of parliament! He was sometimes nicknamed the Cement God because every day of the week aeroplanes were landing on concrete strips laid down by his Rangers. Children played on his playgrounds. Trucks, buses and cars trundled and sped over his concrete roads.

Dan Murray's idea of maintaining a labour pool in Ireland was unprecedented in the English building world – finishing ahead of time was the difference between giant profits and small. With any luck Dan hoped to clear a quarter of a million pounds on his first major contract.

The Contractors is a stirring story of people who were forced to emigrate and work in England in the early 1950s. Before leaving Ireland they were warned about the likely evils that they would confront in that pagan place. John B. Keane, with his wonderful skill and humour, brings them to life in these unforgettable pages as he gives us the fascinating details of their daily existence, their exhilarations and their sorrows.

The Celebrated Letters
of
John B. Keane

'I grew up in a time when there was no alternative to the letter as a means of communication except, of course, in the case of emergency when the phone in the local barracks of the Civic Guards became the extreme resort ...'

In this collection of some of his finest letters, John B. Keane turns the letter as a means of communication into a comic, sometimes surreal, artform.

Includes *Letters of a Successful TD*, *Letters of an Irish Parish Priest*, *Letters of a Love-Hungry Farmer*, *Letters of a Matchmaker* and *Letters of an Irish Minister of State*.

'Hilariously Irish, shrewdly accurate and richly creative.'

Irish Times

'There are more shades to his humour than there are colours in the rainbow.'

The Examiner

More Celebrated Letters
of
John B. Keane

Garda Leo Molair copes masterfully with all the transgressions of village life. He knows when to intervene and when to leave well alone. Yet nothing that he has learnt will help him when he encounters the most serious problem of his career, one that cannot be sorted out with a hard word or a good kick *[Letters of a Civic Guard]*.

Kerry publican Martin MacMee is a confirmed bachelor but irresistible to women, a principled man forgiving of the failings of others, and a brilliant storyteller. Comic, romantic or tragic, the lives of the inhabitants of Knockanee are brilliantly evoked in his letters *[Letters of an Irish Publican]*.

After fifty years as a postman, Mocky Fondoo has developed a shrewd understanding of the human condition. Imparting his hard-earned knowledge to a young postman and reminiscing with old friends, he describes the bizarre characters and hilarious events encountered in a long career *[Letters of a Country Postman]*.

Tom Cram's body and soul have suffered greatly during fifty years of drunken debauchery. In a series of irate letters, his much-abused organs recount hilarious misadventures and missed opportunities and put the case for a healthier, happier future *[Letters to the Brain]*.

THE BEST
OF
JOHN B. KEANE
COLLECTED HUMOROUS WRITINGS

John B. Keane is known nationally and internationally as a successful playwright, handling tragedy and comedy with equal art, and as a prose fiction writer of great invention and skill. Yet an equal claim to fame is made by the hundreds of short pieces which have been published in more than a dozen highly popular collections, their titles ranging from polemical to surreal, from *Inlaws and Outlaws* to *Is the Holy Ghost Really a Kerryman?* Now harvested into a single volume, they represent the distillation of the experience of a funny, witty, wise and passionate observer of the bright tapestry of Irish life.

All human life is there, and he tells its story in a remarkable procession of remarkable characters. There are mouth-watering disquisitions on food and paeans to drink, and since Kerry people do not live by bread alone, there is much about their two other preoccupations – love and words. *The Best of John B. Keane* is a collection to prize and an ideal bedside book or travelling companion.

Three Plays
Sive, The Field & Big Maggie

John B. Keane

Sive is a powerful folk-drama set in the south-west of Ireland which concerns itself with the attempt of a scheming matchmaker and a bitter woman to sell an innocent girl to a lecherous old man.

The Field is John B. Keane's fierce and tender study of the love a man can have for land and the ruthless lengths he will go to in order to obtain the object of his desire.

Big Maggie: On the death of her husband Maggie is determined to create a better life for herself and her children. The problems arise when her vision of the future begins to sit with increasing discomfort on the shoulders of her surly offspring. John B. Keane's wonderful creation of a rural Irish matriarch ranks with Juno, Mommo and Molly Bloom as one of the great female creations of twentieth-century Irish literature.